the Curious Case
of the Missing
Figurehead

recipe:

the Curious Case of the Missing Figurehead

A PROFESSOR — AND — MRS. LITTLEFIELD MYSTERY

from: Diane Noble

a novel

David C Cook®

transforming lives together

THE CURIOUS CASE OF THE MISSING FIGUREHEAD
Published by David C Cook
4050 Lee Vance View
Colorado Springs, CO 80918 U.S.A.

David C Cook Distribution Canada
55 Woodslee Avenue, Paris, Ontario, Canada N3L 3E5

David C Cook U.K., Kingsway Communications
Eastbourne, East Sussex BN23 6NT, England

The graphic circle C logo is a registered trademark of David C Cook.

This story is a work of fiction. Characters and events are the product of the author's imagination. Any resemblance to any person, living or dead, is coincidental.

Unless otherwise noted, all Scripture quotations are taken from the Holy Bible, New International Version®, NIV®. Copyright © 1973, 1984, 2011 by Biblica, Inc.™ Used by permission of Zondervan. All rights reserved worldwide. www.zondervan.com; Scripture quotations marked NLT are taken from the Holy Bible, New Living Translation, copyright © 1996, 2007 by Tyndale House Foundation. Used by permission of Tyndale House Publishers, Inc., Carol Stream, Illinois 60188. All rights reserved. Scripture quotations marked KJV are taken from the King James Version of the Bible. (Public Domain.)

LCCN 2014944484
ISBN 978-1-4347-0497-9
eISBN 978-0-7814-1161-5

The Author is represented by the literary agency of Alive
Communications, Inc., 7680 Goddard Street, Suite 200, Colorado
Springs, CO 80920. www.alivecommunications.com.

The Team: Don Pape, Lorin Oberweger, Amy Konyndyk,
Nick Lee, Helen Macdonald, Karen Athen
Cover Design: Tim Green, FaceOut Studios
Cover Photo: Getty Images

Printed in the United States of America
First Edition 2014

1 2 3 4 5 6 7 8 9 10

063014

To Anna Lou and Doris, my beautiful aunts
Your laughter, joy, faith, prayer life, storytelling,
and the music you make with piano and song,
went into the creation of El and Hyacinth.
At 89 and 96, you are an inspiration. You shine!

To Kris, my precious cousin
Your courage, your giving heart, your sense of humor,
your many talents, your grace … are a
beacon for all who know you.
I am in awe of you, my cousin-
friend, and forever will be.
For reasons too many to list, you are
my hero. You are in my heart.

To Dona, my Idyllwild angel
God gave me the gift of a very special friend during the
writing of this book. As usual, His timing
was perfect. I will never forget
how you "flew" down the mountain to
help when we needed it most.
You were (and are) truly love-in-action.
Your friendship is a treasure.

To Marihelen and Linda, my forever friends
Through the years, we've shared joys
and sorrows, laughter and tears,
good times, challenging times, and
everything in between.
Our "sisterhood" is one of my life's greatest treasures.
You, too, are written into the hearts of El and Hyacinth.
I love you all!

When we find someone who is brave, fun, intelligent, and loving,
we have to thank the universe.

Maya Angelou

Prologue
Madeleine

. . . .

Here is the world. Beautiful and terrible
things will happen. Don't be afraid.

Frederick Buechner

Paris, France, April 1942

Seventeen-year-old Madeleine Dague wrapped her arms around
herself, trying to draw warmth from her thin, worn coat. Hurrying
along the wet boulevard, head down, shoulders hunched, she carried
no form of identity, no papers, nothing that could trace her back to
the Maquis that connected her family to La Résistance Française.

She carried only fear deep inside, fear that she would fail her first
mission.

Along Rue Gabriel, the wet pavement reflected the glint of
streetlights. The time of curfew neared. Shopkeepers slammed and
locked their metal gates. Few people remained on the sidewalks, and

those who did seemed to pull into themselves, just as Madeleine did, in an attempt to go unnoticed. She chose a family hurrying along the avenue and adjusted her speed to match theirs. After they turned onto a side street, she fell in with another small group and hid herself among them.

The tall building with the spindled top rose into the darkening sky. Guards stood at the ornate gate at the entrance. As she drew closer, she saw the glow of their cigarettes and heard snatches of their conversation. She listened carefully, but their talk was only of the nearby cabaret and the women who danced there.

She spotted the flags first, blood red with black swastikas. It would have been difficult to miss them. Falling in with a man and woman, she followed them through the café's open doorway. Music spilled from a stage on one side of the expansive space, and a long crowded bar filled the other. Loud conversation and even louder singing assaulted her ears. A haze of smoke filled the room, and odors of acrid tobacco, cheap perfume, and stale beer twisted her stomach.

Madeleine tried to keep her knees from trembling as she moved closer to the room's center. Turning, she took in the room. A German soldier sitting at the bar caught her gaze and came over to her.

"Guten abend, Fräulein." He lifted a brow expectantly. She felt her face redden, shook her head, and stared at the floor. He started to say something more, but a new act came onto the stage, distracting him.

The sounds of whistles, shouts, and stamping feet roared from the audience, and then the music started again. The cabaret singer glittered in the lights, her clothing so skimpy it barely covered her.

Madeleine blinked in surprise and looked away, feeling a blush creep up her cheeks. She had been warned, but no one could ever have described such a scene to her.

But she had no time to think of such things now. She was expected at the meeting place. She could not be late. Too much hinged on her being there. She fixed her gaze on the back of the room, reciting the directions silently. Go downstairs. Find the door at the end of the hallway. Step through the doorway and into a long room. They'd told her again and again that though the room was largely unused, she would be in danger until she navigated through that space and entered the tunnel on the other side.

In the dark room, she lit a match from the small box she'd brought in her pocket. The brick wall she'd been told to expect stood before her, looking ominous in the dim light.

She moved a barrel out of the way and then counted the rows of bricks from the corner to approximately where she stood. Twenty-two. Then she counted seventeen rows down from the ceiling until she found the brick at the intersection of the two lines. It looked as secure as all the others. But when she touched it, it shifted.

She caught her breath, nibbling her bottom lip, but she knew better than to assume success. The other two messengers had also made it this far and then failed. She lit another match and then moved the same brick. Her fingers were small and nimble. The brick slid forward at the same time her match extinguished. She reached into her pocket for another ... and then heard voices in the distance, speaking German.

She froze.

She had gone over this with her father. *What will you do if …?*

Quickly, she replaced the brick and knelt behind the barrel she'd moved moments earlier, across from some shelves that held crates of Wicküler, Pschorr Bräu, and Kulmbacher beers.

The door opened, and the voices—two, it seemed—carried on in animated conversation. The light flicked on, and footsteps came toward her. She feared to breathe.

She heard the rattle of bottles, followed by a grunt as one of the men picked up something heavy. A crate? A box? More shuffling, more grunts as heavy items were picked up and moved. It seemed the men searched for something they could not find.

A pair of Marschstiefel boots came toward her, heels clacking on the concrete floor. She held her breath as the wearer turned toward the shelves that held the beer. Then came the sound of a case sliding across the shelf and a curse as he picked it up.

The other man laughed and they walked to the door. Seconds later the light went out. Madeleine waited until the doorknob clicked and then struck another match. She made quick work of removing the bricks and dropping them inside the tunnel to replace once she passed through to the other side.

Within minutes, she had created an opening roughly the circumference of her body. Without pausing, she squeezed through, replaced the bricks, and then struck another match to see what was ahead. The tunnel sloped downward. It was narrow enough for her to feel the concrete sides. Squatting, she crept forward in the darkness, willing herself not to be afraid. But her heart thudded so hard she feared it might bruise her ribs. She stopped and rocked back on her heels.

Her mother's image came to her, along with the memory of a psalm she had read to Madeleine long ago. *Yea, though I walk through the valley of the shadow of death … thou art with me.*

She then whispered the words as she crept forward again, the words resonating in her heart like a prayer.

At last, a pinpoint of light appeared in the distance. She breathed easier and picked up her pace. The tunnel increased in size until she could stand again. Soon, she came to a large underground bunker, and two men, standing near the open doorway and backlit by the dim light inside, hurried toward her. One stood a head taller than the other, had thin shoulders and large hands. The shorter man carried himself in a rather haughty manner. A dark mustache and shadowed jawline gave him a menacing look, which she hoped was her imagination.

"You are the messenger?" The taller man spoke French, though his accent was American. He stepped forward and shook her hand. "I am an aide to the ambassador." He glanced at the mustached man standing next to him. "And please meet our curator from the United States. Boston, Massachusetts. Please excuse us for not using our names. You do understand why?"

Madeleine nodded and then shook the second man's hand, studying his face. This man, the curator, spoke flawless French. For a half heartbeat she wondered if it was too flawless. Perhaps she was being overly cautious because so much was at stake. She tried to read his expression. Her father had trusted everything to her judgment. She would do anything to make him proud.

"I will tell you about our work," she said, lifting her chin. Papa had told her that she need not tell them about the thousands of art objects that had been confiscated by the Nazis from France, the Netherlands, and Belgium. They were well aware of these things. They also knew that the objects were brought to a central depot in Paris, the museum Jeu de Paume, for inventory by art historians before they were shipped to Germany—for Hitler's private collection and for that of Hermann Göring.

"The stolen art—," she began simply, and both men nodded, letting her know they understood, "that we are interested in saving is from private collections."

"Jewish collections," the curator said.

"Yes, and from Freemasons, museums, and shops. It seems the Germans have a hunger for the best of the best." She shifted uncomfortably as she spoke. "Jewelry, silver, gold bars. The value surpasses anything Germany has known since the invasion."

The men nodded. "Please go on," the ambassador's aide said.

Madeleine took a deep breath. "We have taken many items from the depot and from shipping points along the way. We have also kept an inventory, quite extensive, listing the identity of the rightful owners and the objects taken from them. This list is hidden with the objects, and new lists accompany each shipment."

The curator watched her intently, an odd glint in his eyes. "How many items are we talking about?" Again, something about his expression bothered her. Greed, perhaps? But she couldn't stop now, could she? Had she given them too much information already?

"Right now, they number in the thousands. But we intend to continue our work until the war is over." Her hands, still cold from the tunnel, now felt as though they were made of ice. She rubbed them together, hoping to warm them even a little. "If we are successful, the number will be much higher. You must promise you will not send anyone to the place I am about to reveal to you until then."

Both men nodded.

She glanced from one to the other. Again, the matter of trust made her determination waver. It was not only because of the treasure. If anything went wrong, her family, the Maquis, all the members of the resistance, could lose their lives.

"I will tell you the location. But it cannot be written down even after I leave you."

"We understand the importance of this. We have worked out a way to get the information out of the country," the ambassador's aide said. "Completely undetected."

The curator nodded. "That's where I come in."

"Can you tell me, so that I can assure my father and the others?"

They exchanged glances, and the assistant to the ambassador nodded. "You may tell her," he said.

"Because we cannot retrieve the treasure while we are under occupation, the only safe place for it is in the United States. It must be disguised as something no one could connect to a buried treasure worth millions, even billions of dollars. It must be something so innocuous that it slides out of the harbor without inspection. It must have good reason to be shipped—to Boston."

The aide stepped forward and dropped his voice. "We have found a ship's figurehead that was designed and carved in Boston and through a series of events ended up in a second-rate museum in Paris. It's a beautiful piece, and the ambassador has convinced Maréchal Philippe Pétain that as an act of goodwill, it should be returned to Boston where it 'came to life,' so to speak, more than one hundred years ago."

She frowned. "Pétain is a puppet. Did he get permission from Hermann Göring?"

"We can't know for certain, but we don't believe he would give permission without it," the aide said. "He is quite old and frail, unwilling to go against the Nazis."

The curator laughed bitterly. "He is a mere figurehead himself."

"How will you get the information inside this ... this ship's figurehead? Remember, nothing can be written down. It is too dangerous."

"We have a plan," the aide said, meeting her eyes. "Even if the Nazis confiscate the figurehead, they will find no clues to the place where the treasure lies."

"It will be in some sort of code, then."

The men nodded.

"How many people will know about this ruse?" Madeleine directed the question to the curator. "How many will know the code?"

"Three people. The two of us and the ambassador," he said. "The ambassador will personally see to the figurehead's shipment to the States, and I will be in Boston awaiting its arrival. When the war is over, we will find the location you're about to give us and the stolen items will be returned to their rightful owners."

"Now, if you will tell us the location ... ," the aide said, looking at her expectantly.

What if this was a trap? She had to trust her father's wisdom, but he didn't know the men, only knew of them through a chain of contacts. What if they were not men of their word? What if she made the wrong choice?

Too much was at stake. The burden of her youth and inexperience settled hard on her shoulders.

As if sensing her reluctance, the ambassador's aide stepped closer to her. He reached into the inside pocket of his jacket, drew out a folded piece of paper, and handed it to her. "Perhaps this will help."

Madeleine unfolded the paper. The likeness of the carving seemed to smile at her. "She's beautiful," she whispered. "Utterly beautiful."

The curator looked over her shoulder at the drawing. "And valuable, even if we didn't give her such an important secret to carry."

She kept her gaze on the drawing, taking in the carving's sweet expression of strength and determination. "Does she have a name?"

"From the beginning she was called *Lady with a Scarf.*"

When Madeleine looked up, his eyes softened. "You may keep the drawing, if you'd like."

She swallowed hard and nodded. She shouldn't keep it, but it was so beautiful. What if she was caught with such a drawing? "No one would know what it means," she whispered, half to herself. She looked up. "Would they? And no one knows her name."

"No one knows her significance, and no one has paid attention to her name," the curator said.

"*Lady with a Scarf,*" Madeleine whispered, staring at the paper. "She's beautiful."

She took in his words, moved her gaze from the aide's to the currator's. Her father had said to trust her instincts. She drew in a deep breath and began. "The searchers will find seven caves. Each is filled with gold, silver, and priceless art of untold worth." She stopped abruptly. "But before I tell you where they will be found, you need to tell me the code."

"It is safer that we do not tell you," the curator said. "In the event of your capture."

She raised her chin. "What if, at the end, no one else knows? Then all will be lost."

Chapter One
The Professor

• • • • • • • • • • • • • • • •

Off the Coast of North Carolina

Huge gray swells marched toward the *Black Watch* like an army of humpback whales, only larger. Outriders of severe weather, they stood tall, growing taller, wider, blowing more wind-whipped froth as they came.

Dr. Maxwell Haverhill, dean of Southern Highlands University's history and social science departments, braced himself against the railing just seconds before a frothy swell lifted the ninety-one-ton salvage ship, took it on a glide along its crest, and then dropped it into the wind-driven chop.

His stomach lurched as the ship shuddered and rose again. He tightened his grip on the rail. Wrapped his fingers around its slick wet surface for support. Waited for the inevitable drop.

It came too soon. The ship groaned as it slammed into the water.

Max, still wearing his wet suit from an earlier dive, glanced up at the bridge. Captain Brady Donnegan looked agitated. His second in command, Rob Marconi, stood next to him, eyes fixed on his instruments, phone to his ear, likely talking to the diving crew about the men in the water.

Saltwater spray stung Max's face. As head of SHU's Semester at Sea program, he was responsible for the fifteen students and three faculty members on board. Dr. Fletcher, a new faculty member, had taken over his duties this morning since he'd been gone on the first dive. The students, curious about the storm, and seemingly unfazed by the danger, were clustered near the dive station. The faculty apparently had better sense; he didn't spot anyone over thirty from SHU. Even Dr. Fletcher was missing.

The winds had come up fast. Too fast. It was early in the hurricane season, and though Donnegan had paid close attention to the marine VHF weather reports, the sudden ferocity of the wind seemed to take even this seasoned seaman by surprise. As late as this morning, VHF predicted the storm would miss North Carolina's Outer Banks. Something had changed.

Now they were in the storm's path.

And they had kids in the water. Divers. Dirk and MacFie, working under his supervision and in partnership with Brady Donnegan's Oceanic Recovery and Salvage. Experts at what they did, but the conditions were deteriorating fast. They were also former students at the university, and he cared about them. And though they were now married with families of their own, he still thought of them as his kids.

The thought of anything happening to them hit him in the gut. He was no expert, but he'd spent enough time on Brady's ship to know when danger lurked. A sudden storm. Divers in deep water. Not a good combination. They could only ascend at a rate of fifteen feet every thirty seconds, and if they hadn't yet started for the surface ...

Max looked out at the building storm clouds. The *Black Watch* creaked and rocked as the wind kicked up again. Marine VHF had predicted the collision of two fronts—one warm, from the south, the other cold, from the northwest—but no one had expected the resulting superstorm to spin this close to the Outer Banks. Or to come up this fast.

He glanced up to see Captain Donnegan striding toward him. "We're pulling up anchor as soon as the divers are out." His friend looked grim.

"I expected it. We've got the coordinates. We'll come back another time." After all these years, he was certain they'd found the figurehead, and now this. He didn't show his disappointment to the captain.

"But we've got another problem. The divers aren't ascending as ordered. They're still trying to dig out that container. They insist on bringing it up." Brady shook his head. "Look, Max. I know what this means to you—so do those kids. But we've got to get out of here.

"You've gotta talk to them, Max. They're doing it for you, you know." The captain frowned, the lines on his weathered face showing more than usual. "And they're putting everyone on board in peril."

Max barely heard the captain's last sentence. He was already halfway to the diving platform and the surface Aquacom.

The crane loomed tall on the far side of the platform. It seemed rock solid, but it swayed in the powerful wind gusts, creaking as if ready to break. It was the lifeline between the divers and the ship. In normal circumstances, the divers would ascend on their own, but in this weather and turbulent waters, they would be safer in the cage, letting the crane bring them up.

He'd just reached the diving platform when Tom Hardy, the dive team member operating the Aquacom, called out that the divers had the pod in the cage. "They're both in the shark cage," he yelled, "with the container—ready to be hoisted up." He signaled the crane operator to start pulling up the shark cage.

Max watched the crane sway once more, and a strange sense of foreboding twisted his gut. The ship rocked violently as another huge swell lifted it. Anything that wasn't battened down rolled, slammed, or slid.

The blast of the ship's alarm startled him.

"All passengers to quarters!" Captain Donnegan ordered over the loudspeakers. He repeated the words three times. The alarm blasted again.

Voices rose as the students trooped to the center of the ship to make their descent. He did a mental count as they passed. Though the winds lashed and his stomach roiled, he tried to tamp down his fear.

A spit of rain hit his face. Then another. In the eastern green-black sky, blasts of lightning lit the storm clouds. The storm seemed to grow to monster-like proportions as it surged toward the salvage ship.

He glanced at the swaying crane for an instant, and then, making a split-second decision, headed to the gear room, grabbed his fins, mask, and scuba tank from his locker. He strapped on the tank as he headed back out to the deck.

The sense of urgency grew stronger. He put his head down against the wind, found the rope ladder, and climbed down.

Whitecaps topped the swells. Clinging to the last rung of the ladder with a one-handed death grip, he slid on his fins, and then put on his mask.

The wind flipped the ladder. He clung to it, gauging his time, watching the crane.

The squalls had closed in on them, darkening the skies. The rain came down in sheets a short distance away, and it was moving toward them.

A huge swell several yards out caught his attention. It grew as if alive, white foam capping its peak.

The closer it came, the higher it rose, in seconds towering above the ship. The captain gunned the engines to turn the bow into the huge wave. As Max put in his mouthpiece, the winds ripped the ladder out from under him. He fell, hit the water. Tried to breathe, but something was wrong. He got a mouthful of saltwater. Sucked it into his windpipe.

The wave grabbed him and dragged him down. He fought to get away, but it was too strong. It carried him in its jaws, pulling him under, holding him, tossing him like a toy. The raging water was as dark as ink. His lungs felt as if they were about to explode. If he couldn't get to the surface fast, he wouldn't make it. Finally, he felt a surge moving upward. He snapped his legs into a scissors kick and shot to the surface.

He broke through, gasping for air. Regurgitating the saltwater he'd inhaled. His heart thudded frantically, from exertion, from fear. Unable to draw in oxygen, he paddled to the ship and grabbed hold of the rope ladder. He coughed. Regurgitated again. Tried to draw in air. He'd always dismissed the notion that a person could drown in an inch of water. Now he knew better.

He'd probably inhaled only a tablespoonful of saltwater from the broken line, but it had almost killed him. He coughed again, spewing saltwater from his lungs. Gasping, he finally pulled air into his lungs. He clung to the rope with one hand, breathing hard, his heart still pounding.

He unlatched the belt that held the tanks in place and examined the hoses. Both the main hose and the secondary hose had been sliced through. It hit him with stark, cold clarity. Someone had just set him up to die.

Above the sounds of the storm, he heard shouting but couldn't make out the words. The ship had taken a direct hit by the wave that pulled him under. A flash of lightning gave him a glimpse of some of the crew looking overboard, yelling and gesturing. He swam a few feet away from the ladder and looked up through the sheets of rain.

The section of deck housing the crane was barely visible. He strained to see through the heavy rain. Jagged lightning flashed. The crane was gone. And with it the cable that tethered the men to the ship. Worse, the divers, still in the cage and tethered to the crane, were being sent straight to a deep underwater canyon.

Max screamed above the wind for someone to throw him a tank. Someone heard him and tossed it overboard. He grabbed it, struggled into it, and tested the oxygen mix.

Another jagged lightning strike gave him light, enough to see the evidence of bubbles and an oil slick. Every second counted. He had to get to his kids. And fast.

He adjusted his headlamp, adjusted the settings on his gear, put in his mouthpiece, and dove deep.

Hit again by the surge of waves and swirling waters, he fought to move through the water, to descend.

He touched his cross and kicked harder. Finally, a glow of light appeared in the murky distance. It blinked a distress signal. He sent a message back with his strobe, swimming hard against the current. It took another two minutes to reach the men. He gave them a hand signal, then swept his light over the cage. It had come to a rest on a shallow ledge about fifty feet below the surface. Still tethered to the crane, which was somewhere below, the cable connecting them was dangerously taut. If the crane moved or shifted with the current, the plunge downward would be fatal.

Fatigue set in, made worse by the strong currents that threatened to sweep him away from the men. He tied his belt to the cage, pulled his diving knife from its sheath, and began to work on the cable.

Chapter Two
Mrs. Littlefield

· · · · · · · · · · · · · · · · ·

I couldn't help doing a little dance step and raising my fist in an air punch with a resounding "Yes!" as I read the front-page headline: LOCAL PROFESSOR FINDS PRICELESS HISTORICAL TREASURE.

I grabbed my coffee and reading glasses and headed to the kitchen table where I slipped into the nearest chair.

Dr. Maxwell Haverhill, local celebrity adventurer, professor of history, and chair of Southern Highlands University's Department of Social Sciences, confirmed at a press conference yesterday that he and his team of researchers, divers, and graduate students have located a rare nineteenth-century artifact. Rumors of the artifact, a figure of a woman originally carved for a ship's figurehead in 1862, have circulated for decades. He said the entire team will reunite here in Eden's Bridge to celebrate their find during the professor's retirement party later this week. With

this news, the guest list has nearly tripled, according
to our sources at the university.

The guest list had tripled? The sip of coffee I'd just swallowed caught in
my windpipe. I choked, coughed, and spewed liquid across the paper.

*What sources? Why wasn't I told? I'm the caterer, for heaven's sakes.
It's Wednesday. The party's Friday. Three hundred, not one hundred?* My
brain went into a spin as I considered what that meant.

My name is Elaine Littlefield, but my friends call me El. I'm a
woman of a certain age and a widow, if you must know. My husband, Herb, passed away back in California thirteen years ago, right
after he asked to be buried with someone named Carmen, but that's
another story.

I stand five-two and three-quarters, providing I hike up my
shoulders and suck in my stomach. I weigh around one hundred
ten unless I have access to chocolate. I keep my silver hair cut
short because I like to race about with the top down on my vintage
Karmann Ghia.

I'm a full-time foodie—at least that's what my best friend,
Hyacinth Gilvertin, calls me—and part-time amateur sleuth, running my investigative services out of the back of The Butler Did It
catering company van. Nothing big, I just look into the odd case that
comes my way from time to time.

Lately, I hadn't had many clients. Mainly because I'd landed the
biggest gig in The Butler's history, Dr. Maxwell Haverhill's retirement party.

I did a couple of deep-breathing exercises to calm my inner self.
It didn't help. I went back to the article.

The figurehead, known as *Lady with a Scarf*, survived three shipwrecks, only to be rediscovered in Paris during World War II and shipped to the States in 1945, its destination a Boston museum near the shop where the piece was carved. The ship capsized in rough seas during a hurricane, and the figurehead, it is said, was thrown overboard by superstitious sailors.

When asked the whereabouts of the figurehead now, the professor refused to say. He did confirm that it has undergone extensive testing, including X-ray analysis and an MRI, to make sure the wood has not deteriorated. "It's in pristine condition," he said. "One of the most beautifully carved ship's figureheads I've seen. A world treasure that will be talked about for years."

Haverhill did not comment when asked for further detail. Neither would he confirm this intriguing artifact is on its way to the maritime museum in Boston. One team member, however, speaking anonymously during a follow-up interview, said it might go to Washington, DC. "Much of the initial testing was done under lock and key in our nation's capital," she told this reporter, "but no one knows why."

World treasure? Washington for testing? Under lock and key?

I stared at the headshot next to the article. The great Dr. Maxwell Haverhill himself. At first glance he looked exactly as one might expect:

tweed vest and coat, a bow tie—of all things—and a hat like the one worn by Sean Connery in *Indiana Jones and the Last Crusade*.

But beneath the turned-down hat brim shone eyes that intrigued me. This was no pointy-headed, dull professor. That spark spoke louder than any faculty photo. Something more than lectures in History 101 was going on behind those eyes. He had something up his tweedy sleeve.

I stopped to consider it again. One of the biggest nights of his career just days away. And he'd recently made what might be the most important discovery in his life. Combine those two events, and what do you get?

I grinned at the photo as a possibility—no, make that probability—came to me. I grabbed my handbag, and headed for the front door. I knew exactly where to look for some answers. Who else but the woman who put together the university's special collections? Southern Highland University archivist Hyacinth Gilvertin had been my best friend since first grade. Now all these decades later, we'd landed in the same university town, a continent away from California where we'd been raised.

It wasn't by happenstance, believe me. Hyacinth landed a plum job at SHU right after she graduated from Berkeley with a doctorate in library science. She loved the South, lived alone following a messy divorce, and encouraged my daughter, Katie, to begin a new life here after her husband, Sandy, left her. For another woman, I might add, but don't get me started. He left my Katie and their precious baby girl. Just walked out on them. Long story short, I wasn't about to let my girls move across the continent without me. Especially given that my BFF already lived here too.

That was seven years ago.

Phone in hand, I hopped into my creamy beige Karmann Ghia, gave the dashboard a pat, and then punched in Hyacinth's number.

She picked up on the first ring. "I thought we weren't getting together until noon."

"Too panicked to wait." I leaned back in the seat, waiting to crank the engine. Hyacinth's voice was of a booming nature, but not loud enough to overcome the noise made by my decades-old Ghia, especially with the top down. "Over-the-top anxious unless you tell me we don't really have two hundred extra guests to feed Friday night."

She laughed. "You must have read the *Chronicle* article. I was going to call you later."

"Cinth, that's not the sort of thing you wait on. Those are huge numbers."

"I wanted to confirm with the powers that be. Which I just now did. We have an edict or two from on high." Though Hyacinth wasn't a partner in my business, she was my self-appointed sous chef and claimed each new dish she came up with brought us more customers. I'd never had the heart to tell her I had to adjust the overabundance of seasonings before daring to serve them. Just like Hyacinth herself, the dishes were flashy and spicy. She especially loved cayenne.

"The admin folks are thrilled with the media explosion over this figurehead. It's putting Southern Highlands on the academic map. They've gotten a rash of late RSVPs in the last few days."

I let out a long sigh. "They may be thrilled, but think about what The Butler's got to do. Hire extra crew, buy more supplies, food, oh me, and order more centerpieces ..." My to-do list burgeoned by the nanosecond.

"The committee discussed the extra help you'll need. They said they'll get the culinary arts students to fill in."

"Are you kidding? I've already hired the sharpest cutlery in the block, so to speak," I said. "I don't have time to train the others."

"I've seen them serve at faculty luncheons. They'll do great."

"And uniforms," I said. "What will they wear?" I pictured kitchen chaos in T-shirts and jeans. "Oh my."

Hyacinth read my mind. "The students have a dress code. They'll stick to it." She laughed, and then added, "There will be compensation, you know."

She had my attention. "As in moola?" I quickly calculated what I would need and gave her a figure.

"You're good."

I chuckled. "I have to be."

She confirmed my quote.

Even so, I breathed, "Holy cannoli."

I could almost hear her grin. "Exactly," she said.

"The figurehead will be here. Don't tell me it's not." She tried to interrupt, but I was on a roll. "It will be on exhibit in the new wing. Word's gotten out, and that's why all these folks are descending on Eden's Bridge."

She laughed. "If I tell you, I'll have to shoot you."

"I take it that's a yes."

"I plead the fifth."

"So you're involved."

Sighing, she said, "Honestly, El. I can't tell you. I promised Max."

That got me to thinking I was certainly right in my assessment. Before I could say so, Hyacinth added, "We do have an edict from on high for adding the extra help and the high price we knew you'd demand."

My radar went up. "What edict?"

She sighed. "Let's wait till we get together. Bad news is easier to give—and take—in person." Amusement tinged her voice, the kind that bubbled just below the surface. The kind that meant trouble. "I tell you what," she said. "To make up for the bad news I have to deliver, I'll help with the extra shopping. I've been at the library more hours than any sane person should admit to. Truth is, I could use some time away. How about a trip out to the pig chalet?"

"I'd like the company."

"Because no matter how you slice it, pigs still die and you get depressed. You need me to cheer you up afterward."

"'Slice? That isn't funny," I said. "Even the thought of escargot makes me—" I laughed, interrupting myself. "Here I go again. Animal rights, even for snails. Hey, thanks, my friend. I can use the help. Ribs for an extra two hundred people. That may not be so easy. I'll be there in five. Get ready."

"I was born ready," she said.

I revved the engine and raced down my driveway, glad the Ghia's canvas top was down. Nothing like the early morning air hitting your face to wake up a girl. As if the *Chronicle* article hadn't already.

Hyacinth was watching for me through her front window. She waved as I drove up, and then trotted from the house in jeans and a wild, colorful poncho. She'd tied her thicket of unruly curls back with a long scarf, and her hair's latest shade of red and fuchsia caught the sun. Part of what I'd loved about my friend for decades was her determination to go against stereotypes.

"Glad we're doing the Thelma and Louise thing," she said, patting the folded canvas top as she passed. "Makes it easier to get in."

I grinned at her as I reached over to open the door from the inside. She sidled in, her spine as straight as a pool cue, and then dropped like a stone into the passenger seat. "New skinny jeans," she said, breathlessly. "They're supposed to make you look twenty pounds lighter, so of course I ordered them."

"That would be great," I said, "if you could breathe." I shaded my eyes with my hand as I studied her. "Internet?"

She grinned as she buckled her seat belt. "You betcha. From If You've Got It, Flaunt It. Dot com. It's for women of a certain size." She looked my slight frame up and down. "But you ain't got it to flaunt, El. Sorry to say, you skinny little thing."

I couldn't help laughing with her as I glanced at my thighs. "Even so, cellulite has no favorites." I was still chuckling as I pressed the accelerator and took the corner without braking. She grabbed hold of the passenger-side armrest, ever the drama queen.

"Okay, spill," I said, guiding the car toward the interstate.

She glanced at me through her oversized sunglasses. "All in good time," she said. "Let's just enjoy the country air for now."

A few minutes later we were on the interstate heading south. A red Peterbilt loaded with chrome roared up beside me, then geared down. The driver shot me a glare, fell back, and pulled in behind me. The shiny grill loomed large in my rearview mirror. The driver hit his air horn.

I frowned. "What's he so upset about?"

"I think you floored it when he was trying to pass," Hyacinth said as if it were an everyday occurrence. Which it was.

By the time I reached the turnoff to Wilber's Pig Farm, she still hadn't spilled the beans about the edict. But for good reason. We'd talked through what we needed to beg, steal, or borrow within the next forty-eight hours. She took notes as I listed the extra ingredients we needed for the rub, the coleslaw, the Beauregard soufflé, the hush puppies, and the cupcakes. She also made calls to the florist for extra centerpieces and to the cupcake designer who was making the custom beauties for the professor.

We were discussing the table placement when we reached Wilber's Pig Farm. The farmer was out feeding his pigs beside the barn and saw us coming. He waved, climbed over a fence, and trotted over to the car before we got out.

"Been expecting you," he said. "Saw the big news in the paper. So you're expecting three-hundurd, 'stead of one. Already got the word out to some of my farmer friends. Not to worry. We'll have all the ribs you need."

"How do your farmer friends treat their animals?"

He stooped and peered into my face with a frown. "All them pigs are bein' raised happy, pigs in clover, just like mine, right up until the minute they're—" He made a slashing motion across his neck. "No factory farms in my circle of hog friends, believe you me."

We took care of the business end of the deal, and then Hyacinth and I were on our way to the tomato farm a few miles down the road. As we drove, we reminisced about some of our recent run-ins with our rival caterers, Bubba and Junior Sutherland, who owned Sons of the South—or SOS, as the young hotshots called themselves.

"They were heirlooms, you know." I was getting riled up just recalling what they had done to my van. "Perfectly ripe and ready for making tomato bisque."

"They might as well have been cannon balls," Hyacinth said. Mirth bubbled below the surface of her words. "You have to admit, it was amusing."

"Amusing, my foot. You were screaming bloody murder as the van careened all over the interstate."

"The EMTs thought we'd been shot." She doubled over with a loud guffaw. "They were about to declare the whole thing a crime scene. Wrap us and the van in yellow tape."

"Wasn't funny. I was the one driving when the tire blew."

"And then there was the Beauregard business," she said, "I'll never forget the look on your face when you found the potato."

"Who puts potatoes in tailpipes anymore? Errant teens, that's who. Not grown boys in their twenties."

"Fess up," she said. "You wouldn't have been half as mad if it had been a russet. You just have a thing for the 'Queen of all Sweet Potatoes,' the almighty Beauregard."

"The head of Greenpeace would've felt the same way if he'd found a baby spotted owl in his tailpipe."

She hooted. "Touché. Cut 'em a little slack. They just wanted you out of the way so they could have a shot at having the winning bid for the gala."

"Wanted me out of the way?" I sputtered. "You're forgetting about the forged letter from my alma mater. They basically said my credentials were a fraud."

"Their signatures were clever, you've got to admit."

"N. Corrigible? D. S. Troy?" I had to laugh with her. "I could have wrung their beefy necks. Still could."

"You're right. They've got a lot to learn. Right now they're dervishes looking for a place to whirl. It's too bad their godfather is holder of the purse strings."

My ears perked up. "What do you mean? What godfather?""

"You know the new board member, Silas Sutherland?"

How could I forget a face that's plastered on billboards all over town? "The real estate guru, right?"

"That's the one."

I glanced at her, but she was staring straight ahead, obviously trying to get up the nerve to tell me something unpleasant.

"Okay, what about him?"

"They say he bought his way onto the board of regents."

"So, that's news?" I laughed, shaking my hair in the wind. "Everybody knows he provided funding for the new library wing. And that was his ticket."

"Sutherland may be new," she said, "but he's got clout. And not just the the kind that money buys." She paused. "He's in thick with the VP of finance, who listens to every word Sutherland speaks as if it's pure gold. If he says no extra funding for The Butler, you'll have to abide by the original contract."

"Uh-oh." I thought for a moment. "Something tells me this has to do with the edict, that we've got some strings attached."

"You betcha." She took off her sunglasses and looked over at me, waiting for the neurons to connect.

They did. In a flash. "Oh dear. You're kidding." In my distress, I swung the steering wheel hard to the right, something I have a tendency to do if I'm looking at the person next to me. A loud screech of brakes followed as a little Toyota of some sort moved out of my way. A feeling of dread swept over me. "What else?"

"Silas wants us to hire SOS as our sous chefs for the retirement dinner."

"You've got to be kidding. They're a couple of kids in grown-up bodies, and that's about the kindest thing I can say about them." The brothers who ran SOS were recent graduates of some unknown New York culinary school, or so they'd led the folks in Eden's Bridge to believe.

She rolled her eyes. "The problem is, Silas wants the boys to be under your tutelage. He thinks they need to learn a thing or two, get better at what they do. He's insisting."

"SOS has been trying to either run me out of town or take down my business for weeks. And Silas wants me to hire them?" I frowned. "As sous chefs? It's a setup for sabotage."

"If you don't," Hyacinth said, "no extra moola comin' your way from the university." She rubbed her fingers together.

I glared at her. "So we have no choice."

She shook her head. "And you can't back out now."

She knew I'd borrowed against the company to have the funds to make this event work. Our success would mean new business, new gigs, money in the coffers to replace what I'd borrowed.

I drew in a deep breath. "Okay," I said. "What's the worst that can happen?"

Chapter Three

When I get nervous about an upcoming catering gig, I bake chocolate-chip cookies. When I get nervous about a case I'm looking into, I bake double-chocolate-chip cookies, adding white chocolate to the bitter-sweet. When my anxiety meter spikes, I bake triple chippers, adding a cup or two of butterscotch chips to the mix. While they bake, I crank up Mozart on my iPod, conduct an imaginary orchestra with my spatula, and then do a boot-scootin' boogie the length of the kitchen.

It was a triple chipper night. Or maybe I should say morning. I'd been awake since 3:17, and this was my third batch. Rather than lying in bed, staring at the ceiling, and worrying about how I was going to pull off tonight's dinner with grace and elegance, I'd risen to do battle in my sock monkey pajamas and my grandmother's faded ruffled apron.

The Sutherland boys had been given a list of their duties, but the closer we got to the retirement dinner, the more I worried they might try to bring us down if not watched carefully. It was in their nature.

I glanced at the clock, which read 6:24. Dawn was about to break, and I needed to get upstairs to change into my work clothes before Bubba, Junior, and their crew arrived. Catering day was always one of organized chaos. Most of the expanded crew—including my daughter, Katie, who played manager when I wasn't there—was already at work at the Encore kitchen. I planned to join them as soon as Enrique and Juan arrived with the ribs.

I pulled out the large tub of sauce, a unique recipe I called my secret weapon. For perfect ribs, you need crisp spiciness on the outside, succulent juicy flavor on the inside, and a burst of flavor from the sweet and pungent glaze brushed on at the last minute. The timing had to be perfect, or the sugary sauce would scorch.

I tasted the sauce, let out a sigh at the heavenly taste, and then closed the refrigerator door.

With Mozart streaming through my earbuds, I treated myself to one more cha-cha slide across the kitchen.

I halted midcrescendo as an off-pitch chime rang out from the percussion section. As the chime sounded a third time, I realized it was my doorbell, not the London symphony.

I left the kitchen for the dining room, stepped up to the lace panels at the window, and peered through. A man appeared to be stretching out his hamstrings, or whatever they're called, on my front porch. I didn't recognize his profile, but he wore running clothes and had a sports towel hanging around his neck.

I pulled the door open and blinked when I saw who it was.

"Dr. Haverhill," I said, opening the door wider. I recognized the professor from his picture in the *Chronicle*, but what was he doing here on my front porch, especially at this time of day?

Dr. Haverhill scratched his forehead and then seemed to take a sudden interest in his running shoes.

I followed his gaze for a second and caught sight of my sock-monkey slippers. And pajamas. And Grandma's faded apron. I didn't remember running a comb through my hair. Or washing the sleep out of my eyes. I felt my face grow warm and wished the floor would just swallow me now and be done with it.

"I need to talk to you," he said. "About tonight's dinner."

He gazed anywhere but at me and my pajamas. Even so, I could see his expression and it wasn't that of a man looking forward to his retirement party.

"Tonight's dinner?" It came out in a squeak.

He nodded. "I'm afraid I have bad news."

I couldn't bear hearing bad news, standing here in my doorway in my sock monkey slippers and PJs. Don't ask me why, I just couldn't do it.

"Cookies," I said, gesturing toward the kitchen. "Uh, why don't you come in and help yourself?" I reached for his arm and pulled him inside, and then couldn't believe I'd done that.

"The cookies are cooling on the counter. Milk's in the fridge." I rambled, while backing slowly to the stairs at the other end of the entry hall, hoping I'd aim right and not land on my fanny. "I need to run upstairs for a minute. I'll be right back. I promise. We can talk. Whatever it is that you need to talk over, we can indeed talk." Finally, I reached the stairs, turned, and trotted out of his sight, the entire time speculating about what bad news he had about tonight's dinner.

I returned to the kitchen in less than ten minutes, ready to roll: face scrubbed, pixie hair fluffed, clad in baggy jeans and a work shirt.

Dr. Haverhill, sitting at the kitchen table, faced the backyard garden and oak trees at the rear of the property. He was chewing a chocolate chipper, something I've found can calm the most troubled soul. Two others, one from each batch, sat on a small plate in front of him. He seemed lost in thought.

He stood as I walked toward him.

"Please, no formalities. We're practically old friends by now," I said with a laugh. "I don't greet just anyone in my pajamas."

He gave me a stiff smile. "I'm Max Haverhill," he said, extending his hand. As if I didn't know.

I shook his hand and smiled into what I realized was a very good-looking face. Strong. Lots of character. With eyes the color of a deep mountain lake. My heart did a little cha-cha slide of its own. "Elaine Littlefield," I said, rather breathlessly. "My friends call me El. And since you're officially a friend …"

"El," he said. "Yes, it suits you." I wondered about that but didn't ask why. "Please, call me Max."

"Okay, Max, how about some coffee to go with your cookies?"

He shook his head. "I really can't stay. I came by to tell you about the cancellation in person. I planned to wait until the hour was decent and phone you, but I saw your kitchen light on."

The thought of him watching me dance made my face burn once again. "I bake when I can't sleep. I play Mozart, *Eine Kleine Nachtmusik*, and—"

Then it hit me. He'd just said cancellation. "Wait, what did you say?" He started to speak, but I held up a hand. "Just hold on a minute."

I went to the fridge, grabbed a carton of milk, and then opened the cupboard door over the counter and picked up two glasses. I had to keep moving or I would bawl on the spot. I set the glasses down and then headed to the cooling rack on the stove and placed more cookies on the plate.

"We have to cancel tonight's dinner."

"I thought that's what you said. But you can't."

"I must."

"No," I wanted to shout, or at least cry. "No," I said, the decibel level increasing. "Why?"

"I can't say."

"You have to have a reason."

"I do. A very good one."

"What is it?" I felt the heat of tears behind my eyes.

"As I said, I can't say."

I stood and moved to the center of the kitchen. Mainly because I couldn't sit still. Not with this news. "You wouldn't believe how much food has been prepared," I said patiently as I paced. "We're expecting three hundred and twelve people. Think of it. And the preparations. The people flying in—your people—historians, dignitaries ... the ... the ..." I ran out of nouns. "Everyone.

"Most people don't know what goes into putting on a dinner party for even one hundred guests. You start weeks ahead of time, hiring a crew of at least two dozen—and in the case of your party, twice that." I was on a roll, still pacing. "I hired a couple of extra sous chefs, at least a dozen extra servers, still others to set the tables and refresh the food warmers. And yet another crew for cleanup."

I grabbed a double-chocolate chipper to give my hand something to do besides shake a finger at him. "You just have no idea what it's taken to coordinate all this—and then to have two hundred people added to the guest list two days ago—" My voice rose an octave higher and threatened to keep rising. "All the preparation and planning and people who are counting on the night's wages and tips. My daughter, Katie, is just one of many." I took a huge bite of the cookie.

The professor just sat there, watching me. I couldn't be sure, but I thought I saw warmth and understanding in his expression. Kind eyes always bring tears to mine. I sniffled.

"And my business ... oh dear, what about my business?" Tears now pooled in my lower lids. "You can't do this to us. We need this event." I grabbed a napkin from the holder and gave my nose a swipe. "And you can't even tell me why the event must be canceled?" I'd put in everything I had, plus some I didn't, even taking money out of my retirement account. If tonight's dinner didn't happen, my little company would be bankrupt by the end of the month.

He was fingering an antique-looking cross I hadn't noticed before. It hung from a leather cord tied at the back of his neck. Since it was a well-known fact among the gossips in town that he'd never married, I wondered if he'd ever seen a woman cry before.

"It's complicated."

I huffed out a sigh as I slid into the chair next to his. "Please reconsider. Whatever's causing you to cancel, can't you deal with it tomorrow?"

"I wish I could. But in truth, we'll all rest easier if we cancel." He stood to go. "I'm sorry about your business and all the work you've gone to. I really am. But it's just too dangerous."

I trotted along behind him as he headed through the dining room. "You must have known that bringing the figurehead to Eden's Bridge means that every Tom, Dick, and Harry who's ever dabbled in antiquities, legal or otherwise, would congregate here too."

He turned, and a smile almost made it to his lips. I saw his mouth twitch in one corner. "I will make inquiries about compensation for all you've put into my dinner. Maybe the food could be taken to Asheville to a homeless shelter, or …"

I looked down, so disappointed I could have cried. Again.

He didn't say good-bye or even "I'm sorry," but turned back around, opened my front door, and jogged down the steps. I stood watching from the doorway as he continued down the driveway toward the street.

Seconds later, Enrique and Juan Fox arrived in The Butler Did It catering van. One hundred fifty pounds of prime baby back ribs lay in big tubs in the back of the van. When they opened the door, the fragrance of the rub wafted out. The crew had applied the rub last night at the Encore, a dinner theater with an adjoining restaurant-sized kitchen, built for Southern Highland University's school of culinary arts and for the drama department. It was perfect for dinners such as this. Or it would have been perfect.

But back to Enrique and Juan and the van full of ribs. I raised my hand in greeting. Enrique jumped out of the driver's side, and Juan exited on the other.

"Okay to leave the ribs in the van while we get the pit ready?" Enrique asked as he closed the door of the van.

I hesitated. What would we do with one hundred fifty pounds of raw baby backs? Or cooked, for that matter?

I walked with them to the barbecue pit in the rear corner of my yard. They had laid the apple wood yesterday, so it was just a matter of lighting the fire, letting it cook down to coals, and then keeping the coals at a constant temperature.

I started to tell them that Dr. Haverhill had canceled dinner. And then stopped as a new thought occurred to me.

The Butler Did It wasn't about to cancel.

I had no idea why Dr. Haverhill thought going forward with the dinner would be dangerous, but I was going to find out. And I had only a short time to do it.

Chapter Four

Enrique had parked the catering van to one side of the garage door, so I had a clear shot out of the driveway.

I sped down Crab Apple Lane, turned onto University Avenue, and spotted Dr. Haverhill jogging along at a fairly nice clip. I was impressed. I wasn't sure how old the retiring professor might be, but he seemed to be in good shape for any age. Very good shape.

I caught up with him, honked, and pulled over. He halted, his face red with exertion. He came over to the Ghia, looking puzzled.

"I'm not a quitter, Dr. Haverhill."

"Max."

"Okay. I'm not a quitter, Max."

"Neither am I, under ordinary circumstances …"

"Have you received threats?"

"Not exactly."

His laugh lines disappeared. Something in his eyes said perhaps something worse had happened.

"Do you want to talk about it?" I removed my oversized sunglasses and propped them above my forehead, headband style. "Before you call off the dinner, I think we should talk."

"I plan to make my calls as soon as I get home." He nodded toward the university campus, which was in the distance. "I'm only a mile or so down University Avenue."

A perfect opportunity to do some digging and perhaps save the day. Or, rather, night. "I'll drive you."

He looked grateful, opened the door, and dropped into the passenger seat. "Thanks."

As soon as he had fastened his seat belt, I checked for traffic and pulled away from the curb. I stepped on the gas, revving the Ghia's little engine as I shifted gears.

After a few moments he frowned and glanced at the speedometer.

"There's something else you should know," he said, "about the figurehead." He glanced at me. "It's here."

I smiled at him. "I know."

"How could you possibly know?"

"I guessed when I first read the article about it, and you, in the *Chronicle*. And it doesn't take a PhD—sorry—to figure out that with that kind of press, you're going to receive threats and all kinds of attention. Am I right?"

"The figurehead was delivered by special transport last night."

I swerved around a car puttering in my lane. Max inhaled sharply. My synapses fired. I needed to stop and process everything the professor—er, Max—was telling me. "Do you mind if I pull over for a moment?"

His eyebrows shot up.

"I think better when I'm not driving."

He looked relieved.

By now we were parallel with the university faculty parking lot. I turned in with only a moderate tire squeal, spotted an empty space, and glided rather nicely into it. I cut the engine and turned to look at him. I had only a short time to convince Max that the show had to go on. My company's very life was at stake.

"Okay, so the figurehead is already here."

He nodded. "Under lock and key."

"You planned to put it on exhibit tonight?"

He smiled. "Am I that transparent? Yes, I talked to Hyacinth and James Delancy—plus a few others in administration—and then I made arrangements for the carving to be transported from DC. The approval didn't come through until a couple of weeks ago."

"Hyacinth knows about this?" I couldn't believe my best friend kept a secret like this from me.

"I know you two are good friends. I swore her to secrecy. As university archivist, yes, she needed to know. She approved the plan and has been on board every step of the way."

He reached in the pocket of his sweatpants, pulled out his cell phone, pressed a few icons, scrolled through some pictures, and then handed it to me. "This is why I need to cancel."

I saw a man in his late fifties, dressed casually, his silver hair stylishly collar length with a bit of curl. Fairly tall, with a slim build. He was turned slightly away from the camera so I couldn't see his eyes. A beautiful woman stood next to him. I could see only her elegant profile and spiked blonde hair. "Who are they?"

"His name is Marcel Devereaux. He's an art and antiquities dealer from Paris. He's well-known in certain circles. And those circles aren't necessarily aboveboard. The woman, I don't know. He's said to have a companion who's connected to high-end thieves. But I don't know how true that is. European skullduggery, I suppose, and really, just hearsay." Max frowned and, taking the phone from me, studied the photo. "He's been following me. I've seen him several times over the past few days. He and the woman were on my train from DC to Charlotte. And then I spotted them here in Eden's Bridge yesterday. I don't believe in coincidences."

"Why do you consider him so dangerous that you would cancel tonight's dinner?"

"There was an attempt on my life during my last dive. A deliberate act. Someone cut both hoses to my oxygen tank. I didn't find out until I was in the water."

"If he deals in antiquities, what if he's here for the event, pure and simple? Maybe he wants to rub elbows with the who's who of the antiquities adventurers." I gave him a confident smile. "If he's on the up-and-up, there's nothing to be worried about, right?"

"Anything is possible with Devereaux. But whatever it is, I doubt that it's on the up-and-up."

"Why do you think he had anything to do with the sabotage of your oxygen tank?"

"After we docked a few weeks ago, I saw him in a pub with a member of our crew. Money was exchanged. There was no reason for this Parisian to be in that spot at that time."

"But you didn't see him while you were in DC?"

Max shook his head.

"How about letting me look into it? See what I can find out." My life suddenly flashed before my eyes. Was I nuts? My company was about to put on the biggest event in Eden's Bridge history and I was about to go AWOL to unmask a possible bad guy. I told myself to count to ten and calm down. If I didn't take time to snoop, The Butler might lose everything anyway.

It helped that Katie could pinch-hit for me as manager of The Butler team. Even so, my brain was spinning to the point I felt dizzy. And Max still didn't look convinced.

I leaned forward, determined to keep him from speaking until I'd finished. "If I can get the skinny on Devereaux and make sure he's not up to something nefarious, will you agree to go ahead with the dinner?"

Max surprised me by throwing his head back and laughing. "Get the skinny?"

"I don't see what's so funny." I put my sunglasses back on my nose.

"I love your tenacity."

"This wouldn't be my first investigation, you know." I lowered my sunglasses to study his expression.

"Hyacinth told me you dabble in PI work."

Something about the word *dabble* hit me wrong. But I quickly felt the irritation fade as I met Max's mountain-lake-hued gaze.

"You said earlier that you had to put on this dinner for financial reasons. You have a stake in my dinner being successful, true?"

"A huge stake." My eyes watered again as I considered it. I pushed my sunglasses back into place. "It will pull The Butler Did It out of the red. If it's canceled, I'll be out a lot ... of ..." My voice caught and I couldn't go on. The thought of losing my company hit me all over again. Sometimes my PI work took precedence over The Butler. The catering side of my business suffered when I did pro bono for friends. And I'd had a string of those lately. Tears stung behind my eyes, but I was proud of myself for being calmer than I'd been in my kitchen.

Max's brow furrowed in thought. "I'll hold off canceling for a short time. How fast can you work?"

"Speed of lightning." I started the engine.

"Somehow that doesn't surprise me."

"You need to text Devereaux's photo to me. And do you mind riding with me back to my place?" I didn't give him a chance to answer. I had little time to spare.

He pulled out his phone, and I gave him my cell number. I heard my phone chirp a few seconds later.

I did a one-eighty and Max grabbed the edge of the worn Naugahyde seat with one hand.

"Not to worry," I said. "It just feels faster because the top's down."

He nodded and wrapped his white-knuckled fingers around the armrest on the passenger-side door. "I like your spirit, El," he shouted over the noise of the wind. His hair blew straight out behind him, and he was grinning from ear to ear.

I'd never heard my name shouted more beautifully.

Chapter Five

My house came into view. I hit the brakes and turned into the drive-way, narrowly missing the catering van. We both lurched forward at the sudden stop. "You can stay here, if you'd like," I said and swung open the driver's-side door.

The humidity was rising along with the sun. The cicadas were out in force this year, and this morning they'd turned up the volume on their buzzing. Several frogs set up a competing racket from the small creek behind my office. Well, actually, it's a potting shed that I turned into an office.

The professor, still a bit white-faced, just nodded as he grabbed a handkerchief from his rear pocket and mopped his brow.

I headed to the back corner of my yard, behind my vegetable garden, where Juan and Enrique were turning the racks of ribs in the pit. The charwood sizzled and sparked, and hickory-scented smoke rose. The scent was divine. Bubba and Junior sat in lawn chairs, read-ing magazines and talking.

"You boys comfortable?" I tried not to sound too sarcastic. "You might lend a helping hand to Juan. I need to take Enrique with me."

The Sutherland boys shrugged lazily and stood to stretch. Bubba yawned and scratched his chest. Lazy or wily, I wondered. They grew very quiet and attentive when I told Enrique that he was needed at the Encore and why. I had the eerie feeling they were watching me like birds of prey, and noting everything I said, especially when I mentioned surveillance.

Enrique, a top student in the culinary arts department, had discovered that he was a talented chef when it came to pit smoking and grilling. I'd also found he was even better at working with electronic devices such as bugs and minicams.

"Right now?" He'd already pulled off his apron.

"It can't wait."

He glanced at his younger brother. "Go ahead," Juan said. "I can handle it."

I pinched off a piece of meat on the end of a rack and popped it into my mouth. It nearly melted on my tongue, it was so tender. "Perfecto," I said as I chewed. "Absolutely perfecto."

I turned back to Enrique. "I've got the Ghia," I said. "And the backseat isn't very big. You know where the equipment is?"

"Same as last time?"

"Yes," I said. "Wireless only."

He trotted off toward the potting shed, where I kept a variety of such gadgets. I followed to make sure everything was in order and to explain precisely what he needed to do.

I hurried to the car, Enrique trotting to keep up. Max had extricated himself and now leaned against the passenger-side door, his legs crossed at the ankles.

I made introductions and then waited, trying not to look at my watch, while they climbed in and fastened seat belts. The morning sun was higher now, the wind warm against my face as I turned out of my driveway and pressed on the gas.

"Mrs. Littlefield always drives like this," Enrique shouted from the backseat as I rounded a corner, the tires squealing. "Someday, I tell her, she will not be so lucky when the sheriff catches her. I tell her this all the time."

Max raised his brows.

I faked a scowl at Enrique in the rearview mirror, and he mugged back. Enrique was the taller of the two brothers, with jet-black hair, long legs, and pecan-hued skin, and dark, expressive eyes. Juan was of a shorter and stockier build and was a little better looking.

With Max shouting directions, before long we were turning onto his street. "Third house down," Max said, glancing over at me. His face held a new expression, almost as if he was seeing me for the first time.

I came to a halt in front of a small two-story English-style house with a high-pitched roof. I almost laughed as I surveyed the front yard. Where most people grew a lawn, seedlings thrived in perfectly aligned rows. Signs made of empty seed packets stood at the end of each row identifying corn, squash, spinach, and tomatoes, among others. Amid a dozen other loamy rows stood a larger sign: Grow Vegetables Not Lawns.

I liked the professor more every minute, and we'd spent only a few hours together. I met his gaze. For a breathless moment, I imagined … well, I didn't want to go there. I had it on good authority from my hairdresser friend, Mabel, one of my best sources for such things, that half the women in town had either tried or were in the process of trying to catch the professor's eye.

I lifted my chin a notch. I was above all such romantic folderol.

Max opened the passenger door, unwound his legs to get out, then hesitated a moment and leaned back in. "I enjoyed our morning together."

Be still my dancing heart. So much for the folderol.

"Let me know what you find out about Devereaux," he said. "I'm still not convinced that the dinner should go on. If we're going to cancel, we must do it soon."

"Give me till eleven," I said, hugely disappointed. I flashed him a brilliant smile and gave him a mock salute, which in my humble opinion spoke volumes about my confidence that all would be well.

He sighed and nodded reluctantly.

Minutes later, I roared into the Encore parking lot and halted in a parking space near the service-entrance side of the building. I checked my watch. My mind spun with last-minute preparations for tonight's dinner: overseeing Enrique's setup, syncing it with the monitor in The Butler Did It van once Juan delivered the ribs, getting the crew working on the table setups, hoping the university maintenance crew had pulled out the extra round tables from storage, placed chairs around each, and laid out the linens.

But before I could get started on all of that, I needed to find out about Devereaux.

Hyacinth must have heard the rattle of the Ghia's muffler, because before I could set the brake, the Encore's side door opened, and she stepped out and waved.

Her red curls glinted in the sun, and her tunic flapped as she approached. She wore a Cheshire smile.

"What on earth …?" I grinned as she approached.

"I've just met the most adorable man."

"You think all men are adorable." I opened the trunk and retrieved my planner, my two totes full of notes and reminders, and of course, my laptop in its case and myriad other tools of my trade. Hyacinth took one of the totes and closed the trunk.

She raised a brow. "Not quite true, but almost."

I laughed lightly and then stopped, thinking about the ticking clock. "Do you have a copy of the guest list?"

"It's on your desk."

"Cinth," I said as I followed her up the stone steps. "Max wants to cancel the dinner."

She halted midstep. Her hand flew to her collarbone. "He wants to what?"

"Cancel."

"He can't. Not now. Everything's in place. Even the figurehead. The dedication of the new wing. It's all for him."

"There was an attempt against his life on the ship. Since then, a man has been following him. He was on the same train as Max and the figurehead, and is now here in Eden's Bridge. Max is pretty sure there's a connection between the two."

"Could be a coincidence."

I shrugged. "Max doesn't think so. I've held him off for now, but can't for very long. I said I'd look into it."

"All the work we've gone to … Your business, the needed income …" She shuddered, dropping her hand. "The giant headache

of canceling with more than three hundred guests." She started up
the steps again, and I followed a couple of steps behind.

"The guy he thinks could be involved is Marcel Devereaux, an
antiquities dealer from Paris."

Her eyes opened wide. "The drop-dead gorgeous man I just
mentioned? He had a French accent."

I stopped in my tracks. "You're kidding."

"I'm not," she called after me and huffed her way up a few more
stairs. "He just happened into the kitchen. Said he was lost. And
believe me, he was no delivery boy. Not the way he was dressed." She
waggled her brows. "Talk about to the nines."

A new thought nibbled at my brain. "Just wandered into the Encore's
kitchen? The theater is hardly a building one would venture into if lost."

"That's what I was thinking." Hyacinth looked distressed. "What
did you say his name was again?"

"Devereaux," I said. "Marcel Devereaux." I pulled out my phone,
opened the email from Max with the photo attachment, and handed
it to Hyacinth.

She went pale. "It's him."

Hyacinth dropped into a chair as soon as we reached the kitchen.
She was head of the planning committee responsible for the evening.
"We can't let this happen," she said, shaking her head.

I sat next to her. "I'm with you, but sadly, the professor is calling
the shots. Now, tell me everything this man did and said to you or
to the crew."

"The crew kids were busy unloading a shipment of fresh shrimp, starting their prep with the vegetables—you know, the usual pre-party chaos."

I tried not to be impatient. I worried that Max would pull the plug before I could clear Devereaux. "Where were you during this time?"

"I'd just stepped out of the walk-in fridge when, above the hubbub, I heard someone speaking in French. Very loudly. As if arguing. I pushed through the swinging door to check it out. And there he was, this gorgeous man speaking French into a smartphone."

I swallowed hard. "Then what?"

"He turned when I came in, looked not the least bit flustered, ended the call, and—get this—said he was checking out our campus for his daughter who was considering applying to come here next year. I gave him directions to the administration building, and off he went."

"You're certain it was the same man?"

She rolled her eyes. "Of course I'm certain. If you'd seen him, you'd know what I mean."

"Did he ask about the dinner, or mention anything related?"

She shook her head. "Not a thing. Just talked about his daughter."

"Why would someone who lives in Paris, the mecca of all things culinary, come to Southern Highlands University in tiny Eden's Bridge?"

"I was thinking the same thing." She frowned as she pushed a stray red curl behind her ear. It sprung out of place immediately.

"Now let's get down to real business," she said. "We've got to find a way to convince Dr. Celebrity Pants that he's as safe and sound here in Eden's Bridge as he would be anywhere."

"Dr. Celebrity Pants?" I sighed. I wondered if she'd ever called the professor that to his face. "And just how are we going to do that?"

She winked. "You're the brains of the outfit. You tell me."

This time I rolled my eyes. "I'll check the guest list to see if by some strange coincidence, there's a Marcel Devereaux. Maybe that will convince the professor that he's here for a legitimate reason."

She fanned her face. "And I, dear friend, will make a supreme sacrifice and run down the gorgeous Frenchman somewhere on campus." She grabbed her handbag and headed toward the door. She hesitated and looked back. "If all else fails with Dr. Celebrity Pants, use your feminine wiles."

"Moi?" I said in mock horror.

Chapter Six
Hyacinth

. . . .

Hyacinth huffed and puffed her way around the nearly empty campus. She tried the administration building first, but it was deserted except for a couple of janitors. Finals week had come and gone, and the students were on a break before the summer session. She headed to the chapel at the far end, skirting a few parking lots along the way. Very few cars, and she passed only a few walkers and a single jogger on her way. It took close to an hour to cover the campus. She stopped near the library and dialed El.

El didn't pick up, so she left a message. "Hey, girlfriend. No cute men of a certain age, French or otherwise, to be seen. I'm heading to the library to check the new security system installed around you-know-what, then home to freshen up. Not to fear, I'll be back to help you with last-minute details. Call me and let me know if you sweet-talked the prof into going forward."

Two security guards were posted at the library door. She greeted them, showed them her ID badge, and then hurried up the steps, unlocked the door, and let herself in.

She flipped on the overhead lights and walked into the new wing, which would be dedicated to the professor during tonight's ceremony. The twenty-four smaller exhibits in glass cases contained various artifacts that Max had discovered through the years, most having to do with American history from the Colonial period through World War II. She had designed the spaces herself and as she passed each one, checked to make sure it was arranged correctly, its signage visible.

She saved the best for last. After ducking into her office, she grabbed her archival gloves and a stepstool, then hurried back. Slowly and with awe, she approached the platform that held the figurehead. It had been removed from the shipping crate, then placed on a platform encased with Plexiglas. It was then covered with a dark royal-blue velvet cloth, to be unveiled during the dedication ceremony here in the library.

She removed the cloth, folded it, and put it to one side. She drew on her gloves, punched in the code to open the Plexiglas encasement, and stepped closer to the figurehead, captivated by its beauty. Its surface held a sheen that made it appear to be made of marble. She knew its worth to be in the tens of thousands. Looking up into the woman's face, she smiled as the whimsical thought came to her: *If only you could talk.*

No wonder Max had spent a lifetime looking for the *Lady*. And his father before him. It would be part of their library exhibit for only one month, and then it would be sent to the Maritime Museum in Boston, finally completing the delivery expected nearly seventy years ago.

She rested her fingertips on the figurehead's arm, almost reluctant to leave.

Just then a scratching sound outside a nearby window caught her attention. Perhaps it was footsteps, or shrubbery moving against the glass. She went over to investigate but couldn't see anything.

She replaced the covering, flicked off the lights, and headed to the front entrance. The guards looked up as she exited.

"I heard something outside one of the windows while I was in the new wing."

"Something?" The taller guard raised a brow, and a slight smirk played at the corner of his mouth. "Can you be more specific?"

"I can lead you to the exact window, if that will help," she said. "Or you two can do your jobs and investigate the perimeter yourselves."

Hyacinth walked to her car in the faculty lot, more than ready to settle in for some time to rest and go over her speech. It had been a long morning, and it promised to be an even longer afternoon and evening. She would put on some soft music and relax in a bubble bath.

With those pleasurable thoughts in mind, she was soon turning into her driveway. She clicked her garage door opener, and watched the garage door rise.

After pulling in, she turned off the ignition, closed the garage door behind her, and stepped out of her vehicle into the stuffy heat damp of the closed garage. Times like this she missed California's dry heat. The South's humidity was legendary. She rummaged through her handbag for a tissue to pat her face as she walked toward the side door that led to a small yard by her house.

Hearing an odd noise that sounded like footsteps, she looked up, startled.

Two people of indeterminate gender, one slightly taller than the other, stepped out of the shadows. They stood shoulder to shoulder in front of her only exit. The overhead garage light cast an odd glow on their masks. One was Emeril Lagasse, the other Julia Child. Strangely, they both wore medical scrubs.

It took just a split second for her mind to leap from fear to irritation. The Sutherland boys were up to their high jinks again. First the tomato caper, then the Beauregard in the tailpipe, the forged letter, and now this.

"Okay, guys. Game's up," she said, shaking her head as she walked toward them. "You've had your fun. Now get out of my way."

They looked at each other and shrugged.

She laughed. "I know who you are, Bubba. Junior. You don't fool me for a second." She searched her handbag for her cell phone. "I suppose you're going after El next. Good luck. I plan to warn her. You're not going to get away with ruining The Butler's big night. Not for a minute."

"You're coming with us," Julia Child said in a poor attempt to imitate the famous chef.

"This is no longer funny," Hyacinth said. "Your pranks are getting old. Very old. Your uncle got you the jobs you wanted. Isn't that enough? I'm not going to let you do any more to harm my friend's big chance at success. This means too much to her." She found the cell phone and then fished around in her purse for her reading glasses. She squinted at her smartphone and pressed the phone icon.

"Put that away," Julia Child said in a decidedly low register.

"Don't you mean, 'put that away, y'all'?" Hyacinth taunted, and started to tap in El's speed-dial number.

"Maybe you didn't hear my partner." Emeril lifted a pistol and pointed it at Hyacinth.

"Oh sure, and now you're Bonnie and Clyde. Or is that made of licorice?"

Then she stared into the unblinking eyes in the masks. Doubt settled in. Fast. Something was off. Dollars to doughnuts, those weren't Bubba's and Junior's eyes staring back at her. Fear twisted her stomach. She swallowed hard, weighing her chances of getting away.

She made a quick decision to keep up the charade. If they thought she'd mistaken them for someone else, maybe she could at least get out of the garage and then make a run for it. Fat chance. But she had to try.

"As if that's real." She'd always had a booming voice, and she turned up the volume, figuring the louder and braver she sounded, the better. "Let me see that. Is it made out of licorice? Somebody did a great job. You'll have to give me the name of the candy store," she boomed, and then guffawed.

The men turned toward each other as if exchanging glances. She could only imagine what they were thinking. *You like that? Wait till you hear me sing, boys.* She smiled and waggled her fingers. "Now if you'll excuse me," she was almost yelling by now. "I need to get some things done."

"One more step, ma'am, and you'll find out how real this is." Emeril waved the gun around.

Hyacinth raised her hands in mock protest. "Bubba, Junior, the fun is over. You've made your point. Now leave. Instead of calling El, I'm about to dial 9-1-1 to get you off my property. Skedaddle."

Emeril took a menacing step toward her. "Give me your phone, ma'am."

She gave them a come-on-make-my-day stare, and continued booming. "I've had an exhausting day and I have an exhausting evening ahead. And I need to make my phone call. You go play someplace else."

She tapped El's speed-dial number, but before she could hit send, Julia stepped up and grabbed the phone. Hyacinth held on with a death grip, but Julia wrestled it away.

"You're coming with us." Emeril grabbed her wrist and propelled her forward. Within a heartbeat, Julia Child stepped behind her and poked the barrel of a very real pistol into her spine. "Now walk," Julia said. "Outside to the car. If you look right or left or use that voice of yours to call for help, you'll see stars without even looking at the sky."

They pushed her through the side door and around the garage toward a fairly new dark-colored Honda Accord.

Julia opened the front door and propelled Hyacinth into the passenger seat. Emeril got in behind her and leaned forward to speak into her ear. "You make one false move and I use this gun," he said. "And believe me, it's not made out of candy."

Julia rounded the car and got in on the driver's side, slammed the door, and put the car into reverse. They took a roundabout route, but it seemed they were heading toward the university.

"I suppose you're going to kidnap El next," she said, attempting to keep things light. "Wait till the *Chronicle* hears about this. You two have stooped lower than low. You'll never have lunch in this town again, let alone prepare it." They were probably too young and too ignorant to get the irony.

"And you talk too much," Emeril said. "Shut your yapper. Now!"

Instead of pulling into a university parking area, Julia instead turned onto a side road and parked near an ambulance.

Hyacinth tried to put it all together. She'd been kidnapped, brought back to the university, and parked near an unoccupied ambulance. It didn't take a genius to figure out what they wanted. The figurehead. She was the librarian and had access to the library. And the ambulance ... of course, what an ingenious plot. She had to warn El, and fast. She made a grab for the door handle.

At that moment, a loud crack shot through her head like a lightning bolt. As the interior of the car darkened and began to spin, she realized the sound came from her own skull. A nanosecond of pain and starlight mixed together, and then a dark velvet blanket pulled her into its grasp.

Chapter Seven
The Professor

• • • • • • • • • • • • • • •

Max walked across his den to the large window and opened the wooden blinds. The room was on the second story of his home and faced the university campus.

He'd been at odds with himself all morning. Mostly, he weighed the pros and cons of going forward with the dinner. So many people had gone to a lot of trouble for him. Yet after the attempt on his life, he couldn't get past the feeling that he might be endangering others. Campus security was tight. A private security company had been hired. But these measures did little to assure him.

The east side of the campus lay before him, its sycamores, pines, and cedars providing a lush backdrop for the multitude of brick buildings, some more than a century old. The late morning sun shone bright on the towering neoclassical-style library, giving its burnished gold an almost ivory glow.

Closer in, the newest building on campus, the Encore Center for Drama and Culinary Arts, was nearest to his home. It stood out from the rest because of its modern design, consisting mostly of glass with sail-like bronze facades that hid concrete columns. It always reminded him of a sailing ship mired in concrete and waiting for a good wind to break free.

Much like himself.

He chuckled. *Where had that come from?*

The window afforded a good view of the parking area next to the Encore. Suddenly El roared in, the Ghia's top still down. She jumped from her car and almost sprinted up the rounded concrete steps leading to the entrance.

His watch read five minutes past eleven. That had been her cut-off time.

He couldn't wait a minute longer to see her again, to speak with her. He told himself it was necessary because of Devereaux, but who was he kidding?

Was Devereaux connected to whoever cut the lines to his tank during the dive? He worked his jaw as he thought about it. That was no accident.

The figurehead was valuable, an artifact that any dealer would want to get his or her hands on. But to what lengths would someone go? He wished he knew.

Max reached El's catering van, which was being unloaded by members of her crew. He chuckled at the logo with its snooty butler and wondered if El had designed it herself.

El marched down the stairs with a clipboard and an air of determination. She headed to the van, then caught Max's gaze and smiled.

The sun seemed to stand still for a moment. She exuded this crazy kind of confidence that drew him to her. Case in point: this morning. He had been determined to call off the dinner. But she had been so confident that everything was under control, and her optimism had been contagious.

As she walked toward him, he noticed how the shape of her face and her hair, short and mussed and pixie-like, gave her a rather mischievous appearance. The sparkle in her eyes and the way her lips curved upward at the corners, even when she wasn't smiling, told him he might not be too far off the mark.

"Max," she said and then hesitated. Sunlight touched her face. The sudden image of the *eldila* came to him, pillars of faint, shifting light. It had been years since he'd read the C. S. Lewis's *Perelandra*. But he'd tucked away that imagery of angelic beings made of light somewhere in his consciousness.

El shaded her eyes with one hand, and he noted her delicate, long fingers, and the lack of polish on her fingernails. Her slender fingers struck him as artistic. And strong.

"I almost made it," she said, checking her watch. "I was planning to stop by and let you know what I discovered about Marcel Devereaux."

Max took in a deep breath. "Let me hear it."

"I don't know if it's good or bad or a little of both."

Max followed her over to the back end of the open van. Inside, dozens of trays of cupcakes were carefully stacked on gleaming stainless-steel shelves. She lifted one to show him. The frosting was a sea green, shaped like ocean waves with whitecaps; in the center sat a ship made of dark chocolate complete with a female figurehead that seemed to be made of some sugary substance.

"You made these?"

She laughed, a musical yet husky sound he'd enjoyed earlier. "I made the prototype. Took some trial and error—the first ones looked like sampans—and then I hired a bakery in town to make the rest. They're quite delicious on the inside as well. We piped a raspberry cream filling into the chocolate-fudge cupcake."

She held the cupcake up to Max. The scent of chocolate and vanilla filled his senses. "How about a taste?"

He couldn't resist. "If you'll share."

She laughed and looked around. "I guess the boss deserves a little break." She broke the little cake into two pieces and handed him the half in the foil wrapper.

He'd just taken his first bite, lost in the silky goodness, when El said, "Devereaux was here earlier."

He felt his eyes go wide as he finished chewing. "Here?"

El handed him a napkin and took one for herself. "He actually came through the Encore kitchen into the dining room. Hyacinth found him. He told her his daughter might apply for acceptance here. She wants to major in culinary arts."

"They live in Paris …," Max sputtered. "Why …?"

"That's what I said." El walked with him a few steps away from the van as one of her crew members picked up another tray of cupcakes. She leaned in. "I checked the guest list, and guess what?"

"He's on it."

"You betcha. And get this—" She finished her last bite of the cupcake, licked her fingers, and then crossed her arms. "The person who added him to the list is none other than our illustrious university president."

Max felt his jaw drop. "You're kidding."

"Not." She captured Max's gaze. "How about this scenario? If it's true that his daughter is interested in coming here, my bet is that he's giving the university a sizeable monetary gift. Ensuring her acceptance, one might say."

Max shrugged. "I still can't shake the feeling that he's got an ulterior motive. And I'm betting it has to do with the *Lady*."

"Security is tight."

He drew in a deep breath. "I know. Tighter than it's ever been for one of these events. Believe me, I've been to a lot of these." As if on cue, a private security vehicle rolled by, already on patrol. "But I also know to expect the unexpected."

She met his gaze. "So we'll go forward with the dinner, right?" As soon as he nodded, her eyes sparkled with victory. She did a little air punch, looking ready to dance.

"The cupcake did it. How can I say no?"

"Good." El pulled her phone from her pocket and punched in a number. "Hyacinth," she mouthed to Max. "She set up the whole shebang, including the extra security."

He raised a brow. "I know she did. I worked with her—" But El wasn't listening.

"She must not be home," El said. "I'll try her cell." She pressed more numbers and then put the phone to her ear. "She's not picking up," she said to Max, and then into the phone, said, "Hey, girlfriend, give me a call. Soon. The dinner is ON!" She almost shouted the last word. She shot Max a dazzling smile and stepped closer.

He tried to breathe normally. His heart skipped a beat and then raced. Was he having his first A-fib attack? Or was it this woman's smile? Or the way she crinkled her nose while shading her eyes from the sun?

How could this be happening? He barely knew Elaine Littlefield, yet in some ways he felt he'd known her forever. He swallowed hard, trying to get hold of his emotions. He needed to think clearly. Already, she had turned his plans upside down. He'd fully intended that morning to cancel the retirement dinner. Yet, because of this woman, he had agreed to move into danger at warp speed.

Chapter Eight
Mrs. Littlefield

• • • • • • • • • • • • • • • •

Two dozen crew kids and the sous chefs, including Bubba and Junior, whirled about the kitchen at the Encore. I peered into the dining room where my daughter, Katie, second in command at The Butler, supervised the setup. She caught my eye and gave me a thumbs-up. Taller than me, she was dark-haired and pleasantly plump in all the right places. Her hazel eyes expressed more than she wanted to reveal, especially of past heartache.

Smiling at Katie, I returned the thumbs-up, then headed back into the kitchen and made my rounds, tasting and adjusting spices.

I was getting more worried by the minute as I raced around the kitchen, chatting with my staff, inspecting everything from uniforms to dishes, making sure everything was spotless. I glanced at the big clock over the walk-in fridge at least every ten minutes. Where was Hyacinth?

She played a huge role in the event. As the time ticked by, I found I wasn't the only one worried about her. A couple of the deans and the vice president of instruction stopped by to see if I knew her whereabouts.

Soon after, President Delancy's assistant called and said her boss needed to see Dr. Gilvertin right away.

"I'm sorry, but she's … been delayed," I stammered, then wondered why in the world I was protecting Hyacinth when something terrible might have happened to her. I should call the sheriff's office.

I considered it as I headed into the walk-in fridge to check the temperature of the sparkling water. What would I say? Normally, she would have been here by now, but she certainly wasn't late. We had forty-five minutes to go before the hors d'oeuvres happy hour. And another hour before the dinner got into full swing.

Meanwhile, I'd shown the photo of Devereaux to my waitstaff, asking them to keep watch as they bustled in and out. I'd already instructed them to report anything unusual to me.

I called Enrique, who was holding vigil in the back of the van. "Have you seen Dr. Gilvertin?"

"No, not yet, Mrs. Littlefield."

"How about Devereaux?"

"Nada."

Taking a deep breath, I told myself that she would sweep in at any minute with her new floaty, artsy fuchsia-print dress and gold strappy heels, her laughter bouncing from the ceiling, her mere presence creating a party atmosphere. She would have a logical explanation, probably humorous, as to why she ran late.

Bubba and Junior were behaving themselves. So far. They exchanged a few mischievous glances, but all I could do was keep an eye on them. They wielded knives, which was a worry as they were very obviously imitating chefs from *Chopped*. Splatters of barbecue sauce flew around the workspace as they hacked the ribs into serving-size pieces. Although they supposedly graduated from a well-known culinary arts school, their skills did not impress me.

I shot them what I hoped was a withering stare on my way to change into my chef's coat and pants. Problem was, my withering stare left something to be desired, according to Hyacinth.

They had settled down by the time I returned. I checked the clock again, and dove into the already-spinning vortex of kitchen activity, checking on this and that, tasting dressings and sauces. Perfection. All of it. I couldn't help the smile that took over, even in the midst of nonstop activity. I was proud of my workers, proud of The Butler Did It. I kept telling myself this was going to be a grand night.

The best night ever.

If only Hyacinth were here.

I checked the clock. It was nearly time to start the prep for my Sweet Beau Soufflé. Already I could hear the jazz trio setting up and practicing scales and the intros to a few tunes. I recognized a favorite, Horace Silver's *Song for My Father*. I stepped through the swinging door.

My setup crew had worked miracles. Festive red linen table-cloths were in place, with sunflower centerpieces and sunny yellow linen napkins poking up from glassware in perky folds. We had achieved a whimsical ambiance that blended a dignified gathering with Southern barbecue.

Even as I watched, early-bird guests began to arrive, mostly faculty and their spouses, some who I knew from the program had speeches to give or tasks they were heading up. As the jazz trio launched into *It's a Wonderful World*, I stepped back into the kitchen.

My daughter, Katie, heading up the team of servers and prep people, had overseen setting out my ingredients. The Beauregard sweet potatoes were cooked to perfection, freshly peeled, and sprayed with orange juice. Ready for me to do my magic.

Katie pulled the first tray of my catfish meunière from the oven, a dish I'd created for non-red-meat eaters. At home I sautéed them in small batches in an iron skillet. I was pleased to see how beautifully the large trays of fillets had browned in the 400-degree oven.

"It worked." I broke off a piece and popped it into my mouth. Katie did the same. "Excellent," I mumbled around the crunchy munch. "Let's try it with a little sauce." I fixed a bite for Katie, giving it a spoonful of the butter-caper-wine sauce.

Katie eyes glistened. "You've done it. Best ever."

I grinned. "Secret ingredient."

"Someday you've gotta come clean with all your secret ingredients."

I waggled my brows. "I'll leave them to you in my will."

She caught my hand, her expression now serious. "I know this isn't the time, but I've got to talk to you after the dinner's over. It's important."

I squeezed her fingers and looked into her eyes, noting the haunted look I had seen too often lately. "It's a date."

I checked the pans of finished food that had been prepared ahead and reheated just before serving. Well, of course, except for the slaw, made with baby cabbages and fresh cherries from the farmers' market, and pine nuts from New Mexico. I felt proud of my team and told them so as I visited the various stations, but also reminded them that the fish needed to stay as crispy as the slaw. I did one more taste test: the baked beans were as sweet as a dessert, and the baby back ribs fall-off-the-bone tender. And my Sweet Beau Soufflé? Well, time would tell. I hoped for the best.

The next half hour flew by. The hubbub of laughter and chatter floated through the swinging doors as my crew went in and out to the dining room.

I glanced at the clock again, took a breath, and swallowed hard. *Hyacinth, where are you?* Sometime in the past hour my stomach had tied itself into a colossal knot. I pulled out my phone again and hit redial three times: home, cell, office. Nothing. Katie caught my worried look and came over to me. "Are you okay?"

"It's Hyacinth. She should have been here a while ago."

Katie frowned. "That's not like her at all."

"I know."

She gave me a smile. "She's probably just running late. Maybe found a stray along the roadside and detoured to Angel Babies."

Angel Babies was the town's animal shelter where Hyacinth and I spent time as volunteers, taming and cuddling the most wild and fearful animals. It was a rare week that passed when one of us didn't find a stray kitten or puppy to drop by the shelter. "You're probably right, honey. I just wish she'd pick up one of her phones ... or better yet, return my call."

Katie went back to the stainless table where Bobby Jo and Liza were setting up to plate the slaw. Behind her, Brooke and Fawna were refreshing the hors d'oeuvre platters. Waylan, a young Elvis Presley look-alike, was mixing the ingredients together for refilling the two punches—one nonalcoholic and the other made with champagne.

From the sounds of laughter and conversation drifting through the doorways, the dining room and adjacent foyer were filling fast.

Katie came rushing through the swinging door. "The punch is going fast. They love it."

Junior elbowed his way to the doorway and peered out. "Need more shrimp cocktails," he yelled to no one in particular.

"Then you can see to it," I called to him. "On the double."

He shot me an exaggerated glare, shrugged, and ambled to the shrimp cocktail prep table.

"Peruvian hot sauce, eh?" Bubba read the label on the small bottle. He turned it to shake into the cocktail sauce. I raced across the room prepared to tackle him. "Nooo," I shouted as I ran. I wrestled the bottle from his hand.

"Please, go help your brother." I hurried him to the door, ready to bodily launch him into orbit if he dared touch my sauce. As he stumbled through the doorway, I scanned the dining area and foyer for Hyacinth. I didn't see her, but maybe she'd run into colleagues who needed to speak with her.

I put on my chef's beret and checked my watch. I had just fifteen minutes until I needed to slip the Sweet Beau Soufflé ramekins into the oven. That left me a bit of time to circulate.

I headed through the swinging door. Several people came up and complimented me on the hors d'oeuvres and the punch. I threaded my way through conversation clusters, smiling and greeting and nodding, all the while looking for Hyacinth.

Where was she?

Something inside me began to crumble. Something was wrong. I just knew it. But what? I wondered if I should call the sheriff. We knew each other well, had worked on cases together. He had called in extra men to cover the library because of the figurehead, but maybe I could get him to send a patrol car out to her house, just to check on things. I was still contemplating the question when Max appeared at my elbow.

"Have you heard anything from Hyacinth?" Because of background noise in the room, he bent down and spoke directly into my ear. His breath tickled, and I almost giggled. If it wasn't for my worry over Hyacinth, I probably would have.

I shook my head. "Nothing. How about Devereaux?"

"Not yet. I hear he's coming with Dr. and Mrs. Delancy. Should arrive any minute."

"Others know of him?"

"Apparently he's had meetings today with a couple of other deans. Visual Arts and Culinary Arts. They both were charmed by him." He shrugged. "I may be reading more into him than is there."

I forgot myself for a moment and patted his arm. "I need to get back to the kitchen. I've got my crew watching for signs of Devereaux. They'll update me when he appears."

I hurried toward the kitchen, reached for the door, but three of the planning committee members stopped me.

"Have you seen Dr. Gilvertin?"

I shook my head. "No, and don't ask me where she is. I don't know." My stomach twisted again as I admitted it.

"She's one of our primary speakers." Dr. Gerry frowned and exchanged glances with his colleagues.

Dr. Perry, an older woman wearing thick glasses and a permanent scowl, stepped forward. "I suppose I can pinch-hit."

The three drifted away, deep in conversation, obviously more worried about Hyacinth's speech than Hyacinth herself. Just then the decibel level in the room rose. I turned to look toward the entrance. A tall, good-looking couple made their entrance with the Delancys and the mayor and his wife.

The tall couple entered the room first. The woman caught the attention of every male in the room. She was a tall, willowy blonde, her hair short and pleasantly spiked. Her jewelry dangled and sparkled, showing off her sequined dress. Her eyes were wide and expressive as she gazed around the room.

Only slightly taller, the man was impeccably dressed in a custom-cut dark suit and carried himself with the confidence of someone used to the finer things in life. His silver hair, swept back from his face, came close to touching his collar. His gaze flicked over the crowd. He whispered something to his companion, and they laughed.

I had no doubt I was looking at Marcel Devereaux and the companion Max had mentioned.

After greeting a few people near the doorway, the foursome made their way to the hors d'oeuvres. Nothing seemed out of order, but I caught Max's worried gaze and gave him a slight nod. My waitstaff had already been alerted to keep an eye on Devereaux and company.

I checked my watch and hurried back into the kitchen. Katie glanced up from the station where I had left my Sweet Beau Soufflés. But the ingredients had been put away and Katie was lifting the heavy head of the mixer out of the bowl. "I got worried that they wouldn't have enough time to bake. So I put the batter together myself."

She had stepped on my culinary toes. I tried not to bristle at times like this, but I wasn't always successful. "I'm sorry, Mom."

I gave her a quick hug. "Not to worry. Did you remember the nutmeg?"

"Fresh ground."

"Good. Let's get the first batch ready, shall we?" We each scooped a large measuring cup into the batter, and poured it in half-cup increments into the ramekins. When they were in place, we closed the oven door.

I called Hyacinth once more, only to reach her voice mail. Still no answer.

My next call was to the sheriff.

I got right to the point with Sheriff Doyle. "I need a favor, Sheriff." I went on to explain that I couldn't find Hyacinth, nor could I leave my post at the Encore. The sheriff knew us both well. We'd gotten into his hair more than once when my investigations overlapped his.

"Odd you should call about Hyacinth," he said. "I had a strange call from her a couple of hours ago. She said the university didn't need extra personnel at the library after all. That campus police had beefed up their own security."

"She did?" That didn't make sense. The sheriff continued, "I questioned her about it, and she was pretty vague as to why. But that's what she said."

"That's odd. I've been trying to get in touch with her most of the afternoon. She won't pick up."

"If you're still worried, I can send someone over to her house to make sure she's all right."

"Thanks," I said.

He paused, probably rubbing his eyes, which he did a lot. "My advice is not to worry. You of all people know how Hyacinth gets herself into fixes." He laughed. "But then you yourself have been known to do the same." He chuckled. "Y'all have a good evening now, Mrs. L."

I pushed through the swinging door into the dining room. The guests were now seated in front of their place cards, eight to ten per round table, with the guests of honor seated at a long rectangular table near the dais. Max sat at its center with an empty chair to his left, President James Delancy and his wife, Maureen, to his right, Mayor Benny Ord and his wife, Cecile, on the far side of the empty chair.

· I searched the sea of faces for Devereaux and his companion, but didn't see them. Max had said they'd met with two deans earlier. I headed back to the kitchen, grabbed my clipboard, and thumbed through my notes until I found Hyacinth's seating chart. The deans were seated at one table near the front. I returned to the dining room, clipboard in hand. Devereaux and his companion seemed to have disappeared. Anxiety threaded through me. Casually, I strolled along one side of the dining room, examining the faces at each table. Still no sign of them.

I started for the kitchen when a young woman with a long reddish braid made her way through the guests until she reached the head table. She wore high heels and a vivid emerald dress and smiled at Max, who looked a little confused as he stood to greet her. She took her seat next to Max and then leaned in to say something that made him laugh. Even from this distance, I could see she was beautiful.

I'd seen her around campus and thought she might be the newest member of Max's department. I'd heard rumors that she was brilliant. And stunning. I squinted in her direction. That had to be her. What was her name again? Jane something. Dr. Jane something. I huffed out a deep sigh, feeling suddenly bereft for reasons I couldn't fathom.

I went back into the kitchen. The hubbub of activity continued to whirl around me with sounds from the dining room dropping to a low drone as the doors swung closed behind me.

A moment later, I heard the distinctive deep voice of the priest from Grace Church offering a prayer of thanksgiving for the meal and the celebration. When he'd finished, I gave the waitstaff the signal to begin serving the salads. They seemed to stand taller, putting their shoulders back and looking like the professionals they were, and headed through the doorway, trays held butler-style. Even the students, new to my crew, looked superb. I needn't have worried when they were added to The Butler's lineup.

I couldn't help smiling.

Katie came over and hugged me. "Couldn't be going better, Mom. I'm so proud of you and what you've done with this company."

"Our biggest and best event," I breathed. "It's just the turnaround the company needs. Though maybe I should knock on wood someplace."

We both laughed. It seemed that everything in this state-of-the-art kitchen was stainless steel. Everything was going well, and I wanted to enjoy the moment. I popped into the dining room to check on the progress with the salads. Most people were finished, with a few still working on theirs. I gave the nod to the staff to begin clearing the salad plates.

Back in the kitchen near the stove, Katie supervised the rest of the staff as they plated the main courses. Soon servers were moving in and out of the swinging doors in perfect harmony.

I zipped around the kitchen, helping here and there as needed, checking on serving sizes, the temperature of the ribs and the catfish, making sure the sauce was simmering but not boiling.

Baskets of hush puppies went out next. It hadn't taken long for this Cali transplant to learn that no decent Southern barbecue could be served without them.

The soufflé ramekins were served with the main course, but went out separately. I heard the oohs and aahs from the dining room and couldn't help smiling.

I gave sous chefs Bubba and Junior the honor of serving dessert—beautifully decorated cupcakes with the sailing motif. They puffed out their chests as if they'd fashioned the cupcakes themselves. When the last one had been served, the diminutive university vice-chancellor, Dr. Isabel Chang, walked up to the podium.

I was heading into the kitchen with a silver coffee server, but stopped short when Dr. Delancy and his wife rose from their seats next to Max. Instead of moving to the podium, as I expected, they made their way across the large dining room to the foyer. As they passed, I could see that Dr. Delancy's skin had taken on a grayish tone. He held his hand to his mouth. I whispered a prayer for him. He had been in ill health earlier in the semester.

Dr. Chang rose and went to the podium. "President Delancy has been taken ill. Keep him in your thoughts and prayers as we continue. I know he is extremely sorry to have to leave. But because of his recent heart surgery, they thought it wise to go straight to the hospital."

People exchanged glances and whispered to each other, looking concerned.

Dr. Chang cleared her throat to regain everyone's attention. "Tonight we are here to celebrate Dr. Maxwell Haverhill," she said, "and his more than three decades of service to this university and community. His outstanding discoveries, especially the latest, will be on display following the festivities here at the Encore."

She smiled broadly and held out her hand toward Max. "It's long been hush-hush, and I'm certain all of us are eagerly awaiting the details." She smiled. "And I'm also certain Dr. Haverhill is just as eager to tell us about his historical find.

"But first I have an announcement to make on behalf of President Delancy. As part of our farewell to our beloved Dr. Maxwell Haverhill and to celebrate the unveiling of the library's new exhibition wing ..." She paused for dramatic effect, and then smiled broadly. "Well, I'm getting ahead of myself. Max, would you please join me?"

Max stood, straightened his tie, and then made his way to the podium to join Dr. Chang. My heart thudded with newfound pride, surprising me. He looked ruggedly handsome, and when he turned to face the audience, his gaze seemed to seek mine. I felt my cheeks warm.

"Thank you, Isabel. It's an honor to be here."

Dr. Chang looked out at the guests and then back to Max. "I'm honored to be the one to announce that our new library wing has been named ..." She smiled at the jazz quartet. "Drumroll, please." The drummer complied, then stopped on cue. "The Maxwell Haverhill Exhibit Hall."

Max's jaw dropped and he took a step backward, then seemed to seek out my face again. I grinned and gave him a thumbs-up.

He turned his focus to his thank-you speech, and I turned mine back to the job at hand. Everything had gone well. The food was perfection itself. The presentation had been beautiful, the staff professional.

Everyone turned to me as I stepped back into the kitchen. With tears in my eyes, I smiled at them. "You all are the best," I said. "You couldn't have done a better job."

I gestured toward the banquet hall. "You may quietly begin removing the last dishes. I'll be just outside, listening to the next few speeches."

Katie came over, wrapped her arm around my waist, and stepped into the dining room with me. "I haven't forgotten about our talk," I whispered.

She nodded. "Thank you."

I nodded absently, my attention suddenly captured by Max, who was just completing his speech. He brought his handkerchief to his forehead and mopped it. Then he stopped midsentence and stumbled off the dais, heading down the aisle toward me. *Me?*

I caught my hand to my throat and tried to move toward him. But the crowd reacted first, and several seated near the aisle stood to help him. Through the forest of bodies, I caught a glimpse of him. He was bent almost double, one arm wrapped around his stomach, running my direction with a look of terrible surprise. He didn't quite make it, but stumbled and then crumpled to the floor.

Still more guests swarmed around him, some kneeling to help.

"Give him air," I shouted. "Please, everyone, get back."

The group parted like the Red Sea, and I moved through to kneel beside him. He was awake, but his skin had the same gray hue that Dr. Delancy's had. He shivered violently. Perhaps in shock? I blinked, feeling sick and helpless myself.

Someone handed me a cloth napkin dipped in water, and I swabbed his forehead.

He attempted a smile and a wink. Neither was successful. "Must've been something I ate," he said. Then he turned his head and retched.

He was joking, of course. But I noticed that the folks around me didn't laugh. My heart twisted in fear. What if …? Surely not. I glanced around the room. No one else was ill.

"What about Dr. Delancy?" said someone at my elbow. "I wonder how he's doing." I turned to find the mayor's wife, Cecile Ord, standing back and holding her stomach. I told myself it had to be sympathy nausea. That had happened when I was pregnant with Katie. My late husband, God rest his soul, had even worse morning sickness than I did.

A few moans filled the room. Frantically, I looked around, telling myself the unthinkable couldn't be happening. I had to get a grip.

The woman I'd identified earlier as Jane appeared at my side. "You might want to roll him on his side," she said. "He could choke on his own vomit." She gently gave him a push in my direction.

I wished I'd thought of that. "Good thinking," I muttered, trying to be generous even in my panic.

"I'm Jane Fletcher," she said with a soft smile. "You know that there are others, don't you?"

"What do you mean?" I looked around at the still-crowded room. "I haven't heard anyone—"

"It's spreading. I just came from the ladies' room. I heard vomiting in two stalls. Several others were holding their stomachs. More were in the lobby, hanging over trash cans.

I sat back, my hands shaking, my heart racing. I didn't think I could breathe. "It's spreading?" It was difficult to get the words out. "How can that be?"

I looked down at Max, whose eyes were closed. His breathing was shallow, and his pallor more pronounced. "Max," I whispered. "You were right after all. Please forgive me."

Tears filled my eyes as I met Jane's kind gaze. "This is turning into a terrible emergency," she said gently. "We'd better get some help here fast." She picked up her cell and dialed 9-1-1.

"The call was made a few minutes ago," I said.

"I know. But earlier we called for just one ambulance—for Dr. Haverhill. Now, we need dozens."

I stood to assess the situation in the room. Suddenly, my knees felt as if they were made of gelatin, and I sank into a nearby chair. Jane was right. Half the dinner guests were either on the floor, curled up in pain, or vomiting.

I didn't want to leave Max's side, but I needed to call Sheriff Doyle. Blindly, I made my way to the kitchen and stumbled through the door.

My catering crew stood as still as death, watching me with large eyes and blanched faces. Behind them, through the window that faced the parking lot, I saw the flashing lights of the first ambulance in the night sky.

I took a deep, shuddering breath and dialed the sheriff. When he picked up the phone, the words just came tumbling out. "I think we have a massive case of food poisoning, and what did you find out about Hyacinth?"

Just then Jane stumbled through the door, clutching her stomach. "You need to come back out. It's Max." And then she wrapped her arms around her torso and ran toward the nearest trash receptacle.

Chapter Nine
Hyacinth

• • • • • • • • • • • • • • • • •

Hyacinth woke with a splitting headache. She didn't open her eyes; one didn't need to have every synapse firing to recognize the feel of a moving vehicle, or a bed, for that matter.

Wait a minute. I'm lying on a bed in a moving vehicle?

She tried to raise her head. Pain shot from the base of her skull to her temples as if she'd been hit by a bolt of lightning. She rested a moment and then tried to move again. Another unbearable jolt zapped her. Nausea followed in waves.

She closed her eyes and let the velvet black nothingness pull her under again. Seconds, or maybe hours, later she crawled out of the fog of pain and nausea once more, the memory of the earlier pain still vivid. She tried to move her head, turning just slightly, attempting to remember how she landed in an ambulance. Nothing came to her. Had she been in a car accident? She didn't remember.

The pain was fierce, but she fought to hold her head up just enough to catch a glimpse of her toes, her feet, her strapped-down arms. She was strapped onto a gurney.

Her heart rate increased, and for a moment beat wildly as she considered what possibly could have happened. A stroke? A car accident?

Whatever it was, she was on her way to the hospital. She couldn't move. She was paralyzed; she just knew it. Tears slipped from the corners of her eyes as her life flashed before her. The people she loved. All the things she wanted to do. Learn to skydive. Trek in the Andes. Fall in love again. Another tear squeezed out and trickled toward her ear.

She swallowed hard and then took a deep breath. She might as well face the bad news and find out how severe the paralysis was. She wiggled her toes. They seemed fine. She wiggled her fingers and moved her hands. All joints seemed to be in working order. Her spirits lifted a notch.

Odd, though, that no attendant sat nearby. One would think a stroke victim might need her stats monitored. She wasn't hooked up to anything. Her dismay turned into a simmering indignation.

As familiar emotions began to surface, clarity gradually pushed away the fog brought on by pain and nausea. And fear. Bits and pieces of her memory floated into focus. She needed to help El at the banquet ... she had a speech to make ... Max's big surprise banquet.

If not a stroke, what could account for her screaming headache and the hallucinations about a gun made of licorice? She would ask the paramedics, but where were they?

These paramedics were flat-out incompetent. Heads would roll over this. She would call their supervisor at her first opportunity. Then it occurred to her that she might not be able to speak. What if the stroke had affected her vocal cords? Hot tears pooled in her eyes again. Unable to speak? Unthinkable.

She ran through a quick do-re-me-fa-so-la-ti-do. Everything seemed to be working, so in her best Helen Reddy voice she sang out, "If I have to, I can do anything. I am strong. I am invincible. I am woman."

The driver slammed on the brakes, and if it hadn't been for the restraints, she would have slid to kingdom come.

"I could use some assistance back here," she called out. "You kids aren't doing your jobs."

"What are you talking about?" The voice came from the front of the vehicle.

"You have a possible stroke victim back here, and no one seems to give a hoot. You should be checking my heart rate, taking my pulse. I should be hooked up to ... well, I don't know. You're the experts. An IV drip of some sort, I suppose."

"Experts?" a different voice said and then laughed.

"Don't you worry now, ma'am," voice number one said. "We've got you covered."

His chuckle bothered her. Also the sound of his voice. She'd heard it before. But where?

She closed her eyes, trying to get past the headache and concentrate on what had happened. She tried to replay her day, but only snatches came back: her early morning at the Encore, El's arrival, the worry over someone named Devereaux? He was French, charming when she met him, somehow considered bad news. Noise outside the window at the library ... the drive home.

She gasped as a darker memory floated just beyond her consciousness. Goulish images of chefs came to her. Emeril Lagasse.

Another strange TV chef. What did they have to do with her lock-down in an ambulance, heading to the hospital?

Images, words, memories flitted about her brain, just out of reach.

The vehicle slowed. She heard a chorus of sirens, all seeming to head for the same hospital entrance, which she assumed was emergency. She took a deep breath, waiting for hospital personnel to open the back door, lift her gurney to the ground, and wheel her into the hospital.

But they didn't come for her. She heard the front doors slam and heavy footsteps heading away from the ambulance. No other hospital sounds. Just the incessant blaring of what had to be dozens of sirens.

A few minutes passed. Her head still throbbed, her stomach was still close to heaving. Her heart pounded. She wanted answers. About her accident or stroke or whatever ailed her. About why she was here.

The hinges on the back door of the ambulance creaked, and a moment later a strange masked figure approached her. She blinked. Emeril. She hadn't been hallucinating after all. She searched her memory bank.

Nothing concrete came to her. Just shadows of events, real or possibly imagined. She remembered being forced into a car, not an ambulance.

He came over to the gurney and unfastened her restraints. She groaned and rubbed her temples as she struggled to sit up. Then, touching the back of her head, she winced. Goose egg. Someone had clobbered her.

Emeril reached for her and grunted under her weight as he helped her to the ground. Another figure, this one in a Julia Child mask, came up as if to guard her, the glint of his eyes showing through two holes in the mask.

They'd parked the ambulance near the library, but the noise at the Encore, just visible through the trees, quickly drew her attention.

She gasped. At least two dozen ambulances and half as many fire trucks, lights flashing, sirens blaring, swarmed in the lot beside the dinner theater. More were lined up on University Avenue. Police and sheriffs' vehicles wailed near the entrance. She had to get to El, find out what happened, help her …

Julia grabbed her elbow. "Not so fast. You've got some work to do for us first."

Emeril handed Hyacinth her purse. "We thought you'd have your keys in there. But you surprised us. No keys except to your house and your car. So we figure, there's gotta be a code to get us past the security alarms."

Julia stepped forward. "You don't want to know what's going on at the dinner right now. But let me warn you, it's not half as bad as what will happen to those you care for—Elaine Littlefield, her daughter, Katie, and her granddaughter, Chloe Grace—if you don't cooperate."

Hearing the names of those she loved brought a chill to her heart.

Hyacinth closed her eyes for a moment. She went to the center of her soul, where no human could touch her, where she could commune in an atmosphere of love, where she knew she was safe, no matter what might happen to her physically. *Be still and know …*

"All right," she said when she looked up. "I'll do as you ask." The same guards still stood by the door, and she prayed they weren't distracted by the goings-on at the Encore.

"This is what you have to do." Emeril gave her precise directions. "We will watch your every move. So don't try to sound any alarms or play the hero."

Hyacinth made her way to the library entrance. She spoke to the guards, frantically trying to convey with her eyes and expression that all was not well. Neither one picked up on her signals.

She signed in, then punched in the alarm deactivation code. She closed the door but didn't lock it, as instructed.

She had just reached *Lady with a Scarf* when she heard gunfire— or maybe fireworks—behind the library. Outside the window, there was just enough light for her to see the two guards sprint past to investigate. *Wrong move, fellas.*

In less than five minutes, Julia and Emeril—along with still another masked figure, Paula Deen, who'd just joined them—rushed into the library with the gurney, loaded the covered figurehead on top, and raced to the door.

Hyacinth stood in front of the door to block them, but Emeril just knocked her to one side and continued to the waiting ambulance.

She tried again to stop them as they fastened the gurney wheels to the floor.

"You can't do this," she shouted. "You don't know what you're doing. You have no idea what this is worth!"

Her heart was about to break over the beautiful *Lady with a Scarf*. Over Max and his lifetime dream, over El and what surely were now her own broken dreams. And she was madder than she'd ever been in her life.

Her feet made the decision. No way would she let these thugs get away with this. Her face flamed and her heels took wing. With a cry that would have impressed Tarzan, she leaped into the back of the vehicle, slamming the door behind her.

The element of surprise was on her side. Emeril was knocked off-balance and fell forward just as Paula Deen stomped on the gas and turned on the siren. Julia fell against the side of the ambulance as Paula screeched around the corner toward the Encore.

Hyacinth looked down at Emeril. He was out cold. Or, heaven help her, deader than a doornail. She knelt beside him and lifted his arm to take his pulse.

Chapter Ten
Mrs. Littlefield

. . . .

Sheriff Doyle barreled through the swinging doors leading from the dining room.

"We need to talk about the food," he said directly to me. His demeanor had turned businesslike, much different from it had been earlier when we spoke on the phone.

I thought of him as a sort of begrudging comrade-in-arms. We'd locked horns over details of cases I'd worked on. I'd gotten in his way a few times. But all in all, we got along.

Now I got the distinct impression that I was under investigation.

Well, duh. Of course I was. You don't have to be the brightest crayon in the box to look to the caterer when people at a banquet experience upper-GI distress. But this might be Legionnaires' disease. Or the kind of quick-acting flu that spreads on cruise ships. I needed to point that out. Lighten things up with a little humor. But truth was, I just didn't have it in me. There was nothing funny about this disaster.

The health of all those who'd taken ill mattered most. And Max. My eyes filled, and I blinked away the moisture. In one day, he'd become important to me. His last gesture while still upright was an attempt to reach me.

The sheriff squinted at my catering crew, studying their faces one by one. The staff looked shaken and pale, and an unnatural pall had fallen over the normally busy, noisy kitchen. Two of the girls wept silently, their shoulders trembling. Katie stood next to me, her arm wrapped protectively around my waist.

I had been close to tears from the moment I saw Max stumble and fall. And to see him—and all the dozens of others—so ill, and to think the food we served might have caused their distress, was too horrible to comprehend. But I tried to keep a professional attitude, to hold it together for my crew's sake. I'd called the hospital a dozen times to find out how the victims were doing. No one would tell me anything. In some ways, not knowing was worse than whatever I might find out.

Bubba and Junior stood apart from the others. I narrowed my eyes at them, and they sheepishly looked away. The Beauregard in the Ghia's tailpipe came back to me, the nail in the van's tire, the resulting tomato missiles, and the half-dozen other antics they'd carried out to get the edge on The Butler Did It. Could they have arranged to work for me to carry out this sabotage?

If so, their plan would certainly work. After tonight, no one would hire me. Bad news travels fast. And this was the worst.

I blinked back the sting of new tears that threatened and drew in a deep but shuddering breath. If I stopped to think about it too long, I would lose it. Just simply lose it.

The sheriff leaned against a tall stainless-steel prep table, his feet crossed at the ankles. "We've got a disease control specialist on his way here, plus some folks from the FDA." Again, he fixed his eyes on me. "I need for you to be around to answer questions, so don't leave the campus. In fact, don't leave the kitchen. Any of you. I've got a lot more questions to ask y'all."

I cleared my throat, but the sound came out like a wounded frog. "Before we get started," I croaked, "can I ask if you've heard anything about Hyacinth? I'm worried sick. Especially after this ..." I gestured toward the dining room.

"So you think these two events are connected? Dr. Gilvertin's disappearance and the poisoning?"

"Oh, goodness, no," I said quickly. "She wouldn't have had anything to do with this. I mean, unless she's a victim too."

"We searched her property. Her car was in the garage, but there was no sign of Dr. Gilvertin. No sign of a struggle. Not that we expected to find one."

"Oh dear," I breathed. Katie gave me a quick side hug.

"Now, back to my questions ..." He pulled out a pad and stubby pencil, but put it down when his cell phone rang.

"Sheriff Doyle here." He listened, and his eyebrows rose to record levels. His face turned red and then paled. His lips went thin as he ended the call. "This will have to wait," he muttered and jammed his phone in a belt holder. "But don't leave the premises."

"What did you find out?" I kept pace with him as he rushed to the service-entrance door. "Is it Hyacinth?"

He shook his head. "It's the library."

"I'm coming with you," I said as we descended the stairs two at a time.

"No, you aren't."

"Yes, I am. If the library is involved, Hyacinth might be there."

He spun quite suddenly, and I almost ran into him. "There's been a robbery."

I brought my hand to my mouth. "Oh my."

"Oh yes. Now go back to the kitchen where it's safe." He might as well have done a John Wayne imitation and added "little lady."

"I'll keep you apprised about what's going on," he added and then trotted down the sidewalk toward the library. I hurried to keep up and I heard an irritated huff. But then, it was hard to tell. Considering his girth, maybe he just naturally huffed and puffed.

"What was taken?"

He didn't answer. I thought of Hyacinth and how she might have been caught unawares, hurt, or worse, if thieves tried to get to the figurehead.

My legs propelled me forward, my mind still reeling over what happened in the banquet dining room. Images of those who'd gotten so very ill haunted me. Especially Max.

And Hyacinth … what had happened to her? I thought my heart might burst with the myriad troubles whirling inside it.

Even in his hurry, the sheriff wasn't moving fast enough. I lengthened my stride and soon scurried ahead of him. Sheriff Doyle—either because he felt the same sense of urgency or because he was about to arrest me for disobeying his direct order—broke into a run behind me.

Out of breath as I reached the library entrance, I had to bend double, gasping for oxygen. When I managed to push my torso upright again, I did a quick assessment. Two worried-looking security guards stood near the open doorway. A couple of deputies appeared to be interviewing them.

From snatches of conversation I overheard, the security guys were trying very hard to shift the blame away from themselves.

Sheriff Doyle moved in, up close and personal, and took over the questioning. I went over to stand beside him, ignoring the glare he shot at me.

"Like I told the deputy, it was the libarian herself who was part of this whole thing. Head of the ring, I tell you. She showed us her ID—though we knew her from before—and put her code in the keypad. The door opened, and in she went, big as you please."

"You're sure it was her?" I furrowed my brow.

The sheriff flashed me a scowl.

I ignored him. "It was dark, right?"

The guard nodded. "But we had enough light to see her face and her ID. And like I said, she stopped by earlier too."

The second guard, a stocky man with a shaved head, cleared his throat. "She had accomplices, at least three that we saw." He stared at the ground for a moment. "They were the ones that set up a distraction, causing us to leave our post to investigate. She left the door open so the thieves could git in."

I moved closer to the guard, out of the sheriff's line of vision. "Do you know that for certain?"

"Does two plus two make four?" If a tone could have a swagger, Head Shave would be on steroids. "She waltzed right in. Then when we were distracted by what we thought was gunfire, she let the thieves in and showed them where the figgerhead was. By the time we discovered it was fireworks, they were gone."

"Well, not quite," the first guard said. "We came around the corner of the libary in time to see them loading up and then peeling off in that dern ambulance. That libarian was the last in and slammed the door. Three of 'em were wearing masks. They looked like those TV cooks, you know the ones. She was the only one that wasn't wearing a mask. She's head of the operation, that's for sure."

"I know Dr. Gilvertin, and she would never do this, I assure you. I'm sure you're mistaken. Isn't that right, Sheriff?"

He ignored the question, keeping his focus on the two guards. "Let's start again from the beginning. I need to establish a timeline. You said this was her second visit. Did you mean second visit today?" They nodded.

"Okay, I want every detail you can remember." Sheriff Doyle pulled out his pencil and pad and started to write.

While he was occupied, I scurried up the stairs and into the library, heading as fast as my feet could move to Hyacinth's office. Apparently, the deputies hadn't searched it yet.

Hyacinth's latest eBay win, a gently used purple Fendi handbag, lay open on her desk. It was a tote style, which allowed me to examine the contents without disturbing the exterior. A fuchsia-and-hot-pink scarf hung from one side of the handle. Her wallet was tucked inside, and in various compartments, her house keys, lipstick, touch-up compact powder with mirror, hairbrush, and day planner, tissues, reading glasses, and breath mints. All things Hyacinth would never leave home without. But where was her cell phone?

I opened her desk drawers and examined the bookshelves and cabinets that lined one wall, careful not to contaminate anything with my fingerprints. I found nothing unusual. Nothing missing.

Heavy hearted, I looked around for hints of a struggle, but nothing was out of order. The handbag seemed to have just been dropped on the desk, as if Hyacinth planned to pick it up on her way out.

I approached the new wing and the special exhibits room. Hyacinth had been in on its design and had looked forward to tonight's dedication to Max. She wouldn't have missed it for all the gently used Fendi handbags in the world.

I rounded the corner and halted midstep. The first thing that hit me was the space where the figurehead should have been.

Oh, Max … if only I'd listened to you this morning. For a split second, I was overcome by emotion and felt the hot sting of tears at the back of my throat … again. I swallowed hard and pressed my lips between my teeth until the feeling subsided.

I spotted three deputies, two of whom knew me and were used to my snooping around during other investigations. I sent a little prayer heavenward, hoping they were unaware of Sheriff Doyle's orders for me to stay put in the kitchen. They caught my eye and smiled. I heaved a sigh of relief and gave them a little wave.

"Hey, guys," I said in a perky tone. "What's up?" As if I didn't know.

"Robbery," said one.

"Inside job, it seems," said the other.

"Nah, I don't think so," I said with an air of confidence. "There's been a suspicious character in town recently. Might be an antiquities thief. I'd check there first. My money's on him."

"That right?" Deputy number one looked up from his finger-printing kit.

"His name's Marcel Devereaux. Hails from Paris—France, that is. Dr. Haverhill himself was worried that he was in town. Apparently followed him from DC."

Deputy number two put down his tools and pulled out his notepad. "Do you know how to spell that?"

Deputy number one sniggered. "T-H-A—"

"Real funny, wise guy." Number two scowled, still working his pencil on the notebook page.

I spelled *Devereaux*. When he seemed to have caught up with me, I added, "You might also check on the Sons of the South catering brothers, Bubba and Junior Sutherland. Though I can vouch for their whereabouts tonight, they've pulled some shenanigans lately in competition for the event tonight. They could have someone working with them. They've been quite upset that my catering company won the bid. I can't believe they would do anything like this, though. Truly."

"Did you file a report?" The third deputy, the one I didn't know, came up to stand beside me.

"No. It didn't seem that serious at the time."

He studied me like a child might study a june bug in a jar. Heat rose in my face as if I were guilty of something. It was time to make my exit as gracefully as possible.

"Well, nice to chat with y'all," I said with a wave. "Let me know what you find out."

I didn't mention Hyacinth. Right now, my intuition told me the less said about her, the better.

I turned back to the entrance, once again examining the carpet and walls for signs of a struggle. Nothing.

Discouraged, I headed to the door. The sheriff looked up as I passed. "Stay on campus, Mrs. Littlefield. I'll be over to question you and your crew once I'm finished here."

Dread twisted my stomach. How could this be happening? Was I a suspect? My brain couldn't take in the possibility. I needed time to think things through. My emotions threatened to overwhelm my logic, to skew my ability to reason through the events of the last few hours.

But try as I might, panic churned in my heart—fear for Hyacinth, for Max, for all those who'd gotten sick, for the future of my company—as I hurried back toward the Encore.

A new thought hit. I halted midstep. Why was everyone assuming the illness was food poisoning? Or food-borne at all? With that assumption, of course, came the accusation, spoken or unspoken, that The Butler really did do it.

By morning it would be all over town. It probably already was. My company would be toast.

I gave my teary cheeks a swipe. No time for such drivel. Indeed, if I let myself, I'd fall on the lawn in a quivering heap and cry my eyes out. But righteous anger took over instead. Besides, I'd actually never allowed myself to become a quivering heap and didn't intend to.

I was ready to swear on a stack of NIVs that the quality of food we served was healthy and good. Never a corner did we cut. Hygienic conditions? You betcha. We were tops.

A frightening thought took hold. What if someone else added a little something, poison or some other sort of contaminant, to our food. But who?

Bubba, Junior, or perhaps their ma? Maybe their godfather was involved at the top of the scheme.

What about Marcel Devereaux and his beautiful companion? They'd conveniently disappeared just before people started getting sick.

Or had it been someone else entirely?

The first two would soon be investigated by the authorities. I'd seen to that. As for "someone else entirely"—that investigation was left to me.

If only I knew where to start.

Chapter Eleven

When I reached the kitchen, a sick feeling came over me as I surveyed what the crew had done while I was gone. They hadn't wasted a minute scrubbing the kitchen and everything in it until it gleamed. Even the floor was spotless.

Why hadn't I thought to tell them not to?

Bubba, Junior, and Katie were telling the others what to do to get rid of the abundance of food and garbage. They worked surprisingly well together. Well organized. But dead-on wrong to scrub a crime scene.

Steam belched out of the top of the noisy dishwasher, its sanitizer cycle light shining. Serving trays had been hand washed, dried, and stacked on the counter, awaiting transport to the catering van once the sheriff gave us all permission to leave the premises. Even the garbage cans had been emptied. The smell of disinfectant filled the air.

Katie smiled as I inspected the shining stainless-steel surfaces. "We thought it would lift all our spirits to clean up the mess."

"Oh, me," I said as I scanned the kitchen again. "It's clean as a whistle, all right."

"You don't look pleased."

I swallowed hard, hating to tell her. "You just destroyed key evidence."

She frowned, not understanding, and then after a moment, she said, "Oh, Mom. I never thought about that. Evidence that would have cleared us."

I nodded. "If it comes to that, yes."

I pursed my lips, torn between wanting to tell her how she'd jeopardized the whole company and wanting to hug her because she looked so bereft.

A ruckus rose outside, and floodlights streamed through our windows. I ran to the door and stepped outside to see what was happening, Katie right behind me, Bubba and Junior behind her, muttering they needed to "get outta town." I turned around, glared at them, and then looked back down at the parking lot.

News vans were parked haphazardly next to the Encore. Reporters with microphones and camera crews swarmed around Sheriff Doyle.

He hesitated, glanced up at me as if sending a warning, and then stepped to the microphone and leaned forward. His eyes glinted in the bright spotlights. "This is what we know at this time," he said, bouncing on his toes.

"We know that one hundred forty-three people of the three hundred–plus attending the dinner at the Encore have taken ill. Many are in area hospitals, and their conditions are unknown at this time." He glanced at his notes. "We will update you as times goes on." He looked up. "Secondarily, we have just discovered the theft of the priceless object that Dr. Maxwell Haverhill planned to unveil at tonight's retirement dinner."

Someone asked if Dr. Haverhill was one of those taken ill.

"I don't have specific information on that," the sheriff said. "We don't yet have a list of victims, but we will get it to you as soon as we can."

"What kind of poison was it?" a reporter called out.

"Again, the investigation is just beginning," he said. "Details will be released as soon as we know anything concrete. And we don't know if it was food poisoning or something else."

"How about the caterers?" another reporter said. "Did any of them get sick?"

The implication was clear, and as the sheriff answered, I turned and herded the others back into the kitchen. I'd heard enough.

Sheriff Doyle turned purple the minute he stepped into the kitchen. "Did anyone stop to realize this is a crime scene and not to be tampered with?"

"Where's the yellow tape, then?" Bubba smirked.

"Watch it, buddy." The sheriff glared at the young man. "You're part of this investigation. You'd better mind your p's and q's or you'll find yourself in the back of my patrol car."

"Like I'm scared," Junior said under his breath.

The sheriff stalked over and grabbed him by the collar. "Look, buddy, you knock it off or I'll throw the book at you. Arrest you right now."

"On what charge?" His voice came out in a squeak as the sheriff's hand tightened around his collar.

"For starters, tampering with a crime scene."

"But all of us were doing it," he squeaked. He pointed to Katie. "She's the one who told us to. And she said to hurry up, we wanted to get the kitchen clean as a whistle, not leave even a fingerprint in sight."

The sheriff let go of his collar and turned to Katie, who stood next to me. "Is that true?"

Katie's voice trembled when she spoke. I reached for her hand and squeezed it.

"I said 'fingerprints' only as a standard I use for cleaning, Sheriff. I tell my daughter the same thing when she's helping me in the kitchen or cleaning her bedroom."

He studied her for a long moment and then turned his gaze to take in the others.

"Let's finish what we started earlier, shall we?" He leaned against the stainless counter and pulled out his notepad. "Did any of you notice anything or anyone suspicious this evening—or even this afternoon during your preparations?"

Everyone started to talk at once.

Dolly raised her hand. "I saw this French guy hanging around here while I was opening the champagne. He was on the phone, arguing with someone in the dining room. Dr. Gilvertin went in to talk with him. Calmed him right down."

"Uh-huh," the sheriff said, writing in his notebook. "Anything else?"

"I saw him too," Will said.

"Was he talking with Dr. Gilvertin?"

"She was smiling and laughing with him, and he was following her down the stairs."

"She smiles and laughs with everyone," Katie said. "She was just being nice. He told her he was looking for the administration building, and she pointed out how to find it. I overheard their conversation."

"But not all of it," the sheriff said.

"No."

"Mrs. Littlefield, I'll need you to supply us with samples of everything you served tonight—both food and drink. As I said earlier, representatives of the FDA and a disease control specialist from the CDC are on their way."

I looked at Katie, who frowned. "We didn't save anything. I thought it would be especially important to clean it up, sanitize everything as fast as we could."

"We have leftovers in the walk-in fridge, don't we?" I gave Katie a questioning look.

She shook her head. "I'm afraid not. We tossed those, worried someone else might get sick."

The sheriff let out a deep and troubled sigh. "You've just tried to obstruct the investigation. Nice try. It just makes it harder to get samples, but believe me, it will get done." He flipped his notebook closed. "Okay, you can leave now, unless anyone has anything else to tell me."

"Only that the food we threw out is in the receptacles outside," Katie said.

"Pleasant," he said without looking up. He jotted a few notes in silence and then fixed his gaze on me. "I need to talk with you further," he said and then looked at Katie. "And you too."

My dejected crew shuffled to the door and quietly exited.

"If this turns out to be something food related, you two are suspects, perhaps others in your company as well. I advise you not to leave town."

"Please, Sheriff, you know me better than that. Get off your high horse and look at this realistically. You know Hyacinth. We've worked with you on other cases. And Katie, you know her too. None of us would do anything like this. Why would I—or any of us—sabotage my company?"

"I don't think you realize the seriousness of what's happened here."

"I do," I snapped. "And I'm terribly upset over it. Excuse me if I've got it wrong, but I thought, in our country, people were assumed innocent until proven guilty. You are acting as if my catering company is at fault for this. The investigation hasn't even begun. The folks from CDC and FDA haven't arrived."

"Go, Mom," Katie said under her breath.

"May we go now?" I said, my voice calmer. "We're all very tired. It's been a long day." I turned to leave.

The sheriff heaved a sigh. "It may be a murder investigation now."

I whirled around. "What?"

"I just received news that Dr. Delancy died a short while ago."

"Oh no."

Katie put her arm around me again. "I'm so sorry."

Just then, Juan barreled through the service-entrance door. "The van is missing. My brother is gone too. We looked everywhere. There's blood. And broken glass."

Chapter Twelve
Hyacinth

. . . .

As soon as Hyacinth had attempted to unmask Julia Child, one of the thugs in the front seat must have bonked her on the head again. They certainly had a bad habit of head clunking. As consciousness slowly returned, another roaring headache seemed to split her skull in two—*déjà vu* all over again.

It was either evening, or she was losing her eyesight from blows to the head.

This time, her arms were secured with duct tape to a rolling stool. Apparently the gurney was in use. She looked across the dark interior of the vehicle, her memory still fuzzy. She'd made a giant leap into the back of the ambulance; she did remember that. Why had she done such a risky thing?

A bulky object wrapped in a sheet lay strapped to the gurney next to her. It was past dusk now, and the lights from the instrument panel cast an eerie glow across the interior of the vehicle. The sheet took on a ghostlike appearance.

The *Lady*. Of course. Her heart quickened. Max had told her about the secret it held someplace inside, the secret that even the experts in Washington couldn't find.

The memory of flashing lights and pulsing sirens came back to her. Near the library? She couldn't picture it. Or in the distance? As if near the Encore. She blinked as ideas filled her head.

A covered object, resembling a human body. An ambulance that probably pulled into a line of others.

Her heart twisted as she thought of the sirens. There had been many. Too many. Tears threatened. How serious was it? El ... Katie, who was like a daughter to her ... the catering kids ... the faculty, all of them her friends of many years ... Max ... had something harmed them? She prayed the thugs had just set off a false alarm, calling out emergency vehicles to create a diversion.

Hyacinth had a choice to make. She'd jumped into the vehicle to save the figurehead, in essence "kidnapped" herself. Should she remain with the *Lady*, or try to get back to El to see if she needed her help with whatever disaster had happened on campus?

She wasn't one to be snooty about such things, but it seemed the robbers had little education, especially when it came to *objets d'art*. First clue was when Emeril compared the figurehead to a statue at Caesars Palace in Las Vegas. Second was when the man wearing the Julia mask peeked underneath the *Lady*'s cover, giggled, and said he preferred his women with fewer clothes.

Maybe they would change their minds with a little education about the value of the piece—not the secret value—but the other, known value as a piece of American history.

But first things first. She needed a phone to call El. And fast.

If El needed her, she'd find a way to extricate herself from the ambulance.

"Hey, guys," she called to the masked men. "A ladies' room certainly would be appreciated right about now."

The men were deep in animated conversation and, with the road noise and hum of the engine, they obviously didn't hear her.

She blinked. Only two men sat in front. Apparently, they'd dropped Paula Deen off when she passed out.

She vaguely remembered being driven from her home to a side street in a dusty Honda Accord. How did that fit in? Her head hurt too much to think about it now. Besides, there was another pressing matter. Getting a phone.

"Hey, guys!" she shouted. "I need a ladies' room. I also need my handbag. Now."

The captain's chair on the passenger's side swiveled toward her, and she got her first look at the unmasked man, his cold eyes, his expressionless face. Her level of anxiety shot up like a rocket. These were the real deal. Thieves. Thugs.

"Who are you?" She tried to sound bolder than she felt. "And why did you kidnap me?"

"We didn't nab anybody. You did it yourself. We had it planned so you wouldn't see our faces. We were gonna leave you at the library. But now you're stuck with us. So get used to it."

"I just came along for the ride and now I need a restroom."

"Deal with it," said the man, the one she'd been calling Julia Child. He swiveled back around to face forward.

The driver, who'd worn the Emeril Lagasse mask, glanced back at her, his thinning blond spiked hair reflecting the dim glow of the dashboard. "Do we look like some sort of valet service? We're on a job, and you got in our way. You weren't supposed to get in this vehicle, and now you pay the consequences. You hear?"

"As for your phone, I believe you accidentally dropped it in your driveway." He snorted when he laughed. It wasn't a pleasant sound.

Her stomach dropped. She pondered the problem for a few minutes. She would just have to take one of theirs.

"We can talk about those consequences right after you stop at the next rest area."

"Rest area?" The snorter laughed. "Look around. Does this look like the interstate?"

In the glow of the headlights, she could see the winding road had a thick forest of pines on either side. They passed no other vehicles, and she saw no houses or even fences that showed a sign of human habitation. Now that darkness had fallen, the forested terrain loomed dark and frightening.

Hyacinth's mind reeled. She couldn't stop thinking about what had happened at the university. She was thirsty—she was telling the truth about the restroom thing—and she had to get hold of a phone.

Lagasse slowed the vehicle and turned again, this time onto a narrow mountain road. The headlights showed more curves ahead. The forest seemed to be thicker than before.

"Hey, guys," she called up to them. "I've got an idea. Just stop here. I'll go off in the forest a bit, behind a bush. You can wait. I promise, I'll be right back."

They looked at each other and shrugged. Their profiles were anything but attractive. They looked better with their masks on.

"Hey, Lagasse," she said, sounding braver than she felt. Neither one turned around, so she shouted the name again.

The man on the passenger side finally laughed. "She's talking to you, bro," he said.

"I'm not your bro, and I'm not Emeril LaJassy, or whatever his name is."

"Lagasse," Hyacinth corrected. "You need to stop. Like right away."

"Hear that, Emeril?" chortled the second thief.

"Yes I did, Julia," said the driver, going falsetto.

"I mean now," Hyacinth said. "I need you to stop. And if you're not going to introduce yourselves properly, you're now known to me as Child and Lagasse." She hoped her chatter would keep them off-balance.

"Believe me," Lagasse said. "It's bad enough that you've seen our faces. You think we're gonna tell you our names?" He pulled off on the side of the road and stopped the ambulance.

Child opened the side door, came round to the back doors, and flung them open. He hefted himself up with a grunt, then made his way toward Hyacinth. He pulled out a box cutter and cut her loose from the chair.

"Now, do your thing and hurry right back," he said. "Got it?"

"Got it." She stood and rubbed her wrists, jingling the bangle bracelets she'd planned to wear to the banquet. On the fly, she'd grabbed them from her Fendi handbag before tossing it on her desk and racing out to the ambulance.

Some people carried prayer beads as a reminder to pray for their loved ones. Her bangles served the same purpose. Even their sound was a comfort, a reminder of family, especially of Chloe Grace, her goddaughter who'd given them to her, one each Christmas for the past few years.

She scanned the forested terrain, and shivered. Night had fallen, and everything except where the headlights aimed was pitch-black. She jingled the bangles again to give herself courage and then turned back to Child.

His shirt pocket sagged with something the size of a cell phone. She stepped close to him and faked a stumble.

"Oh, sorry," she said, feigning embarrassment. "My legs aren't as strong as they used to be. I'm a bit weak from all this excitement." She fanned her face, the bangles jingling.

Child stepped back quickly to let her pass, his eyes narrowing suspiciously. She gave him an innocent smile and dropped his phone into the front pocket of her jeans.

She climbed down the few steps to the ground, letting the bracelets jingle. When she was out of sight, she grabbed the cell and turned it on.

It was locked. She needed a passcode to use it. Without the code, it was useless. There was also no signal. She examined the number pad on the lock screen. At the bottom was an emergency button.

She tapped it, but nothing happened, so she tried it again. Still nothing.

Child had given her some privacy for her bathroom break but stood leaning against the ambulance a few feet away.

She had to make a quick decision. If she ran into the woods, she might get away and reach higher ground where she might have a cellular signal. If she stayed with the thieves, they would discover she had the phone and take it away from her. Now that she'd seen their faces, who knew what they would do? And to compound her problems, her head ached something fierce, and her dizziness was doing battle with her nausea to gain the upper hand.

She glanced at Child, who faced the other direction. She made her decision—she would make a run for it.

Head pounding, she headed into the thick brush, frantically looking for a hiding place. It was so dark once she stepped away from the ambient light of the headlights she could barely make out a footpath. She tried to walk quietly on the loamy soil, but branches scraped and tore at her clothing as she passed. She pushed away thoughts of critters that might be living in those branches as she brushed against them.

Behind her, she heard an exclamation followed by some expletives that grew louder as the men argued about whose fault it was that she had disappeared. So far, no one crashed through the brush in pursuit.

She kept moving, careful to make as little noise as possible. Even if she had a flashlight, she wouldn't use it. The night seemed even darker than before. Even the flicker of a match would be seen.

It would be only a matter of minutes before they found her. The woods were quiet except for the chirp of crickets and a few frog croaks from a nearby stream. The men's voices were but a faint murmur in the distance. They were together, probably still near the ambulance.

She pulled the phone out of her pocket again, and using her body as a shield so the men wouldn't see the glow of the screen, she hit the "on" button. Half a bar showed, which gave her an inkling of hope. She tapped the "emergency" button again, and waited for a callback, a text ... anything.

But the phone remained silent.

After a few minutes, the rumble of a vehicle sounded in the distance. The ambulance was on the move.

Hyacinth didn't know whether to be relieved or worried. She waited for a few more minutes and then made her way back to the clearing, formulating a plan as she went.

It made sense that wherever the two were headed might have some measure of civilization. Maybe she could get a cell phone signal. And at least know her emergency calls were getting through. She didn't intend to let the crooks get away, but before she caught up with them, she needed to get a 9-1-1 call through for help. She prayed for a house, a cabin, an RV, maybe some nice family here for a weekend. Someone with a phone that worked.

Using the dim light from the lock screen as a flashlight, she made her way to the spot where Lagasse parked earlier. She removed one of the bangles from her wrist, gave it a quick kiss as she pictured little Chloe Grace's face, and then hooked it on a small Christmas tree-shaped pine near the clearing. Hansel and Gretel made the mistake of leaving an edible trail. Hers would last longer, she hoped.

She let out a deep sigh as she trudged along. Here she was on a deserted country road in the dark, humid air settling on her like an unwelcome damp blanket, waving away the gnats that fussed about her face. And who knew what lurked in the dark forest? The sound of the vehicle had long since disappeared. The noise of frogs and toads seemed louder than before, and eerie. An owl hooted, and another answered from farther away. A cacophony of crickets joined in.

Hyacinth hummed a bit of "His Eye Is on the Sparrow" as she trudged along, trying to ignore her thirst. Her head ached terribly, but that was the least of her worries. She stopped to rest, but being skittish about creepy crawling critters, she decided she'd rather deal with the headache than rest too long in one place.

She walked along in the dark, flashing the lock screen every minute or so to make sure she remained on the dirt road. Her legs were ready to give out when she saw lights through the trees. Hopefully the distant lights were that of a home or cabin. Her feet seemed to take on minds of their own, and she almost flew toward the glow behind the silhouette of pines.

She pictured pleasant folks with a working telephone.

Panting, she stopped to catch her breath. Just yards away stood the cabin, now clearly visible.

Her spirits plummeted.

Outside a small cabin sat two vehicles: the ambulance and a rental truck. From a familiar company, Coast to Coast, the truck sported a picture of a happy family standing in front of Half Dome at Yosemite National Park. The rest of the truck was painted bright orange. She stopped behind the truck just long enough to memorize the license number in her usual way, making up a silly sentence with the letters and numbers. N8724H. Nancy ate 724 hamburgers. She almost giggled. Poor Nancy.

Then she checked for keys. None in either vehicle.

A light glowed inside the cabin, and she heard voices—more than just Lagasse and Child talking. She crept to a window and peered in. A big man in jeans, a navy Windbreaker, and dark beret sat with his back to the window. His angry shouts pierced the night air. He leaned forward, his words a constant stream of criticism.

The wide porch was filled with junk, old tires, stacks of news-paper, a rusted outdoor barbecue, a sofa that had seen better days, a shelf with a rusted hammer and a wrench or two, and a glass lantern that looked one hundred years old. An idea took root in her brain, and she tiptoed over to the lantern. Kerosene gleamed inside, and she caught her breath, thinking of the possibilities. She needed a match, and fast.

Hyacinth crept over to the window again. "Find that woman and make sure she doesn't see the light of day," said the man she didn't know. "She can identify you. We don't need her causing trouble. Not now. Finish her off. We have no time for such foolishness."

Lagasse said they would take care of it, but Child didn't appear as eager. He finally agreed, and then said he had some business to take care of first.

Her heart racing, she backed away from the window and franti-cally searched for a place to hide. The back of the truck was open, and she ran for it, but before climbing in, she waited, almost afraid to breathe.

Lagasse and Child went around back, and she figured she knew what kind of business they had to take care of. The third man came out of the cabin but turned around before she could get a good look at his face. He walked around the corner of the cabin, and looking out at the forested hills, lit a cigar. Hyacinth crept around the truck so that he was barely a stone's throw away. She waited while he lit another match and puffed away, apparently still not able to get a good draw.

Okay, girlfriend, it's now or never. He struck another match and she hurled the lantern at him with both hands. It struck him in the back of the head. Kerosene and match found each other. Exploded. The man dropped like a stone.

She ignored the screaming and stomping and swearing that ensued, leaped into the back of the truck, assessed her best hiding place, and squeezed behind a large crate that she supposed the figurehead had been packed in. Other crates were stacked as close together as a jigsaw puzzle.

By now, the other two men had joined the melee. The smell of smoke grew stronger, and even from her hiding place, she saw the glow of a fast-moving fire. The men yelled that they had to get out of there fast, before someone in town called the fire department. She couldn't help smiling as someone, probably Child, yanked the truck's sliding door down, locked it, and hopped in the front cab with the others.

Soon they were on their way back down the bumpy road. Her wrist jingled softly with the bumps, and she realized in her hurry to start the fire she had missed her opportunity to leave another clue for El. But she had more than that to contemplate: How was she going to remain hidden once they stopped to unload?

Chapter Thirteen
Mrs. Littlefield

. . . .

Just an hour earlier, the university parking lot was swarming with law enforcement personnel. Now it seemed that anyone remaining after the departure of the ambulances and EMTs was at the library, scratching his or her head and trying to figure out what had happened.

Even the sheriff gave the spot where my van had been parked only a perfunctory look. It didn't matter that shattered glass and what I thought might be blood spatters were left nearby. His attention was locked on getting back to the library. I couldn't blame him.

I thought about Hyacinth being in danger, and the ache came back to my throat and tightened in my chest. I swallowed hard to maintain control. Too much was at stake to let my emotions get the better of me. Best to get back to business. I pulled out my phone and snapped a few shots of the glass. Then I dialed the sheriff's office and reported the missing van with my employee inside. I figured the sheriff had too much else on his mind to think of reporting it.

I told the dispatcher about the broken glass, hoping to get quicker action with my description of what might have happened.

"Ma'am, with what we've got going on tonight, you'll be lucky to have someone stop by to investigate three weeks from now."

"Now, listen here," I said. "This young man may be in danger—"

"So are the more than one hundred victims of food poisoning in area hospitals," she said. And then she added, "What did you say your name was again?"

I told her.

"So you're that Elaine Littlefield."

"The one and only."

"Thank goodness for that," the operator said and hung up. I was beginning to feel like Typhoid Mary.

I came through the kitchen doorway to find Katie still waiting for me. She leaned against one of the serving counters, her shoulders sloped wearily, her arms crossed. Her eyes were red.

Her worried gaze met mine. "Are you okay, Mom? This has been a nightmare from start to finish. Those sick people …" She started to cry. "I don't understand why anyone would do this, would want to hurt people, to hurt you and the company." She wiped her tears with a soggy tissue. "I'm sorry. I waited for you so I could be strong for you, to help you get through this. But look at me, I'm a mess."

"The Butler doesn't matter right now," I said. "Getting people well is all that matters. Finding out what caused it is more important than who. If it's poisoning, we need to know what the antidote is. If it's something else, we'll deal with that when we find it."

"So many of them are our friends," Katie said, her eyes filling again.

"I know." If I let one tear slip out, I might dissolve into a puddle. I tried to keep my mind off the friends I'd seen carried out of the dining room on stretchers. I tried to keep my mind off one man in particular: Max.

"I think we know why," I said. "It was a diversion so someone could pull off a robbery. The figurehead is missing."

As she drew her hand to her mouth, I realized she hadn't known.

"There's something else, honey." I went over to stand beside her and put my arm around her shoulders. "Somehow, during the theft, Hyacinth got involved."

"What do you mean 'involved'?"

"Her purse, keys, and phone were on her desk. There was no sign of struggle, but she's missing."

Katie put it all together immediately. "So while the deputies and EMTs were busy here at the Encore, the thieves attacked the library. And Cinth."

"She'll give them a run for their money." My mind jumped from Hyacinth to Enrique to Max, and then back again to Hyacinth and the figurehead. And, of course, the poisoning. It was nearly too much to take in. I felt a headache coming on.

"Did Enrique pick up anything with the cameras?" Katie asked. "Maybe he caught something, or someone, having to do with the poisoning."

She grimaced as I told her about the broken glass I'd found in the parking lot. "I tried to get him on the phone several times. He's not picking up."

"So we don't know the whereabouts of the van or Enrique—or even if he's injured." Katie let out a long sigh, and for a moment neither of us spoke. "Mom, I really don't like to see you involved in something like this. I worry about you. You're not as young as you used to be."

I shook my head, too weary and worried to laugh. "Well, that made my day." Then I nodded. "I've always said I won't get involved with anything that gives me nightmares. If it weren't for Hyacinth, I would just let law enforcement and the CDC handle this. I can only imagine the nightmares this one will bring on."

She stepped closer. "You still have nightmares. When Chloe Grace and I stay over, I sometimes hear you."

I shrugged off her worries. "Just leftovers from childhood." I laughed. "Monsters in the closet." We hugged once more and she headed to the door.

"You said you needed to talk with me earlier," I called after her.

She turned back and gave me small smile. "After what we've been through tonight, it's small potatoes. Our talk can wait."

Not more than thirty seconds after she closed the door, my cell phone buzzed. I pulled it out of my pocket and tapped the screen to accept the call.

"Mrs. Littlefield?" The woman sounded businesslike and detached.

"Yes?"

"This is Sheriff Doyle's office. We found a van registered to you. It's apparently your catering van, has a logo and The Butler Did It on the side. And there's some sort of electronic equipment in the rear."

Relief flooded through me … for about a half second. Then I remembered the blood, the shattered glass. "Was there anyone in it?"

"We've arrested a young man and charged him with grand theft auto. He was driving erratically, speeding, and endangering the lives of others. Caught him over by Waynesville. He insists he's your employee, and that he was following somebody on your orders. He's also being charged with assaulting a police officer, as well as trying to escape."

"Enrique Fox?"

She sounded surprised. "Well, yes. Do you know him?"

"Yes, I do. He's an honors student at Southern Highlands and works for me part time."

She had the audacity to snort. "Even if you can vouch for him, we still have the charges of excessive speed and endangering the lives of others."

"Tell Enrique I'll get there as fast as I can."

"He's already in the holding cell, ma'am, which is downstairs. So I can't tell him anything."

My head was throbbing by the time I ended the call. I glanced at the clock, thinking it surely must be midnight. It was barely nine o'clock. First things first. I needed to get Enrique out of jail before he was deported or something worse. Besides, he might know something about the poisoning or Hyacinth's disappearance, or the theft if he caught something on camera. I thanked God he was alive. I wished I'd thought to ask if he'd been injured.

I hurried across the parking lot to the Ghia, and as I slid onto the driver's seat, its scarred and worn Naugahyde seats gave me some element of comfort. The top was still down. Taking a minute to breathe in the fresh air before I started the engine, I looked up at the sky and blinked.

On this inglorious night, the stars were glorious. Brilliant. A sense of calm, even peace, came over me as I stared at the night sky. My little world and its troubles seemed to shrink for just a heartbeat.

I found it difficult to let go of the moment, so I closed my eyes and breathed deeply.

I turned the key in the ignition, revved the engine, and headed for the street. Just before pulling out of the drive I stopped, looked up once more, and gave God a smile. I almost believed He winked back at me; but maybe it was just the twinkling stars.

I floated on that feeling of peace until I swung into a parking place next to Sheriff Doyle's SUV at the back of the courthouse. I took in the dismal entrance to the sheriff's office, its barred windows and worn concrete steps.

When I reached the small landing at the top of the steps, I tried calling Max's cell phone. He picked up on the third ring, sounding weak, his voice raspy.

I didn't realize I'd held my breath while waiting to hear his voice. I let it out slowly as relief flooded through me.

He said he was still in the ER, but on a gurney in the hallway of the crowded Eden's Bridge Memorial Hospital, along with many of the others who'd gotten sick.

"How do you feel?" After all that had happened since this morning, a funny little flutter of my heart accompanied the question.

"Better," he said. "You know how it is after a flu bug; you're just glad to be alive." He paused, either because he was too weak to go on, or because there was something he didn't want to tell me. I worried it was the latter. "Several of us—I don't know how many exactly—will be released after they get the paperwork done. Probably not till morning at this point. The staff is overwhelmed by the sheer numbers. I've heard the CDC is flying in an investigator, but last I heard, he or she hasn't arrived."

"You said 'several.' What about the others?" I prayed there hadn't been any more fatalities.

When he sighed, it was so deep he must surely have pulled it up from his socks. "Most have to wait for the paperwork to be completed." He paused. "But there is one in ICU."

New, raw guilt swept over me. I had to be the one to tell Max the latest about the university president. "Do you mean Dr. Delancy?"

"Yes. How did you know?"

My eyes filled, and I blinked rapidly, willing them to stay put. "He died, Max. I'm so sorry."

He fell quiet, and I wondered how close the two had been. Probably quite close, considering Max had been a professor at Southern Highlands for nearly as long as Delancy had been president.

"I'm so sorry," I said again, softly.

I'd tried to keep it at bay, but the truth was, The Butler Did It was involved. Not just in the event, but in Dr. Delancy's death. I hadn't kept proper watch over our foods and beverages. If I had, maybe none of this would have happened. Maybe the president would still be alive.

I paused again and then said, "He was on a blood thinner, and the vomiting apparently started some internal bleeding."

"I can't help but feel responsible," Max said. "If I hadn't brought the figurehead here …"

Again, my throat tightened. I had been the one who talked him out of putting off the party. The full weight of it all fell on my shoulders. I swiped my tears away. They would serve no purpose now.

"There's been a lot of talk here about the cause," Max said, "but no one's come to any conclusions."

"What did you eat?" I leaned against the metal railing at the top of the steps. The cold seeped through my chef's shirt, and I shivered.

"A little of everything. It was delicious."

"How about drink?"

"Water from the pitcher on the table. It had a lemon slice in it."

I ran it all through my mind for the ninetieth time. "Katie and I both tasted everything to adjust the seasonings, including the hors d'oeuvres," I said. "If it was in the food, we would have gotten sick." I paused. "Did you have any of the punch?"

"Only a few sips when I was toasted."

"The nonalcoholic one or the one with champagne?"

"I didn't know there was a difference. Jane Fletcher picked up a glass for me for a toast. Others came over and toasted as well. If it had champagne, I couldn't taste it."

"Did anyone else say how much of anything they ate or drank?" Something was taking flight but refusing to land in my brain. It was as if I knew the poison. Had possibly even used it. Sort of like a word on the tip of your tongue that you can't find. The words *heart fibrillation* flitted around the edges of my mind but refused to tell me anything more.

"I've got to go," I told Max. "Enrique was arrested for stealing my van. I'm at the courthouse right now, hoping to straighten things out."

"I'll check in with you later," he said with a note of regret, which surprised me. Regret that I hadn't had other news for him? I hadn't told him about the missing figurehead. And now wasn't the time, not when he was still dealing with the news about Dr. Delancy.

"I'll let you know if I hear anything," I said.

I headed for the sheriff's office at the rear of the building, turned a corner and met up with a sliding-glass window. Behind it, a woman was busy with what appeared to be a phone bank with blinking lights of different colors. It seemed hopelessly old-fashioned in our techie age. With a moment of chagrin, I realized she must be the dispatcher.

I cleared my throat, and she removed her headset. "Can I help you?"

"I'm here about Enrique Fox," I said. "He's been accused of stealing my van, which he didn't do."

"You must be the woman I talked to earlier." She looked none too eager to be talking with me now. "What did you say your name was again?"

"Littlefield. Mrs. Littlefield." I smiled "Was and still is."

Still unsmiling, she wrote my name on a pad.

"I would like to clear this up without delay," I said. "Enrique isn't guilty of anything. He works for me."

A scoffing sound came from someplace between her nose and her throat. "Working for you fifty miles outside city limits, driving at speeds up to ninety miles per hour? It turned into a car chase." She shook her head. "And you think he isn't guilty of anything."

I sighed heavily. "With everything that went on tonight, I'm sure he had good reason."

She laughed. "Yeah, right. He's still good for resisting arrest and assaulting an officer. Those charges won't be dropped." Her mouth puckered, prune-like.

Since this morning, it seemed that troubles had piled upon troubles. The destructive mass whirled in my mind like a tornado, picking up speed and creating greater and greater havoc as it moved.

"I would like to talk with Sheriff Doyle."

She made that scoffing sound at the back of her throat again. "He's a very busy man. Especially tonight. I'm not even sure he's in."

"He's in. I saw his car in the lot. We talked earlier. I think he'll want to see me."

She tapped the eraser end of her pencil on the desktop, and then, with her free hand, punched one of the blinking lights on her console.

"He said to come right in, Mrs. Littlefield."

"I know the way," I said, and smiled, attempting to try to cheer her. She sniffed and donned her earphones.

Deputies, male and female, passed each other as they scurried here and there. They looked harried. They wouldn't want to relive this night anytime soon. Make that anytime at all.

I found the sheriff's door, knocked lightly, and then heard a gravelly, "Come in."

Sheriff Doyle stood as I entered. His expression was business-like and cold, very different from the man I'd come to know and admire through the years. "Quite a night. Have you heard anything from Dr. Gilvertin?" He gestured for me to sit in the chair facing his desk.

"No, and I'm still worried sick."

"Our dispatcher received a couple of 9-1-1 calls earlier. They came from a burner phone, no GPS."

"There's no way to trace them?"

He shook his head. "No way to know who or where they came from. I mention it only because cell service is sporadic in these mountains. Calls without connections are common." He shrugged.

I leaned forward. "But because it came into your dispatch office, it's likely to be fairly close."

"Still a large area," he said.

I leaned back. "Dr. Gilvertin is not in on this," I said. "You've got to believe me."

He gave me a stare that said the jury was still out.

"I'm here about an employee of mine. He was picked up speeding in my catering van tonight. He was watching a person of interest on behalf of Dr. Haverhill."

The sheriff leaned forward, narrowing his eyes. "Person of interest?" He pulled out a legal pad and clicked his ballpoint pen.

"You'll need to speak to Dr. Haverhill about the details, but a man named Marcel Devereaux had been following him."

He sat back. "That's old news. Dr. Haverhill already alerted us to this Devereaux person. We checked him out. He's legit."

"Dr. Haverhill was worried enough to want to cancel the banquet."

"Is that right?" His eyes remained fixed on mine. "Cancel the banquet that was to be in his name? What made him change his mind?"

"I talked him out of it," I said. "I told him that we would keep an eye out for Devereaux."

He made some notes and then looked up. "And did you?"

I nodded, suddenly feeling that I was on the witness stand. Again.

I stood to make my point. "I intend to work as hard—make that harder—on this case than any I've ever been involved with. It's Hyacinth, my best friend, for heaven's sake. It's my company's reputation on the line. Why do you keep coming back to point the finger at Hyacinth, at me, at my company, and earlier, even at my daughter?"

He stood then too, towering above me. "I have to go where the trail leads, Mrs. Littlefield. Your catering company puts on a meal and more than half the attendees end up in the hospital. A valuable artifact is stolen at the same time from your best friend's library. Eyewitnesses saw her open the door for the thieves and jump into the getaway vehicle on her own accord. Now, you tell me, Mrs. Littlefield, why I shouldn't suspect either—or both—of you."

I blinked at him, and my hand flew to my chest. "You've got to be kidding."

"I'm not kidding at all. Just know, Mrs. Littlefield, that our past 'working relationship,'" he said, making air quotes, "doesn't mean a thing."

He sighed heavily and let his body drop into his chair, then removed his glasses and cleaned them with his handkerchief. "Circumstantial evidence speaks loud and clear. You've got to bring me something concrete that tells me—and the DA—that you didn't have anything to do with this."

"What would be my motive?"

He laughed mirthlessly. "The treasure in the library. Who needs a catering company if you nabbed the figurehead?"

I put my hands on my hips. "Do you know how laughable that sounds?"

He nodded. "Unfortunately, yes, I do. Better get used to it. I've heard it's tomorrow's headline in the *Chronicle*."

"A special edition?" I stifled a groan. Of course. All this was big news. But making headlines wasn't something I wanted to think about right now.

"Let's get back to Enrique." I leaned forward. "I think he saw something, or someone, suspicious. Maybe his cell phone was damaged or taken by whoever it was that accosted him. He knew I'd want him to follow. My guess—with a high degree of probability—is that's why he was arrested for speeding fifty miles from here. I can vouch for him, Sheriff. He's never been in trouble before. I can't imagine he assaulted an officer—that's just not like him."

The sheriff reached over to pick up his phone. "Sergeant," he said when the other end picked up, "bring that Fox kid to my office." He listened for a moment, his face immobile. Then he said, "I don't care what the charges are; we'll handle that later. Just get him up here ASAP."

Enrique arrived a few minutes later. I gasped and stood so fast my purse fell to the floor. Blood and soil covered his face and arms. His clothes were torn and covered with dried blood.

He stood, handcuffed, with his head down and his shoulders sloped.

"Enrique," I breathed. "What happened?"

Enrique looked up, and despite the smudges of blood and grime on his face, he attempted a smile. "I tried ..." was all he got out before the sheriff told him to sit down.

"This is not protocol," Sheriff Doyle said. He went on for a bit about regulations and the seriousness of the charges. Enrique nodded that he understood.

Not being one to let an opportunity go by, I interjected. "Sheriff, can we hear Enrique's side of things? If he's seen something, or knows something, we're wasting time not listening. And by the way, do you really think he needs handcuffs at this point?"

Sheriff Doyle scowled a bit at my interruption, made a call, and a moment later, an officer arrived to take off the cuffs.

The sheriff turned again to Enrique, who was rubbing his wrists. "Tell us what happened."

"I, uh, it happened so fast. And I didn't, well, I tried …" Enrique looked at me, tongue-tied. It was no wonder. He'd been through a lot.

I leaned forward and drew his attention away from the sheriff, who now glared at me.

"What did you see?" I kept my gaze on the boy, willing him not to glance at the sheriff and risk being intimidated again.

"You know the monitor in the van?"

I nodded.

"Well, it was picking up the feed from the library camera. I was watching it when two men went by with something on a stretcher. It looked weird so it caught my attention."

I leaned in closer. "Weird? Like how?"

"It was a block-like shape. If it was a person, it was covered with a tent or something." He shrugged.

"The people who carried it, were they firemen or medical people?"

"I don't think so."

Enrique was an eyewitness. He witnessed the robbery. I wanted to yell yahoo and give the air a punch, but restrained myself. "Did you see their faces? Anything that could identify them?"

"It happened so fast I almost missed it. It seemed fishy because they were coming from the library, not the Encore."

"Then what happened?" I could hear the sheriff's loud scribbling on his notepad. At least he wasn't interrupting or scaring the young man.

"I got out of the van and ran over to where I'd seen them."

"And where was that exactly?"

"On the service road the gardeners use. You know, the one just below the library."

"Good," I said. "This is really good information, Enrique. What else did you see?" I resisted shooting a look of triumph in the sheriff's direction.

Enrique hiked his shoulders up a notch. "Well, that was when I saw the ambulance."

The scribbling sounds continued from the sheriff's desk.

"Can you describe it?" I kept my eyes locked on Enrique's.

"It was red and white. It looked just like most of the others. The only reason I noticed it was because of where it was parked—over by the library, like I said."

"Okay, that's good," I said. "What else did you see?"

His eyes darted to the sheriff's and then back to mine. It seemed he didn't want to go on.

"It's all right," I said. "Please, tell us everything. Why don't you start with what they looked like?"

"I couldn't see their faces. They wore rubber masks, the kind that look like real people. But I saw that one was tall with blond hair sticking out the back of his mask, and the other one was very short." He shrugged. "Maybe that one was a woman. I don't know."

"Go on," I said.

He cleared his throat. "They put the stretcher into the back of the ambulance, and then, while I was watching, Dr. Gilvertin ran out of the library and climbed into the ambulance with them."

"Dr. Gilvertin," the sheriff repeated. "Did she appear to go willingly?"

Enrique turned to me again, as if for permission. I held my breath. What if I was wrong about Hyacinth? What if …? I didn't let myself go there. I had faith in my friend no matter what.

"It's okay," I said. "Tell us what you saw. Every detail."

"She seemed to know what she was doing. She almost jumped into the back of the ambulance. I didn't know what to do." He shook his head slowly. "I was too far away to stop them. I decided it would be best to follow them and then call and report what I'd seen." He glanced at me again.

"You made the right choice," I said.

"You said they were carrying someone on a stretcher," the sheriff asked without looking up from his notepad.

"That's what I thought at first. But now I think it must have been the figurehead from the library covered with a white sheet. At least, that's what I think."

Sheriff Doyle cleared his throat. "So, just to be clear, in your opinion Dr. Gilvertin left with them voluntarily?"

Enrique glanced at me, and I could see how sorry he was. "Yes, it seemed like she went along because she wanted to."

I jumped to my feet. "I know my friend. If she went voluntarily, she had good reason." In my agitation, I paced in front of the sheriff's desk, then stopped short. "If Hyacinth got into the ambulance on her own accord, it was because she couldn't imagine that piece of history and art leaving without her."

The sheriff didn't appear to be moved. "No one in their right mind would voluntarily get in a vehicle with a couple of thieves. Unless ..."

He made a few more notes and then looked up again at Enrique. "So you went back to the catering van. What happened next?"

"I had just started the engine when an explosion happened next to me. At least, that's what it sounded like. Somebody in a dark hood hit the window with a crowbar. It shattered the window on the driver's side. He reached in and unlocked the door, practically lifted me off the seat, and threw me on the ground."

He stopped for a minute and picked at his bloodied arm. "In the glass. He broke the equipment"—Enrique looked at me, and I knew he meant our audiovisual monitoring equipment—"with the same crowbar. Then he grabbed the keys to the van and next, came after me. He only got in a couple of good licks before I rolled out of the way."

"He took your keys," the sheriff began, "then how—?"

Enrique smiled and shrugged. "Hot-wire."

I took over the questioning. "That must have taken some time—all that breakage and beating. How did you know which direction the ambulance went?"

"I guessed they would hide in the line with the other real emergency vehicles. So I pulled alongside the stream of vehicles headed to different hospitals. I didn't know if I would find the right one with all the others mixed in. But as I followed, I saw one ambulance veer out of line and head up the on-ramp to the interstate. I took off after him."

"Smart thinking," I said, feeling tremendously proud of Enrique. "You said your plan was to call in what you'd seen as soon as you were tailing the thieves ..."

"After the man trashed the van, he grabbed my phone and squashed it with his boot."

The sheriff scribbled another line or two and then looked up. "And the rest of what you are accused of is, as we say, history. You still have serious charges made against you by an officer of the law."

I jumped in again. "It may be history from the cop's point of view. I want to hear Enrique's version."

Enrique shot me a look of gratitude. "At first, the ambulance blended with traffic. The driver made no sudden moves, and I stayed far back so I wouldn't be seen. I followed for a half hour or so, ducking behind cars and trucks and big rigs. Then they began to pick up speed. Soon they left the rest of the traffic behind. I think they must have figured out I was following them.

"Suddenly it was like they were in a NASCAR race. I was going ninety, and I couldn't catch them. When they saw the cop car coming toward them from the other direction, they flipped on their lights and siren, obviously to look legitimate."

"Giving them a 'reason' to be speeding." I frowned as I thought of Hyacinth dealing with those scoundrels.

Enrique went on with his tale, now seeming to enjoy being the center of attention. "The cop swung a U-turn and shone his lights on me. I pulled over to tell the officer what had happened. I suppose I got carried away. I wanted him to follow the ambulance. But he wouldn't listen.

"He slammed me up against the van and cuffed me. Said I needed to calm down, that I must be high on something. He said my story was the best one he'd ever heard from someone trying to beat arrest." Enrique sighed and his shoulders went down a notch. "I've

never been in cuffs before. Makes you feel … like you're a bug about
to be squashed."

I had one more question, hoping against all hope for a clue to
Hyacinth's whereabouts. "Did you see the ambulance turn off the
interstate?"

"No, ma'am. I was too busy trying not to get arrested."

The sheriff called the switchboard again and asked that all paperwork on Enrique Fox be brought to his office. "Fox, eh?" he said.
"Any relation to the former president of Mexico?"

"Never been asked that one before," Enrique said with a straight
face. "I usually get asked if I'm related to Michael J. Fox."

I almost snorted with laughter. Even the sheriff's grimace almost
turned into a smile.

Chapter Fourteen

I picked up my bedside clock and squinted at its face. Three o'clock in the morning. I'd climbed into bed at midnight, and when I wasn't punching, fluffing, or flipping my pillow, I'd been staring at the ceiling. The events of the previous day continued to haunt me: Dozens of people in the hospital after eating and drinking food and drink my catering company prepared and served—under my direction; the university president dead; my dearest BFF missing, presumed to be in the custody of thieves; and Sheriff Doyle suspicious that Hyacinth and me were in cahoots. And then there was Max, ill and in the hospital.

It was cookie-baking time. I leaped up, grabbed my robe, and headed downstairs to the kitchen. My iPod was on the counter by the landline phone. I stuck it into my wireless speaker, tapped Mozart's *Eine Kleine Nachtmusik*, and went to work.

I didn't know when, but I'd worked in time the night before to freeze the batches I'd made. I opened the freezer and there they were, perfectly stacked inside a thin container on the shelf atop a seven-bone roast. How long ago yesterday's baking and line dancing seemed. Tears threatened again. I selected the country music play-list on my iPod, pulled on my cowboy boots, and tried a bit of the cowboy cha-cha across the floor.

It didn't help much. So I tried a surefire heart starter, the watermelon crawl. I brightened a bit, and even threw in a couple of shake-your-bootie moves as I grabbed ingredients. Might as well whip up another batch.

Still moving to the music, I turned on the mixer and creamed the butter and eggs. I'd just added the vanilla when a thought that had been at the back of my brain for hours shot through my corpus callosum and lit up both sides of my brain. Stunned, I paused my iPod and stood as still as death itself as two specific memories came to me.

The scent of vanilla brought with it a memory of Katie as a tiny girl. A few nights before Christmas, when I was busy at my sewing machine in the other room, she climbed out of bed, slipped into the kitchen, and ate several scoops of cookie dough. The next thing I knew, she was by my side crying and holding her tummy. I fretted that her stomach would warm up the dough and make it rise, but it came up instead all over the bathroom floor.

The memory triggered one of Katie picking poisonous green holly berries from a bush in our backyard. I was working on the vegetable garden when she came over to me, proudly holding several in her little hand. "Peas!" she declared with a huge smile that showed bits of the berry on her tongue and caught in her teeth.

Frantic, I called our pediatrician, and he recommended what all mothers and fathers kept in their medicine chests in those days: syrup of ipecac, used to induce vomiting in the event of poisoning. I grabbed my bottle of the gel-like liquid and carefully measured out a teaspoonful. What followed was much the same as the reaction at the Encore, though far less severe.

Could it be something as simple as that? Syrup of ipecac? I hurried over to my laptop, which I'd left on the kitchen table the night before, typed it into my search engine, and hit enter. A list of websites appeared, and I clicked on those that appeared to be genuine medical sites. The first site stated that the remedy was no longer available in the United States, though it could be purchased illegally.

I clicked on to another site. A photo of Karen Carpenter, a singing star from the seventies, caught my attention. A brother-and-sister team, the Carpenters had produced some of the songs I loved most. I leaned closer to read the article. Karen used the syrup to keep her weight down. It played a part in her death. A big part.

I clicked on a few more sites, making notes of the information: where ipecac grows, its various forms, and the fact that it's no longer sold in the United States because of anorexia.

When I glanced at the clock, it was after four. I was exhausted. The cookies had barely begun baking, but I had one more task to take care of before trying to get more sleep.

I dialed the sheriff's office, though I knew he wouldn't be in. If he checked his messages while out of the office, I wanted him to know right away what I suspected so he could pass it along to the CDC and any other investigators working the case.

A dispatcher picked up on the second ring.

"Sheriff Doyle's office, please."

"I'm sorry," she said. Though female, the voice sounded older than the dispatcher I'd dealt with earlier. "The sheriff won't be in until eight o'clock."

"Could you forward me to his voice mail?"

"Certainly."

"Sheriff," I said to his voice mail a moment later, after identifying myself, "have your investigators test for ipecac. It seems to me that it could easily be dropped into something liquid at the dinner, or stirred into … something." I hesitated, wishing I could take back the "stirred into" phrase. That action would implicate someone on my crew—or Katie, or me. My heart skipped a beat at the thought. "Or sprinkled onto," I added quickly. "It can cause heart fibrillation as a side effect, which may have contributed to—" I gulped a deep breath and finally added, "Contributed to Dr. Delancy's death." A chill traveled up my spine as I spoke the words.

I disconnected the call, put the mixing bowl in the fridge, and went back upstairs to try to get some rest.

On my way to the kitchen later in the morning, I glanced toward the dining room windows and noticed a newspaper on my porch. Puzzled, I hurried back to the front door, opened it, and picked up the paper. It was the special edition of the *Chronicle*.

I tossed it on the kitchen table and started the coffee. While it brewed, I sat at the table and unfolded the paper.

The headlines, in two-inch block letters, screamed, SPECIAL EDITION! Beneath that headline were two featured articles, titles in large print, with prominent photographs. "Dozens Rushed to Hospital after Catered Banquet," read one. The other, with a photo of the figurehead, read "Robbery of Priceless Artifact at University Library."

My heart threatened to drop into my toes right then and there as I read the articles, written by two of the reporters who'd attended the dinner. Then I turned the page and saw yet another headline: INVESTIGATORS HAVE A LEAD.

I pressed my hand to my mouth as I read.

> Unnamed sources in the sheriff's office revealed early this morning that they received a call from someone with firsthand knowledge of the type of poison used. The sheriff's spokesperson said that the connection between the two events is obvious. What isn't known is how these two major events— the catering disaster and the library caper—are connected. The head of The Butler Did It catering company, Mrs. Elaine Littlefield, and the library archivist, Dr. Hyacinth Gilvertin, are longtime friends. Though Dr. Gilvertin is missing, the unnamed source said both are persons of interest.

Persons of interest? Me? Hyacinth? She was a victim. We both were. Stunned, I sat with my head in my hands. I didn't think things could get worse but they just had.

I nearly jumped out of my skin when the doorbell chimed. The last thing in the world I needed right now was a guest, no matter who it was. I hurried to the front door and flung it open, ready to tell whomever to take a hike.

Good heavens, it was Max. Out of the hospital, and looking wan but glorious, at least in my humble opinion. I restrained myself from hugging him—barely.

I opened the door, wide. "You're free."

"They released me just an hour ago. I couldn't wait to get over here"—my heart lifted at that, and then he added—"to find out about the figurehead." He wore his jogging clothes, a towel slung around his neck. A good sign that he was indeed feeling better.

Oh yes, the figurehead. I'd almost forgotten that important piece of the puzzle after reading the morning paper.

"Oh dear," I said. "You don't know?"

He shook his head.

"I think you'd better come in."

He followed me into the kitchen. I pulled two mugs out of the cupboard and filled them with coffee. We sat at the kitchen table, just as we had the morning before.

"I take it this is not good news." He watched me over the rim of his mug as he took a sip.

I barely shook my head and looked down at the newspaper. "Here's the latest," I said. "A special edition."

I left him to read through the articles and went to the freezer to retrieve some of the frozen cookies, put them in the microwave to thaw, and then sat back down.

He'd just finished the article about Hyacinth and me being persons of interest. He met my gaze, and as terrible as I felt, I still found myself melting into those eyes.

"Oh my," I said, standing abruptly before I did or said something I might regret. Like kiss him. Just the thought made my cheeks burn. "Milk or sugar?" I tossed nonchalantly over my shoulder as I headed to the fridge.

"I need some this morning," I babbled. "All this drama …" I retrieved the plate of cookies from the microwave, sat again, milk carton in one hand, cookie plate in the other. Why hadn't I gotten the cream pitcher? Where was my mind this morning?

His face had turned three shades lighter, either from the physical trauma or from reading about the figurehead. Or both.

He rubbed his eyes and then dropped his head into his hands. "A lifetime's quest," he said softly. "I'd already figured out that whoever caused the ruckus at the Encore planned a heist. This confirms it."

I reached for his hand, surprising myself. I held it between my hands, and he looked up, met my gaze again and made my knees go weak. I was glad I was already sitting. "You found it once," I said. "You'll find it again." Now I had to make the awkward decision of whether to put his hand back where I'd found it, or continue to hold it.

"More coffee?" I finally said, though he'd barely taken three sips. After what he'd been through, I couldn't blame him.

As I stood, I had the strange sense that he knew my thoughts. I grabbed the carafe and hurried back to the table.

He leaned forward. "I need to know everything that happened after the EMTs wheeled me out. Please, every detail you can think of." He tapped the paper. "I've read the sensationalized version. Now I want the truth"—he gave me that little hint of a smile again—"your version. Your insights. What do your instincts tell you?"

I nodded and gave him an almost minute-by-minute rundown, including the thoughts that led to my search for ipecac.

"I couldn't sleep, so I got up to bake cookies …"

Something flickered in his eyes, and for a nanosecond his serious expression disappeared. *"Eine Kleine Nachtmusik?"*

I grinned. "And the watermelon crawl. Anyway, while I was mixing together the dough, a memory came back to me. Two memories, actually. They say that the sense of smell brings memories to mind faster than any of the other senses. In this case, it was the vanilla."

I told him about my experiences with my daughter and about the research I'd done online, and then I added, "Because it's not available in the States—legally, that is—we may be able to trace its origins and find the buyer, who might lead us to the person who's behind the theft."

"If only it could be that easy," he said.

"What about Marcel Devereaux?"

He drew in a deep breath. "He was in the hospital with me, just as sick as I was. He and his companion. We were right across the hall from each other last night. I can't imagine putting yourself through that, just to throw off suspicion."

"That's odd," I said. "I watched them closely, and they left without eating. I specifically looked for them when people started getting sick."

"You're sure?" He looked worried.

"I am." I smiled. "Though considering we had three hundred people in attendance, I might have overlooked them. I say, keep them on the list."

"The problem is, we don't know who's at the top."

The word "we" caught my attention. Was he suggesting we work together on this? It made sense. "My number-one priority is finding Hyacinth," I said, "and making sure she's okay."

"Human life is more important than a thousand figureheads." He stood, took his cup to the sink, and rinsed it, which made me smile. "Besides, where Hyacinth is—"

"The figurehead will be too," I finished. "At least, that's my greatest hope."

As we walked to the front door, he stopped and looked down at me. "There's something I haven't told you about the figurehead." He searched my eyes. "About its value. We'll talk later." He touched my arm.

"It's a date," I said, flustered by his touch. I feared I was as foolish as every other single female in the county. I needed to put a stop to this flirting. And this new heart-fluttering thing.

Chapter Fifteen

My cell phone rang as I scooped coffee into the filter basket the next morning. As I unplugged the charger, I spotted the sheriff's office number on the display. I'd just been there the night before. He wouldn't call unless he had news. I closed my eyes, said hello, and prayed that Hyacinth had been found.

The disembodied voice sounded familiar. "Mrs. Littlefield?" I pictured the woman at the switchboard.

"This is she."

"This is Ethel Adams at the sheriff's office. Sheriff Doyle asked me to call you. Said he wants you to stop by this morning."

My stomach dropped. It had to be news about Hyacinth. "Did he say why?"

"No, ma'am. Just that you need to get here right away."

"Give me half an hour." I hesitated before hanging up. "Did he mention anything about my friend Dr. Gilvertin?"

"No, ma'am. He didn't mention any names. He was all business, though, like something is bothering him something fierce."

"Okay. Thanks. Tell him I'll be there soon."

What was so important that it couldn't be shared over the phone? I finished making coffee, poured it into a travel mug, and then hurried upstairs to shower and change.

I was dressed and out the door in record time, coffee in one hand, a frozen chocolate chipper in the other. There's nothing better for breakfast, especially if one dips the cookie in the coffee. Tricky to do while driving and I do advise against trying it.

"Hi, Mom," Katie said. "Is there any news about Cinth?"

"Nothing yet. I'm on my way to the sheriff's office right now, though. He wants to see me. Maybe he knows something."

"Call me as soon as you hear. She's like part of our family."

As much as my daughter loved Hyacinth, I had the feeling something else was troubling her.

I lightened my voice. "Hey, I miss you and Chloe Grace. It's Saturday. Let's make a night of it. Why don't you and Chloe Grace plan to sleep over tonight? We'll do popcorn and a Disney movie. Besides, I want an update on how things are going with Sandy." I cringed as I spoke my former son-in-law's name. "Maybe we can finally have that talk."

"The talk can wait. It's important, but not as much as everything else you've got on your plate right now. As for Sandy," she added, "things are going great. In fact, maybe he could come with us for the popcorn and movie time."

"Oh yes," I said after I'd swallowed hard. "That would be great."

We ended the call, I dunked the cookie and took a bite, then peeled out of the driveway. I pointed the Ghia in the direction of the courthouse. When I arrived, I parked around back, just as I had done the night before, and trotted up the concrete stairs.

I stopped at the sliding-glass window and asked to see Sheriff Doyle. The same woman who manned the station, so to speak, must have drawn weekend duty.

She opened the window. "Do you have an appointment?"

I reminded her that she had just called and asked me to come in. "Tell him Elaine Littlefield is here," I said, watching for a reaction.

"Oh, that Elaine Littlefield." She pressed a button on her console, uttered a few words into the headset, and then looked back to me. "Do you know where his office is located?"

Good heavens, what happened to the girl's short-term memory?

A few minutes later, I was knocking lightly on Sheriff Doyle's door.

"Come in."

I pushed open the door, surprised to see Max with the sheriff. Both men stood as I entered. Both looked somber. My stomach dropped to the floor. I looked around for a chair to drop into. Pronto. I settled into one next to Max and glanced from one man to the other.

The sheriff let out a long sigh. "I'm afraid I don't have good news," he said.

My mouth went dry. "Hyacinth?" I could barely get the word out.

"We found the ambulance early this morning before sunup. Someone reported a fire near Waynesville. When the fire crews arrived, they found a cabin and a vehicle—an ambulance—in flames. We're not certain it's the ambulance we're looking for, but it seems unlikely there would be more than one out there. And it's near where Mr. Fox said he'd last seen it.

Their expressions told me they were holding back.

"I sent deputies to the scene immediately," the sheriff continued. "I heard from them a short while ago. The fires are out, but it's still too hot for anyone to go in to gather evidence." He glanced at Max before going on. "Also, they said there appeared to be a woman's body in the back of the vehicle."

I caught my hand to my mouth. "Oh no." I put my head down for a moment, trying to get my bearings, and then added, "But we don't know it's the right ambulance ... or that the woman is Hyacinth ... It can't be. I'm sure of it. Really, it's not her." Denial wasn't working. I felt the sting of approaching tears behind my eyes. When I cry, it's not a pretty sight. My nose runs, my eyes puff up, and I shake all over. I avoid that kind of behavior in public at all costs. I stood abruptly, grabbed my handbag, and headed for the door.

I trotted through the rabbit warren of little cubicles and, once I was outside, breathed in huge, shuddering gulps of air. I heard the door open and close behind me, and then I felt a hand on my shoulder.

"Easy now," Max said, his voice low. "Just as you said, we don't know for sure that it's Hyacinth."

I rummaged around in my purse for tissues, grabbed a handful, and dabbed at my eyes. Then I nodded. "It can't be."

He let his gaze drift from mine to where I'd parked the Ghia. "Would you like for me to drive you home?"

"I'm not going home." I lifted my chin a notch and gave my eyes another swipe, glad I had avoided the runny-nose-and-trembling stage. "I'm going to the crime scene."

"You mean the scene of the fire?"

I nodded. "If there's a body in that ambulance, it's a crime scene."

"Do you mind if I come along?"

"Not at all, but one of us needs to get a map and directions."

He headed back toward Sheriff Doyle's office.

I shuddered, thinking about Hyacinth, thinking about my recurring nightmares. This was no time to dwell on it, so I stuffed it deep inside, in that place where I usually kept such things locked tight. I hoped this one would stay there.

Chapter Sixteen

Once we reached the interstate, the drive from Eden's Bridge went by in a blur. I drove slower than usual because my eyes kept filling with tears. Max didn't say so, but he seemed more comfortable at this speed. At least, his knuckles weren't as white as they'd been during previous rides. Or maybe it was because he was too busy handing me tissues.

About a half hour from town, I turned left off the interstate onto a gravel road and then in a half mile or so, turned left onto a single-track dirt road that led into a dense forest.

I tried to keep my heart filled with hope that the call to the sheriff had been in error. My brain didn't cooperate with my heart. It kept trying to calculate the improbability that another female had hooked up with the thugs who stole the figurehead.

Max pulled out his cell. "I'll see if the sheriff's heard anything new."

My words came out in a whisper. "Good idea." I was having a difficult time keeping my grief below the surface.

He handed me another tissue, balanced the phone on his knee, and tapped the number. "No signal," he said after a few seconds. "It says it's searching."

"The sheriff did say last night that someone tried to call 9-1-1, but they couldn't trace it because of the dead spots in these mountains." Dead spots. I started to tear up again. Max handed me another tissue. I blew my nose and then said, "Maybe it was Hyacinth."

He didn't bow his head or close his eyes, but I got the sense he was praying. I didn't want to interrupt, so I remained silent.

Our gazes met a few moments later. His eyes were bright with unshed tears, which made that place at the top of my throat sting all over again. I swallowed hard to keep the tears under control. It didn't work. Max handed me another tissue and took one for himself.

"I've always counted Hyacinth a friend," he said. "We haven't spent a lot of time together—only at faculty functions. But she's a character you never forget. One of a kind."

I smiled. "And then some." I looked across at him. "Thanks for not using past tense."

He gave me a crooked smile. "I can't imagine our world without Hyacinth."

I reached for his hand. "Thank you for saying that." He grasped mine and squeezed it, causing me to nearly run off the rutted road, even in my grieving state. Reluctantly, as I headed toward a skinny pine, I decided it was the better part of wisdom to keep both hands on the steering wheel. We missed the pine by inches.

I aimed the Ghia back to the center of the road, and we bumped along for several more minutes. The scent of loamy damp soil, mixed with pine and a host of other growing things, filled the air.

The forest grew thicker and darker, the soil now damp enough to leave clearly marked tire prints and footprints. I squinted into a shady area ahead, where it appeared a fairly large vehicle—the ambulance, perhaps?—had turned off. As we approached, I slowed the Ghia, came to a halt, and turned off the engine.

Max jumped out of the car before I did. I didn't want to admit he might have spotted the tire tracks first; after all, I was the PI.

He bent over the tread marks left by a single vehicle. I came up beside him and squatted, rocking back on my heels for balance.

"Deep, meaning a heavy vehicle. Good evidence that it might have been the ambulance," he said.

Not to be outdone, I said, "Also a wider wheelbase than most cars."

I glanced around at the thick brush and a crescent-shaped turnout that appeared to lead back to the main two-track road. I walked farther and found more tire marks and footprints. "It looks like they stopped here," I called to Max.

My breath caught in my throat. "Smaller footprints. Tennies. Female. They could be Hyacinth's. She had them on yesterday." *With her skinny jeans and bright top,* I remembered, tamping down a fresh sting of tears.

Even if they were hers, it didn't prove she was alive.

"I see one set of larger prints," Max said, stooping again for a closer look.

I tried to imagine what had happened there, but shook my head. It could have been anything. Maybe she tried to escape, but was chased. My friend was resourceful, and I hoped she'd pulled out all the stops, no matter what had taken place.

I walked a few feet up the road, scanning the brush. I spotted a single set of small prints leading out of the clearing, and my heart lifted. She'd gotten this far by herself. I scanned the foliage again, the soil beneath the trees, and then began looking higher. I narrowed my eyes as something sparkled at eye level in the distance.

"Oh my," I enthused, scarcely able to imagine my eyes weren't playing tricks on me. "Oh, my goodness gracious." My heart felt light enough to make my feet go into a cowboy cha-cha.

Max grinned and came over. "What'd you find?"

I pointed to a small pine near the edge of the turnout, then walked over and plucked a golden bangle bracelet from an upper branch. It sparkled in the dappled sunlight of the forest.

"Hyacinth was here." I held the bracelet up to inspect it in the light. There was nothing unusual about it. The shape hadn't altered, and there were no signs of blood, thank heavens. "Katie and Chloe Grace give her one every Christmas. She has quite a collection."

"She knew you'd be coming after her."

His expression was kind as I looked up at him and nodded. "She would count on that. She is counting on it," he amended. "And the footsteps lead on, alone, it appears."

She'd been alive before reaching the cabin and the ambulance. She had tracked the thieves. I concentrated on that image rather than the scene we were heading for. "It's just like her to do that."

"Do what?" Max turned and gave me a quizzical look.

I'd almost forgotten that he couldn't read my mind. I managed a watery smile. "Track the thieves. It's just like her to do that."

I looked back at the car, then turned to follow the track up the hill. The footprints eventually disappeared as the soil became dryer. Within a few minutes, we saw the burned-out cabin with a vehicle in front of it.

As we drew closer to the clearing at the front of the smoldering cabin, or what was left of it, two large fire engines came into view, along with a smaller double-cab truck and two SUVs, one marked with the county coroner's seal and the other with that of the sheriff's office.

I slowed the Ghia and tried to draw in a deep breath, but my chest was too tight for oxygen to enter. I hunched over and dropped my head into my hands. "This is too hard," I whispered. "I can't do this. I just can't."

Max scooted over as close as he could get, considering we were both in bucket seats with a console between us. But, bless his sweet heart, he tried. He patted my right shoulder, the only one he could reach, which did bring me some comfort.

"Why don't I take it from here? I'll ask some questions and get all the information I can, including the body ID."

I nodded gratefully and tried not to think about Hyacinth being in the burnt shell of a vehicle.

The passenger-side door opened and closed, and then all was quiet. The acrid odor of wet ashes and charred wood mixed with mud and decaying leaves turned my stomach. I looked up to see Max striding toward a group of firefighters and a couple of deputies.

I moved my focus to the burned-out vehicle and felt my throat tighten. I couldn't draw in a breath. I thought of Hyacinth. What would she do if our roles were reversed? She would march right up to that clearing and demand to know what had been found out about the body.

I took a breath—this time it went deeper than my throat—girded my loins, so to speak, and got out of the car at last, the strap of my handbag that contained my forensic kit slung over my shoulder as I marched toward the clearing. *I can do this, I can do this, I can do this*, I chanted silently. The smell of damp, burnt wood was overwhelming, and more than once, I came close to turning back.

Images came to me from so long ago that they seemed like shadows. Or faded black-and-white photographs from my childhood. I remember neighbors standing over me, and behind them, flames shooting out of a dark, charred building that once was my home. The horrible aching in my heart as I watched my mother and father being wheeled to ambulances. I'd tried to go with them. No one would listen or let me go. And my mother wouldn't wake up and hold her arms out for me. Neither would Daddy. I shuddered as I returned to the present. I'd been four when it happened and I'd been terrified of fire since. Not many people knew of my fear; I'm not one to put such things on display.

I had almost reached the ambulance when my knees turned wobbly, and I worried they might give out any minute. The men were still talking about the case. I couldn't hear everything, but a few words drifted toward me: "APB." "Could've used a rental truck." "Size of the tires tells us it's a …"

I sidled over to the ambulance, not necessarily to be secretive, but to save myself the embarrassment should I fall apart when I saw Hyacinth's body. The shell of the burned-out ambulance seemed to be untouched. I frowned. By now, surely the coroner had retrieved the body. Why weren't they gathering forensic evidence?

I stepped closer and, holding my breath, peered inside. The body, at least what was left of its charred remains, lay facedown. I turned away, feeling the urge to either upchuck or run. What if this was Hyacinth? I closed my eyes to shut out the image. It didn't work. I told myself that if the tables were turned, Hyacinth would be strong and tough on my behalf. I needed to have the same courage to take another look.

On closer inspection, something about the body didn't seem right.

The charred head seemed misshapen, but then, I'd never seen a charred body before. I touched the metal of the ambulance, and found it warm but not unbearably hot. Then I moved around the rear of the shell and climbed inside. I held my breath and moved slowly toward the body.

I reached out to touch it but jerked my hand back when I heard a voice behind me say, "Are you okay?"

I turned to see Max standing behind the ambulance. "I just had to see for myself."

He started to say something, but I waved him away. I wanted to concentrate so I could get a better look. "What on God's green earth is this?" I gasped. "These are the remains of the body they called in?"

I turned to Max. It took only seconds for my huge, soul-buoying relief to flare to anger. "How could they make such a mistake? They couldn't tell the difference between a mannequin and a real person? Couldn't they have waited until they knew for certain?"

"Apparently Resusci Anne had them fooled. She'd been sprayed with some sort of a fire retardant so she was visible through the flames—for a while, at least. It wasn't until they put out the fire that they found poor nearly melted Annie." He chuckled, and the sound calmed me somewhat.

"I don't think it's funny." I clambered out of the smoldering shell and brushed myself off. "I grieved all the way over here," I said with a sniff, though if it hadn't been for the audience, I would have done a watermelon crawl, complete with the bootie shake.

"They did call the sheriff's office to clear up their mistake, and he's been trying to reach us."

"But how did they get a sig—?" It came to me before I got the question out. "Satellite phone. Of course. They can get a signal anywhere." I made a mental to get one, then remembered I might be going into bankruptcy if I didn't turn these accusations around pronto.

By now, the two deputies and the firefighters were getting ready to leave. The coroner was just pulling out onto the road, the fire truck behind him.

Max and I walked over to the deputies. "Did you find any evidence that will help locate these guys?" I asked.

The tall, lean dark-haired deputy spoke first. "We put out another APB about their last known location. We believe they met up with someone here who probably was waiting with another vehicle. Judging from the distance between the front and back tires, it appears to be a seventeen-foot truck, a common size for a rental." He adjusted his stance somewhat. "Of course, that doesn't mean it is a rental."

"A pretty good move on their part," I said. "A great way to blend in. Those are popular rentals."

"We're checking to see if nearby agencies have reported anything stolen." The shorter deputy adjusted his belt buckle. "If so, that will be our first break."

"Sorry about the false alarm," the first deputy said. "My bad."

My bad? I wanted to throttle him. *My bad?* His *bad* had caused me unspeakable heartache.

"Well, we're all done here," the shorter deputy said and hitched up his belt buckle. "We'll let you know if we get any hits on the rental truck."

"Is it okay if we nose around?" I planned to anyway, but it didn't hurt to ask.

"Go ahead," Belt Buckle said. "We're done."

They waved at us, then went around to their vehicle and got in, soon disappearing down the two-lane road.

"You look as pale as death," Max said, his concern showing in his eyes.

I glanced at the burned-out cabin and the shell of a vehicle, knowing I had forensic work of my own to complete. My nostrils filled with the stench of smoldering charred wood and plastic and who knew what else. "You don't know the half of it."

My nightmare again threatened to surface and carry me back to that other time and place when the smell of wet, smoldering embers filled my tiny nostrils, coughing sobs filled my throat, and I thought I was going to die. But again, I tamped it down deep, and determined it would stay there.

Chapter Seventeen
The Professor

· · · · · · · · · · · · · · · ·

Max had been cast under a spell. No doubt about it. An alien had taken over his heart and mind. He'd been a confirmed bachelor for more decades than he cared to admit. He had come close to marrying once when he was a graduate student, but the girl returned his engagement ring when she found someone with better prospects for future income. Too bad that someone was Max's best friend. He'd dated some fine women through the years, a few even seriously. But he'd never before met anyone like El Littlefield.

He thought of El bustling around the Encore the night before, dressed in black and white, her pixie hairdo perfectly framing her face. Remembering her hand signals even made him smile. And the way she'd surreptitiously woven her way through groups of the guests, her face blandly innocent, but catching his eye from time to time, lifting her eyebrows to signal one thing or another. All of it made him want to chuckle, despite the way the evening turned out.

When she'd wept earlier, he had wanted nothing more than to gather her into his arms. The vision of holding her caused his heart to pick up speed. He almost shook his head in disbelief. What was going on? A place in his heart, long unoccupied, seemed to be filling with something good. Something beautiful. He let out a deep sigh. He'd be listening to country-and-western songs before long. He needed to get over this ... this schoolboy crush. It was not in his life plan. Besides, who was he kidding? Falling in love at age sixty? He was quite comfortable with the way he'd organized his life, thank you very much. His home, modest as it was, had no mortgage. His future travel would be taken care of by those who were already hiring him to lecture throughout the country and overseas.

Yes. His life was arranged quite nicely. Research. Lecturing. Searching for historical artifacts. Writing. And working in his garden.

Thirty years ago, he had taken his vows as a lifetime Franciscan. Not as a monk living in a monastery, but a Third Order Franciscan in the Episcopal Church. His vows included a rule of life, following the example of the thirteenth-century monk Saint Francis of Assisi: living simply, joyfully, and generously.

It wasn't something he talked about. He was more comfortable living by the quote some said originated with Francis: "Preach the gospel at all times; if necessary, use words."

Like others in the Third Order, his only habit was the cross that hung on a leather cord around his neck.

The women he'd spent time with felt his way of living out his love for God was too intense. Too quiet. Too contemplative. They wondered about his yearly silent retreats. How anyone could go seven days without speaking. Until he found someone who understood his Franciscan nature, he would remain a single man.

He gazed over at El, wondering. She didn't seem to have a contemplative bone in her body. She was lively, gregarious, transparent with her sorrows and joys. He'd never forget the morning he'd caught a glimpse of her dancing in her pajamas. Nor would he forget how she opened her heart to sorrow when she thought her friend had died.

As attracted as he was to her, he needed to put the brakes on his feelings. It was time to turn one hundred percent of his energy toward finding Hyacinth and the figurehead. Even then, his work wasn't done. The figurehead held a puzzle that he had to figure out. That would occupy his time quite nicely.

He realized that he'd just come full circle in his thinking. His life was nicely ordered. He didn't have the time or inclination to change things. He had a worthy quest to complete, other quests to pursue, lectures to give, and silent retreats to attend.

And that was that.

Max picked up a twig and knelt to sift through some broken glass near the ambulance. El reached into her handbag and rummaged around. A minute or two later, like a magician pulling a rabbit out of a hat, she produced a forensic kit with a number of implements, including two pairs of rubber gloves.

"Here you go, Sherlock." She grinned and tossed him a set.

After he'd pulled on the gloves, she handed him long-nosed tweezers and a few plastic ziplock bags, which he stuffed into his shirt pocket.

"Do you always come this prepared?"

"You think this is prepared?" Her gaze seemed to reach into his soul. He held her eyes for a breathless moment and then looked away as she added, "You should see what else I've got in here." She laughed lightly.

The resolve he'd felt just moments ago was already melting. He stood and went over to the burned-out vehicle and nosed around inside, but found no evidence of either Hyacinth or the *Lady with a Scarf*. He turned when El came up behind him.

"Anything?"

Max shook his head. "If there was any evidence to start with, I'm afraid it's long gone. The blasts of the fire hoses took care of it."

"I wonder if it was arson."

He raised a brow. "Why do you think that?"

She looked up at him, shading her eyes. "Maybe I'm grabbing at straws. But think about it. The glow from a fire this size lights up the night sky. This close to Waynesville, someone's going to notice and call the fire department."

The light dawned. "Hyacinth."

El smiled. "She's creative." She glanced at the cabin, and a shadow crossed her face—a bad memory, perhaps—then disappeared just as quickly. She swallowed visibly. "Besides, I found the flash point. And this." It was a shard of thick glass.

"Follow me," she said, and moved to what probably had been the front of the cabin and a charred hulk of what might have been a sofa. She picked through several more shards of glass and laid them on the ground. "Not a perfect fit," she said, "but do you see what this might have been?"

"A lantern?"

She nodded. "Kerosene." Again, she motioned for him to follow. "And over here." She led him to a small patch of land beyond the yellow tape that had escaped the burn. She knelt and, using her tweezers, carefully picked up a cigar and dropped it into a plastic baggie. She grinned. "If we're lucky, we might get prints. Or DNA."

She stood and brushed herself off. It didn't help. The mud and ash just streaked across her jeans. "I know how Hyacinth thinks. My theory is that she was looking for a weapon, found this old lantern, and threw it at someone who was lighting a cigar." She lifted the baggie for a closer look. "You can see by the length that he didn't have much of a chance to smoke it. She probably took aim when he lit a match." She shrugged. "It may be far-fetched, but it's a theory."

"And it's a good one," Max said, admiring her skills of deduction.

El again dropped to her knees and crawled the entire length of the cabin, her expression intense as she examined more scorched bits of glass. "This piece has blood on it," she said, holding it up for Max to see. "And here's another." She laughed. "If I'm right, and I just bet I am, Hyacinth packed quite a wallop." She dropped the pieces in a separate baggie and zipped it closed. "Let's get this back to the sheriff's office. The lab might get lucky and find some DNA."

She stood, took off her gloves, reached for his, and then dropped both pairs into another ziplock baggie. "One more thing," she said. "I need to do one last sweep."

El walked slowly around the outer perimeter of the clearing, scrutinizing every rock and tree and twig, it seemed. She seemed to pay special attention to trees, especially pines that even vaguely resembled the shape of a Christmas tree.

"I had hoped for another breadcrumb." El looked pale and shaken, but she held a small cluster of pine branches to her nose. "Reminds me of Christmas—and helps get rid of the smell of death."

"The smell of death?"

She joined me and we turned toward her Karmann Ghia. "The smell of smoldering ashes," she said.

Chapter Eighteen
Mrs. Littlefield

· · · · · · · · · · · · · · · ·

I turned onto the interstate ramp, and we zipped along like a hound after a hare. I half listened while Max was on the cell phone with Marcel Devereaux. It sounded to me as if he was giving Max a snow job, though I couldn't exactly hear Devereaux's side of the conversation.

Besides, I was dealing with the aftermath of the journey into my worst nightmare. I'd been shaken to the core. I wondered if Max had any idea how close I'd come to being ill while we searched for evidence.

After he dropped his phone into his pocket, I picked up speed, wanting to get our newly collected forensics evidence to the sheriff's office. Even so, the results would be delayed. Eden's Bridge didn't have a forensics lab so everything had to be transported to Asheville. I pressed harder on the accelerator, and Max held on to his bucket seat.

I signaled to change lanes and pulled around an eighteen-wheeler with a bumper sticker that said "Jesus is coming: Look busy." We were on an incline, and the Ghia struggled to make it to the top. I pressed harder on the gas.

Max cleared his throat. I glanced at him and tried to avoid moving the steering wheel the same direction.

"How about stopping for lunch? I'm famished." He sounded apologetic.

"Now that you mention it, I am too. How about a drive-through? I wouldn't want anyone to see me covered with this muck and grime."

"On you, it looks good—the muck and grime."

I peeked at him and saw that he was grinning. The Ghia wobbled out of my lane briefly, and someone in my blind spot blasted his or her horn. I jerked the steering wheel to the left for a quick recovery.

"Thanks," I said, keeping my focus on the road.

The following ramp looked promising. A variety of artery-clogging choices raised high their banner-like signs. "Burritos, tacos, hamburgers …?"

We agreed on the burrito place, and I turned into the drive-through and stopped in front of the menu. As a California transplant with exceptionally high standards for Mexican food—with a few exceptions in Salisbury—I'd given up on finding any Southern offerings that lit my fire, so to speak.

But I had to admit, when we pulled over at a rest stop with a tree-shaded picnic area, the burrito I ordered had a scent like spicy manna. It had been a long day, and I didn't realize how famished I was.

After we'd visited the restrooms and freshened up, we met back at a rough-hewn table with fewer bird droppings than the others. I spread my paper napkin out as a placemat, unwrapped my burrito, and prepared to say grace.

I reached for his hand out of habit. When I'm with Katie and Chloe Grace, we hold hands when I say grace. I have a tendency to cover everything that's happened up to that point in my day, and more than once Chloe Grace has tugged at my hand and asked me to please hurry.

But it appeared Max was already praying silently. And it wasn't lengthy. When my hand touched his, he looked up, puzzled.

"I was about to ask God to bless our food and the hands that prepared it," I said. I blushed. Goodness, I hadn't done that in years. "My family and I … we always hold hands."

"I thought maybe that was it." He reached for my hand and bowed his head.

I kept my prayer short, though I did get rather revved up thanking God for the mannequin that turned out not to be Hyacinth. And then I quickly drew it to a close, keeping Chloe Grace's oft-repeated request in mind. When I looked up, he seemed to be studying me.

"You pray a lively prayer," he said, raising his eyebrows.

"I like to let God know how much I like the life He's given me. I think He loves it when we notice." I took a bite of my burrito and savored its goodness. "I like to try to make God laugh."

He threw back his head and laughed out loud. "You do?"

"Yes, I do, though I think this is the first time I've admitted it to anyone. It just seems to me that if we're made in His image, and we take such amazing delight in our children or our grandchildren, wouldn't God look at us in much the same way? Taking delight in us …"

"'ADONAI your God is right there with you, as a mighty savior. He will rejoice over you and be glad, He will be silent in His love, He will shout over you with joy.'"

"Zephaniah 3:17, but I haven't heard that version before."

"It's from the Jewish Bible."

"Do you ever sit still and listen to God?" he said after a few minutes.

I laughed. "I'm too busy talking."

"Most of us are."

I pictured a voice thundering from heaven. Or Max standing beside a burning bush. Realizing I was holding my dripping burrito inches from my mouth without taking a bite, I lowered it to the table. "He talks to you?"

He went back to eating his burrito, and I just sat there a moment, trying to take in this new side of the professor.

"Not with words," he said. "But with love, compassion, mercy, gentleness … whatever it is I need from His Spirit."

"I don't think I could sit still long enough to hear Him. I've tried some of the ancient ways of praying, the labyrinth, contemplative prayer, lectio divina. It felt awkward. I was too aware of myself, not of God." I grinned. "Give me a good gospel song to belt out, a Bible to read and underline and take notes in, a fiery preacher, and I'm a happy camper."

"Church isn't necessarily the place I find God, or connect with Him. And I'm pretty sure I haven't confessed that to anyone before. For some people He can't be found there at all."

"I'm surprised at that," I said. "He sure can be found at my church."

"I see Him everywhere, in every circumstance, if I'm attentive." Then he laughed. "How did our conversation take this turn?"

"I think I started it."

He nodded thoughtfully, looked off at the horizon for a moment, then turned back to me, his expression serious. "While you were in the restroom, I called our VP, Isabel Chang, for an update. All the victims are much better."

"Except Dr. Delancy," I said, letting my gaze drift from his.

I closed my eyes briefly, wishing the previous day had never happened. "I won't feel better until they're out of the hospital and this part of the nightmare is over," I said. And that didn't even take into consideration Hyacinth and the figurehead.

My cell phone rang. I fished around in my handbag and picked it up on the second ring. I sighed. Chance Noseworthy.

"Mrs. Littlefield?"

"Yes."

"Yes … this is Chance Noseworthy, an investigator with the CDC. I need to talk to you about the banquet last night at the Encore, and the mass poisoning that your company caused."

"You've got it wrong. We don't know that it happened through my catering company."

"It's important that we meet right away."

"Of course. Have you found out the origin or makeup of the poison?"

For a moment, dead silence reigned, then he said, "I'll meet you at the sheriff's office in Eden's Bridge at two o'clock this afternoon. We'll discuss it there."

❧ ❧

"He can't order me around like that, can he?" We tossed our burrito wrappers in a waste barrel by the picnic table and walked back to the Ghia. "I mean, does Noseworthy have the legal authority to treat me as if I've done something wrong? I'm one of the victims here. My company may never recover from this terrible publicity. The Butler Did It will always be synonymous with upchucking." The thought depressed me.

"But that's not what's important now," I continued, on a roll. I opened the door on the driver's side and slid behind the wheel, steaming at the tone Noseworthy had used with me.

Max got in on the other side, quiet in the face of my rant.

"We—I—have more important things to do. Not that I'm not curious about who did it and why, but the main thing now is to find Hyacinth and the figurehead." Tears stung my eyes again. Hyacinth. My forever friend. Missing. And right now, I had no idea where to start looking.

"True," Max said, finally edging in a word.

I started the engine, and surprisingly, I worked the clutch correctly and the car didn't leap out of the parking space with my usual speed. I noted Max's grip on his seat wasn't as tight.

"The important thing," he continued calmly, "is to get the forensics to the sheriff's office. Maybe they can shed some light on who's involved. That, in turn, might lead us to Hyacinth and the *Lady*."

"Providing they get fingerprints or DNA off the cigar and glass," I said. "And providing the prints and DNA are in the system."

"Yes."

I drew in a deep, cleansing breath and let it out slowly. Max did have a sense of calm about him, an odd peace that affected me somehow. Maybe because he listened to God instead of trying to make God laugh.

I revved up the ramp and onto the interstate again, checking my rearview mirror for the eighteen-wheeler that always seemed to lie in wait to roll over the Ghia at such times.

"You said that there's more to the figurehead than meets the eye."

From the corner of my eye, I saw him turn toward me. "There is," he said. "Its worth is in the quarter-to-half-million range right now, at auction. Of course, our intent is to keep her in her proper place in a Boston museum, near where she was carved."

"That would make a collector sit up and take notice." I glanced across at him. "But you've said it holds a secret that makes its value even greater."

"My father heard about the figurehead at the end of the World War II. He wrote down the details so he wouldn't forget and then passed them on to me.

"He enlisted when he was only seventeen—lied about his age—and was stationed in France in 1944 until the end of World War II. During the Nazi occupation, artwork worth millions was stolen from museums, homes, and public buildings. They took anything of value, anything they would get their hands on."

Astounded, I turned to him, though I tried to keep the Ghia from wobbling out of our lane. "So that's why this is so important. The *Lady* has to do with finding the hidden artifacts."

He nodded. "Yes."

"How many people know about this?"

"We don't know. But the paintings, sculptures, and artifacts were hidden by a courageous group of men and women in the French Resistance. In caves somewhere in the Pyrenees."

"And they've never been found."

He shook his head. "No. But now that we've found the figurehead, that may change."

"That's why you're worried others may be after the *Lady* too." I spoke slowly as a few more pieces to the puzzle began to fall into place. "Other families, maybe descendants of those in the Resistance, may be on the lookout for her."

"I didn't realize the news would travel so fast," he said. "I'm still unused to the speed of the Internet, especially how fast things spread through social media." He fell quiet for a moment and then continued.

"The French Resistance meticulously documented the rightful owners and where each piece came from. They succeeded, at least for a time. One night, they were betrayed by one of their own. They were caught and taken to the camps, never to be heard from again. Rumors about the location of the caves have cropped up through the years, but no one has been able to find them."

I could barely breathe when he finished. I turned to him again. "This is big. I mean, really big. You're talking about items that might add up to millions, perhaps billions of dollars."

"There are those who are driven by greed. Who want to find the hidden message that the figurehead hides."

I let his words sink in as I passed a dusty SUV with a group of rowdy teens, glad to see them disappear in my rearview mirror. Max glanced at the speedometer, then quickly looked away.

"It's broken," I said and gave it a little tap. "They don't make parts for it anymore."

"So you have no idea how fast you're going."

I shook my head. "It's been stuck on eighty-three for years." I passed another car. "So, how did the map get into an American figurehead?"

"*Lady with a Scarf* has quite a history." He leaned back in his seat, taking his time before answering.

"I'm listening."

"My dad did all the initial research. She was carved by a Boston artisan in 1812, mounted under the bowsprit of a small schooner and put into service soon after. She went down in a sudden storm on the Great Lakes in 1826. The figurehead was recovered by a Canadian seaman who sold her to the owner of a fleet of three-masted barks. The flotilla set sail for Europe with our *Lady* in the lead. The bark she was attached to sank in a storm off Nova Scotia. All men on board were lost."

"Good heavens, she sounds like bad luck to me," I said, letting out a whistle.

"Some seamen say she was cursed. That's why, though someone brought her out of the water, she was never attached to another ship," Max said. "She was sold at auction and ended up in the Musée National de la Marine in Paris."

Up ahead, I could see the turnoff to Eden's Bridge. Three miles. My stomach was in knots. Max's story had taken my mind off Chance Noseworthy, which helped, but nausea from this morning's adventure seemed to be catching up with me.

"And then what happened?" I needed Max to keep talking. Anything to distract me.

"She remained in the museum until her final crossing in 1944 on the USS *Andrea Rae*, a crossing that few people knew about. Officially, it was to return the figurehead to Boston, where she had originated. But she held other more important secrets and was being shipped to an undisclosed location in Washington, DC.

"Once again, however, the ship carrying her hit bad weather and capsized. All on board were lost—except for one soldier."

I signaled to change lanes to make the off-ramp. Apparently the woman in the car to my right didn't notice my signal. She laid on her horn as I crossed the lane and zoomed onto the ramp.

"And that lone seaman who made it," I said as I braked for a stop sign. "That was your father?"

Max nodded. "As the ship began to capsize, there was a lot of talk again about the curse of the figurehead. Someone suggested they throw her overboard in order to save themselves. And a desperate group actually found the container in the cargo hold and hoisted her into the stormy waters. My father described the scene, even her watertight pod, down to the last detail.

"But one of the officers—apparently, the only person on board who knew the *Lady's* true purpose—screamed for someone to save the pod. He screamed loud enough for those who stood nearby to hear, even above the storm. He cried out that she carried inside the only directions to the treasures stolen by the Nazis and hidden by the French Resistance."

I felt my jaw drop. "So that's how your father came to know about it. Did any of the others survive? Maybe there were survivors he didn't know about. Could they be after the hidden cache?"

"My father said that he thought maybe one officer had worked with the underground, that's how he knew. As for the others, he believes they all perished."

I turned by the courthouse, drove around back to the sheriff's office, and parked.

I looked at Max thoughtfully. "When you retrieved the figurehead, you said you sent it off to be inspected."

He nodded. "I didn't send her off. I went with her to some people I'd been in contact with in DC. For one thing, I worried that being in saltwater off and on through the years might have caused deterioration."

"And did it?"

"The museum in Paris did some restoration when the figurehead first arrived, which helped. And after that, she really didn't touch seawater again. The pod had remained amazingly watertight for all those years."

"Was there any mention of a secret compartment? Or did they do any tests to see what might be inside?"

The door to the sheriff's office opened and a tall, balding man in a dark suit stepped out. He seemed to zero in on me as if he knew who I was.

"Methinks this is Chance Noseworthy." I gulped a deep breath as I reached for the Ghia's door handle.

Max got out on his side at the same time. I expected him to go to his car, but instead, he walked with me toward the dreary entrance where Noseworthy waited.

Noseworthy introduced himself, and I introduced Max, and then offered my hand to shake. He ignored it, asked us to follow him to his office, and gestured to two chairs opposite a bare desk. The office looked temporary, devoid of anything that would make it homey. Probably just an extra space made for visiting investigators.

"We need to find out from you, Ms. Littlefield, how you identified the poison. It strikes us as quite a coincidence that you immediately knew its identity." He leaned forward. "You even called here at two o'clock in the morning to report the information."

"I was a mom back in the days when ipecac was the responsible thing to have on hand to induce vomiting if your kids ingested something poisonous. I happened to remember how quickly it worked, and the sequence of events at the Encore seemed to fit." I was moving quickly from surprised to steamed. "Mr. Noseworthy, do you have kids? Grandkids?"

He blinked and shifted in his seat.

"If you did, at your age"—which I guessed was close to mine— "you would have had syrup of ipecac in your medicine cabinet too. And if your child had ingested something poisonous, and you had to administer this syrup, and then clean up the aftermath ..." I stood and leaned over his desk. My index finger took on a life of its own, and shook itself in his face. "Believe me, you would remember it too."

His Adam's apple moved up and down as he swallowed. "I see," he said.

"One more thing." I paused for added emphasis. "Holy cannoli! If I did it, why on God's green earth would I call and tell you what I used?" I settled into my chair again, glanced at Max, who seemed to be struggling to keep his face straight, and then looked back at Noseworthy.

"To throw us off track." The investigator folded his hands on the desk. "Is it true that Hyacinth Gilvertin is your friend?"

"Yes, but what does that have to do with the price of tea in China?" I was on a roll with my food clichés. If I weren't so worried about Hyacinth, I might have enjoyed coming up with a few more.

"Is she your friend, or isn't she?"

I rolled my eyes. "I thought you were from the CDC, not the FBI."

"Did Ms. Gilvertin have access to the food your company served?"

"Of course, she's my sous chef—or thinks she is," I said with a small laugh.

"Was she ever alone with the food?"

I dragged in a deep breath, remembering what she'd said about being in the walk-in fridge when Devereaux paid his first visit. "Yes."

"And what about your daughter, Katie?"

I leaned forward. "What about her?"

"Two questions. Is she Ms. Gilvertin's goddaughter? And was she ever alone with the food?"

"What are you getting at?" The hair on the back of my neck stood tall. I forced my hands to remain still in my lap.

"Please answer my questions."

"Many of my crew kids were alone with the food at any given time yesterday. Not just Katie or Hyacinth." I was ready to leap over the desk and get mean-faced, nose-to-nose with the despicable Noseworthy, but I was afraid my meanest face might be laughable at best and pathetic at worst. "And yes," I continued, holding back the growl that threatened to roar out of my voice box. "My friend Hyacinth is my daughter's godmother."

I stole a look at Max, who seemed coiled and ready to spring into attack mode himself. He worked his jaw, curled and then straightened his fingers, only to repeat the actions.

Noseworthy didn't seem to notice. "We've located the source of the poisoning—the flash point—one might say."

I looked back to him, suddenly cold to the core. I wasn't going to like where he was going with this. But I kept my voice even and calm. "And where was that?"

"As you recall, your daughter, Katie, ordered her crew to clean up before the sheriff's office could even surround the crime scene with caution tape. The food was thrown into the trash, but not otherwise disposed of. I had a team working on it all night, collecting samples from the bins outside the building. We narrowed the source to one specific food you served."

I leaned forward again. "You did?" Unfortunately, my words came out in a squeak. "What was it?"

"We analyzed the contents—sweet potatoes, the Beauregard to be specific, white truffles, eggs, milk, butter, and"—he gave me a smug smile—"ipecac—dried, ground very fine, and liberally sprinkled either in or on top of the mixture." He paused, staring at me. The room was deathly quiet. "We've already interviewed the members of your crew, and they confirm that your daughter, Katie, prepared the sweet potato dish last night. She was seen sprinkling the ipecac onto the small serving dishes."

"You can't be suggesting—," I said, icy fear twisting itself around my heart. "Katie? You can't be serious."

"And not just your daughter," Noseworthy said, sitting back and steepling his fingers. "Considering there was no sign of struggle at the library, considering the origin of the poison, your familiarity with it, your daughter's preparation of the dish that brought on the terrible epidemic of poisoning, I have to inform you that you will be placed under arrest." He hit an intercom button. "Sheriff, get someone in here to read Mrs. Littlefield her rights. And pick up her daughter and bring her in."

"You can't do that. She's a mother." I jumped to my feet, appalled. My head spun so fast I couldn't think straight. "Besides, she's innocent."

Max stood quite suddenly. "This has gone far enough. You are making serious allegations based on pure speculation. You have no proof. You're here to investigate, but it seems to me you rather enjoy intimidating and playing wanna-be cop. This woman is innocent. She's a victim, not a criminal."

My mouth dropped open. Was he talking about Hyacinth or me? We were both as pure as the driven snow. Well, almost. There was that time back in the seventies, involving a break-in at the zoo, a blinking caution sign, and the dean of women, but that's another story.

Max walked closer to Noseworthy so that he towered over the seated investigator. "Mrs. Littlefield gave you a lead. That's all. Nothing nefarious in that. She wanted to help. No crime in that. She's frantic to find her friend, and she's upset over the lost reputation of her catering company. She feels terrible because of those who got sick. Not because she's guilty, but because it happened under her watch. And because she's a caring person.

"Now, if you will excuse us," Max said, "we need to get some forensic evidence to the sheriff." He then turned to me, reached for my hand, and helped me out of my chair. With our spines ramrod straight, we marched to the door.

"There's one more thing," Noseworthy said. We both looked back at him. "As you've probably heard, President James Delancy is dead. His doctors confirm that it wasn't his previous heart condition that took him. It was the poison. This is now a murder investigation."

Then he pointed to me. "And you ... you ...," he sputtered. "You haven't heard the last of me."

Chapter Nineteen

When Katie and Chloe Grace arrived just before dinnertime, I was still reeling from my encounter with Noseworthy, and at war with myself about whether to worry her with his accusations.

After we got Chloe Grace settled in with a Junie B. Jones book, Katie and I sat together at the kitchen table, and I filled her in on the details of my drive with Max out to the site of the burned-out cabin.

Katie took my hand when I told her about going into the charred ambulance. "I know that was hard for you, Mom."

She was aware of my nightmares, though I'd never told her about their origin and why I was terrified of fire.

I squeezed her hand. She wasn't a little girl anymore. She deserved to know, and to process, the charges that might be brought against us. "There's something else you need to know." I told her about Chance Noseworthy's threats. She looked as worried as I felt when I'd finished. But her words comforted me.

"We're innocent and justice will be done. It's Cinth I'm worried about, not us and this Noseworthy character. Who all is on the case, besides Noseworthy?"

"Sheriff Doyle is heading up the investigation. Until he determines it's a kidnapping, then the FBI will take over. Right now, Hyacinth is considered a person of interest who's missing. That's all. Because of the theft, all the local law enforcement agencies are working together. There are APBs out all over the state, and photos of Hyacinth have been sent to every precinct and spread over the Internet."

"How about the thieves?"

"No one got a good look. They can't be identified."

"And the car they're in?"

"Also unidentifiable." It sounded so hopeless. Thoughts of Hyacinth brought a cold chill. I hugged my arms to myself, closed my eyes, and whispered a little prayer.

Katie touched my arm. "Are you all right?"

I looked up. "I'm fine. Just want to get started on my own search for Hyacinth. I'd leave this minute if I could."

"Mom, you look like you haven't slept for days. Promise me you'll get a good night's sleep and not go off hunting for Cinth in the middle of the night."

I laughed and held up a hand, as if it was a ludicrous thought. She didn't know how close I'd come the night before to doing that very thing.

"You've got a tendency to do that anyway, and now because it's Cinth—"

Chloe Grace came flying through the doorway to the kitchen. "Gramsy!" she shouted, and I knelt to scoop her into a hug. "I'm hungry. What's for dinner?"

"C.G., what is the proper way to ask?" Katie said.

Chloe Grace held me tight around the neck, then leaned back and smiled. "Gramsy, please, can we have pizza for dinner tonight?"

"That's exactly what I had in mind," I said.

"Yay!" she yelled and then quieted when she saw her mother put her finger to her lips. "Yay!" she then whispered loudly.

"Little Italy okay?" Hands down, our favorite pizza. "And what delightful delicacies do we want on it?" I already knew but asked just to hear her explain in her special way.

"Hawaiian, but with no onions, ham, or pineapple," Chloe Grace said, just as she always did.

"Which is—"

"I know, I know," she said, nearly giggling. "It's a cheese pizza and not really Hawaiian, but that's how I like it. The cheese tastes better after all that stuff is scraped off."

Katie smiled at her daughter. "I'm always ready to eat the pineapple and ham you don't like."

Yay!" Chloe Grace yelled and took off for the living room.

I peeked in to see her cuddled up in my favorite overstuffed chair with her nose in the Junie B. Jones book.

"She makes everything else pale in importance," I said to Katie. "We are blessed."

Katie smiled gently. "She makes everything different."

What an odd thing to say. "That sounds like a segue. Are you about to make an announcement of some sort?" I was half-joking when I said it, but her eyes told me she was serious.

"It is, but let me place our order before C.G. starves, and then we'll talk."

She called in our order—a large pizza, half Hawaiian and half nearly everything but the kitchen sink. I remembered that she'd asked if Sandy could join us. I refilled our iced tea glasses, poured milk for Chloe Grace, and then set an extra place at the kitchen table for Sandy.

Katie came over and sat on one of the tall bar stools between the counter and the table. I sat beside her.

Her eyes were luminous, bright, as if a long-smoldering fire had been ignited. The stress lines I'd seen so often after her divorce seemed to have disappeared. She was wearing new earrings, and they looked expensive.

Sandy. Of course.

"What time will Sandy be here?"

She smiled. "Should be any minute. He has something he wants to ask you."

I could only imagine one thing, and it was the one thing I dreaded hearing from this man who'd left my daughter for a woman who he said was more suited to his life. The woman had been in his class at Duke and his lab partner.

"Has something changed?"

She nodded. "He's talking about reconciliation. He says he's willing to go to therapy, anything, to right the wrongs of the past so we can become a family."

I took Katie's hands in both of mine. "It's taken you years to get over the heartbreak, to get your life back." I glanced through the doorway toward the living room, making sure Chloe Grace was still buried in Junie B. Jones.

"I hope you said it's too little too late." I should have bitten my tongue. I'm an advocate of forgiveness, believe you me, but after what this man had done …

"He's asked me to marry him." She gave me a little smile. "Again."

"Oh, honey, he did?" I didn't think anything could make my heart ache more than it already did this day, or could cause it nearly to break with one more trouble piled on all the others. But Katie's words came close.

"And did you give him an answer?"

I waited while she stared at her folded hands. When she looked up, her eyelids brimmed with tears. She brushed them away. "I want us to be a family, whole and healthy. I want C.G. to know the love of her father. But I don't know if I can trust him again. I can forgive and have forgiven him, but I just don't know about trust. What if I give him my heart, and C.G. gives him hers? I know I can deal with anything, but when it comes to my daughter …" Her tears spilled, and I handed her a tissue. We seemed to be going through quite a few of them this day.

"It's hard enough to open yourself to such vulnerability in a loving relationship. But after you've been betrayed—and by the same man who is trying to win you—it must be a hundred times harder."

She nodded. "I told him I needed time." She blew her nose and gave me a watery smile. "He knows it's an issue, and he wants to talk to you about it."

I drew in a deep breath. "Whoa. Me? One more question," I said and reached for her hand. "Does Chloe Grace know Sandy is her father?"

"No. She thinks he's my friend."

The doorbell rang, and I grabbed my wallet and headed for the door. Saved by the delivery man.

Except, when I opened the door, Sandy grinned at me with the pizza box in his hands. Behind him, I saw the familiar pizza sign on the top of a car pulling away from the curb.

"I intercepted your delivery man," he said, and when I reached into my wallet, he shook his head. "Please, put that away. This one's on me."

Katie's face lit up as she stood and watched him come toward her. He was still as good looking as ever. Tall, broad shouldered, coloring the same as Chloe Grace's. Even his eyes were the same shade.

He strode to where Katie stood waiting, set the pizza box on the counter, and gave her a hug. She smiled into his eyes, but the moment had ended—thank the Lord—before Chloe Grace came running into the kitchen.

"Let's eat, shall we?" I said, my voice perkier than I felt. "Chloe Grace, help me set the table, will you?"

"Let me help you, C.G." Sandy winked at her, making her grin stretch even wider. They went together to the kitchen sink to wash their hands. He gave her a lesson in scrubbing thoroughly the way surgeons do before operating. Her eyes were wide.

"You do that every day? Operate on people?"

He squatted so he was at eye level with the child. "Not every day, but lots of times during the week. The rest of the time, I see patients in my office." He stood again and reached for the pizza as I handed Chloe Grace the flatware.

"Holy cannoli," Chloe Grace said, looking up at him with wonder as he placed the pizza at the center of the table. "Would you operate on me if I got sick? Or how about Gramsy? Or Mommy?"

Sandy laughed, patted the top of her head, and then sat down beside her. "Sure," he said. "But I don't think we need to worry about that for a long, long time. Look at you, you're as healthy as any seven-year-old I've ever seen."

I sat across from him and had a good view of his eyes. I thought I detected a shadow of regret as he mentioned her age. He'd lost all those years with her. There was no getting them back. He and Katie might reconcile, perhaps remarry, but that kind of desertion can never be completely erased.

I didn't know if I could hold my tongue when it came to telling him how I felt. Knowing myself, I probably couldn't.

After Katie took Chloe Grace upstairs to brush her teeth and get into her PJs, Sandy helped me load the dishwasher. "I'd hoped to have a private conversation with you," he said when we finished. "Is now a good time?"

I nodded. "Yes. Please sit."

He waited while I popped some frozen cookies into the microwave. And then I sat opposite him.

"Katie told you about us … what's been happening over the past few weeks."

"Yes."

He leaned toward me earnestly. "It started with a longing to see my daughter. I wanted to be part of her life. I knew—know—I made a huge mistake when I left them all those years ago. I'd hoped that I could just see her from time to time."

"You never sent a penny of child support. Katie put you through medical school, and as soon as you graduated, you left her for

someone else. She sacrificed everything for you. You left her penni-
less and devastated with a newborn infant." I stood, unable to look at
him. My hands were trembling when I reached for the plate of cookies. I closed my eyes and counted backward from ten to calm myself.

When I turned, concern was written on his face. "I know I have
no right to ask this of you, but do you think you could give me
another chance?"

"It's taken Katie years to get over you, to get her life together.
She's done a stellar job of raising Chloe Grace. It's taken her almost
seven years to complete her degree—she'll graduate with honors this
coming year. She did that while working two jobs most of those
years.

"And now you come waltzing back into her life and want to
patch everything up?"

"Everything you say is true," he said quietly. "I have no right to
ask for another chance. To ask for your daughter's hand in marriage
again." He shook his head slowly, his shoulders slumped.

For a moment, neither of us spoke. Then he said, "Is there any
way I can prove it to you?"

"Prove it?"

"Prove to you, to Katie, and to my daughter, that I want us to be
a family. I've changed. I'm not the same man I was seven years ago.
How can I convince you?"

I thought again about the need to forgive seventy times seven.
Much easier said than done, in my thinking. How I wished Hyacinth
were here to be part of this conversation. She knew firsthand the
heartache Katie had endured; she'd been there once herself. She'd
have some choice words for the man sitting in front of me.

She was also all about forgiveness. And deep down, so was I. And about second chances, when it came right down to it.

But that was an easy position to hold when considering anyone except my beloved daughter and granddaughter. After what he'd done, after the devastation my daughter suffered, I really didn't think I could live it out.

I stood and placed my hands on my hips. "You have some nerve, waltzing in here—the great Sandborn Ainsley, MD—to sweep my daughter off her feet the way you did seven years ago.

"You don't deserve reconciliation. You don't deserve Katie or Chloe Grace. You hurt Katie deeply and that's very hard for a mother to forgive. You are asking too much."

He stared at me as if I'd stolen candy right out of his hand.

"As for second chances," I said, taking a step closer to him, "I don't think so, at least not from me. Not yet. Already, I can see that you are stealing my granddaughter's heart. I only hope you don't trample it the way you did her mother's. And you've said nothing about love."

Instead of giving me the sharp retort I expected, he moved his gaze to the entrance to the dining room.

Before I turned I knew who was standing there. Chloe Grace. Big tears filled her eyes and her light spray of freckles stood out against her white face. I knew she'd heard my scathing words. My heart threatened to break.

Chapter Twenty
Hyacinth

· · · · · · · · · · · · · · ·

Hyacinth settled into the space she'd made for herself in the rental truck. She'd tucked some dirt-smudged quilts into place behind the crate that she assumed held the *Lady*. It was the right size, but then so were others. She fought the urge to drift off. She needed to be awake if someone opened the back of the truck.

She checked the phone she'd lifted off the thief she called Child. It had gone from "no signal" status to zero percent battery power. Frowning, she put it back in her pocket.

The rental truck bounced along the road on its way to heaven only knew where. They stopped for gas; she heard voices outside the truck, the click of the gas cap, and then the flow of gasoline. She held her breath, waiting for one of the men to open the back of the truck to check on its contents.

The problem was, as usual, she needed a ladies' room. And she was thirsty. And hungry.

She pondered the problem. Even if she could slip out without being seen, there was probably a parking lot to cross. She might be a bit tattered because of all she'd been through, but there was no mistaking her bright curly red hair with magenta streaks; her bright, though wrinkled and dirty, colorful top; and—she sighed—the skinny jeans with rhinestones on the derriere.

She stood, the image of a restroom with running water taunting her. She moved to the door and tried to raise it. It was one of those lift-up types that rolled up into the ceiling of the body, so it would make a lot of noise. The men were likely to notice immediately.

Hyacinth gave the door a quick once-over, mentally measuring how much she'd need to open it in order to slip out. She was a beautifully built woman of a certain size—she never thought of herself as a double-digit number on a clothing tag, only in terms of being beautifully built. Or wonderfully made, if she thought about it in biblical terms.

She was nimble and quick. She could do this. The image of a bathroom became fixated in her mind. Thirst became stronger than caution. She knelt and gently pulled up on the handle, so she wouldn't make any noise.

It wouldn't budge. She tried it again. And again. She fell back onto a short stack of moving quilts in dismay. Maybe it was just as well. She still hadn't solved the dilemma of being seen … and recognized.

She looked down at the quilts, and an idea took root. She grinned and yanked at the handle, harder this time. It moved. She pulled it up just far enough to squeeze through. A gust of fresh air entered the truck, and she breathed it in gratefully.

She dropped to the floor and peered out. The rear of the truck faced a dollar store in the center of a strip mall with half its storefronts boarded up. Rusted grocery carts were scattered in every direction. She smelled fast food, which made her stomach growl but also told her the men might be taking a food break.

She wriggled underneath the rolling door and dropped to the ground, thankful she'd landed feetfirst. She reached back into the truck for a quilt, shook it out, and wrapped it around her head and shoulders.

Hyacinth forced herself to walk with slow steps, shoulders stooped and head down, to the nearest rusty shopping cart. She tried to push it forward, but it had a wonky wheel and wobbled sideways, jerking her along with it. She almost giggled. The wonky wheel added a nice touch. She'd never been inebriated in her life, but she imagined that someone watching her right now might think she was.

The thieves had no idea she'd hitched a ride. Even so, she didn't feel entirely safe in her disguise.

Creeping around the gas pumps, she got a better view of the mini-mart and adjoining fast-food joint. Sure enough, there were Lagasse and Child sitting at a counter, facing her way. They seemed to be in a heated conversation, animated hand gestures flying between bites of greasy burger.

She huddled closer to the wire cart and wobbled faster to the mini-mart entrance. Now out of the thieves' range of vision, she removed the quilt, dropped it into the cart, and scurried across the store to the restroom area.

She knew she didn't have much time, so she gulped as much water as she could hold, drinking straight from the faucet. A middle-aged woman with thin permed hair and glasses came in, stopped and stared, her mouth dropping open.

"Sorry," Hyacinth said, water dripping from her chin. "I'm just so thirsty." She bent her head and drank again.

"Is there anything I can do for you?" the woman said. "I saw you come in with the cart. Are you going through tough times?"

She reached into her purse. "Is there anything you need? Bottled water? Food? I can buy you a meal next door."

Her kindness touched Hyacinth, but every second counted if she was going to make it back to the truck undiscovered. "I'm in a hurry, but I need you to get in touch with someone for me. Would you do that?"

The woman nodded.

"Do you have paper and a pen?"

The woman reached into her purse again and pulled out both, and handed them to Hyacinth. She wrote El's name at the top and then her phone number. "Call her, tell her you saw me and that I'm fine. I would do it myself, but my phone battery is dead. Tell her where we are ... "

The woman studied the paper. "Yes, fine. I'll do that." Then she looked back to Hyacinth as if she recognized her from someplace.

"Thank you," Hyacinth said. "You have no idea how fortuitous your coming in here right now is. Thank you."

Hyacinth raced into one of the stalls to do her business, and the woman left without another word.

A few minutes later, she left the ladies' room and headed for the cart and quilt, just beyond the glass door. The woman she'd given El's cell number to was talking to the clerk at the cash register. She gestured toward the restroom as if telling him who or what she'd witnessed. Puzzled, Hyacinth quickly ducked behind a shelf filled with paperbacks and DVDs.

She had put her trust in this woman's kindness, but now it appeared she might have turned her in to the management. Her heart fell as the clerk strode over to the hallway leading to the ladies' room.

Hyacinth hurried back out the front entrance, grabbed the quilt, and wrapped it around her body, covering her head. She revved up the speed on the cart, its wobbly wheel rebelling every step of the way. After a glance into the fast-food joint—where she saw the men emptying their wrappers into the trash can—she abandoned the cart. With a fast shuffle, she moved toward the truck, rounded the corner, and dove into the opening, slamming the door behind her.

It was only then she realized she'd left the quilt on the ground behind the truck. And it was too late to retrieve it.

She plopped onto the stack of quilts behind the crate, breathing hard as she tried to catch her breath. Several minutes passed. She scrunched her eyes closed and waited to hear the doors of the cab open and close. It didn't happen.

Suddenly she heard voices from outside. They moved toward the back of the truck. She cringed, wishing she'd remembered the quilt. There was an expletive, some questions, and then laughter.

She sat up to hear better as the back door lifted and someone tossed in the quilt. "Somebody's loss is our gain," one of the men said, laughing. It sounded like the one she called Lagasse.

Then Child said, "Wait a minute. These look exactly like the ones in the truck. Here's the logo."

"You don't suppose …?" Lagasse said, his voice taking on an edge. "You don't suppose that … that woman somehow caught up with us."

"You're paranoid," Julia Child said. "Of course not. How'd she get here, anyway?" His laugh was condescending. "Thumbin' a ride?"

"Well, I'm gonna just have a look-see for myself. Make sure all's clear. You know how the boss can be. He thinks we got rid of her."

She heard the creak of metal as one of them pushed up the door.

Hyacinth's entire body ached something fierce. She kept her eyes closed for a few minutes, trying to determine where she was and how she got there. And why her head felt like a watermelon that had been dropped on concrete.

The scent of damp, freshly mown grass filled her nostrils, birdsong twittered down from overhead, and from a short distance away, the sounds of a rollicking spiritual sung by heavenly voices carried toward her. Clapping accompanied the music, peppered by several hearty shouts of "Amen" and "Praise the Lord." The organist played with such enthusiasm that Hyacinth pictured a bouncing bum on the bench and dancing feet on the pedals.

She opened her eyes, slowly sat up, and looked around. Tombstones. Old tombstones. She was in a graveyard, of all things. How did she get here? She tried to remember, but she was still too groggy to make sense of it. Judging by the tombstone nearest her, she'd apparently spent the night near a man named Samuel "Uncle Sam" Johnson, who was beloved by his family and had been born in 1830 and died in 1879.

At the bottom a gentle grassy slope sat a small country church. Its steeple rose from a pitched roof, and its windows and front doors were flung wide open.

The congregation launched into another song, just as rollicking as the one she'd woken to. "Oh, happy day …!"

She stood and stretched, looked down at her tattered and soiled clothing, and shuddered. A glance around told her the thugs she'd been with had finally succeeded in getting rid of her. They hadn't even given her one of the quilts.

The vision of that quilt, the one she'd wrapped around herself to slip into the convenience store, brought it all back to her. She reached up and touched the back of her head. When she felt a lump the size of Rhode Island, she nearly cried out. One of the thieves had certainly knocked her out cold. Again.

She was thirsty and famished, so the first task at hand was to make her way to the church and ask for help.

It took some doing, given her hunger, thirst, and the state of her throbbing head. But she made it. She spotted a rusted bike leaning against a shed at the back of the church. She certainly didn't feel like hopping on and riding away right now.

The singing faded, and as she drew closer, she heard the preacher working up a head of steam, preaching about being ready for the Second Coming. He paused after each fiery sentence and the congregation shouted "Amen" or "Preach it, brother!"

Hyacinth hesitated at the entrance, worried about interrupting the sermon just when he seemed to really get going. But she took a deep breath and stepped inside. A woman about her age and robust size stood by the door with a stack of bulletins in her hand. She started to hand one to Hyacinth, but instead of taking it, Hyacinth motioned for her to come outside.

"I'm in need of some help," she said, after they'd stepped away from the open doors and windows.

"Then you've come to the right place." The woman's expression was kind, her dark eyes seemed to see more than just a tattered and tired woman on the church doorstep. "You look like you've been on quite a journey."

"And you'd be right, but it's a long story and it isn't over yet."

"What do you need?"

"Food and water and transportation. And a couple of aspirin would be lovely too. I'm also in need of a telephone—if you've got one I can borrow just to make one call."

The other woman opened her arms to give Hyacinth a hearty hug. "Welcome, dear. My name is Josie Mae Washington. My husband, Marshall, is the pastor and the one you hear preachin' right now."

"Is it Sunday?"

"It sure is, and a beautiful one too."

Hyacinth felt safe and at home. She wished she didn't have to leave.

"We can take care of the things you need. As for a phone, we don't get much signal out here. Possum Grove's not high on the telephone company's list of folks deservin' a close-by tower, we figure."

"Is there a landline?"

"Oh goodness, no. We don't even have a church office. Most folks just put up with a mobile phone that works about half the time." She smiled. "But don't you worry. I've got an old phone that sometimes gets one bar at the top of the cemetery. You can try it as soon as I find it."

"Thank you. It's very important." She looked around. "But if I do reach someone, I don't even know where I am."

"Honey, you've arrived at Possum Grove Holy Ghost Revival Church. Possum Grove proper's about four miles down the road." Josie Mac gave her a curious look. "How'd you get here?"

"I don't know for certain. I just now woke up in your graveyard. My head hurts, and I think I was knocked out and dumped there. I need to catch the culprits, so I'm in a bit of a hurry."

Josie Mae's eyes widened considerably. "Lord, have mercy! Let's see what we can do to help you out." She motioned for Hyacinth to follow her. "Let's get you that phone."

She opened a door off the entryway that led down some stairs to a basement. The room had tables and chairs to accommodate maybe twenty-five people. The smell of ham and baked beans wafted from a nearby kitchen, making Hyacinth's mouth water.

"Wait here just a minute," Josie Mae said and hurried down a hallway. Seconds later, she returned and handed an older-model cell phone to Hyacinth. "It doesn't work half the time. I need a new one anyway. So you can keep it." She handed her a plug-in car charger, which Hyacinth placed in her pocket.

Josie Mae then took Hyacinth into the kitchen, handed her a bottle of water, opened a cupboard, and grabbed a bottle of aspirin. She dropped two into Hyacinth's outstretched hand.

Without a word, she cut some thick slices off the ham and pulled some homemade rolls from the oven. She made sandwiches and placed them in a plastic container. Next she placed a half-dozen plastic bottles of water in a grocery bag and then dropped in the bottle of aspirin. "Just in case you need more," she said, glancing up at Hyacinth.

Hyacinth was touched by the kindness this woman offered to a complete stranger. A simple "thank you" seemed inadequate. She still wore the bangles on her arm and decided then and there where the next one would go.

"I'd like to stay …," Hyacinth began.

"I know, honey, but somethin' tells me you're on a mission."

"I am."

"Then you must be hurrying along. Do you want to try the phone now? I'll go with you and show you the spot we come closest to getting through."

They climbed the stairs to the ground level. The preacher was winding down as they climbed the hill to the cemetery.

"Over here," Josie Mae called. "Usually, I get a little something right here by Uncle Rufus."

Hyacinth followed her to a spot not far from where she'd spent the night. She flipped open the phone and smiled. A single bar. She moved the phone around to see if the signal strengthened. It didn't.

She closed her eyes, then punched in El's cell number. El picked up on the first ring. "Hello."

"El, it's me. It's Hyacinth. Can you hear me?"

Nothing.

"El," Hyacinth said louder, at the same time moving around and checking the bars on the phone. "El, it's me. Don't hang up," Hyacinth yelled. "It's me on a borrowed phone. El—!"

The line went dead. Her shoulders drooped, and discouragement filled the place where hope had been.

Josie Mae climbed higher up the hillside. "This spot by Grandpa Jones is always worth a try," she said, and headed toward a large sycamore.

Hyacinth trudged up the hillside behind her, reached the spot, and hit redial. This time the call went straight to voice mail. "El, if you can hear me, it's Hyacinth. I'm in Possum Grove, trying to find the thieves. I was hiding out in the stolen truck but lost them. Run a check on N8724H. That's 'Nancy ate 724 hamburgers.' It's a rental truck. These guys are pawns. I'm trying to find out who they're working for and get the figurehead away from them. I'll try calling when I have a better signal."

The phone made no sign that the call had gone through. When she looked down at the phone, it showed the home screen, not the phone app. Had the call lasted long enough for El to get the message?

She followed Josie Mae to the shed where she'd seen the bicycle. They stooped and examined the tires, looked at each other and smiled. "Not bad," Josie Mae said. A tattered basket was strapped to the handlebars, which nicely accommodated her bag of sandwiches and bottles of water.

Behind them, the congregation sang again, this time "Joshua Fit the Battle of Jericho." It felt appropriate. She was ready for battle. She only hoped that El had received her message.

"Wait here a minute," Josie Mae said. She hurried off toward the front of the church. A few minutes later, she ran back with her pocketbook. "I want you to take these." She opened the grocery bag in the bike's basket and dropped in a few dollar bills. Then she gave Hyacinth a long, searching look. "I couldn't help but overhear what you said to your friend. You take care now. It sounds like you could get yourself in a whole lot of trouble. I'll hold you in my prayers."

"Thank you."

The congregation was still singing about Joshua. By now a number of tambourines had joined the organ, and it sounded as if folks were dancing in the aisles.

"One more thing." Hyacinth nearly had to shout to be heard above the music. "If you were a thief with 'hot' goods in a rental truck, which direction would you go?"

Josie Mae gave it some thought. "Possum Grove is in the middle of nowhere. They must have picked this spot to drop you off because of that. If I were you, I'd head back through town to the interstate, and ask around with the description of the truck. Ask folks if they spotted it. Did you get a good look at it?"

Hyacinth grinned. "Yes, I did. It's a Coast to Coast truck with a picture of Yosemite on the side."

"How about the plates?" Josie raised her eyebrows. "Was that what you were trying to get across to your friend? That Nancy ate 724 hamburgers?"

"You're good," Hyacinth said, grinning.

"I'm about the only one in these parts who didn't get a lick of musical talent when God was handin' it out. So while the others are goin' to choir practice or such, I read mysteries or watch whodunits on TV."

Hyacinth held her new friend's gaze for a moment. "You've taken care of a stranger today," she said. "I pray you'll be blessed double for doing so."

Josie Mae nodded, her dark eyes shining. "I believe you would do the same."

With some effort, Hyacinth got herself up and onto the bicycle seat and headed in the direction Josie Mae advised. Her balance was wobbly at first, but she soon picked up speed and the ride became smoother. Not to mention more interesting than the stationary exercise bike she rode every morning.

"Thank you," she called back to Josie Mae, who waved and then returned to the little church.

Now, to catch the thieves. Her mind raced with ideas of what she would do once she spotted the truck.

She pondered the timetable as she pedaled. It had been evening when they caught her in the back of the truck. By the time they drove out to Possum Grove, it would have been after dark. They would probably have returned to the interstate and, she hoped, stopped at a motel for the night. And, she hoped, because it was Sunday, maybe gave themselves a later start and big breakfast.

She pedaled faster, glad the road was smooth and flat, but kicking herself for not asking exactly how far it was to the interstate. She stopped every once in a while to check for a signal on the cell phone. There was none.

Up ahead, the road turned wavy with a heat mirage. Strange, because it was still early and didn't feel all that warm to her. Although she was getting warm due to the exertion, of course. She could have sworn she spotted the thieves' truck up ahead, but it faded into a mirrorlike puddle. She pushed the thought from her mind, and instead concentrated on her pedaling.

She found a comfortable speed and stuck to it, watching the scenery pass by. No other vehicles were on the road, probably because it was Sunday morning, and many of the people who lived in the area were in church. Which reminded her of her favorite way to calm her nerves. Singing. Loud and joyous, just because it was a beautiful day and she was alive to enjoy it.

This wasn't a day for "I Am Woman, Hear Me Roar." The singing at Possum Grove Holy Ghost Revival had put her in the mood for a different kind of singing altogether.

As she pedaled along, she belted out all the verses she could remember to "Joshua Fit the Battle of Jericho," and then moved on to "Swing Low, Sweet Chariot." It was so pleasing to feel the wind in her face and the sun on her shoulders that she moved right into "When We All Get to Heaven."

She was singing the last verse, pedaling in time with the beat of "Onward to the prize before us! Soon His beauty we'll behold …" when a vehicle roared up behind her.

She glanced over her shoulder. It was the rental truck, the two men in the cab and aiming straight for her. In her hurry to get over to the shoulder and out of their way, she lost her balance. She wobbled uncontrollably, and the front wheel of her bike hit a rock. She flew off the bike and landed with an undignified grunt in the dirt.

Raising her head, she blinked as she stared down the road. The two thugs had exited their truck and were coming toward her. It looked like Lagasse was in the lead. And they were arguing.

"I tell you," Julia Child said, "this is the stupidest thing you've ever done. We were told to get rid of the woman, once and for all. And here you go, getting all soft on me. Sayin' she reminds you of your grandma. You kiddin' me?"

Lagasse didn't answer, but made a beeline for Hyacinth. "Maybe I just want to make sure we finish the job."

"Yeah, right," Child said. "So, now that you found her, you gonna save her or do her in fer good?" He spat. "The boss is gonna have yer hide."

Lagasse shrugged and kept coming for her.

"Soon the pearly gates will open," Hyacinth sang in a whisper. "We shall tread the streets of gold."

Chapter Twenty-one
Mrs. Littlefield

. . . .

Sunday morning, my eyes flew open before dawn. My brain had been working overtime while I slept. I loved it when that happened.

Memories, ideas, plans marched into my consciousness, those of Hyacinth first in line. I remembered a book report she gave in ninth grade on the O. Henry story "The Ransom of Red Chief." She laughed so hard she nearly fell on the floor while relating the story of a bratty and obnoxious ten-year-old boy whose kidnappers were so desperate to get rid of him they paid the boy's father two hundred fifty dollars to take him back.

She could be bratty and obnoxious if the circumstances called for it. I'd seen her in action.

Hope soared. I wanted to jump up and down on my mattress, the way we did when we were kids, or at least laugh out loud. I chose the latter. If anyone was tenacious, it was Hyacinth. Always had been, always would be.

The thieves' plan was clever, but from my point of view, they hadn't covered all contingencies. From what Enrique told us,

Hyacinth launched herself into the back of the ambulance. The perpetrators had been taken by surprise or were powerless to stop her.

Now to the thieves. I leaned back on my pillow and tapped the end of the pen on my chin. What if they nabbed Hyacinth at home? I considered it for a moment and made a note. We'd all assumed she'd met up with (per the sheriff) or been forced into, as I swore to be true, the "ring" at the library. What if evidence had been overlooked at her home?

I sat upright and almost forgot to breathe. Holy cannoli. Had the thieves nabbed her in her garage? Sheriff Doyle had indicated they had seen no signs of a struggle, but some evidence might have been overlooked. And perhaps there were clues in her house or on the driveway that would lead me to Hyacinth, to the thieves, to the figurehead.

I jumped out of bed. No way would I wait till morning to have a look. Finding Cinth was too important. I ran to the closet, grabbed some jeans and a sweatshirt, and threw them on. Slipping into my tennies, I flipped on the outside lights and raced out the door.

As I drove to Hyacinth's house, another idea marched into mind. The cabin. Who owned it? How was that owner related to the thieves? How would I find that out?

It felt impossible. Sometimes I loved impossible. This was one of those moments.

The county records office was closed on Sundays, but I could call a realtor in the area. Most worked weekends and had access to such information. First to come to mind was Mr. Hotshot Realtor whose photo was plastered on interstate billboards. I made a mental note to call him later.

By the time I reached Hyacinth's, the sky was turning a pinkish gray and the humidity was rising. I parked on the street behind a muscle truck, and left the headlights on for a moment as I took in the truck's back end. A shotgun hung in the back window, and a couple of faded Confederate flag decals and a plethora of bumper stickers had been stuck haphazardly on the tailgate.

I'd seen them before, and a few had imprinted themselves on my brain: I Love Jesus and Bluegrass Music; Tomato Whisperer; I Believe in America, God, and the Right to Bear Arms; and Keep Honking, I'm Reloading.

The same Dodge Ram had been parked on Crab Apple Street just down from my house the morning Bubba and Junior helped Juan with the barbecue. Later that same afternoon, I noticed it in the Encore parking lot.

It must belong to Bubba and Junior Sutherland. How did they fit into this increasingly complex puzzle? Nothing made sense. Yet here was their truck, parked in front of Hyacinth's.

No time like the present to find the pranksters and question them. So I marched across the street and did a search around the property. Nada.

Hyacinth often asked me to watch her house when she traveled, so I knew where to find the hide-a-key. I stooped near the flower bed that ran along the side of the garage, opened the little fake river rock, and took out a key ring. The key I needed first was marked with diva-pink nail polish.

The side door to the garage was just a few feet away. I would start there. In dire need of WD40, the lock took a few jangles and twists to get the key to work. Finally, it clicked and I pushed open the door.

Immediately, two heads popped up from the opposite side of Hyacinth's car.

"So there you are," I said with a note of triumph. "What's going on?"

Bubba and Junior started talking at the same time, each obscuring what the other was saying.

I interrupted. "If you can't tell me, maybe you'd rather talk to the sheriff." Unfortunately, I'd left my handbag, and phone, in the car.

They stood and sauntered over to me. No doubt about it, Bubba's size was intimidating. The size of his neck and arms didn't help. Neither did the tattoos. His brother wasn't as big, but his sneer made up for it.

Maybe they were indeed part of the ring of thieves and had been sent to clean up the crime scene. I had a flashback of how attentive they were when I asked Enrique to help me wire the Encore.

"Okay, tell me what you're doing here," I said.

"None of your business." Junior adopted a cocky, intimidating look and stared at me belligerently.

"So you two are in on this whole thing." I was fishing, and I had the feeling they knew it.

Bubba rolled his shoulder, and stood up taller. I backed up as he cracked his neck, flexed his muscles, and took a step toward me.

"Stay where you are," I growled. I don't growl well at all, but I gave it my best shot.

"What are you doing here?" Junior's tone took on a singsong imitation of mine, which irked me to no end.

"Okay, guys," I said. "I'm serious about getting the sheriff in on this. You had the opportunity to use the ipecac. You were in the right place at the right time. And now here you are, cleaning up the crime scene." I was fishing, but I needed to see their reaction. "If you won't tell me, maybe you'll tell the authorities. Who are you working for?"

"Can't say." Junior slumped his shoulders again.

"What's ipy … kak?" Bubba looked at his brother, who raised his brows and shrugged.

"So we're busted," Junior said. "Go ahead. Make our day."

"Just remember," Bubba said, "everything you say is circumstantial."

"Trespassing isn't," I snapped. "You've been caught in the act. At a crime scene. And, I might add that at the very least, you're fired."

The boys looked at each other and laughed. "Fired from what?" Junior couldn't keep the giggle out of his voice. "Your nothing company? Do you know what everyone is saying about you now? The Butler Did It is gone. It's a joke, and you're the laughing stock around town. No one will hire you in a million years."

They knew exactly how to deliver the knockout punch. For a moment, I was afraid to breathe. I struggled to keep my expression bland, my emotions in check.

"Not only that, but you owe us a wad of money," Bubba said. "Take a look at the contract we signed. You owe us big money whether or not you get reimbursed for the gig that made everyone sick."

"And killed one person," Junior added. "Whoo-ee, the lawsuits that are a-comin' round the bend." He laughed. "They're comin' at you so fast they're already smokin' up the road. At least, that's the talk around town. I can't wait."

"And does that ever open the door for new talent." Bubba looked triumphant. "You wanna know why we got involved, Mizz Littlefield? It was for that reason alone. To bring you down."

"Besides, it was fun," Junior said.

"See ya in court," Bubba said as they moved toward the door. "You think trespassing is a crime? Wait till you see where you land when those lawsuits hit."

They took off at a run. "Who's fired now?" Junior yelled back at me. Minutes later, the rumble of their engine and the bass of their stereo carried toward me in the humid air.

I went back to looking for evidence that Hyacinth's kidnapping had happened here. I found nothing around her car. I tried to concentrate on the task at hand, but all I wanted to do was curl up in a fetal position and cover my head with a blanket. For the rest of my life. Tears were close, but I refused to let them flow. I'd cried enough for a lifetime in the past two days.

Finding my friend was more important than saving the reputation of my company. The Butler was my lifeblood. I'd built it from scratch after Herb, God rest his sweet soul, passed on thirteen years ago.

How could I go on if it ceased to exist? What would I do when people laughed as I drove by in the catering van? What if the boys were right about the lawsuits? What if the sheriff went through with his plans to arrest me, arrest Katie?

Precious Chloe Grace would have to live with her father.

That thought almost pulled me out of my pity party. But this party wasn't one I'd made up; it was real. The circumstances were acutely, irrevocably real. Of course, I'd already thought about lawsuits. Also talk around town. But to have them validated knocked me for a loop.

I dropped to my knees at the side of the driveway near a flower bed. I needed to have a little talk with God, and it wasn't to make Him laugh.

"Okay, God," I said. "It's me again and I've had about enough." Tears formed and I brushed them away. "I'm not talking about me, really, but everyone around me. Hyacinth, my precious friend; Katie and the decisions she is making; Chloe Grace—oh, God, how will we keep her safe? And Max … Oh, dear God, I just need You to know how important each one is to me, how much I love them … and how afraid I am for them.

"People who know more about these sorts of things than I do say that prayer doesn't make You change Your mind, but it changes the heart of the one who's praying." I sniffled. "I don't know if my heart needs changing—well, it probably does, but You know what I mean. It's not all about me. I just ask You to give comfort to those I care about. That's all. Just wrap Your great big wonderful arms around the people I love and let them know You're with them." I paused, thinking of His love. Our church nursery has a pastel print of Jesus holding a tiny child. When it came to mind, I smiled. Was this what Max meant when he said he listens to God? I waited for a while, listening to the silence of the morning, the birdsong, the waking cicadas. "Well, that's about it for now," I said. "I'll check in later."

I was still kneeling when I spotted a piece of plastic and bent lower to inspect it.

It was part of a scattering of tiny electronic parts. Like those that might be found in a cell phone. I stood and parted some branches in a nearby hedge. More pieces. Not enough to make a whole phone, but someone had smashed it to smithereens. It had to be Hyacinth's.

That meant she was accosted here, in her driveway. It wasn't much, but it was a start.

I ran to my car and grabbed my handbag and drew out my stash of baggies, my tweezers, and my cell phone.

Chapter Twenty-two
Mrs. Littlefield

• • • • • • • • • • • • • • • •

It took me only a few minutes to pick up the pieces of Hyacinth's cell phone, but I was emotionally wrung out by the time I turned onto my street.

Most Sundays by this time, I would be at choir practice, warming up with some of my favorite gospel songs. And Hyacinth, who was scheduled to sing a solo in this morning's worship service, would be practicing upstairs in the main sanctuary with the organist. She had chosen "He Giveth More Grace," an old hymn that she loved. No matter what she sang, she delivered it with such emotion that Pastor Newborn, known to cry over just about anything having to do with God's love and grace, would weep so hard that he could barely get the words out when he preached. The church secretary finally suggested the order of the service be changed so the solo came after the sermon.

Pastor Billy and I had talked by phone twice since Hyacinth disappeared. I knew he would offer special prayer for her this morning. The prayer phone tree had been in action since Friday night. It was a comfort to know others were praying too.

But here I was, bone tired after my jaunt to Hyacinth's house in the middle of the night, just now turning into my driveway. Max was waiting for me in an old but well cared for Land Rover Defender. It suited him. Besides, I had this thing for old cars.

"Good morning," I said, feeling my spirits rise for the first time in hours. He opened the door for me, and I wearily got out of the Ghia.

He smiled and gave me a quick hug, which brought on a new flood of tears.

"My dear," he said, standing back and looking stricken. "What has happened?"

I gave him a brief rundown of what I'd been up to. When I got to the part about the Sutherland brothers and their hurtful accusations, his hands fisted at his sides and his face turned red.

"Excuse me a moment," he said quietly. And then he heaved out a couple of deep breaths, took a few steps away from me, and looked up at the morning sky. After a few minutes, his hands uncurled, his shoulders relaxed, and he seemed to be letting go of something. When he returned, the serenity I'd noticed in his eyes the day before had returned.

It was catching. I breathed in his peace. I needed to concentrate on Hyacinth. That was all.

"You need sustenance," he said. "I came by to see if you wanted to go with me to Grace Church this morning. But you need some TLC of a different kind right now. Do you have any eggs?"

I nodded.

"Bread?"

"Yes." I gave him a small smile.

"I know you have milk, so I won't ask about that. How about vegetables? Scallions, tomatoes—I know, I know, it's a fruit—cilantro, spinach?"

I was grinning now. "Yes to all of the above. Plus avocados, cheese, and whatever else you might need for an omelet."

"Not just any omelet," he said. "The best you've ever had in all your picked-up-and-put-together."

I laughed. "All my what?"

"Old saying of my grandma's." He led me to my front porch, and I unlocked the door.

When we stepped inside, he guided me to the sofa and I settled onto it. He brought over my hassock and I put my feet up.

"Soul rest," he said, his eyes full of compassion. "That's what you need most right now. When you're rested, I'll have a meal for you that will feed both body and soul."

I closed my eyes, listening to the whisk of eggs in a bowl, the chop of a chef's knife on my wooden cutting board, and after a few minutes, a hum that turned into a psalm sung as if with a lyre in ancient days. "I lift up my eyes to the mountains—where does my help come from? My help comes from the LORD, the Maker of heaven and earth. He will not let your foot slip—he who watches over you will not slumber ..."

I must have drifted off, because when I woke, the fragrant mix of fresh-ground coffee and fried potatoes and onions greeted me. I rose and went into the kitchen, drawn there as if by a magnet. The table had been beautifully set. How he'd found placemats and flatware, I couldn't fathom, but he had.

A smile spread across his face as he waited for my reaction. I was too moved to speak. Surely, my eyes weren't going to tear again. I rushed from the room and ran up the stairs, tears spilling. This had to stop.

I went into my bathroom, scrubbed my face and teeth, combed my hair, and took a deep breath.

When I came through to the kitchen again, he was sitting at the table. He didn't look up when I approached. "Let me explain," I said.

But before I could speak, my cell phone rang. I ran to the living room where I'd left it in my purse. I grabbed for it and said "hello," but the connection was dead. The caller ID said Marshall Washington and listed a phone number in an area code I didn't recognize.

I tried to call back, but the call didn't go through. Frowning, I returned to the kitchen and sat at the table across from Max. An edible piece of art awaited me. The omelet, perfection itself; the hash browns, gloriously golden and perfectly spiced; the grits, as creamy as pudding. I dove in with relish.

"This is heavenly." I reached for his hand. "Thank you, my friend. You don't know how much I needed this right now, what it means to me ..."

My phone rang again. This time I picked it up on the first ring.

"El—" The connection was weak. The voice cut in and out, mostly out, making it almost impossible to hear. For a split second, it was clear. "El, I need help—" And then it went dead.

I stared at the phone in disbelief. "It was Hyacinth," I whispered. "I recognized her voice. She needs help." I quickly hit callback, but the call went to voice mail. And the mailbox was full. I dropped my head into my hands. "Just hearing her voice ..."

Max came around and put his hand on my shoulder and gave it an affectionate squeeze. "Is there anything on the phone readout? A number? Caller ID? Anything?"

I lifted the phone to show him. "The caller ID says Marshall Washington."

"That's good. We've got something to go on." He grabbed a notepad from my desk and wrote down the information, frowning as he did so.

"But she said she needs help … also something about a possum right before she cut out."

He sat down next to me. "This is more than we had to go on before."

I nodded as he handed me a tissue. I dabbed my eyes and then reached for the phone.

Max got up and cleared the table, rinsed the dishes, and put them in the dishwasher, while I kept trying to return the call to Hyacinth. Each time I got the same result: a full mailbox.

I dialed the sheriff's office and asked for Sheriff Doyle.

"What is it?" He was still all business.

"Two things. I just received a call from Hyacinth. The signal was too weak for me pick up all she said. But I did hear her cry for help. That should settle the matter of whether she went willingly or unwillingly with the thieves."

He didn't comment one way or the other. "Number on the phone? Caller ID?"

I gave him both and then added, "The connection was terrible, but I thought I heard her say the word *possum*."

"That area code covers a large area. Mostly unpopulated. I'll send a couple of deputies up to have a look." He fell quiet for a moment and then said, "You said there were two things."

"I found the remains of Hyacinth's cell phone to one side of her driveway. It looks like it was purposely destroyed. I think that gives us evidence that she was abducted at her home. She wasn't a willing partner in the robbery."

"You pick it up?"

"It's in a Ziploc. I'll bring it by."

Max came over to the table, dish towel in hand.

"I've got to find her," I said. "There's got to be a way. We have to go wherever that area code is."

"There is a possibility that the owner of that phone no longer lives in the area," Max said. "Lots of people have cell phones unrelated to where they live."

"I know it's a thin hope," I said, "but I have to start somewhere." I narrowed my eyes in thought. "*Possum*. What if that has to do with where she might be? Is there a town or landmark with that name?"

"I haven't heard of it," Max said, folding the dish towel.

I opened my laptop and did a search for "Possum, North Carolina." Several possibilities appeared. I felt like cheering. "There it is. Possum Grove. And if I'm right, it corresponds to that area code." I pulled up an area-code map and enlarged it.

Now for Marshall Washington and the name of the town. I typed it in. I sat back, grinning. "Well, glory, glory be." I turned the laptop so that Max could see.

He smiled. "Possum Grove Holy Ghost Revival Church. Marshall Washington is the pastor."

"Let's go there," I said, standing. "This is our first real lead." I was almost dancing.

"I'd like to," Max said. "But I can't today. I'm sorry."

"You can't?" I swallowed my disappointment, wanting to tell him how much he'd come to mean to me in just a few days. How much I would miss him. But I didn't know where to begin.

He placed the towel on a rack at the end of the counter. "I need to go." He hadn't met my eyes since the phone call when he rested his hand on my shoulder. And it seemed he was keeping his gaze anywhere but on me now.

"I'll walk out with you."

We reached his Defender and he stopped and finally looked at me. His eyes were just as warm as before, but there seemed to be an awkwardness, a distance, between us. "I'm really glad I came by. It's been nice."

Nice? How could things have changed so quickly? Nice? I thought it was wonderful. I blinked and opened my mouth to tell him so, then thought better of it.

He attempted a sideways hug, something I've never liked—a hug is a hug in my book—so I gracefully twirled out of his reach, and instead, stuck my hand out to shake his.

He started the Defender and rolled down the driveway. The sun was high, the afternoon sunny, but something cold wrapped itself around my heart. What had come over him? Had I said or done something to upset him? One minute he places his hand on my shoulder, his eyes warm and sympathetic, the next minute he's doing the dishes and acting as if he can't wait to be out of my presence.

But truth be told, I didn't have time for this kind of rumination. I had to get to Hyacinth. The sound of her voice calling for help haunted me.

I raced back into the house and sprinted up the stairs. My jeans were filthy from crawling on the ground while searching for Hyacinth's phone parts, so I grabbed another pair, kicked off my shoes, and slid into them.

Downstairs again, I grabbed my electronic tablet and a gadget that I hoped would boost the signal. I kicked myself for not having upgraded my phone to a model that had GPS. As a backup, I picked up a paper map of North Carolina.

I packed a couple of sandwiches, a thermos of coffee, and some frozen chocolate chippers.

I was just getting into the Ghia when my phone rang again. I held my breath, hoping it was Hyacinth.

"Mom, can you watch C.G. tonight? Sandy and I need to talk privately about what happened last night." She hesitated. "I think you need to talk to C.G. about it too. After hearing what you said, she's terrified of Sandy."

My heart fell. I'd spoken the truth to my daughter's ex and put my foot in my mouth at the same time. How could I explain what I'd said, and why, to a child who didn't know the man was her father? That I was speaking harshly because of my love for her and her mom? That I'd been upset with him because he'd betrayed them both when she was an infant? I couldn't.

"I do plan to have a talk with her. But I can't tonight. I'm on my way out of town."

"Hyacinth?"

"I'm in the car, just now leaving the house. Every minute counts. She called for help and I've got a general idea where to find her."

"Nearby?"

"Possum Grove up by the state line." I hesitated. "Can you get a sitter?"

"Maybe we'll just postpone," she said.

A great idea. How about for a lifetime?

"By the way," she said, "Sandy said you were entirely justified for firing away at him the way you did. He said he deserves every bit of it."

"Well, that's a side of Sandy we've not seen before." I was immediately sorry for my snarky attitude. One thing to feel like a mama bear protecting her cubs; quite another to voice those feelings.

"Mom ..."

I started the car and backed out of the driveway as we talked, the phone cradled with one shoulder. "I'm sorry, honey, this is difficult for me. You'll have to give me some time. I'm trying to get used to the idea that he might be trustworthy. I've disliked him for so long, it's hard to flip that switch off."

"He's working hard to regain trust," Katie said.

"How long has he been back in your life now?"

"A month."

"That's not nearly long enough to test a relationship, especially one that was so terribly broken. And not by you." I softened my voice. "Do you really think you can trust him again, honey? What about the back child support he owes you?"

"He says he's going to pay every penny."

I'll believe it when the check clears. "That's thousands of dollars ..."

"I know, believe me."

"Just be careful with your heart, honey. Take it slowly."

"I will. I promise."

"Tell C.G. I'm sorry I can't have her come over tonight. We'll do it another time."

"She's right here. Why don't you tell her?"

It was a setup; I knew it the minute Chloe Grace came on the phone. "Gramsy, can I come over? I was so sad we had to leave last night. I'm scared and I want to be with you."

I would walk over hot coals for this little girl. In my opinion, the most beautiful sound in the world was Chloe Grace calling me Gramsy. I melt. I'm putty in her hands. Always will be.

I tried to stick to my guns. "I have some work I need to do, sweetie. We'll have to plan a sleepover for another night."

"I don't like Mama's friend anymore," she said. "I don't want to be here when he comes. You looked mad at him last night and now he scares me."

Oh dear. I'd been had. I went over the alternatives in my head. With Chloe Grace along, this would have to be a reconnaissance mission. Visual contact only. If by some miracle I encountered Hyacinth and the thieves, I would have to stay back—hard for me to do, but necessary because of the little treasure in the backseat. I would step aside and let law enforcement take charge. Above all else, I would do anything in my power to keep my granddaughter out of danger.

"Okay," I said, trying to ignore the niggling doubts still alive and well in my brain. "Let's make a new plan. How about if you come with me? You can be my assistant."

"Yay!" I held the phone away from my ear as she screamed. "Mama says you're looking for Auntie Cinth."

"I am."

"Then I can help."

"That's what I'm thinking. Put your mom on."

In the background, Chloe Grace squealed and laughed. Katie took the phone. "So what's the plan?"

"If it's okay with you, I'll take her with me." I explained my plan to do research and not get into anything dangerous. I shot up an arrow prayer while Katie thought it over.

"To Possum Grove?"

"Yes. I'll have my phone. I'll keep you posted along the way. But we may not get back until late. Pack her jammies and she can spend the night."

More squeals of delight as Katie relayed the news.

"I'll be right there."

Chapter Twenty-three
The Professor

. . . .

Max had good reason to visit his dad. He enjoyed their weekly visits immensely, but today held special significance. He needed to jog his dad's memory about the sinking of the *Andrea Rae*. The last time they spoke, he felt his dad knew more than what he'd revealed through the years.

But as he drove away from El's, his dad and the *Andrea Rae* weren't what occupied his mind.

No, he wondered about his sanity. Never in his life had he fallen so quickly and completely for a woman. Not even the girl he'd been engaged to marry eons ago, the one who broke his heart.

He left El with mixed feelings: sorry he couldn't go with her to search for Hyacinth; also relieved to get away from her before he did something foolish—like pull her into his arms and kiss her thoroughly.

His feelings took him by surprise. He'd known since Friday morning that he was falling hard, but when he saw her priceless expression as she entered the kitchen today, he knew he'd never be the same. It was as if he looked into his own soul. Her face, her eyes, told him she was—in that one instant—filled with joy, disbelief, vulnerability, and fear.

Yes, he was afraid. He'd trusted a woman once a long time ago, so long ago it was almost laughable. Still, it took years to get over her. Sometimes he wondered if he still feared relationships because of the one that failed. Human beings were odd that way, their memories selective and tending to turn toward the negative if allowed.

But just thinking about El made his heart rate increase. Her laughter, velvet and husky; the way she talked with her hands; the tears that seemed to embarrass her yet flowed freely and somehow pulled from him a tenderness he never knew he had. Her eyes and the way they sparkled with mischief and made his heart soar.

He downshifted and turned onto a mountain road just east of Asheville. He traveled north for a good way; he'd memorized the route years ago. The cottage, his destination, had been in his family for generations, though he associated it more with his grandpa than with his dad, who moved there after retiring from the navy.

The closer he got to the cottage, the more eager he was to see his father. And to talk about the figurehead. Maybe he'd left out something in his story.

Max had called him after he found the *Lady*, but he hadn't talked with him about the theft. He probably already knew. Gray Ghost couldn't get and didn't want broadcast TV, only a radio signal. He would likely have heard about it on the local news station.

He turned the Defender onto another smaller road, a two-tracker. The average traveler would have no idea that, in the midst of these thick woods, a thriving community of two dozen people and a few herds of deer existed, independent of the outside world.

Mostly, they were older but hardy souls. They lived separate from society, but took care of each other. It had been that way for generations. Some nights, it was one's turn to cook for the others; another night, someone else provided the victuals. Nothing was ever planned. It just happened. There was dancing and storytelling, fiddling, hunting, and fishing. His dad thought he'd found himself a little piece of heaven when he got out of the navy and moved to his own father's cottage in Gray Ghost.

When Max's grandparents lived there, he had often stayed with them for long stretches of time. Now, it felt as if he were coming home.

He spotted his dad's cottage from where the two-tracker ended a ways down the mountain. Max caught his father up on the latest news about the *Lady*, but his father obviously had something on his mind.

"Son, I came across something the other day that I'd forgotten about. Hearing the news of the robbery got me to thinking about the sinking of the *Andrea Rae*, about the day it went down, and a letter I received sometime later."

He got up and went into the cottage. "You stay there, son," he said from the doorway. "I'll be right out."

He came back out a few minutes later with an envelope. "I want you to read this." He handed it to Max.

Max opened the envelope and pulled out a letter.

March 25, 1945
To: Wallace Haverhill
Dear Sir:

It may come as a surprise that someone besides you survived the sinking of the Andrea Rae. *You have become quite the hero as the lone survivor. Since finding out about your celebrity in my local newspaper, I thought it would be wise for us to compare notes. I, too, was on board that fateful night. I remember hearing someone speak of a treasure. Things went black after that, and the next thing I knew I had washed ashore with no memory. My memory returned when I saw your photograph in the newspaper and read your story.*

I hope to receive a reply from you. My address is 41771 Mountain View Avenue, Wilmington, North Carolina.

Cordially yours,
William B. MacDonald

His dad reached for his US Navy mug and sipped his coffee. "I put the letter away, at first thinking the seaman was a crackpot. He called me a celebrity. All I did was get pulled ashore. I didn't even have to swim. And surviving a shipwreck when everyone except you perishes is worse than dying with your friends and comrades, believe you me. I was no hero. And I didn't want to meet someone else going through the same sorrow I was. Then, later on, I got to thinking maybe it was for real. I replied to the letter, but it was returned with a stamp that said no one at that address."

"What do you think now?" Max examined the type. It clearly was from the 1940s or thereabouts, and not something recent. "You remember when you got it?"

"Oh, yes. It was right after the war. The date on it is authentic."

"May I take it with me?"

"Of course. I'd hoped you would. Maybe it will help to run down this MacDonald or his descendants. Maybe they had something to do with the robbery." He shrugged.

"We certainly haven't had much luck so far."

"Son, do you still have a passion for finding it?"

Max smiled. His father always got to the point. Saw things no one else did in him. "I do, but it's tempered somewhat. I'm just now beginning to realize there's been a shift in my thinking." He leaned forward, pondering his dad's question. "I think it's because I've come to understand that an object, no matter its dollar value, can't come close to the sanctity of life. The value of even a single life. A lot of people have been placed in danger, one even died on Friday night, because of an object." He paused, surprised at the difference three days made.

They sat quietly together.

"Better late than never," his father finally said. "What's her name?"

Max laughed softly. "El. El Littlefield."

"Ah, one of the Eldila."

Max grinned, appreciating his father's knowledge of the writings of C. S. Lewis and his Space Trilogy. "I thought of them too when she told me her name. She is full of love, laughter, and light." He was quiet a moment and then added, "Strangely, if it weren't for the justice of returning the millions, perhaps billions, of dollars' worth of treasure to the families of the victims, the rightful owners, it would have little meaning."

"And that from a historian. She must really be something."

Max threw back his head and laughed. "It's not just about her, Dad. I take my vows seriously, my vows of living simply, in poverty and chastity. An overabundance of wealth, unless generously helping the poor among us, is troubling. But these treasures, and the families they belong to, are not mine to judge. My quest is to find them."

"Hmm. Does El know of your Franciscan vows, that you follow Christ's footsteps in the manner of Saint Francis, a simple monk?"

Max grinned. "You really know how to spell it out for me, don't you?" He studied his father's weathered face, the flowing white beard, the lively blue eyes, and nodded slowly. "I need to tell her. It's only fair."

"Especially the chastity part."

"It doesn't mean what you think, Dad."

"I know that, but she won't, so you better talk fast when you explain it." He laughed. "I would love to be there when that happens." He leaned forward and gave Max a playful slap on the knee. "Bring El with you next week."

"As if that will ever happen." Max grinned at his dad. "I would like to bring her up her with me, but you've got to promise to behave yourself."

His dad's eyes brightened. "You mean I can't talk about the heirs I'm hoping you'll give me?"

Max was still laughing as he walked down the mountain to the Defender. His dad never failed to lift his spirits.

Chapter Twenty-four
Mrs. Littlefield

. . . .

After three restroom breaks and one ice cream stop, we made it to a faded roadside sign that pointed to Possum Grove, five miles away.

Chloe Grace had been a little trooper and kept a lively conversation going with either me or with the doll that sat next to her in the backseat. She'd even drifted off for a brief nap. Now she was getting antsy, and I didn't blame her. I was too.

"How much longer, Gramsy?"

"We're almost there, honey. Help me watch for a church."

"What does it look like?"

"I don't know. But we might see a sign that says Possum Grove Holy Ghost Revival Church."

"That's a big name for a church. I don't think I can spell that. Those are big words."

"They are."

"Is that where Auntie Cinth is?"

"She might be. She called me from a telephone that belongs to the pastor here."

"I see it, I see it," she squealed a little bit later.

I too saw the small brick building in the distance, but as we drove closer, it turned out to be a Baptist church.

Dusk set in, and I wasn't too keen on driving after dark. Not only did we need to find the church, and the pastor, we had to make our way back to Eden's Bridge. I began to wonder if I'd been out of my mind to bring Chloe Grace along on this trek. I'd just been so sure that this phone number might lead to Hyacinth. So sure of a happy outcome.

The what-ifs marched in and took up residence in my stomach.

We came to the town of Possum Grove, which boasted a general store, a café, a gas station, and a dollar store. All were closed.

I kept my foot on the accelerator, and we soon left the little town in the distance.

"There it is, Gramsy," Chloe Grace squealed again. "That's gotta be it. I just know it. Let's stop and see!"

In the waning light, I spotted a small white clapboard church down the hill from what appeared to be an old graveyard. As we drew closer, I slowed to have a better look. I didn't see a sign, but there was a steeple on top of the roof.

The church looked friendly, with its windows and doors open wide and light spilling out into the darkening dusk of evening. A few cars were parked on one side of the building, and as I pulled up, parked, and turned off the engine, I heard singing drifting from inside.

"Music!" Chloe Grace unfastened her seat belt and scrambled from the car. She stretched her arms and legs, allowed herself a loud yawn, and then took off running for the church.

I trotted along behind.

"Gramsy, come look. Hurry!" Chloe Grace called when she reached the doorway. "It's a choir, and I know the song." They were singing a rollicking, syncopated version of "This Little Light of Mine." "I love that song," she said. She started singing with the choir, at first mouthing the words, then growing bolder and louder.

Several members noticed us and smiled, and then the choir director turned to see what had caught their attention. He clicked his baton on his music stand and the singing stopped.

The organist, a middle-aged woman with a graying cap of curls, halted, reluctantly it seemed to me, in the middle of "I'm going to let it shine, let it shine, let it ..."

"Hello, there," the choir director called to us. "Can we help you?"

"I'm looking for the Possum Grove Holy Ghost Revival Church," I said, walking briskly down the aisle.

"Well, now." His smile spread. "The good Lord has led you to the right place. You're standing on holy ground in the very church you're looking for. What can we do for you?"

I took Chloe Grace by the hand, and we walked toward a choir of about fifteen men, women, and teens arranged on risers.

"We're practicing for a contest in Nashville the end of the month," the choir director said. "Normally, we don't meet on Sunday nights, but because of the contest, we're working in an extra rehearsal. I'm glad we're here tonight. The Holy Ghost must've put it in our hearts so we'd be here for you."

I smiled my thanks. "I'm Elaine Littlefield, and this is my granddaughter, Chloe Grace."

"And I'm Cleon Washington, the pastor's son." He shook hands with Chloe Grace and then with me. "Now, how can we help?"

"We've driven a long way today, looking for my missing friend. We're from Eden's Bridge."

"That is a ways." His expression reflected his concern.

"I received a call from her today on a phone that had this number on it, and the name Marshall Washington." I pulled my phone from my purse, tapped a few icons and showed him the number.

"That's my parents' number," he said, appearing even more puzzled.

The choir members drifted from their positions on the risers and gathered around us.

"I remember my mama saying something about a woman she helped out this morning during our worship service."

My spirits leaped up inside me. "Did she give her name?"

A younger woman stepped forward. "I'm Cleon's sister, Natasha. I remember Mama sayin' that the woman was in a hurry and never gave her name. Mama gave her some food from our potluck, and some bottles of water. She must've given her the phone too."

"Did this woman say where she was going?"

"If she did, Mama didn't say. She and Daddy were pretty excited about leaving on their mission trip."

The choir members nodded and started talking about it. Something to do with helping out the less fortunate, going where the Holy Ghost leads, but not knowing where that might be when they first get on the road out, how many they'd helped through the years, just depending on the Holy Ghost to lead them to those in need.

My heart plummeted. I couldn't help thinking I could use a little help from the Holy Ghost myself about now. So could Hyacinth. "It sounds like there's no way to get in touch with them."

"Especially now that they don't have the cell phone," Cleon said. "It only worked half the time anyway."

"If they happen to call, would you give them this number?" I jotted down my cell phone number and name and handed it to Cleon. "Have your mother call me about my friend? She might know some details that she didn't mention to anyone else."

Cleon studied my face, probably noticing how my spirits had fallen. "You look in need of refreshment. We have potluck leftovers downstairs."

I shook my head. All I could think about was how we'd come so far for so little. We did find out that Hyacinth had been here, but we didn't know where she'd gone next. "I promised Chloe Grace that we'd stop by the Cracker Barrel out by the interstate for supper."

Cleon nodded. "Little 'uns love that place." Then he smiled, looking straight down at Chloe Grace, who I could see was getting more fidgety by the minute. "How about joining us for another round of "This Little Light of Mine"? I heard some mighty fine singin' a few minutes ago comin' out of your mouth."

Chloe Grace brightened considerably. She looked at me for approval and I nodded. "You'll have fun. Go ahead."

The choir trooped back to the risers and took their places with Chloe Grace in the center front, and I sat down in the nearest pew, my heart growing heavier by the minute.

As the choir and organist listened to Cleon give direction for their next run-through, I leaned forward and dropped my forehead into my hands. I thought of Max's ongoing conversation with God, and his prayer of gratitude. Ongoing? I could only think of one thing to say right now, and it wasn't, *Hey, thanks*. It was, *Help!*

When Chloe Grace began to sing, I brought my head up with a snap. She stood up tall, beaming like a sunflower in a patch of sunlight, her voice loud and clear. Behind her, the choir clapped and swayed and almost danced. Someone handed Chloe Grace a tambourine, and she shook it in time to the music as the choir and organist joined in for the chorus.

We all clapped when the song was over. Her little face flushed, Chloe Grace ran to me, her arms open to get a hug. For a moment, I forgot my huge disappointment and anxieties about the drive back to Eden's Bridge.

"You ever want to join our choir, you just give us a holler," Cleon said as we stood to leave.

They started over at verse one, this time in syncopated rhythm, as we moved to the aisle. I took Chloe Grace's hand and we headed to the back of the sanctuary and the door that led outside and into the dark night.

Chapter Twenty-five
Mrs. Littlefield

• • • • • • • • • • • • • • • • •

I had just parked the Ghia in the Cracker Barrel parking lot when my cell phone rang.

"I bet it's Mommy," Chloe Grace said from the backseat.

"I bet you're right," I said, smiling, something I'd been doing a lot for the sake of my granddaughter. I picked up my phone, saw the ID, and answered.

"Katie."

"How is everything going?" She sounded tense.

"Very well. We've just stopped at the Cracker Barrel for a bite to eat."

"I thought you'd be back by now. I was getting worried."

"I'll explain when we get home …"

"Let me talk! Let me talk! Let me talk!" Chloe Grace bounced up and down in the backseat. I handed her the phone.

"Mommy, I got to sing with a choir. It was the coolest thing ever. They let me sing a solo with them and play a tambourine. It was so cool."

They chatted a bit more, and then Chloe Grace handed the phone back to me.

"I know you don't like to drive at night." Katie sounded worried. "Would you like for us to come pick you up? Sandy could drive your car, and you and C.G. could ride with me."

"Us?" Really? I took a moment to count backward from ten.

"No, dear. I'm fine. Really. We'll grab a bite to eat and be on our way. I'm going to take the interstate home. It'll take longer for us to get there, but I think it's safer than the shortcut at this time of night."

"We sang 'This Little Light of Mine' a thousand times." Chloe Grace yelled from the backseat so her mom could hear her. "It's my new favorite song ever."

Katie laughed. "She loves being with you." Then she paused. "Did you have any luck tracing Cinth's path?"

I sighed deeply. "No. That's been a disappointment."

We said our good-byes, and then Chloe Grace and I got out of the car and headed into the Cracker Barrel.

"Fried chicken and mashed potatoes," she declared as we stepped through the door. "I can't wait."

We gave our name to the hostess and then looked around the country store. I'd promised she could buy one toy, and she was still methodically examining the shelves of children's items when our name was called.

We followed the hostess to our table through a large room that seemed to be filled to capacity.

"Lots of people like this place," Chloe Grace said. "Did you know so many people liked it, Gramsy?"

"It's probably because it's near the interstate. It's a handy place for a restroom stop, and they have good food."

"I need to go," she announced, bouncing up and down.

"How about waiting until we order, then we'll go."

She nodded, still bouncing.

Finally, the waitress came for our orders and we headed to the restroom. I stood guard at the stall door, while Chloe Grace used the toilet, then we switched places.

"Stay right by this stall," I said. "It's important. Do you understand?"

We'd had this conversation before in public restrooms, and I was confident she knew the rules. I chatted with her through the closed door. She chatted back, giggling and happy. Then suddenly she didn't answer.

"Chloe Grace!"

No answer.

I pulled up my jeans and undies and flew out of the stall. The area around the basins and mirror was crowded.

"Chloe Grace!" I called, fighting the feeling of panic. "Chloe Grace?"

I moved through the knots of women and little girls washing their hands.

"Chloe Grace! This no time to be hiding, if that's what you're doing. Come out right now." It didn't matter that she'd never hidden from me before in her life.

By now everyone in the restroom had fallen quiet. Several women stooped to look under the occupied stalls, but my granddaughter had disappeared.

I ran out the door into the waiting area. I still didn't see her. I found the hostess and told her my granddaughter was missing. She remembered seating us, and said she hadn't seen the child.

"Why don't you see if she decided to return to your table? If she isn't there, we'll call the police. Meanwhile, I'll alert the manager."

I ran into the dining area and spotted our table. It was empty.

In that moment, I wanted to die. This was a thousand times worse than my fire phobia. A million times worse: a lost child. My beloved grandchild.

Time stood still, and then I heard, "Gramsy! Over here. Look what I found."

I looked two tables over from ours. There stood Chloe Grace at one end with a bangle bracelet on her arm. Seated at the table was a middle-aged couple, looking at once confused and delighted.

"You scared me to death, honey." I knelt beside her so we were eye to eye. "How many times have I told you stay put when we're in a public restroom?"

"I'm sorry," Chloe Grace said, big tears filling her eyes. "I saw this bracelet. It's just like the one I helped Mommy pick out for Auntie Cinth last Christmas. See, it's got a little heart 'graved on it."

I hugged her close, promising myself I would never let her out of my sight again, squeezed her gently once more, and then stood.

The woman gave us an understanding smile. "Your granddaughter must have spotted it when I was washing my hands. I didn't know she'd followed me out here until just a moment ago. I'm so sorry to have frightened you."

"I'm sorry," Chloe Grace said, tears still streaming. I kept my arm wrapped around her shoulders. She handed the bracelet back to the woman, who smiled and thanked her.

"It was a gift," she said. "I'm glad your aunt has one like it. It's very pretty."

From the corner of my eye, I saw our food being delivered to our table. I thanked the couple for keeping watch over Chloe Grace.

As we left, the man said, "I hope you don't have far to go tonight. I hear we may get showers."

I wondered if any worse news could be delivered before this day ended. Slick streets. Glaring lights on wet pavement. My night-vision problems.

"Oh dear," I said, trying not to sound as discouraged as I felt. "We do have a few hours ahead of us. We're headed to Eden's Bridge."

"Godspeed," the man said, looking concerned. He exchanged a glance with his wife, which puzzled me.

Chloe Grace's tears had disappeared by the time she picked up her drumstick and began scooping up her mashed potatoes and apple-sauce like there was no tomorrow. She passed on the peas and sweet potatoes, and then decided on chocolate ice cream for dessert.

We talked about the toys she'd seen earlier in the general store. Her eyes were bright as she told me about a ballerina sock monkey she spotted on a top shelf. "And he's dressed in a tutu." She giggled. "Except he's a girl monkey."

We paid for our meals, visited the restroom once more, and then stopped to buy the sock monkey.

"She's beautiful," Chloe Grace whispered when the sales clerk laid the toy in her arms. She looked up at me. "I'm going to name her Pumpkin, 'cause that's what you call me sometimes."

We walked out into the parking lot. I smelled rain in the air, and shivered, thinking of the drive ahead. There weren't as many cars now as there had been when we arrived.

We'd almost reached the Ghia when Chloe Grace looked up at me and smiled. My breath caught in my throat as I remembered the panic I'd felt when I thought she was lost. I hugged her close, taking joy in that moment just knowing she was with me.

As I unlocked the Ghia, Chloe Grace started singing "This Little Light of Mine" in perfect syncopated rhythm, swinging the monkey by its arms in a made-up dance. I leaned against the car for a moment, watching her and feeling my heart lift at the sight of her face, now beaming as bright as an August moon.

I was about to get her to hop in the backseat, when the couple we'd talked with earlier appeared just a few feet away.

"We heard your little one singing just now," the man said. "That's an unusual rendition of that little song."

I smiled. "She just learned it. We stopped by a church a couple of hours ago during choir practice. The director asked her to sing with them. I don't think she's stopped singing it since then."

"A church here in town?"

"Possum Grove Holy Ghost Revival."

They looked at each other and then back at me. "That's our church," the woman said. "My husband's the pastor. And it was likely our son leadin' the choir. My name's Josie Mae Washington, and this old man"— she grinned—"is my husband. You can just call him Pastor Marshall."

The Holy Ghost indeed. I laughed and hugged them both. "Is there a chance you met my friend Hyacinth Gilvertin? She called me from your phone yesterday."

"Well, lands, yes. I did indeed meet her. Sweetest lady ever." She shook her head. "She told me she's gotten herself in some big trouble, though. I tried to get her to stay with us for a spell, rest up at least one day. But she'd have none of it. She got on an old bicycle we gave her and pedaled on down the road. Said she was after some bad guys who stole something she wanted to get back."

"Did you see which direction she went?"

"Oh yes," Josie Mae said. "She was coming this direction. Straight down this same road. But I don't have any idea where she went next."

She thought for a minute and then said, "The last I saw of her was on the road leading from church toward town. Just before she left, she asked me if I were a thief with hot goods which direction would I go. I told her back to the interstate. So that's the direction she went. She planned to look along the way for the rental truck that dropped her in the graveyard. She said it was one of the ones you see all the time on the highway. 'Coast to Coast,' I believe she called it. The ones with a picture of Yosemite on it. She said to tell you, let me see if I can remember it, yes, she said, 'Nancy ate 724 hamburgers.' Do you know what that means?"

"No, but I'll figure it out." I could have hugged her. This was the most information I'd received so far. "Anything else?"

Josie Mae shook her head. "I told your friend that if it was me, I wouldn't try to find someone who would do such a thing, but your friend, Hyacinth, seemed determined. Said they took something of value that she wanted to get back."

She glanced down at her bracelet and then knelt so she was level with Chloe Grace. "Child, I want you to take this back to your mama to keep safe until your Auntie Cinth gets home, you hear?"

Chloe Grace nodded solemnly, holding her ballerina monkey close.

"'Cause it was your pretty eyes that spotted it as belongin' to your auntie. That sort of thing doesn't happen very often. And when it does, I always think it's because God sends His angels to give us little clues about things. I think a little angel gave you a clue tonight. You hold that thought dear to your heart, okay?"

Chloe Grace smiled and nodded. "An angel?"

Josie Mae laughed as she stood. "Yes, ma'am. A real angel."

Then Pastor Marshall stepped up. "We're traveling in that Winnebago over there. It would please us if you'd like to tuck in behind us. It'll keep you outa some of the wind and sheltered from the rain and oncoming headlights."

I shook my head in wonder, then realized they might think I was saying no. I grinned. "Thank you. You have no idea how—"

He held up his hand. "Think nothing of it. We're going the same direction anyway." Then he laughed. "By the way, where are you headed again?"

I remembered what the choir members had said about them being led by the Spirit, and my smile widened. "Eden's Bridge."

"Lotta good folk there," the pastor said. "Maybe we'll stick around for a while."

"I hope you do. Our town could use a couple of angels like you two."

They chuckled as they walked back to the Winnebago.

Chloe Grace and I climbed back into the Ghia. In less than five minutes, the Winnebago rolled to the parking lot exit, and I followed.

Not that I wasn't nervous. Truth be told, I was quaking in my tennies. Especially with my little angel in the backseat, and me unable to rid my mind of the horror of those few minutes I'd thought she had been kidnapped.

Even so, as I followed along, protected from the storm, I figured if there was ever a "Hey, thanks," moment, this was it. I might yet get the hang of this ongoing conversation with God after all.

"Gramsy," called a little voice from the backseat. "I'm worried about my heart. How can someone steal it? You said Dr. Ainsley was going to steal it like he did Mama's. That scared me. He ... operates on people. Cuts them open." She started to sniffle and I knew she was crying.

This called for emergency measures. I flashed my hazard lights at the Winnebago and then signaled the need to pull over. The big RV lumbered to the side of the road, with us right behind.

As soon as we stopped, I got out and reached for my grand-daughter. She came into my arms and clung to me. "I don't want anyone to steal my heart."

"No one ever will unless you let them," I said softly into her hair. "I promise you." I pulled back and smiled. "Besides, that's not really what it means when people say that. Your heart will always be right here"—I gently thumped her chest—"beating strong and healthy, just like always. 'Steal your heart' is an expression people use when they talk about your feelings inside." I watched her face in the glow of the Winnebago's taillights.

I sat on the edge of my driver's-side seat and pulled her into my lap. "I spoke harshly to your ... to your mom's friend last night. It wasn't the right thing for me to do. He wants to be friends with you and your mama, and I just want him to give your mama time to decide if she wants to be friends again."

"They were friends before?"

"A long time ago. But your mama will have to tell you that story."

"So he's not going to steal my heart."

"No. I promise."

Chloe Grace heaved a big sigh. "Can I be his friend again?"

Now I sighed and prayed for grace. "Absolutely, sweetie. Absolutely."

Chapter Twenty-six
Mrs. Littlefield

. . . .

The next morning as I showered and dressed, I went over my mental to-do list: call realtors about owner of property/cabin fire scene; find out what the Sutherland boys were doing at Hyacinth's; call Sheriff Doyle to see if the officers he'd sent out yesterday found anything; investigate how someone bought illegal ipecac; call Silas Sutherland about cabin ownership. And I wanted to return to the intersection of Possum Grove Road and the interstate with a photograph of Hyacinth and ask if anyone had noticed her.

How could anyone miss a healthy-sized woman with bright red curls, riding a bicycle, for heaven's sake?

And what in the world did "Nancy ate 724 hamburgers" mean?

As soon as I finished dressing and fluffing my hair, I went down the hall to check on Chloe Grace in the guest room. She was still sleeping soundly, the ballerina sock monkey tucked under her arm. The sight warmed every part of me. Grandchildren had to be one of the greatest gifts of getting older. I studied the curve of her cheek, so like her mother's at that age, the soft strands of hair splayed on her pillow, the relaxed curl of little fingers, the soft rise and fall of her breathing.

I heard my cell phone ring, but I'd left it plugged into the charger on the kitchen counter. By the time I picked it up, the call had gone to voice mail. I waited for the chirping signal and then touched the icon to listen.

"Hi, Mom, I thought I'd stop by on my way to work, if it's okay. I wanted to fill you in on my conversation with Sandy. If C.G. is awake, then we'll wait to talk until later. No need to call me back. Put on the coffee and I'll see you around seven thirty."

My shoulders sagged, and I sank into a chair and rubbed my temples. I was fighting a headache from last night's drive, and I had planned to get started on my to-do list as soon as Chloe Grace awoke.

I made another pot of coffee, placed it on a tray with two cups and my favorite fixings, then carried it to the potting shed and placed it on the corner of my desk.

The air smelled of damp loamy soil and fragrant herbs—rosemary, basil, and thyme—growing in my garden. I felt the need to keep moving, and though sitting in my wicker chair near the garden was a favorite pastime, I couldn't bring myself to sit still.

It struck me that something wasn't right. I didn't hear any birds, for one thing, and I wondered about the silence. I told myself it was my imagination, but the nagging thought kept nipping at the back of my brain.

I checked my watch as I paced: 7:17 a.m. Katie had to be at her preschool job at eight o'clock, so that didn't give us much time.

Still antsy, I went over to see how my vegetables had made it through the rainy night. I was glad to see they were thriving. So were the weeds. I knelt and pulled a few, then spotted more, and went to work on them. I didn't realize how furiously I was pulling on them, until I stood and looked down at the piles of oxalis and dandelions.

Katie finally arrived at seven twenty-five. She spotted me in back, opened the side gate, and let herself in. She looked dazzling in the early morning light. There was color in her cheeks, and she wore makeup for the first time in a long while. Not a good sign. I was beginning to say that to myself a lot.

I gave her a hug and then pulled back to search her face. Her luminous eyes were questioning, but the hint of sorrow from Sandy's betrayal remained. With a deep breath, I reminded myself that, after all, she was an adult, and no matter what I thought about Sandy, I loved her and wanted to support her.

I went into the potting shed and poured coffee into both mugs, then handed one to Katie.

"Let's walk," I said. "For some reason, I just can't sit still this morning."

"You've got a lot on your mind," she said. "Trying to find Aunt Cinth and hitting dead ends. The bad publicity about The Butler. And now this situation with Sandy."

"I'm trying not to think about the publicity," I said. We walked toward the small peach orchard at the back of my property. "That's the least of my worries." I took a sip of coffee.

Katie didn't need to tell me that the news was already all over town. What wasn't known before was certainly known now, thanks to the *Chronicle's* special edition. I was certain it was the hottest topic to hit Eden's Bridge in decades.

We reached the orchard, and Katie turned to me. "Sandy wants to set a date."

I spun, my coffee sloshing, and walked away, my emotions hitting my stomach with a nausea-inducing thud. For a moment, I just stood there, staring at the cold coals of the pit barbecue in the opposite corner of the yard. I remained there for a few minutes, thinking of at least a dozen warnings I'd already given her.

"There's something else." She paused, watching me. "He's leaving the medical field." The set of her jaw said she would stand by her man. I knew better than to point out how long it had taken him to get through medical school. While she worked to pay their bills.

I tilted my head. "So he's decided medicine isn't for him after all? He didn't say anything about that the other night."

"It's complicated and he didn't want to get into it. He never married the other woman. The new federal regulations are getting to him, and he just wants a clean break from the practice."

"What's he going to do?"

"Medical research. He's accepted a position with one of the biggest research companies in the world." She looked proud. "This career move will make all the difference. He'll be able to pay off his student loans within the next couple of years."

I poured out the rest of my coffee, having lost my taste for it.

Seeing her tense expression, I circled my arm around her waist. "You know how much I love you," I said as we walked back to the house.

"When you say that, it's always followed by a 'but,'" she said.

I was sure the smile I attempted was pathetic. "His track record isn't great. It feels to me like he's pushing you into a decision."

"I know what I'm doing, Mom."

A few minutes later, Katie kissed me good-bye. "If you need to, just drop C.G. by the school. Otherwise, I'll pick her up after work."

I walked her to the door, and watched as she drove away. Again, I noticed the absence of birdsong, and wondered why.

I dropped a slice of bread in the toaster, and while I waited for it to pop up, I called Enrique. He picked up on the first ring, sounding tired.

"Don't tell me you've taken a third job," I said.

"No, but I did cover my brother's late shift at Little Italy." He yawned.

"Did I wake you?"

"Oh no, I needed to get an early start today. I am going to the campus bookstore to buy books for my summer-school classes. I hope I can find used ones. They go the fastest. I will also keep a lookout at the café for skinny girls who might be using that drug ipecac." He chuckled. "Though if I did have time for girls, I want them to have meat on their bones."

I laughed with him. "You can just buy books today." The café was a hangout for students, a good place to watch for exchanges of nefarious kinds. "I'm going to do some investigating today and may go there myself."

"You?"

"Yes."

"Pardon me, Mrs. Littlefield. You cannot pass for a student."

"Well, for one thing students nowadays can be any age. Not long ago, a woman got her doctorate at age ninety. Besides, who's to say I'm not an instructor?"

"What you say is true. But you yourself said these guys might be dangerous. They provided the poison that made people sick and killed the president of the school. You said they are ready to strike like cornered rattlers." He took an audible breath. "Take extra care, Mrs. Littlefield."

"I usually say that to your brother and you."

I spread peanut butter on my toast, added a drizzle of honey, and poured myself a small glass of apple juice. I congratulated myself for passing up the frozen cookie. Though just thinking about it made me grab one out of the freezer and put it by my coffee mug for later. I also knew it wouldn't last till later.

I reviewed my list again. While Chloe Grace slept upstairs, I would spend my time in diet forums to find out where I could buy ipecac. I would set a time and place to make the buy, find the source and, through him or her, a client list. Pretty straightforward, if I could pull it off. And if I had the time.

After Chloe Grace was awake, I would turn my energies to finding Hyacinth. I needed a large recent photo, maybe several copies, to show around. She was recently featured in the Who's Who Around Town section of the *Chronicle*. The photograph that accompanied the article was spectacular. A former client on the PI side of things worked at the paper and we'd become good friends. I picked up my phone to give her a call.

She picked up after the first ring.

"Suzanne, it's El."

A half heartbeat of heavy silence followed. "El," she said. "How are you?"

"After last Friday night, I'll never be the same."

"It was terrible, wasn't it? I feel so sorry for those who became ill."

"Yes, it was, and so do I." I frowned. She sounded distant. Distracted. Certainly not friendly. I plunged ahead anyway. "You're probably aware that Hyacinth Gilvertin disappeared Friday night as well."

"Yes, I believe the whole town is aware of that." Now she sounded impatient, like she wanted me to get off the phone.

"Your photographer took a great photo of her when you featured her in the who's who piece. I wonder if you could get a copy for me. I'll stop by and pick it up. I want to show it around in the area where she was last seen."

"That's not such a good idea, Elaine."

Elaine? She'd never called me that before. "Why not?"

"It would be better for you not to stop by, or even come near downtown."

"You're kidding."

"People are pretty steamed. They're blaming you and your company for James Delancy's death and the other illnesses. I'm writing our feature article for Wednesday's edition right now. I shouldn't even be talking with you."

I sat back, too stunned to respond for several seconds. "Shouldn't you interview me for this article? Get my thoughts, my point of view?"

"I've talked to the sheriff's office. I'm writing it from their unbiased perspective, as well as doing some digging of my own."

"So you're not interested in my guilt or innocence?" My world was slipping out from beneath my feet with dizzying speed. I didn't think I could breathe, and closed my eyes to try to shut out all that was happening to me and to the world I knew and loved. I inhaled deeply, exhaled slowly. *Breathe. Breathe. Breathe, girl. You can do it.*

Finally I said, "I feel terrible about President Delancy's death. But I can assure you, I had nothing at all to do with it." I let more silence fall between us and then said, "I thought we were friends." The sting of tears hit me again at the top of my throat. I ignored them, or tried to.

"I did too, El. Until this happened. Now along with others, I wonder if any of us really know you at all. We find that to be true with so many transplants, especially from places like California. Here in the South, you're really only one of us if your great-grandpa knew my great-grandpa."

"I see." I thought of several comebacks, some of them clever, but decided the better part of wisdom said to keep them to myself.

"Heed my warning and stay away from town, Elaine."

I was too upset to answer. Bubba and Junior's hateful accusations swept over me again. I felt as if I were standing helpless before a riptide, nothing to hold on to. Nothing solid to cling to. I breathed that one little word again: *Help!*

I stared out the window, noting again the quiet of the morning. No lawnmowers or leaf blowers, no joggers. A strange silence.

I shivered as I picked up the phone and called Max, hoping he'd gotten over whatever was troubling him yesterday.

"How about joining me for a road trip to Possum Grove?"

"Your voice tells me you found something." His tone was warm, which made me smile.

I filled him in on what I'd discovered. "We know Hyacinth was there just twenty-four hours ago. She was free as a bird, but chose to go after the thieves on her own. I met a pastor's wife who gave Hyacinth food and water and a bicycle. She was last seen cycling to Possum Grove to look for the rental truck she knew the thieves were driving. The rental company's name is Coast to Coast Rentals."

"They're trying to get rid of her, and she won't be gotten rid of." He chuckled. "I know it's not a laughing matter, but—"

"—the O. Henry story comes to mind?" I laughed with him.

"Exactly. Do you think that's what she's doing?"

"If anyone could pull it off, it would be Hyacinth." I pictured such a thing and wanted to laugh, but the worry in my heart overruled.

"Do the authorities know the latest?"

"I filled them in yesterday, but haven't yet today. The sheriff sent a couple of deputies up to Possum Grove. I didn't see them, but I called the department after I heard about the rental. They've put out an APB, but they can't trace it without the license plate number. I haven't heard a peep from the sheriff this morning."

"How about if we take the Defender?" Max said. "Or do you prefer to drive?"

"I love my Ghia, of course, for sentimental reasons, and someday I'll share my stories. But if I could have my number-one choice in cars, it would be an old Defender. The kind the Brits once took on safari."

"You're kidding, right?" His voice seemed to catch. "An old Defender. Really?"

"Really."

"What time?"

"Give me a couple of hours. My granddaughter is still asleep. I need to fix her breakfast and then drop her by her mom's work-place."

"Great," he said, with such enthusiasm that my cheeks warmed and my heart did that little dance again. The coolness I'd sensed the day before was gone. I breathed easier.

We said our good-byes, and I went upstairs to wake Chloe Grace. But when I stepped to the doorway, she was sleeping so soundly I didn't want to wake her. Plus, it would give me time to do some research on my laptop in the potting shed office.

I checked the front door to make sure it was locked and then headed through the kitchen to the back door.

I sat at my desk, turned on the laptop, and opened a search engine and typed in "anorexia." Pinterest had more boards and pins on dieting and fitness than I could have imagined. The theme? Thin was in. What I read sickened me. Most pins I scanned seemed to be written with the express intent of making women believe that you can't be too rich or too thin. They included helpful hints to stay thin. Many suggested menu plans featuring lettuce and rice cakes. I suspected that many of the models were airbrushed, making them appear thinner than they were in real life.

One forum I found in my search caught my attention. I double clicked, only to find that it was a locked site. I would have to ask to join. A photo was required, which stumped me. I would have to lie about my age and use someone else's picture. I chose Katie, and copied a shot of her the night of her senior prom.

It irked me no end to be deceptive. But if my actions saved lives, I would do it. I uploaded Katie's picture, named my fictional self Amanda MacLean, and asked to join.

The moderator must have been sitting at his or her computer, because I received an immediate reply. I was in.

I typed a forum entry, asking—innocently, I hoped—if anyone had tried syrup of ipecac as an appetite suppressant. Just as I hit Enter, a racket rose from the street in front of my house. Brakes squealed, followed by a loud crash, the sound of breaking glass, and then more squealing brakes and the fast rev of an engine.

I ran out the side gate and down the driveway to the street. Broken glass was scattered on the pavement. My across-the-street neighbor, Cecilia Ann Potts, ran out of her house at the same time. Her husband, Harold, came down the driveway, shaking his head.

"Kids," he said, narrowing his eyes. "Probably from the university. Little hellions." His mouth always seemed permanently turned downward at the corners anyway, and now he looked even more disgusted. "But I got a partial plate."

"Did you see what happened?" I asked.

"Hit-and-run," he said. "Probably didn't have insurance."

Cecilia Ann frowned. "I swear one of the cars has been up and down the street before. More than once, and slowing right about here where the accident happened. Right in front of my house."

Or mine.

Just then a strange whistling sound came out of my mailbox, a beautiful miniature Victorian house on a pole at the end of my driveway.

"Take cover!" Harold grabbed his wife and dived to the ground.

A bright flash of light shot up from somewhere near my house, followed by a loud boom and orange billowing smoke. Heart pounding, I threw myself to the ground as a ball of orange-black smoke rose into the morning sky.

Another loud boom shook the ground a nanosecond later. Followed by more smoke. I shaded my eyes and looked up in time to see a sky full of splinters and chunks and flames that seemed to float for a moment before raining down again.

A wall of flames stood between the street and my house.

Chloe Grace!

I felt dizzy from the blast, my limbs too weak to be of any use. But I had to get to my granddaughter.

I half limped, half crawled to my driveway, unable to see through the heavy smoke and the orange glow beyond it. I couldn't see through the flames—or what was in flames. My house?

The fear that sliced through my heart was as searing as the flames. I doubled over, unable to go on.

Then I remembered. Again. A child, a little girl inside a house, screaming, flames licking higher and higher. I was the little girl. No. Not me. Chloe Grace. Inside. Sleeping.

My knees were ready to give out, but I kept moving forward. Someone grabbed me from behind. Harold? Another neighbor? Trapped me in steel-banded arms. Wouldn't let me go where I needed to go.

I thought I heard crying. "Chloe Grace!"

At once, my arms turned into windmills. My tennies grabbed hold of the pavement. I kicked and fought. Broke loose and ran with strength I didn't know I had. Straight into the heavy smoke.

I kept running. Coughing. Eyes stinging. Tears streaming. Couldn't catch a breath.

Then, through the smoke my front door became visible. I ran for it. Locked.

Shrieks from somewhere above me. "Gramsy! Gramsy!"

I flew to the kitchen door, and threw it open. Smoke filled the rooms downstairs, but no flames. I flew up the stairs, and into the guest room.

Chloe Grace sat on the edge of her bed, holding the ballerina sock monkey. She smiled up at me, her cheeks still wet with tears. "I knew you'd come get me. I told Pumpkin you'd be here soon."

I hugged her tight and gathered her into my arms. She was still light enough to carry, thank heavens. I made my way downstairs with Chloe Grace and the ballerina monkey in my arms.

The smoke began to clear, and I could see the damage had been contained to the front of the property. My mailbox had been blown to smithereens, a nearby rose arbor destroyed, and a favorite ancient dogwood partially burnt.

The main house hadn't been touched.

I stood by the gate, waiting for my knees to stop shaking, and assessed the damage. That was a close call. Chloe Grace slipped out of my arms and stood beside me, holding my hand. With wide eyes, she said, "What happened to the mailbox?"

"It caught fire," I said shakily.

Fire trucks had arrived while I was in the house, and now the firemen were all over my property, searching for anything suspicious. A sheriff's deputy questioned Harold and Cecilia Ann from across the street. Judging from their animated gestures and what I knew of

Cecilia Ann's propensity for making a good story better, there was no telling what version authorities would end up with.

I hadn't moved from my place by the gate when Max drove slowly past in the Defender, did a one-eighty and then parked across the street.

When he exited the vehicle, his face was pale. He spotted me and ran toward us without hesitation, giving Chloe and me a giant bear hug.

I thought my knees would give out before he let us go. I had forgotten the feel of masculine arms wrapped around me, especially those of someone you cared about and who cared about you. Somewhere deep inside, I'd ached for such a moment. I just didn't know it until now. My eyes watered and my throat stung, but Max's hug made me think it wasn't so much from the smoke as being gathered into his arms.

He stepped back and put his hands on my shoulders, studying my face as if to make sure I really was unharmed. "I heard the sirens, saw smoke from the interstate, and then when I got closer"—he swallowed hard and then shook his head slowly—"I thought the worst. But you're okay?"

I nodded.

"My monkey was just a little scared," Chloe Grace said, still clinging to my hand. "But I wasn't."

Max ruffled her hair. "I think I would have been." He looked around. "That must have been a pretty big boom."

She nodded solemnly. "It was. It shook my bed and woke me up."

Just then, a young teen with red hair and freckles trotted up the driveway and headed toward me. He held an envelope in his hands. "I found this in the street just now," he said. "Are you Mrs. Littlefield?"

"I am."

He thrust it into my hands and took off back down the street.

My name was typed on the outside of the envelope and it was sealed with wax. I ripped open the seal, pulled out a single sheet of paper, and unfolded it.

Typed on an old typewriter, the message read:

> You are playing with fire. Already it turns on
> you. Taste it. Smell it. Know it will return. Not
> in your nightmares, but in living flame, a wild
> beast to devour you and those you love.

My knees threatened to buckle, and I reached for Max, who put his arm around me as he read. He became more disturbed with each line. Beside me, Chloe Grace danced with ballerina monkey, singing "This Little Light of Mine."

The monster who wrote this knew my weakness, my fear of fire. He had put it together with my love for my granddaughter, creating a powerful weapon to use against me.

How could this monster know such intimate details of my childhood, my life?

~~~

An hour later, I dropped a very chatty Chloe Grace by her mother's preschool, then stopped by the sheriff's office. I didn't wait for the dispatcher to inform him that I had arrived. As soon as she unlocked the door from inside, I sailed past her station and through the rabbit warren of cubicles.

When I reached the sheriff's door, I knocked lightly, and in a rather bold move (if I do say so myself), I stepped in without waiting for his invitation. Mercy me, he could have been in conference with the governor.

He looked up from his paperwork.

I handed him the note I'd received, which I'd placed in a large ziplock bag.

He scanned it and then looked up at me. "Are you taking the threat seriously?"

"After what happened to my property today, yes, I am."

He placed the letter on his desk. "We'll send it over to forensics, see what comes up. Maybe we'll get lucky and find some prints." He removed his eyeglasses and rubbed his eyes, and then pinched the skin above the bridge of his nose. "I think you ought to back off," he said, putting his glasses back on. "This is a threat that someone means to carry out. Let us do our jobs."

I counted backward from ten, taking a calming breath or two as I did so. "This is personal. More now than before. My catering company may go under because of the sabotage meted out on me." I could feel my face getting red. "My best friend has been kidnapped—"

He held up a hand. "Now, now. Let's not go there again."

I was on a roll, and I barreled on. "My best friend was kidnapped. My property has been damaged with a sophisticated explosive and fire." I leaned forward. "And worst of all, whoever did this endangered the life of my granddaughter."

I stood up, placed my palms on the edge of his desk, and with elbows unbent, I leaned forward, close enough for my breath to fog his glasses. "And what have you and your staff done in the past three days to catch the thugs behind all this? How close to cracking the case are you? What forensic evidence have you brought in? Does anyone think that what happened at my house today might be connected to the poisoning at the university, the death of the university president, the disappearance of a world treasure—*and* the disappearance of Hyacinth Gilvertin?"

"I'll get someone out there to investigate," he said.

I pulled a plastic sandwich baggie from my handbag, placed it in front of him, and settled back into my chair. "No need," I said. "I collected this in and around the trigger point. Inside the bag you'll find a piece of red cardboard, two end caps, and some pieces of plaster. That tells us that the explosive that was placed in my mailbox was an M-80."

"Military grade." He looked up at me with new respect. If I hadn't been so tired and more than a little annoyed, I would have appreciated his expression.

"From the debris, I could tell more than one explosive was used. The explosion was a thousand times greater than you might get on the Fourth of July with an old-fashioned cherry bomb."

I let the information sink in and then stood and girded up my loins, so to speak. I'd never before been quite this bold with law enforcement officials, but this time I'd been pushed too far.

"This case is getting more complicated by the minute. If we leave it to the 'professionals' to solve, it will soon be a cold-case file stuck in a box in the basement. So far the only hypothesis I've heard is that

Hyacinth Gilvertin is somehow connected, as if it were an inside job and she's to blame. As if that explains the whole thing." I narrowed my eyes. "And if you think that could be the case, why aren't you out there looking for her?"

I didn't give the sheriff a chance to answer but spun and headed to the door, my spine as straight as a billiards cue.

I crawled into the Ghia and slumped in front of the steering wheel. I'd never carried on like that with a law enforcement officer, especially not the county sheriff himself, for heaven's sake.

Maybe it was because I'd never had a case like this before, a case with so much at stake for me. It seemed that since Friday morning, troubles had piled upon troubles. It seemed as though I would follow one lead, only to be distracted by another, and then the same thing would happen all over again. Each led to more information, but not to anything of substance. Not to a solution.

I went over what I knew for certain: We had an eyewitness who said Hyacinth had jumped voluntarily into the ambulance with the thieves. We knew she had been at the site where the ambulance and cabin burned. In my opinion, evidence showed that she may have set the fire to draw the attention of nearby Waynesville. We knew from an eyewitness that she had been left in the middle of nowhere by the thugs who were last known to be driving a rental truck, and that she was last seen trying to catch up with them on a bicycle.

I also surmised that unless they had stopped for the night some-where nearby, she had no chance of catching them.

How was the fire at my house connected? Someone had been watching me and had planted the explosive.

But who?

As soon as I arrived home from the sheriff's office, I turned on my computer and picked up where I left off in my search for illegal sources of ipecac.

I clicked through sites on anorexia, bulimia, and other eating disorders, and in the course of my research I happened upon the word *purge*. That's what I wished I could do now with all the accusations and bad news about The Butler Did It and me: purge.

There had to have been a grand mistake somewhere in the universe. Maybe my guardian angel was busy with other folks. Or got bored with my life. Until now, it truly hadn't been very exciting. No romance. No cases taken on that would give me nightmares. No threats of arrest. No one telling me I might be guilty of manslaughter.

I thought most folks liked me, or at least didn't dislike me enough to want me imprisoned. Or tarred and feathered.

Now, I'm told the people in town practically think I'm the sum of all evils. Things really couldn't get worse.

I thought about that for a minute, then sat back and chuckled. "Well, this is a fine fix I've gotten myself in," I said to God. "I think I need to say more than 'help,' if You know what I mean. And I believe You do. I need to tell You that I'm royally ticked off. I just need to get that off my chest. Purge, if You will.

"You know my thoughts before I even think them, as it says in the Psalms. So I don't need to rehash what I've been thinking or how I feel. You know, but enough already. Help!"

I found an ipecac dealer ten minutes later. Maybe my angel figured that what I was up to now warranted at least a flyby.

The kids in the chat room seemed eager to help me find the drug and a dealer they said was cool. Someone with the sign-in handle *skinny_minnie* wished me well, and said to drop in later and tell them all how it went. No one asked why I needed the drug. No one asked about my health. I saw at least a dozen names in the forum.

Someone really should monitor these sites, in my humble opinion. A nurse maybe, or some other medical person. Or a psychologist, for heaven's sake. Or maybe an adult who cares and can tell these people that self-image has nothing to do with size.

Mostly I was mad at those who bombard kids with images of perfect bodies and glowing skin. Most little girls want to grow up and look like Barbie. I'd rather they'd look up to women of substance, women like Helen Keller, Eleanor Roosevelt, Amelia Earhart, or Marie Curie. Or Mother Teresa, for the love of God. But then, maybe I'm just old-fashioned.

I huffed out a sigh and made the call. For some unknown reason, my voice dropped to a whisper when I spoke to him.

"Hello?" I said when he picked up.

"Yes?"

"I want to buy some ipecac—in liquid concentrate form. What sizes do you have?" So far, so good for someone who'd never before talked to a drug dealer. "What are the prices? And how soon can you deliver?"

He chuckled. "I don't deliver. You need to come to the meeting place at the time I give you. You'll find an empty cardboard box by the trash bin where you'll put your envelope of cash. Close the lid, walk into the campus bookstore, and browse for ten minutes. Or hit the café for a cup of coffee. Your choice. Just make sure you are gone no longer than ten minutes."

"That's it?"

"Did you expect something different?"

"It's just so easy. Who is your supplier?"

"What does it matter?"

Uh-oh. I worried he'd made me, if that's what it's called. "Purity," I said. "I want to know the percentage of ipecac to binding liquid." I'd done my homework and was talkin' the talk. I hoped.

"It's good stuff. You lookin' to sell?"

"I don't have to say, do I?"

"My price is different for dealers."

"Oh. Hmm. Well, let me see. First I want to know more about you. Who do you buy from?"

"This game is over."

"Wait," I said. "Please. I need the stuff. No more questions, I promise."

"You sound … older. Why do you need it?"

"No more questions," I threw back at him. I sounded 'older'? Maybe because of the whisper. I forced my voice to get a bit louder.

"How much can I buy at one time?" I'd already calculated how much ipecac would be required to poison three hundred people.

He laughed. "How many people you gonna treat?"

"A couple hundred. Maybe more."

He disappeared from the phone for a few minutes. I almost ended the call. "I've got it for you." He gave me the number of pounds I'd need, and what the price would be, including a discount for a first-time buyer.

That much ipecac would not be cheap. That narrowed the field. My brain went into a tailspin as I went over the suspects. A student wouldn't have that kind of cash available. Maybe a group, if they pooled their funds.

He interrupted my thoughts. "So do we have a deal?"

"Yes, we do," I said. "I'll need to stop by the bank first. You can't get that kind of money out of an ATM."

He laughed. "True. Remember, cash only, all twenties. I'll see you in a half hour."

That didn't give me much time for the setup. "I understand."

We ended the call. I punched in Max's number and told him the arrangements. "Does this give you enough time?"

"I'll leave right now. You won't know I'm there."

"Neither will he, I hope," I said.

On the way to the bank, a warning flare went up in my brain. Was it really this easy for someone to buy enough ipecac to poison a room full of people? I had a hard time believing it.

I went in the bank and withdrew what I needed, then stuffed the twenties in an envelope. I was counting on the fact that I'd somehow pull this off and my money would be returned.

I pulled into the student parking lot near the café a few minutes early. I looked around for Max, but didn't see him or the Defender. Maybe he had parked in the faculty lot.

I stared at my phone, watching the minutes march by. Right on schedule I got out of my car, and as casually as I could, walked to the back of the building that housed the bookstore and café.

I spotted the garbage bin and next to it the box, sidled over to it, and dropped in my envelope. A lid lay nearby, and I stooped to pick it up and place it on the box. Then I casually walked back to the front of the building and entered the student bookstore. Several students and a few faculty members milled about. Two women I recognized and counted as friends looked up. I started to wave, but they turned their backs. I swallowed hard and pretended I didn't notice. Or the whispers and snickers that followed. I told myself it didn't matter. I was working undercover anyway.

I went over to the greeting-card section, straight to a humorous brand I liked. They reminded me of Hyacinth, which brought the threat of tears again.

Ten minutes passed and I hurried to the door, exited, and trotted to the box by the Dumpster. Stooping, I opened it. My envelope was gone, and in its place were stacked several Mason jars filled with liquid.

I picked up the box, which was heavier than I expected. This drug-buying business was not for the faint of heart. Struggling with my awkward burden, I slowly made my way back to the Ghia.

Standing beside my car were Sheriff Doyle and Chance Noseworthy.

Chapter Twenty-seven
Mrs. Littlefield

· · · · · · · · · · · · · · · ·

Chance Noseworthy adopted an arrogant pose next to the sheriff's SUV, sniffed, and shot me an "I told you so" look.

The sheriff just seemed annoyed as he opened the back door of his vehicle and gestured for me to get in. He hefted himself up and sat beside me. "This is serious. Intent to buy an illegal substance." His tone was low, maybe because he didn't want Noseworthy to overhear.

"You've been itching to arrest me since Friday," I said. "So, go ahead."

"I suppose you have an explanation."

"I'm following the trail of the real perpetrator"—I thought about adding *duh* but restrained myself—"to find out who sold the drug and then trace it back to its source." I looked around. "By the way, did you see Dr. Haverhill?"

"Dr. Haverhill was in on this?"

"Yes. Max is my lookout." Speaking his name calmed something inside me. It was a strange feeling, one I didn't remember experiencing before. It made me want to say it again. "Max is around here somewhere." *Max*.

Sheriff Doyle took off his glasses and cleaned them. "He'll vouch for you?"

I sat forward, more than a little annoyed. "Sheriff, enough of this game playing. You know me better than that. What's with all this tough-guy cop nonsense?" Good heavens, I was getting brave. Until recently, I'd never been so bold when voicing my opinions. Maybe that's what love does to a person. Love? I felt my cheeks warm. Love? I'd known Max for only a few days. What was I thinking?

And then Max strode across the parking lot toward us. The tiniest bit of fear seeped into my heart, surprising me. And so soon after all those lovely romantic thoughts.

I was beginning to lose myself in his presence. Wanting to hear the sound of his voice, his laugh, to get lost in his gaze … Wait, maybe that was where the fear came from: losing myself in someone else after all these years of independence.

No matter the cause, my stomach did jumping jacks as he approached.

Max arrived at the vehicle on the driver's side next to the sheriff. He smiled, met my eyes, then winked. My stars and garters, the famous Dr. Maxwell winked. At me. I felt like fanning my face, but thought I might look too much like a Scarlet O'Hara wannabe.

I turned to the sheriff. "Are we through here?"

"Not quite, little lady," he said.

I narrowed my gaze and squared my shoulders. "I'm no little lady." I moved toward the door on my side to get out of the SUV.

That term had long secured a place in my top-ten list of least favorite things people say and do, right up there with air quotes. I didn't wait for an apology. I grabbed the handle above the door and swung out—unfortunately forgetting to account for my short stature, and landed with a thump. I pretended not to notice and stomped over to the Ghia.

"And don't forget my reimbursement for the drug sale," I called to him before sliding behind the steering wheel. "And I prefer a check to a fistful of twenties."

I didn't care if the sheriff sent a deputy to my house to read me my rights. I just hoped Max would follow me home.

Once home, I watched for him by the dining room window for several minutes, then turned away, feeling strangely bereft. Perhaps I'd set my hopes too high.

I walked back to my office in the potting shed. When I powered up the laptop, it opened the last site I'd visited, the chat room on ipecac. Elbows on the desk, I propped my chin in my hands, staring at the screen.

My thoughts went again to Hyacinth. Because we'd grown up together, we were as close as sisters, and I missed her. Several times over the past few days, I'd actually caught myself reaching for the phone to tell her all about what was going on in my life—just as we always did.

Memories of our childhood would flood my heart if I allowed them to. And now, more than ever, I needed clear focus.

I reached for the list I'd put together Saturday night and checked to see if anything I'd looked into had actually paid off. Too many dead ends, and yet I still felt they were all somehow connected.

I still hadn't called Silas Sutherland to set up a meeting with the owner of the cabin that burned. No time like the present. I pulled out my cell phone and tapped in the number I'd memorized from his billboard ad.

A receptionist answered and then connected me to his office. Put on hold, I was forced to listen to spa music punctuated by static. Just when I thought I couldn't take another Indian flute trill, Sutherland's executive assistant picked up.

"Thank you for calling Silas Properties. This is Darla speaking. How may I help you?"

I told her I wanted to make an appointment to see Mr. Sutherland, the sooner the better.

"May I ask what this is regarding?"

"Real estate."

"You've come to the right place." She sounded like a mechanical doll. "Let me see …" A few clicks of a mouse came from her end. "He will be out of the office all next week. I don't see an opening until the week after. How will that work for you?"

"It won't. This is an urgent matter. Does he have any time this afternoon?"

A short laugh erupted from the young woman. Obviously, getting in to see Silas Sutherland was akin to making an appointment to see the pope. "I'm sorry. Mr. Sutherland is a very busy executive."

"I'm sure he is. We are all very busy and put a high value on our time, don't you agree?"

"Yes, of course." She heaved a sigh, and I pictured her rolling her eyes. "May I ask your name and what this is regarding?"

I gave her my name and then added, "I'm interested in a real estate transaction." I wouldn't get past the front door if I mentioned that I also wanted to find out about the money due me from the university.

"You said that it's urgent. Let me see what I can arrange. May I place you on hold?"

"Yes, I'll wait."

Flute music and static made my ears ring. I put the phone on speaker mode and placed it on the desk.

"Good news," Darla said when she came back on the line a short time later. "He says he'd like to talk with you. He has a few minutes between clients. If you could give me your phone number, he'll return your call."

"How about a Skype call?" I blurted without thinking. I wanted to see his face—especially his reaction to my questions.

"So you do Skype?"

I didn't know one "did" Skype. Rather, it seemed to me something one would use. "Yes," I said.

"He can speak to you in ten minutes."

"Yes, all right, that will be fine," I said. I gave Darla my Skype account info.

"Great. Get set up and I'll connect you when Mr. Sutherland is ready."

Holy cannoli, what had I just suggested? I'd never "done" Skype before. Katie had showed me once how to turn on the camera and make the call, but when I saw how washed out and grim I appeared in the reverse shot, I vowed it was one piece of technology I would never use.

This was terrible. I ran back into the house, sprinted up the stairs and into the master bedroom. I quickly changed to a colorful floaty top that reminded me of Hyacinth. In fact, she'd given it to me on my last birthday. I ran to the dressing room, put on a dab of mascara and a swipe of pink lip gloss, and fluffed my hair. With a last look in the mirror, I pinched my cheeks.

Nine minutes later, I was seated in my chair behind my desk, computer open to Skype, hands calmly folded in front of me. I checked my appearance on my webcam and adjusted the lighting accordingly.

A minute later a new video call came through, and I accepted the call. Immediately, a well-appointed office appeared on my screen. My focus went from the expected masculine executive furniture to a large framed print depicting Saint George slaying the dragon. Interesting choice.

Sutherland sat down in front of his computer a moment later, obscuring my view of the print. Holy cannoli. I caught a glimpse of something else: a framed photo that sat on the corner of his desk, just beyond the frame of the camera.

I squinted, trying to focus on it. The people in it looked familiar, but oddly out of place. Then I remembered I was on Skype and Silas Sutherland had a great view of my puzzled squint. I plastered on a wide-eyed friendly look.

"Mrs. Littlefield, it's a delight to see you again."

"Hello, Mr. Sutherland. Good of you to work me into your schedule."

"What can I do for you?"

Relax. Smile. Breathe. I sat back and folded my hands. "I'm looking into some property near Waynesville, and I want to find out its value." I remembered to smile. "You were the first realtor that came to mind."

"Are you looking to buy?"

"Actually, I'm conducting some research."

"You're on a case, then."

I laughed. "You caught me. Although it might be crazy after everything that's happened since Friday."

He nodded. "Not a good night to remember. What's the address of the property?"

I studied his expression as I gave him the address, looking for any reaction to the address. If he or his godsons were in any way connected to the heist, he didn't show it. He typed in the address and tapped a few keys.

"Here it is," he said a moment later. "Josiah Meyer is the name on the original deed, dated 1883. It was passed along to male heirs for two generations. The current owner is ..." He squinted at the screen. "That's odd. The name is blacked out." He tapped on his keyboard as he spoke. "I'm looking on other sites, county and state, and then back at a central database. It's blocked on every site. Very odd indeed." He turned back to me. "What is your exact interest in this property?"

"The owner may be involved in the crimes committed Friday night." I gave him the details, watching his expression change. The muscles in his jaw tightened visibly, and he pressed his lips into a straight line.

When I finished, he said, "I will look into the current owner's status and get back to you." He stood abruptly, leaving me again with the image of Saint George slaying the dragon … and the two young men in the photograph taken at what appeared to be a graduation ceremony. Then the screen went dark.

I closed my laptop. The legend of Saint George was one of heroism and sacrifice, with the dragon representing Satan. Why would it appeal to a man like Silas Sutherland, godfather to two redneck yahoos? Or had it been chosen because the colors matched his furniture?

What about the two young men in the photo—who I now knew were Bubba and Junior, looking nothing like rednecks? What was their game?

I was still pondering the blocked-out property owner's name, the framed print on the wall, and the strange photo of his godsons, when I remembered I'd forgotten to ask about reimbursement for Friday night. My stomach twisted again at the thought of losing The Butler Did It. I blinked rapidly and swallowed hard. How could I have let this opportunity slide by when I was about to lose everything?

Chapter Twenty-eight
The Professor

. . . .

After El stormed off and the sheriff and Noseworthy drove away, Max sat in his car in the parking lot, contemplating his vow of peace and goodwill versus the anger he felt at the town's treatment of El.

Following in the footsteps of Francis and patterning his life after that of Christ wasn't always easy. Make that never easy. It helped to remember Jesus's anger over the moneychangers in the temple. He breathed deeply and unclenched his hands.

He couldn't get El off his mind as he drove home. She was all he could think about as he knelt in his garden and plucked a few weeds. Things were moving too fast, and his emotions were becoming involved. In three days, he'd gone from not knowing El at all to thinking about her constantly.

Could it be possible that she shared his feelings? They had exchanged looks that made his stomach do flip-flops, and his heart raced each time he touched her. But they had never discussed such things.

He rocked back on his heels and focused on the row of radishes, considering his dilemma. He longed to hear the velvet sound of her voice. He longed to see her. Be near her. Take her in his arms. He brushed off his hands and stood, feeling like a shy schoolboy.

He needed to get out of his fantasy world and back to the real one. The world where he was desperate to find the figurehead, where he was desperate to help El find Hyacinth, where he was not spending hours daydreaming. His feelings were distracting him, and he needed to get over them.

Yeah, right. He almost chuckled. *Nice try, buddy.*

He went inside and changed into his jogging clothes, immediately thinking that he had been with El the last time he wore them. Stuff and nonsense! He took off at a trot toward University Square, glad for the sunny day with relatively low humidity.

His church, Grace Episcopal, was coming up on the right. The rector, his friend Father Rob, stood in front, watering some droopy looking plants. He looked up and waved.

Max grinned and headed over to chat. "Don't tell me you're taking up gardening too." Grace was such a small parish that Father Rob often filled several roles. He'd been known to fill in at the piano, though he preferred to play jazz, which breathed new life into some of the church's venerable old hymns. Of course, it also brought consternation to some of the older parishioners.

Father Rob laughed. "One never knows what God will put in His children's paths to teach them patience. The sprinkler system is on the fritz. Stopped working the minute the temperature began to climb, wouldn't you know." He aimed the hose at some rosebushes in a flower bed to the left of the entrance.

"I've been meaning to stop by and talk. An issue has come up recently …"

Father Rob studied Max. "It sounds serious."

"It is." Max took a deep breath, thinking of El. How could he explain all that she had come to mean to him in just a few short days? Finally, he said, "I think I'm falling in love."

Father Rob raised his eyebrows and smiled. "That's wonderful."

"It is, but also confusing at my age."

The rector smiled. "Do you want to talk about it?"

Max shook his head and glanced at his watch. "Thanks. I can't right now, but maybe another time."

"Anytime you want to talk, you know where to find me."

They shook hands again, and Max continued his jog. It was time to say more to his Friend than *Thanks* or *Help*. He didn't need words during times like these. He let the utterances of his heart speak for him. He jogged the circumference of the university and beyond and finally turned toward home, his heart full of new resolve.

He jogged into his kitchen, grabbed his phone, pressed the speed-dial key he'd just this morning set up, and waited for her to answer.

"I'm so glad you called." Her voice held a note of joy, and his stomach did another of those flip-flops.

"I am too," he said. "We need to talk …"

"I agree."

"I don't know if you're feeling anything like I am."

"I am," she said. *Glory of all glories!* "It's overwhelming."

"I've never felt like this before," he said.

"Neither have I." Then she added with a little laugh, "At least not for a long, long time. Wouldn't it be better to talk to each other face-to-face?"

He laughed with her. "I'll be right over."

"I can't wait to see you," she said, sounding breathless.

Max sprinted out the door and was halfway to the Defender before they ended the call.

El was waiting for him on her porch, looking fresh and beautiful, a breeze ruffling her hair.

Her expression warmed him to his toes. He opened his arms as he walked toward her. She quickened her steps, almost running as she closed the distance between them. He thought he might melt right then and there. He'd never in his life had anyone run toward him with such abandon.

He drew her close, and she wrapped her arms around his neck. "Oh my," she said as she leaned against his chest. "This is nice, isn't it?" She smelled of violets and jasmine.

"Yes, oh yes, it is," he whispered. He stepped back, touched her cheeks with his fingertips, and then, gently holding her face, he kissed her.

Chapter Twenty-nine
Mrs. Littlefield

. . . .

Max and I put together a wonderful meal that night using whatever we could find in the fridge. Being a confirmed foodie, I always keep a nice selection of interesting tidbits of this and that. My frequent trips to the farmers' market and specialty shops kept my larder quite nicely stocked.

I stood back, unable to stop smiling as I watched Max's reaction to the treasures he found: jars of homemade jam, packages of prosciutto, English cheddar with dried apricots, another with caramelized onions, dried fruit, a carton of hummus, a tube of ready-to-bake phyllo dough. His sighs and utterances of appreciation were music to my ears. I was grateful the man I was falling in love with didn't eat only meat and potatoes.

Falling in love? I let the words flow through my mind like beautiful music.

He pulled out his favorites, I added a few of mine, and we put together a cheese-and-fruit tray, a basket of petite french rolls and crackers, some jams and jellies and specialty mustards, a bottle of

Gewürztraminer, and a bottle of sparkling water. I spread a table-cloth on the floor in front of the fireplace, and Max brought in two plates, the flatware, napkins, and stemware. We made a few more trips to the kitchen for the food and wine, which we placed on the nearby coffee table, and then I lit the fireplace candles and dimmed the lights.

I tried to settle gracefully onto the floor, wishing I'd somehow worked yoga into my schedule during the past year. The creak of my knee joints sounded anything but romantic as I eased myself down. The only consolation was that Max's knees popped and cracked even louder than mine. We looked at each other and laughed.

"Maybe this wasn't such a good idea," I said.

He laughed and opened the wine. "It's romantic. That's what counts." His eyes caught the candlelight as he handed me a wine glass.

The candlelight, the picnic, my dancing heart … and a queasy stomach. This was wrong. A celebration? How could I think of such a thing? My thoughts flew to Hyacinth, and I set my glass on the nearby coffee table.

Max seemed to study me for a moment. "You need this, El," he said softly as he poured his own glass. "You need another few hours of soul rest. Please, don't feel guilty."

I blinked rapidly and bit my bottom lip. His words touched me. He obviously understood me. The strange fear that had troubled my heart earlier faded as I allowed myself to be drawn into the warmth of his expression.

I let out a cleansing breath. "I can't help wondering where Hyacinth is tonight and whether she's safe."

He reached for my hand and said the best thing possible: "I have a new plan for finding her."

I sat up straighter, ignoring the ache in my lower back from my attempt to find a floor-friendly, dainty-looking position. "What is it?"

"Let's get together an army of kids—maybe from culinary arts, your crew kids …"

"We can ask Enrique and his friends." I leaned forward and chose a cracker from the basket. "He's a planner. He'd be a good one to put in charge."

Max nodded as he reached for a cluster of red grapes. "I know a printer that's open twenty-four hours. If we got something designed tonight, we could hand them out—"

"—tomorrow at a meeting place." Land sakes, we were already finishing each other's sentences. "Maybe the parking lot by the Encore. They can fan out, cover all the main roads, and keep watch for the rental truck."

I was so taken with the idea, I stood quite suddenly, wobbled a bit, and then grabbed the hand that Max extended. "I'll call Enrique to get the ball rolling." I shot him a smile and headed to the kitchen for my phone. I got as far as the dining room and turned to him. "You know what? You're a genius."

"It's still a gamble, a needle in a haystack," he warned.

Even so, I was cheered by the prospect. "But it's a needle worth looking for," I called from the kitchen.

When I finished filling Enrique in on the plan, I came back to our picnic spread, tried out a yoga move I remembered from an infomercial, and dropped to the floor with a minimum of fuss. I picked up some walnuts and dried apricots, nibbled a few, and then took a sip of sparkling water, watching Max over the rim.

"Think about this, though," I said. "The good folks of Eden's Bridge are ready to run me out of town on a rail. There's no way they'll be willing to help if they find out Typhoid Mary is involved with getting our 'army' together." I sipped my water again.

He threw back his head and laughed. "You underestimate our town. Those few bad apples who've slandered you are in the minority. I think we'll have as many as we need. No more. No less."

When we finished eating, Max put away our picnic things while I retrieved my laptop from my office and placed it on the kitchen table. We brainstormed the flyer content and finally settled with:

Phone one of the numbers below if you spot a
Coast to Coast truck with an exterior picture
of Yosemite or another National Park.
Do not contact the people in vehicle if you
see them. Do not let them see you.
Cooperate fully with law
enforcement if confronted.
Contact phone numbers: (Sheriff's office,
Enrique's cell, and both of ours)

I chose a large, easy-to-read font and typed in the information. I searched my laptop's photo folder for the right shot of Hyacinth, cropped it, and dropped it into the top right-hand corner of the sheet. I stared at her beaming face, remembering that I'd taken the picture last Christmas. Before cropping, Hyacinth was pictured with Katie and Chloe Grace on either side of her. Katie had just given Cinth her bangle bracelet and, with arms wrapped around each other, all three wore smiles as bright as the Christmas lights behind them. I closed my eyes for a moment, whispered a prayer, and then tapped the Print button to send the document to my wireless printer.

Chapter Thirty
Mrs. Littlefield

. . . .

Before sunrise the next morning, I headed to the Encore parking lot, the meeting place for the group of volunteers. I'd hoped for a dozen, or two dozen at the most, but when I turned onto University Avenue, I slowed the Ghia and gaped. The lot was filled to overflowing.

Some two hundred motorcycles and twice as many other vehicles revved, idled, or rumbled their engines. The cacophony was the sweetest music I'd ever heard. I pulled over to watch the action in the predawn light. Enrique and the other volunteers threaded their way through the vehicles, handing out stacks of flyers that seemed to multiply like loaves and fishes as they were passed along.

I spotted Max halfway up the stairway of the Encore. He had the rapt attention of a dozen or more helmeted cyclists. It struck me that he might have started a phone tree of his own after he left my house. The thought warmed me to my toes.

After a few more minutes, the group dispersed, a veritable caravan winding along University Avenue. Each carried a map with a marked section assigned to him or her, and the plan was to fan out when they reached the interstate, keeping in touch via cell phone. As they drove by, I noticed some had tied fuchsia kerchiefs to their antennas—Hyacinth's favorite color. Many of the volunteers were university students or alumni who likely remembered her with warm thoughts.

She would have loved this. Deciding to come down on the side of hope today, I shot a video with my phone to show her later. The sight I'd just beheld—and this parade in her honor—called for it.

Just as the taillights of the last vehicle faded into the distance, Max spotted me and crossed the street. "How do you like them apples?" he said, his grin stretching nearly to his ears.

"You've gone Southern on me." I laughed. "And I like them apples very much, thank you very much." I didn't want to consider that we were still looking for a needle in a haystack.

❧ ❧

As volunteers in our own impromptu army, Max and I headed for the interstate toward Possum Grove. Our earlier plans to go there had been interrupted by the mailbox explosion.

As soon as I revved the engine and started up the incline to get on the interstate, the traffic came to a dead stop.

I glanced across at Max. The night before, he'd read me the letter from William MacDonald to his father, and we'd talked about where it might lead us. "Any more thoughts about your dad's letter?"

He chuckled. "I did another search online last night, and tried some ancestry sites and census bureau lists. Nothing popped up."

Then he narrowed his eyes in thought. "If my father is wrong and William MacDonald was a survivor, it follows that he or his descendant might have been searching for the figurehead all these years."

"Or," I added, "if your father is right, could this William MacDonald have been a cover for someone else?"

"You mean the Nazis—if they got someone in the French Resistance to confess?"

"I can see how that might account for the international interest. It's also a strong motive all wrapped up in a nice not-so-small package."

The traffic moved forward a few feet and then came to a dead stop again. The foot I used for the clutch was going numb.

My cell phone rang, and since the traffic was at a standstill, I picked up. Enrique's excitement caused him to use a mix of Spanish and English.

"Whoa, slow down. I can't understand you."

Max met my gaze and leaned over so he could hear. I pulled the phone away from my ear and put it in speaker mode.

"Two sightings so far," Enrique shouted into the phone. "Same truck, two sightings—one by a cyclist, the other by someone on a Hog. Both saw two men in the cab. They were just getting off the Blue Ridge Parkway onto Sweeten Creek Road heading east—maybe toward Charlotte or Raleigh. I don't know yet."

"Tell them to stay on their tail, but to keep their distance. We still don't know whether that truck is the right one."

"It's Coast to Coast with Yosemite on the side."

"That's the right description, but let's wait until we know for sure."

"Better yet, I put the word out and everyone in the area is headed their way now. I'm on my way too. I can catch up with the truck in five minutes."

My hair nearly stood on end. "Enrique," I said, forcing my voice to remain calm, but of course, it didn't. "Call everyone back. If they descend on the truck, and it's really the thieves, they may figure it out and panic. Remind everyone they are to notify the sheriff. Did you call the sheriff?"

"It's too late," he shouted. "They're already on their way. And, Mrs. Littlefield, I forgot to call the sheriff." He ended the call.

I looked at Max. "They were supposed to watch and report only."

"We don't know if it's the right truck." He patted my hand, which did nothing to slow my heart rate. "Let's not worry till we know more." He raised his brows. "You want me to follow up with the sheriff?"

I let out a sigh of appreciation. "Yes, please do. He'll respond better if you contact him, I think."

The opposite side of the interstate was moving slowly, though it hadn't come to a complete stop. We crept along at a snail's pace while Max phoned the sheriff's office. Sheriff Doyle wasn't in, so he spoke with a deputy and told him the situation, including the location where the truck had been spotted.

"There's a ramp up ahead," Max said. "I say we get off and take back roads—"

"—to Blue Ridge Parkway and Sweeten Creek Road?"

He grinned. "My thoughts exactly. Plus, I'd do anything to get off the interstate right now."

"Can you see how far it is to the next off-ramp?"

He craned out the window, and I rested my clutch foot, thinking it would have been nice if Herb, God rest his soul, had considered an automatic transmission.

"No, can't even see a sign."

I made a snap decision, pressed hard on the accelerator, and signaled to get onto the right shoulder. Max held on with a white-knuckled grasp as I revved the engine, leaving a cloud of dust floating over the cars in my rearview mirror.

"Oh dear," he said quietly. "This could earn you a ticket."

I flicked on my hazard lights. "I consider this an emergency." I spotted an off-ramp a couple of miles ahead. We reached it without mishap, though Max looked pale as I zoomed off the highway.

My cell rang again. "Mrs. Littlefield," Enrique said. "They're on to us. Now they're playing cat and mouse. They've doubled back to lose us. Heading toward Interstate 40 I think. I'm following with the others and will report."

"Who's with you?"

"Some of the motorcyclists have joined in the chase."

"How many?" I felt my face grow warm.

"A couple dozen," Enrique said.

"Holy cannoli," I said, glancing at Max. "Did any of these guys consider they might be seen?"

"Maybe they want to intimidate the thieves."

"So much is at stake. If the thieves get scared, Hyacinth's life may be in danger."

"Okay, just got another report. This time from a bicyclist on Sweeten Creek Road. The truck is heading west."

"That's where we are."

"Then you're about to run into them, Mrs. Littlefield." He was again yelling into the phone. He let out a whistle.

"Enrique," I said sternly. "Tell everyone to back off. This may get dangerous."

But Enrique ended the call. I dialed him back, but the call went to voice mail. In his excitement, there was no telling what he was passing along to our "eyes on the road." I left a voice message asking him to call back. I wanted to arrange to meet him, so he could accompany us.

I headed off road toward a stand of trees. "This baby doesn't have four-wheel drive, but she's a tiger when we get in tight spots."

Max's eyebrows went up. He was doing the white-knuckle thing again.

I grinned. "These used to be called gutless wonders ... but this one isn't, at least not when I'm driving." I patted her dash. Hidden in her innards someplace was some sort of supercharger that Herb had put on her. That plus a little lift gave her the extra oomph she needed.

I had just pulled behind some spindly pines when a cloud of dust approached at a high speed a mile or so down the road. A wave of apprehension swept over me. What if it was the right truck? What if it wasn't? Should we give chase? Or should we do as we had cautioned the others, call the sheriff and report?

I grabbed my binoculars from the glove box, held them to my eyes, and then handed them to Max. "That's the right color rental," I said. "And it's got a painting of Half Dome." I moved the binocs to the license plate. N8724H. For some reason that number rang a bell.

"Wait," I shouted. "It's them; I know it is." I pounded the steering wheel. "Josie Mae relayed an odd message from Hyacinth—Nancy ate 724 hamburgers." I handed the binoculars to him. "Look at the license plate."

"How did you figure that out?"

"It's a game we played as kids. Making up weird sentences from license plates. I'd forgotten until just now. It's N8724H. Yes!" I did an air punch and then dialed the sheriff to tell him. He was out, so I left the information on his voice mail, and then I called Enrique to spread the word about the license plate.

As the truck moved closer, three motorcyclists appeared in the distance. I hoped the men in the truck were so busy worrying about the Hogs that they wouldn't look in our direction. Even a glint of sunlight on chrome might give us away.

The vehicle passed our copse of trees, soon followed by the motorcycle gang, now consisting of another half-dozen riders. They continued in the direction of Interstate 40. I waited a minute and then followed.

The traffic on the interstate going toward Eden's Bridge now moved at a nice even pace. I drove up the ramp and spotted the truck, flanked by the cyclists, about one hundred yards ahead. I threaded in and out of traffic, trying to catch them. The truck's tall profile helped me keep track of it. Not to mention the motorcycle escort.

Max picked up my phone and dialed Enrique again. This time he answered. "I don't know how you can do it," he said, "but you've got to call off the gang. Someone's going to get hurt. This isn't a game. We've now got the truck in our sight and will contact authorities."

I thanked him with an appreciative glance and then cut around an 18-wheeler. When I cut over to the rental truck, I must have alarmed the semitruck driver. He blew his air horn, long and loud.

At about the same time, the gang of motorcycles peeled off and zoomed ahead of the rental.

The Coast to Coast truck took off like a rocket.

My heart thudded wildly. Was that really the truck? Was Hyacinth inside? Was she alive and well?

I didn't want to consider anything else right now. I had to keep moving toward my number-one goal—getting to my friend.

I practically stood on the Ghia's accelerator, tires screeching as I changed lanes each time the truck attempted to lose me.

Chapter Thirty-one
Hyacinth

. . . .

Things had definitely taken a turn for the worse. Hyacinth was now handcuffed to a steel loop in the cargo space behind the window that opened into the cab. Luckily, the two thieves usually forgot to close the small sliding window, which gave her plenty of opportunity to eavesdrop on their conversations ... and to figure out what made them tick.

Lagasse was obviously in charge, with the younger and milder Child following his lead. Neither was the brightest crayon in the box, but they seemed compatible.

Her plan of action—which included getting them to understand the historic value of the figurehead and return the piece to the library—had been going well until several hours earlier when she realized her intentions had backfired.

"We'll keep it, then," Lagasse had shouted and then pounded the steering wheel. "If it's that valuable, we'll fence it ourselves and keep the proceeds. Maybe hold it hostage. I like that idea." He pounded the steering wheel harder.

"Can't do it." Child spoke with a slight lisp because of his missing front tooth. He had an especially difficult time with *s*'s. "The boss's got people who'll come after us, and make us pay. Big time. They're prob'ly already on their way. We were supposed to be in Wilmington yesterday. He's not one to mess with."

Now after arguing, exploring their options, putting in calls to folks who might fence the figurehead for them, arguing some more—and at the same time dealing by speakerphone with the boss and his growing impatience and anger—they still couldn't decide what to do.

They'd driven north on Interstate 40 as far as Possum Grove twice. Mostly, she thought, because they liked the pancakes at the Cracker Barrel. They'd started toward the coast twice, only to change their minds and turn back. Once they spent the night in the parking lot of Trinity Oaks Lutheran Home in Salisbury, because Lagasse had a contact in a biker bar across the street.

His contact never showed, so they started back to Possum Grove for breakfast. That's where they'd been this morning, when Lagasse made the decision.

"This is an impossible item to fence," he growled. "Whose idea was it to keep it anyway?" He glared at Child, who lifted his eyebrows.

"Yours, bro. I ain't takin' the credit for any of this. All we've done is make the boss mad enough to spit nails."

"We blamed the woman, the trouble we had with the fire and all, him makin' us go back and get her. He can't blame us for stuff that's not our fault, can he?"

Two hours earlier, before sunrise, the boss called. As soon as Child picked up, the boss let loose a string of expletives that carried through the truck. Apparently he'd flown into Charlotte during the night and driven from there to the meeting place. "Two hours," he said at the end of the conversation. "Be there, or you'll regret it. You know what that means."

When they reached the interstate, traffic came to a standstill, so Lagasse took an alternate route, now following directions to a new meeting place.

All was proceeding as planned until they ran into the swarm of motorcyclists.

"The boss sent 'em, I just know he did," Child said as the Hogs surrounded the truck, forcing it back to the interstate.

Hyacinth sat back and closed her eyes, feeling a headache coming on. And this one wasn't from a blow to the head. There aren't many things worse, she decided, than getting yourself kidnapped on purpose and then having the tables turned on you. It was time to implement Plan B (aka, the O. Henry story). If that didn't work, she would move on to Plan C (act like a cute grandma).

The truck jerked to the right, knocking Hyacinth off her pile of quilts.

"Whoa," Child said. "That was close. I told you. The boss sent 'em. No telling what they'll do once they catch us. Buzzin' around us like a swarm of hornets."

"You're paranoid," Lagasse said. "They're just bikers sowin' their oats. They think they're macho or somethin'. The boss didn't send 'em."

The phone rang again. "I gave you two hours, so you should've been here by now."

Lagasse and Child both started talking at once about the traffic on the interstate, getting lost near the Blue Ridge Parkway, and how they thought they were being tailed by bikers.

"Imbeciles," the boss spit. "Do what you have to do. Guard the figurehead with your life. You've got weapons. Use them. But get to our meeting place ASAP. Got it?"

Hyacinth leaned closer to the window, holding her breath. She listened to his voice, the cadence of its rise and fall. Had she heard it before? He had a Southern drawl, but something else about him chilled her to the bone. Something she recognized. But what was it?

He took a few more minutes to chew them out, then ended the call.

She laid back on the packing quilts, thinking of home, of her family—El, Katie, and Chloe Grace—of the university, of The Butler's big night. She wondered how that turned out ... her breath caught in her throat as the image of ambulances around the Encore came back to her.

The Butler's big night ... Max Haverhill and his prize. His lifetime quest rested here beside her.

It was for this piece of history—and for Max—that she'd clung to the figurehead when the thieves tried to pry her off. Her reasoning had been simple. If she stayed with the *Lady*, she wouldn't be lost. It was a lark at first; she had been living out one of her favorite short stories, "Ransom of Red Chief." But things had changed. As the thieves fell quiet, she smiled. No time like the present. *Plan B, commence ...*

Hyacinth filled her lungs with air, opened her mouth wide, and moved closer to the window. "Heavenly sunlight! Heavenly sunlight!" she sang. "Flooding my soul with glory divine; Hallelujah! I am rejoicing, singing His praises, Jesus is mine!"

In the short pause before she began the chorus, her captors groaned in unison. She made certain to use her most piercing tone on the "hallelujahs," and almost laughed as the men tried to cover their ears. When she wanted to boom, she could really boom.

Lagasse turned on the radio, found a country music station, and cranked up the volume.

Hyacinth sang louder.

Lagasse pulled over, parked, and turned around to face her. "I've got duct tape," he said. "I'm gonna use it if you don't shut your yapper. I'll put a piece right over your mouth, believe you me."

"Actually, we don't have any," Child said. "I looked for some a couple of days ago, but couldn't find it."

Lagasse sputtered as he wagged his finger in Hyacinth's face. "You stop this, you hear? You're driving me crazy."

"Singing when I was frightened is a habit I picked up as a child." She smiled sweetly. "I just happen to have a big, booming voice."

"We noticed," Child said as Lagasse pulled back onto the road.

She let them have a moment of quiet, as she hummed "His Eye Is on the Sparrow," keeping it just above a whisper for herself alone.

When they were sufficiently relaxed, she sat forward and belted out "When the Roll Is Called Up Yonder."

Both men jumped and grabbed for the radio controls. Together, they spun the volume knob to loud, as she fought to outsing someone who sounded a lot like Tammy Wynette.

Lagasse pulled over at the next gas station mini-mart. "Earplugs," he cried, as he leaped from the truck and ran inside.

Child turned to Hyacinth. "What can we do to make you stop singing?"

She opened her mouth to tell them to let her go, then thought better of it. When it came right down to it, she wanted to know where they were taking the *Lady*. She had to know. She'd come this far, why not go all the way? So she said instead, "Unlock the cuffs." At least she might have a chance to run, should the need—and opportunity—arise.

"Tell you what," he said, "think you can outsing earplugs?"

She grinned. "I can try."

"Good," he said and winked.

Winked? She sat back astonished. Maybe she would move to Plan C sooner than planned. "You have a grandma?"

"Nah, never knew her." He shrugged. "Don't have much family."

"Aunts or uncles?" Her efforts to make a connection with him were not panning out.

"There was a lady who raised me. I was a foster kid. Orphan, I guess you'd say. This lady didn't adopt me, but I wanted her to. She seemed to care. Wrote to me when I was in Afghanistan."

"Do you still see her from time to time?"

"She died while I was gone." He stared straight ahead.

"I'm sorry."

"She was old." His voice had softened. "And had bad joints. She's better off."

We fell quiet, then Child added, "Those songs you sing. I make a big deal of hatin' 'em 'cause of my partner. But this lady, her name was Pearl, she used to sing the same ones. When it's quiet, I hear you humming another one about a sparrow ... I remember Pearl singing that to me when I was real little. It was about the nicest thing I ever heard."

"What do you want me to sing when Lagasse gets back?"

He glanced back at her and tears pooled in his lower lids. "Do you know 'Peace in the Valley'? Pearl loved Elvis and sang along when she played his records."

"I know it, though I'm not so sure it's one to bellow out."

Without comment, he turned back to stare at the mini-mart Lagasse trotted toward the truck, holding up two small packages of earplugs.

Chapter Thirty-two
Mrs. Littlefield

. . . .

We'd arranged by phone when and where to pick up Enrique, but when we stopped, we nearly lost sight of the rental truck. The driver turned onto a dirt road and then took off like a bat out of the fiery furnace.

"I have seen this road before, Mrs. Littlefield," Enrique said from the backseat. "On a map. It leads to a rock quarry. It's a scary place. People have died there."

"Let's hope that's not where they're going," I said.

The truck screeched around a corner or two before practically flying through a maze of rural dirt roads. I hadn't known a rental truck could do what the driver was making it do. But I tromped on the gas and hung back just enough to keep out of sight. The low-slung hills helped. Also the abundance of roadside foliage.

"Some driving, Mrs. Littlefield," Enrique said. "See, I told you so, Dr. Haverhill. Remember that?"

It seemed like a long time ago, and it had been only last Friday.

"I do," Max said with a chuckle.

I kept pace for a while and then fell back, catching a glimpse of orange from time to time. Max sat forward in his seat, concentrating on the truck, reporting when he spotted them. The chase went on for ten minutes or so, and then we glanced at each other and grinned. It seemed the thieves didn't know they were being chased at all.

Though they were a mile or two ahead of us, when we hit the top of a rise, we saw them slow for a turn.

We followed but pulled off near the road they'd turned on and parked under the shade of a large tree draped with a fine crop of kudzu. The nondescript creamy beige of the Ghia blended into the dappled sunlight and shade. We opted to stay in the car, well hidden, I hoped.

"Well, my goodness," I said to Max. "That was a first. I've never been in a car chase before."

"I don't think the driver knew he was being chased," Enrique said. "It would have been more fun if he had." He grinned.

I handed him the binoculars. "Okay, now it's up to you to see if we've followed the right guys."

He lifted them to his eyes and found a place between the kudzu vines to peer out.

Chapter Thirty-three
Hyacinth

· · · · · · · · · · · · · · · · ·

Twice Hyacinth sang "Peace in the Valley" for Child, but she didn't bother trying to boost her volume to be heard through their earplugs. She noticed Child hadn't inserted his earplugs so she sang softly, just for him, while she aimed a little prayer at heaven.

The truck flew around the curves, picking up speed as it went. She felt motion sickness coming on. Child reached into a plastic grocery bag and pulled out some sodas and candy bars, and handed Hyacinth one of each. She sipped slowly as they wound around some low-slung mountains before coming to a stop.

She pulled herself up to her knees, and peered out as Lagasse and Child got out of the truck and started up the road toward a small farmhouse. Child carried a small nylon duffel. The meeting place, she supposed. But no other cars were around. Just fallow fields and a plethora of weeds.

The place looked abandoned. Except for Lagasse and Child. And, she presumed, their boss. What she wouldn't give to get close to the farmhouse, see who was inside.

She examined the handcuffs, and for the hundredth time, tried to figure a way to break loose. As she sipped the soda, her gaze fell on the pop-top ring. With her left hand she worked the tab loose and then measured the broken end against the keyhole in the cuff. Too wide and too short. But the metal was soft. Pliable with a tool. The only tool she had at hand? Her teeth. She could hear her mother scolding her for even thinking of such a thing.

Sorry, Mom. She squeezed the tab attached to the metal ring with her molars and felt it bending to the shape she was going for—an object just long and narrow enough to pick the lock.

It took three tries but finally, the lock clicked and she was free. She had no time to celebrate. Another vehicle approached. Drawing herself up to window level, she looked out. A black SUV with dark windows drove past the truck and parked near the farmhouse.

A man wearing a white shirt and tie stepped out on the driver's side, opened the backseat door, and grabbed his suit jacket. Shrugging it on as he walked, he rounded the back of the vehicle and then opened the door on the passenger side. He reached in and, a moment later, a woman emerged, holding his hand.

Hyacinth squinted, hoping to get a clear view of their faces, but they were deep in conversation, facing away from her. Even so, something about them struck her as familiar. It was like seeing someone you knew out of context. The couple disappeared into the farmhouse.

Seconds later, the pop of a gunshot reverberated across the field. Followed by two more.

Shocked, Hyacinth flinched and cowered closer to the floor.

Lagasse and Child raced down the dirt road and hurled themselves into the truck, Lagasse in the driver's seat.

"Move it," Child yelled, and slammed the opposite door. He flung the duffel onto the floor. "We've got to get out of here."

Lagasse cranked the engine, threw the truck in reverse, stepped on the gas, but the vehicle sputtered and stalled.

Stunned, their faces gray, they looked at each other helplessly.

"Try it again," Child yelled. "Hurry!"

"Do you have the .45?" Lagasse yelled at Child. When there was no answer, he growled, "Get it out. Now. We're gonna need it."

A .45? For self-defense? Or did the boss tell them to do her in? Hyacinth's heartbeat picked up speed. Dizziness hit, and the inside of the truck spun. She closed her eyes as fear hummed into every fiber of her body. *Oh, Lord* ... She heard the rustle of Child opening the duffel bag, followed by the cocking of the trigger. At that moment, Lagasse got the engine started.

Hyacinth breathed easier. As the truck backed down the road, she opened her eyes and rose to her knees again to peer through the sliding window.

Movement near the farmhouse caught her attention. The couple she'd seen earlier now hobbled from the porch to the car, both bent low as if injured, moving at an angle that kept their faces hidden.

Even so, the familiarity she'd noticed earlier struck her again. She was still pondering the sensation when two men emerged, scanned their surroundings, and hightailed it to the same SUV.

Hyacinth sat back in shock, then blinked to clear her vision. Surely that wasn't—? She looked at them again to be sure and then gaped as she recognized Bubba and Junior Sutherland.

She rocked back on her heels. Of course they were involved. Had to have been from the beginning. Their positions at The Butler had been a setup … by their godfather. Her eyes opened wide. Silas Sutherland. Was he the boss Child and Lagasse had been speaking with? Was he still inside the farmhouse?

Chapter Thirty-four
Mrs. Littlefield

. . . .

The rental truck had parked on a dirt road, about a half mile between us and a farmhouse. Two men got out of the rental truck, one on either side. Their backs were toward us as they walked toward the farmhouse in the distance. One was tall, the other short. I shot a glance at Enrique. He grinned, still holding the binoculars to his eyes.

"Yes, they are the same men. See the blond hair on the tall one? Sticks out even without his mask."

I didn't plan to wait. If Hyacinth was in that vehicle, I wanted to get to her now. I studied the rear of the truck, considering our options. Before I could decide, the sound of another vehicle came from behind. The car, an SUV, passed us and turned right onto the dirt driveway leading to the farmhouse.

I drew in a deep breath and turned a steady gaze on Max. "I've been so focused on Hyacinth that I almost forget you've got something of incredible value in that truck too."

"True, but not as valuable as Hyacinth." He gave me a quick hug. "And believe me, I haven't forgotten."

I got out of the car to get a better view of the SUV, pulling back a few strands of kudzu. By the time I got into position, I saw only someone's back as he or she entered the house.

"I've got to get to the truck to see if Hyacinth is in there," I said.

"I'll go with you," Max said. "We'd better get a move on while the kidnappers are inside the house."

I nodded.

"And I will have the getaway car ready," Enrique said.

I grabbed a small tool kit from the backseat, and with Max at my side, hurried toward the truck. Ducking low, we made our way to the cab on the side facing away from the farmhouse.

I reached for the door handle but halted at the sound of gunfire. So many things happened simultaneously my head could scarcely take them in: a man and woman running out of the farmhouse, Enrique backing the Ghia toward us in record time, Max catapulting me into the backseat … But one image stood out: Hyacinth. She was facing away from me when I peered in, but I'd seen her, alive and well.

We weren't out of danger yet, any of us. Even so, I couldn't stop smiling as we flew out of the driveway, rounded a corner, found another bunch of draped kudzu, and hid the Ghia once more.

We had just switched drivers and I was again behind the wheel, when the rental truck shot out of the dirt road, turning right without a glance our direction. Soon after, the SUV roared from the driveway, hesitated, and then followed the rental truck.

The truck now headed southwest, with the SUV in hot pursuit. I followed slowly to avoid being noticed, though truth be told I figured we already had been. My mind had already played out a few scenarios, the most concerning of them in which the vehicles were in cahoots and playing a game of cat and mouse with the mouse—us— bringing up the rear as they led us into a trap.

I glanced at the gas gauge and my stomach dropped. "We've got a problem," I said. "We're almost out of gas. Less than a quarter of a tank."

"Not a problem," Enrique said from the backseat. "If you can find an old car, I can siphon some out."

Except for the truck and the SUV at least a quarter mile ahead of us, the terrain seemed empty and barren. No vehicle of any kind. No farmhouses or man-made structures. The ground seemed less fertile and more rocky. I sensed we were near the rock quarry, which didn't exactly bring me comfort. I'd seen photos of the huge gaping hole in the ground, the water at the bottom so deep it made me dizzy just thinking about it. Enrique was right; it was a scary place.

I leaned back into my seat, trying to come up with a solution. Even if we could see a gas station, when we stopped we'd lose both the SUV and the truck. But running out of gas out in the middle of nowhere was not a good option. We needed to make a decision.

I met Max's gaze. He looked as worried as I felt. I noticed him fingering the cross that hung around his neck.

"I think we'd better try the quarry," I said reluctantly. "We might find some old equipment with gasoline, maybe even a gas pump."

We bumped along the road, the truck and SUV still in sight ahead of us. Reluctantly, I cut my speed and let them go. If they were playing some sort of cat-and-mouse game, I didn't want either vehicle to guess where we were headed. I nibbled my bottom lip.

"The quarry is to our left," Enrique said.

The sheriff hadn't called and I didn't know if he'd retrieved my earlier message about the license plate. And now we couldn't get a signal. I was getting more nervous by the minute. No one knew we were following the thieves.

About a mile farther on, we hit the next unmarked road. I turned left, and we traveled along for a couple more miles, the rocky landscape becoming bleaker by the minute. We came to a rise, giving us a better view of what lay ahead.

"There it is," I said. "Abandoned, though I guess we expected that." But as we drew closer, I noticed recent tire tracks leading to a large wooden gate, which was open. Someone had been here recently. A good thing, I told myself.

I shifted into low gear and bumped along the damp rock-strewn road to the entrance.

Max was unusually quiet, and I wondered if he was having the same second thoughts about stopping here that I was. The giant hole yawned before us. It had no guardrail or barrier around it. A shiver traveled up my spine.

I couldn't think about standing near the edge without my toes curling and my stomach getting queasy.

Hands clenched on the wheel, I drove into a large open area that had probably once been used for parking. Hulks of rusting rock-crushing machinery dotted the landscape. No vehicles. No gas pumps. Nothing.

To put as much distance as possible between the Ghia and the edge of the quarry, I did a three-point turn so we would face the gate. If nothing else, we could make a quick getaway.

I made the last of the tight turn and stopped dead, the Ghia's engine still running.

The dark SUV blocked the exit.

Out of the corner of my eye I saw Max pull out his cell. "One bar," he said and tapped the screen.

"No time," I whispered.

He looked up. "We need to get out. Fast."

"Hail Mary, full of grace. Our Lord is with thee. Blessed art thou …," Enrique whispered from the backseat.

The SUV moved slowly toward us. I sat there, stunned, as if watching someone else. My mind couldn't grasp what was happening. "What're they doing?" My voice came out in a squeak.

"I don't know, but I think we need to get out of here."

"They cannot do this!" Enrique yelled. He shook his fist at the SUV. "Hey! You cannot do this!"

By now, the SUV was nose-to-nose with the Ghia.

"They're going to push us over," I cried. "We're trapped."

Max had his door open. "Get out, now," he yelled. "El, jump! Enrique out—now!"

The little Ghia was already scooting toward the edge of the quarry. I tromped on the brake. It did no good.

"Jump," Max yelled again.

The SUV backed up and revved its engine. Its tinted windows seemed almost opaque, giving it a blank-faced look.

The monster machine revved its engine again and almost seemed to leap forward to give the Ghia its final nudge. I jumped out and Max did the same. Enrique was already out.

I didn't stay to watch my little car tumble into the abyss. But the sound of its demise carried toward me, sounding like a dozen metal garbage cans rolling down a hillside. A splash echoed at the very end.

Max grabbed my hand, and we ran to hide behind the large rock crusher, Enrique a few steps ahead of us. The SUV turned around and drove slowly around the equipment, looking for us. Not once did the windows lower for a clearer view.

"Whoever it is knows us," I whispered to Max. "That's why they don't get out to search, or even roll down the windows. They know we'll recognize them."

"And that's why they meant for us to die—because we can identify them."

The SUV slowly drove around the quarry, searching. They never got far enough away for us to make a run for it. Though where would we run?

I looked up at Max. He took my hand and held it, this time not letting go.

Standing a short distance away, Enrique stared at the quarry. "I told you it was a scary place," he said.

Chapter Thirty-five
Hyacinth

. . . .

Lagasse and Child were arguing again—this time over her. The boss had made it clear that they needed to get rid of Hyacinth once and for all. She was a witness and had to go. The argument came down to who would do the deed.

The only thing she had going for her was the fact that neither one wanted to. And when they'd been ordered to do it back in Possum Grove, neither man had the heart to do it there either.

But since their meeting with the boss, they seemed to have new determination, which chilled her to the bone.

"If it has to be done, let's get it over with," she said. "The sooner, the better."

Lagasse and Child glanced at each other, and Lagasse shrugged. "Have it your way. But we still need to decide who's gonna do it."

"You don't have to do this. Just stop and let me out. I'll never tell."

"Yeah, yeah, yeah," Lagasse said.

Child was unusually quiet.

Hyacinth saw her opening. "Stealing is one thing. Murder is quite another. Even if you don't get caught, you'll remember what you did forever. And you'll be haunted by my singing till your dying day."

Lagasse groaned. "Don't tell me you're gonna do that again." He reached for the radio, but Child stopped his hand.

"Let her sing one last song."

She chose Elvis's version of "Peace in the Valley" and pulled out all the stops. Even Lagasse seemed moved as she gave it every bit of emotion she could conjure up.

Apparently, it had no effect. Child checked his watch. "It's time to get to the quarry."

The quarry? Her stomach lurched.

Minutes later, the rental truck turned onto a dirt road, moved through a large wooden gate, and onto a flat area that might once have been a parking lot. The outer rim of the quarry lay in front of her, until Lagasse turned the truck around so that the door faced the edge of the quarry. She closed her eyes, picturing her next move in great detail.

She would have only one shot at success. That one shot meant the difference between life and death.

The thieves weren't going to help her after all. But perhaps Child had done so inadvertently when he brought her that soda.

Lagasse set the brake, leaving the engine running, then, with one more glance at Child, opened his door. Child did the same. As they fiddled with their seat belts, Hyacinth quietly moved to the rear door. She waited, and at the exact moment the doors slammed in front, she raised the rolling door, just enough to escape. She scrambled onto a metal ladder fastened to the side of the truck and jumped to the roof, not exactly an easy thing to do quietly, considering her build.

She crawled along the top of the truck as the two men headed to the back, still arguing over who would throw her in. By the time they decided her size would require them both to do the toss, Hyacinth had reached the cab.

She looked at the ground, feeling dizzy and faint, her heart racing. How in the world would she clamber down and get into the cab in time to make her getaway?

She heard the boys open the back of the truck and froze.

Chapter Thirty-six
Mrs. Littlefield

• • • • • • • • • • • • • • • • •

We'd just stepped out from behind the gravel crusher when we heard the sound of an approaching vehicle. Alarmed, we looked at each other, then at Enrique. Then the three of us ran to hide behind another large piece of equipment.

The rental truck drove in, two men in the cab. They did a three-point turn, put the truck in reverse, and backed up almost to the edge of the quarry pit.

I gasped, bringing my hand to my chest.

"Hyacinth! … Oh, Max, you don't suppose—?" I couldn't finish. I pictured my friend in the back of the truck. What were the thieves doing? We had guessed they wanted to get rid of witnesses and she was their number-one witness. "Oh no!"

The words had barely left my mouth when I saw movement at the back of the vehicle. At the same time, the two men exited the cab and, arguing loudly, walked around to the back.

That's when Hyacinth appeared on top of the truck. She lost her balance and then crawled to the cab. The men argued louder.

Still, it seemed, they had no idea their captive was no longer inside.

I ran as fast as I could toward the truck. I heard panting and footsteps behind me. Enrique had youth on his side. He reached the cab first, put one finger to his lips, and pointed at the cargo area.

A slow smile crept across my face. It was a mirror of the smile on Max's. "You do the honors, if you would."

Max headed around back and, within seconds, the rolling door slammed shut. The click of the padlock carried toward us. Soon the captives' howls were drowned out by Hyacinth's cheers, Enrique's laughter, and my joyful greetings as I hugged my friend.

We all squeezed into the cab, Enrique at the wheel. "Always wanted to drive one of these," he said, revving the engine.

"Just make sure you don't put it in reverse," Max said. He then did a quick search of the floor and glove compartment. No phone. No maps. Nothing.

"No phones?" Hyacinth said. "That means Lagasse and Child have theirs with them. It also means that as soon as we get a signal, they'll be in contact with the boss."

"Not good," I said glancing at the sliding window behind us. My few minutes of euphoria in finding Hyacinth slipped into a low-decibel hum of fear. "Lagasse? Child? As in Emeril and ... Julia?"

She nodded. "Long story. Has to do with the masks they wore the night of the heist. More details to come, I promise."

Hyacinth sat next to Enrique, and I sat between Hyacinth and Max. Four people on a bench seat was a squeeze—quite a nice one, I decided when Max leaned back and draped his arm around my shoulders. I smiled up at him and he met my eyes. I felt my cheeks flush.

Hyacinth, as usual, didn't miss a beat. She nudged me with her elbow. "Looks like I've missed out on quite a lot these past few days."

I sobered, thinking of the poisoning, the illnesses, President Delancy's death ... "You don't know the half of it. But that too can wait."

"Did you get a good look at the people in the SUV?" Max asked Hyacinth.

She shook her head. "A male and female are in the front seat. But I saw only saw them from behind and at quite a distance. I thought they looked familiar but couldn't place them." She gave me a tired smile. "You won't believe this—guess who's with them?" She paused dramatically. "The Sutherland boys—Bubba and Junior. There was this farmhouse meeting."

She filled in details that we hadn't seen, and we told her that we'd been there to rescue her, heard the gunshots, and had to take off before we were spotted.

"Bubba and Junior were apparently in the house ahead of time, waiting for the others," she said. "But how they fit in, I don't know."

Max leaned forward again. "Could Silas Sutherland have been the man you couldn't identify?"

She shrugged. "I don't know him well, but it's possible. It did occur to me that he might be involved. He was so adamant about getting his nephews hired for the dinner."

"Which would have given them plenty of opportunity for the poisoning." I realized she didn't know about that.

"Poisoning?" Hyacinth was thunderstruck. "At the dinner?"

I nodded. "Hundreds of people were rushed to the hospital ..."

"The ambulances," she filled in. "The perfect cover. Do you know who did it?"

I shook my head. "Even Katie and I are considered 'persons of interest.'" I decided, with all she'd been through, I would wait to tell her she'd also been a prime suspect responsible for the heist.

The shadows were growing long by the time we reached the turn-off for the farmhouse. As we had all been doing for miles, I checked the large side-view mirrors. This time, my heart nearly stopped. The black SUV was behind us and gaining fast.

"Fasten your seat belts, kids," I said. "We've got company."

The men that Hyacinth called Lagasse and Child knocked on the small window between the cab and the cargo area. One held a phone to his ear. Hyacinth turned and slid open the window.

"The boss says to pull over now and turn over the truck to us," he said.

"Tell him no dice." I turned to emphasize my words with what I hoped was a no-nonsense look.

"He says do it, or you'll never see your daughter and grand-daughter again."

Oh mercy, I cried silently, thinking of Katie and Chloe Grace. I blinked back the tears that threatened and hitched up my shoulders. *O Lord, have mercy …*

"Whoever your boss is, he's bluffing," I said with as much confidence as I could muster. "You can tell him for me that he doesn't know what he's talking about."

"He has something he wants you to hear." He turned the phone on speaker mode. The familiar hurtful words came through in a fake mechanical voice: "You are playing with fire. Already it turns on you. Taste it. Smell it. Know it will return. Not in your nightmares, but in living flame, a wild beast to devour you and those you love."

A chill traveled up my back, but I held my positive pose. "That's just a child's rhyme he—or she—made up to scare me. I don't scare that easily." But the tremble in my hands told the tale. Hyacinth whirled in her seat so that she looked straight at the thugs. "Now, let's make a deal. I offered it to you when the tables were turned, and you opted to pass."

"Okay, shoot," said the taller of the two.

"I'll put it out there again," she said. "Even though you were about to throw me in the pit—"

The two started to argue, saying they wouldn't really have done such a thing.

Hyacinth held up a hand. "As I was saying, I like you two. You took good care of me while I was with you. I told you I would see to it that you get a fair trial. Think of it. You didn't go through with the murder you were supposed to carry out, and the DA doesn't need to know how close you came. I'll vouch for you, and so will my friends here."

"So what do we have to do?" the shorter man asked.

"Turn off your blasted phones and keep them off," I said, imitating her tone. We exchanged a conspiratorial glance, just as we'd done since first grade. "We're gonna lose the creeps behind us, and I don't want you to give away our location. Got it?"

"He'll kill us." The shorter man furrowed his brow.

"Not if we get you in protective custody first," I added. "That means we've got to get to the courthouse without the SUV running us off the road."

The two conferred, arguing, agreeing, then arguing again. "Okay, cells are off," one said.

"Thank you," Hyacinth said. "Now give them to me." She held out her hand.

After a lot of moaning and complaining, a hand reached through the window and dropped the phones into Hyacinth's hand.

"Can you lose the SUV?" Max glanced at Enrique, who shrugged, grinned, and hit the accelerator with skill akin to my own. I gave him a thumbs-up.

Hyacinth handed me one of the phones and gave Max the other. I checked the signal. "We've got coverage," I said, and then dialed Katie. It rang four times and went to her voice mail. I tried not to worry and left a message to call me right away.

Max quickly figured out how to make a call on the unfamiliar phone. "First call, sheriff's office." He punched in the number. He was put through to the sheriff immediately and gave him a quick synopsis of what had happened and our location. The call was interrupted by a loud thump on the back of our truck.

The SUV was right behind us now. It zoomed to the left and nudged the side of our vehicle, trying to force us off the road.

Enrique floored it, but we were on an incline and the truck didn't have enough power to pull ahead of the SUV.

One of the thieves—the tall one with blond hair—again popped up at the window. "There's a gun under the driver's seat."

"Let's leave it there," I said. "Save it for a real emergency."

"Like this isn't?" the shorter thief said.

As the SUV sped up behind us and then alongside us again, it banged against us. Hard.

"Aye-aye-aye," Enrique yelled as the truck skidded sideways onto a sandy shoulder. He turned the wheel into the skid like a pro and somehow got us back on the road.

I tried to take a deep breath, but my throat closed.

Max leaned forward, squinting. "Up ahead," he said to Enrique, "about a quarter of a mile. Wait until the last minute and then make a quick right turn."

A moment later, Max shouted, "Now!" and Enrique yanked the steering wheel to the right. The SUV missed the turn and continued going straight. The highway sloped downward, and we flew along what seemed to be a main artery. It was paved and actually had a line down the center. We passed cars and farm vehicles, and houses and patchworks of crops dotted the landscape.

It took another half hour to reach the outskirts of Eden's Bridge, just as dusk fell. I let out a huge sigh of relief when I saw the courthouse loom in front of us. "Boys and girls, I believe we've made it."

Just before Enrique turned the truck into the parking area behind the courthouse, I spotted the SUV. It slowed as if to send a menacing message, stopped at the curb, and then slowly pulled away.

Hyacinth knew what I was thinking, just like when we were kids. She handed me one of the phones, and I again dialed Katie's cell.

She didn't answer.

Chapter Thirty-seven
The Professor

. . . .

As soon as the officers took the two thieves into custody, Max climbed inside the cargo area and went straight to the large crate. He knelt beside it, ran his hands over the wood grain, and checked the seams. It looked sturdy enough but not professionally constructed by any means. He only hoped there had been no damage to the figurehead during the rental truck's rough ride around the countryside.

Once Hyacinth was safe, all he could think about was the *Lady* and her well-being. Well, perhaps that wasn't quite all. There was also this delightful woman beside him, close enough to encircle with his arm so he could breathe in her violet scent all the way home.

Glancing out at the parking lot, he spotted El in animated conversation with Hyacinth. They'd been talking nonstop since getting out of the truck.

He noticed again how she talked with her hands, laughed often, and let her emotions show. Sometimes she met his eyes with so much affection in hers that he lost his breath.

She looked up and smiled at him, gave Hyacinth a quick hug, and hurried toward the truck. He walked to the rear of the cargo area and helped her climb aboard.

"The grand opening?" she said, her eyes bright with interest.

"If I can find a crowbar."

She trotted off without a word, heading toward one of the deputies. He willed her to sprout wings on her tennies. His anticipation was palpable.

As if by magic, El reappeared at his side at that moment and handed him a well-used crowbar.

She climbed up into the truck and knelt by his side as he pried the top of the crate loose with the crowbar, and then pulled away the packing materials. Relief flooded through him.

The figurehead was there, still locked in the Plexiglas case. The *Lady* was so secure, she hadn't moved an inch.

El gasped. "She's stunning."

It was her first look at the piece, and he knew from the awe in her expression that she didn't just see the beauty, she *felt* it. Just as he did.

"That she is, indeed."

Hyacinth climbed into the cargo area and came up beside them. "She's here and real, after all," she said with a note of wonder. "I'll admit I worried that Lagasse and Child made a switch somewhere along the way, and I was putting my life on the line for nothing."

"Thank you," Max said. "There are no words to describe the gratitude that's in my heart. What you did … what you gave of yourself—and I'm sure we don't know the half of it—" His eyes filled with tears, something he just did not do in front of others. Blinking, he started to turn away. El touched his hand, and smiled up at him, as if saying that tears were okay, even for a man.

Hyacinth seemed too moved to speak. Instead, she stepped toward him and gave him a hug.

They'd been debriefed by a deputy and were now free to leave. Almost as if ticking off a list, details came together and questions were answered. The decision was made to impound the rental truck and check for prints or anything else that might lead to the kingpin who had put the theft together.

It was assumed, now, that the poisoning was directly related, and that it was indeed ipecac. One of the deputies drove Hyacinth home. Max and the sheriff agreed that until the head of the organization was captured, it would be foolish to take the figurehead back to the university for exhibition. The sheriff offered him a secure room with a large safe in which to keep the *Lady* temporarily, and Max nodded his assent.

As the uniformed men headed to the truck to move the crate, Max went over to El.

"I just tried to get Katie again."

"Still no answer?"

She shook her head. "I'm going to run by her apartment."

"Do you want me to go with you?" He needed to oversee the positioning of the figurehead, but suddenly—or maybe not so suddenly—El had become more important.

She laid her hand on his arm and shook her head. "You've got things to do." She nodded toward the men moving the crate from the rental truck. "I'll call you later."

She stood on her tiptoes, and he kissed her.

"I like that," she said, smiling into his eyes.

He found himself grinning like a schoolboy. "So do I." The feeling in his heart was so new to him he didn't know what to do. Except—if he could—turn cartwheels across the parking lot, an image that caused him to grin again.

Chapter Thirty-eight
Mrs. Littlefield

. . . .

I hurried through the security gate leading into Katie's complex. Her condo was on the ground level toward the back on the far side of a greenbelt. Even though it had grown dark, no lights shone in her windows.

Stomach churning, I knocked loudly on Katie's door, called her name, and rang her doorbell, nearly all at once in my frantic state.

I paced back and forth in front of her door, and then pounded on the door again.

Katie's neighbor stepped out of her unit and gave me a curious look. "Oh, it's you, Mrs. Littlefield," she said. "What's wrong?"

"I'm looking for Katie," I said. "And Chloe Grace."

She walked over to me. "I haven't seen them since this morning when they left together. They seemed quite upbeat, especially your little granddaughter. She told me her mama had gotten the day off, and that they were going someplace special, she didn't know where."

I frowned. Katie hadn't said anything to me about a surprise, but I'd been gone all day and unreachable by phone for much of the time. "Were they carrying duffel bags or totes or anything like that? Could they have been planning to spend the night somewhere?"

"Chloe Grace had that cute little ballerina sock monkey." She narrowed her eyes. "Though now that I think about it, Katie was carrying a couple of totes and big bright towels like maybe they were going to the beach." She shrugged. "That is rather odd, don't you think? We don't have a beach around here, do we?"

Beach? My heart thudded a little harder. Something didn't ring true. "Beach?" I said. I tried to calm my frazzled nerves, telling myself that at least Katie and Chloe Grace had been seen recently.

I thanked her and headed back to the gate. The sky continued to darken as I walked to the catering van. I glanced over my shoulder to make sure I wasn't being followed. The last phone call from the mechanical voice, chanting the childish phrases, had me spooked. I couldn't deny it.

What if they—and I didn't even know who "they" could be—had taken my girls? What would be their motive? I pondered the question for a moment or two and then stopped with a gasp. What if they wanted to exchange them for the figurehead? The thought sliced through me like a knife.

The window on the van's driver's side had been destroyed, so I had no way of locking the vehicle. I flipped on the interior light to check for intruders. A noise in the cargo area made my hair stand on end.

I didn't breathe until a yellow tabby meowed and jumped back out the window.

Katie and I live on opposite sides of town, so it took me a good half hour to reach home. As I turned into my driveway, the visible effects of the earlier blast greeted me. Someone had raked up the debris, and I wondered if a neighbor or Enrique's brother Juan had performed the good deed. The thought cheered me somewhat, but the scarred dogwood and partially destroyed rose arbor left harsh reminders.

I unlocked my front door, stepped inside, and then pushed the deadbolt into place. I walked to the kitchen to check my voice mail. I picked up the receiver. Two beeps told me I had two messages. I checked caller ID and saw both calls were from Katie.

I punched my password into the keypad and listened to Katie's first message.

"Hi, Mom, just wanted you to know C .G. and I are going away with Sandy for the day. He and I arranged a little surprise for her—a trip on his boat. We're excited about it, and hope you'll be excited for us too. But don't worry, I'll be smart about everything."

I sank into a chair at the kitchen table. Sandy was moving too fast. My heart pounded a little harder as I waited to hear the second message.

"Gramsy," chirped Chloe Grace. "I'm so sad I didn't get to tell you good-bye. But I'm sooooo excited about Mommy's surprise. I get to go sailing! Mommy's friend has a big, big boat. It's in Wilmy-something. Yay! I wish you could come too."

Then Katie took the phone again and added, "Well, you'll know where we are when you get home. I'll call you if I can. I've got my cell on me, but service in some of the areas we'll be driving through is spotty. Love you, Mom. Keep praying that we make the right decision, even if it's to move forward slowly." She laughed lightly. "You know, one step at a time."

I hung up the phone and dropped my head into my hands. That was how she got through the divorce, one step at a time. I'd prayed with her, held her as she wept, and together we tried to focus on the good things. Now she was opening herself up to more hurt. I drew in a deep breath, trying to push away my fears for Katie and Chloe Grace.

I checked the clock and weighed my choices, my hand hovering to pick up the phone again. It was late but not that late. She did want to talk with me, and I would be returning her call. So technically that wouldn't be meddling, would it?

In the end, I decided I would call in the morning. Right now, I wanted nothing more than a hot bath and to slip into bed. When I did talk to Katie, I would try my best to be supportive and let her make her own decisions. Then I thought of Chloe Grace, and that vow slipped away in an instant. My arms ached to hug her.

What if Sandy and Katie reconciled? He had just taken a new position with a pharmaceutical company near the coast. I couldn't imagine him moving to Eden's Gate and giving that up. Oh my heavens, I thought, standing wearily. I might lose them both.

With that thought nagging at my heart, I went upstairs to take my bath. I was just settling under the bubbles to enjoy a long, fragrant soak when something that had been niggling at the back of my mind returned. The puzzle pieces began settling into patterns.

Quickly, I soaped and rinsed and almost leaped out of the bathtub. I wrapped myself in a towel and padded across the carpet to my bedside table, where I saw the copy of the threatening note I had received.

And where was it that Chloe Grace said they were heading? Wilmy … Wilmy? Could she have meant Wilmington?

William MacDonald, who sent Max's father the letter about the figurehead, was from Wilmington. Coincidence? Or not?

I sat on my bed, putting the pieces together in my mind. The salvage ship Max was on last summer had also been out of Wilmington. Everyone on board knew about the half-million-dollar value of the figurehead. Had one of the crew discovered that there was also millions of dollars worth of treasure hidden inside? More pieces flew into place.

Then there were the personal details. The person who was behind all of this obviously knew how much I loved my daughter and granddaughter, and my fears about fire. Katie knew all about them. She might have mentioned them to Sandy when they were married or during one of their recent talks.

Sandy? He couldn't be involved ... could he? I was feeling so many emotions all at once, and a knot formed in my stomach. I didn't care for him because of how he had treated my daughter and granddaughter, but was he capable of this?

Yet, I couldn't ignore the connection: Sandy. Wilmington. Pharmaceuticals.

Where had the ipecac come from? Brazil was a huge supplier. I'd done enough research to come up with a scenario. A ship could have docked at a legitimate port to pick up merchandise—ninety-nine percent for legal sale, one percent for the street. The legal drugs head for a drug company. The illegal drugs to a supplier. The question was: Who was that supplier?

Still wrapped in my towel and sitting on the bed, I leaned forward, shivering.

As I picked up the bedside phone to call Max, the phone rang in my hand.

"Mrs. Littlefield?" said the mechanical voice. "Do you remember the note?"

My heart started to thud so hard I couldn't breathe. "Of course," I finally managed.

"We have your daughter and your granddaughter. Do you understand?"

My body began to tremble like an autumn leaf in a windstorm—ready to fall. I brought my elbows into my sides, wrapping my free arm around the other and held on tight. *Lord, have mercy ...*

"What do you want?" My voice came out in a whispery squeak.

"What do you think?" A bizarre laugh followed. "We are going to make a trade. Your family for the figurehead. I will give you an address by noon tomorrow. You get the figurehead from wherever it's being held, transport it in a rental truck of your choice, safe and secure, and we will make the exchange. You are to bring no one with you, or there will be serious consequences."

I drew in a deep breath, my eyes closed, trying not to think of my granddaughter, my daughter, and all they meant to me. Only the world. "What is the address?"

"You will find out tomorrow after you have secured the figurehead. We will call you. And Mrs. Littlefield, you are to come alone. You will tell no in law enforcement."

"I ... I won't, but I don't ... ha-have a cell phone."

"Now you do. You will find it on your front porch."

A wave, make that a tsunami, of fear swept over me as I imagined that someone might still be out there in the shadows, watching me.

"Let me speak to my daughter," I said, finding my voice. "I need to know my family's okay."

"How about the little one instead? Come here, little one," he said, his voice still disguised. A minute later, Chloe Grace came on the line. "Gramsy, I wish you were here. This is the best boat I've ever seen. It's beautiful—"

"Sweetie, are you okay?"

"I love this big boat, Gramsy. And the ocean is pretty."

The ocean? Had they already set sail? Fear knotted inside her. "Let me talk to your mommy, okay?"

Chloe Grace didn't answer. After some scuffling sounds, the disguised voice came back on the line.

"You got it, Mrs. Littlefield? Tomorrow noon. Without fail. Or you will never see your family again."

The following morning, in the predawn light, I turned the catering van into the lot at the sheriff's station. I parked near the door, got out, and turned when I heard footsteps.

Max strode over to greet me. We'd been on the phone half the night, planning our strategy. His laugh lines drooped a bit from fatigue, but I'd never seen a more handsome—or welcome—face.

He drew me into his arms. "I've thought about it all night, and I'm not letting you do this alone."

"I have to, Max. Katie's and Chloe Grace's lives are at stake. I don't have a choice."

"I can ride in back, hidden from view."

I thought of Hyacinth's recent adventure and smiled. "It means a lot that you would do this, but I really do need to do as they say." I reached up and touched his cheek. He caught my hand, held it there, and then kissed my palm.

"I've seen you in action," he said. "So I know you're more than capable. I just want to be there if you need me."

"I'll be careful, I promise. I have a lot to come home to."

I didn't want to think about what could go wrong with the deception we'd planned—a borrowed life-size angel statue from the Christmas crèche at Max's church. It weighed about the same as the figurehead and Max told me its face was beautiful enough that it might pass for the *Lady*. If we packed the angel statue just right, we might just pull off the ruse. I couldn't bear to think what might happen if the kidnappers found out I'd double-crossed them.

"I brought you coffee," he said, and handed me a travel thermos. He looked reluctant to leave. "I need to go oversee the packing of the 'figurehead.'" He hugged me, drawing to me as if he never wanted to let go. I blinked a few times, trying hard to keep from tearing up. "My thoughts and prayers will be with you."

Then cold reality hit. I was leaving safety behind and heading into a life-and-death situation. My decisions would tip the scales one direction or the other. Icy fear wrapped itself around my heart.

Minutes later, four men carried the Christmas angel in its crate to the back of the truck, slid it in, and slammed the rear door closed. I climbed into the cab and started the engine.

The air was heavy with moisture, and thunderstorms loomed.

I had just turned onto Main Street, wondering if I should head to the interstate when the phone rang. I made a quick right turn into a service station with room to park the monster rental truck.

"Yes?"

"Here are your instructions." The mechanical voice gave me step-by-step directions to Wilmington on Interstate 40. From there, I was to proceed to the Cape Fear River Road and then drive south. The voice then said, "You will be contacted with further instructions when you arrive," and then disconnected the call.

I closed my eyes for a moment, trying to overcome my panic and toss it out the window. I had to find my courage. All great things to strive for, but I was still shaking. I tried praying, but my words seemed to bounce off the ceiling. I thought of Max's one-word prayers and simply uttered *Help!* Even that seemed to bounce back as if tethered by my fear for Katie and Chloe Grace.

I put the truck in gear, pressed on the gas, and sped up the ramp onto Interstate 40.

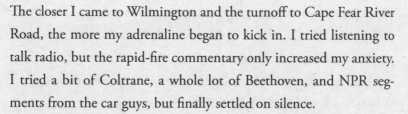

The closer I came to Wilmington and the turnoff to Cape Fear River Road, the more my adrenaline began to kick in. I tried listening to talk radio, but the rapid-fire commentary only increased my anxiety. I tried a bit of Coltrane, a whole lot of Beethoven, and NPR segments from the car guys, but finally settled on silence.

The phone rang, and though I was expecting it, I nearly jumped out of my skin. I looked for a wide spot on the side of the road and pulled off onto the shoulder. My hand trembled as I reached for the phone.

"Yes?"

"Where are you?" demanded the voice.

I told him.

"You are making good progress. You will need to take the exit for Cape Fear River Road, and turn south." He continued to give me complicated directions that included side roads and traveling by ferry across the Cape Fear River to Southport. "Do you understand?"

"Yes," I said, my knees again threatening to turn to rubber.

"Are you being followed?"

"No, I … I don't think so."

"The only way you can save the lives of your daughter and granddaughter is to play it straight. We will deal with any attempt to double-cross us with swift and deadly force." The phone went dead.

I swallowed hard and considered my situation. Not good. I almost laughed when it hit me. I didn't like this guy's intimidating attitude. I decided I'd had about enough of it.

I leaned forward, hitting the gas pedal harder, and watching for the Cape Fear exit.

Now my brain had to work overtime to come up with a plan. I should have been doing that all along instead of trying to soothe my achingly worried thoughts with music, NPR, and prayer. Well, the prayer wasn't a waste of time.

I went over my assets. Besides my own wits, what tools did I have in my arsenal? I had my kit of tools and my binoculars, always handy to have along. I was nimble and good at surprise attacks; I could sound tougher than I am; I could play the sweet-little-lady role quite successfully, throwing people off guard. I could think fast on my feet. I didn't believe in weaponry, but I had used cherry bombs quite effectively in the past, and I always carry them in my tool kit.

I came to the Cape Fear exit, signaled, and drove down the off-ramp. I turned left and jostled along, watching for the first side road that would lead me to the ferry crossing. It took about a half hour, but I finally saw the ferry looming on the horizon.

It had grown more humid by the hour, and when I rolled down the window to buy my ticket, the air felt heavy and damp.

"Round trip?" the man in the booth asked.

"Yes," I said and handed him a bill.

He gave me change, and smiled. "Y'all have a good day now."

I almost laughed at the odds. "You too," I said and drove down to the ramp to await boarding.

I continued going over my plans as I drove onto the ferry, and then again as I drove up the ramp on the Southport side of the river. Lightning flashed in the dark sky, and large drops of rain began to splat against the windshield.

The phone rang again.

"Okay, where now?"

"Well, well, well," mocked the voice. "Feeling a little feistier, are we?"

I didn't give him the satisfaction of an answer.

"Continue on River Drive until it turns into Moore. It will dead-end at West Brunswick Street. That will lead you to the marina. You will be met at the gate. I hope for your sake you are alone."

I followed his instructions, except for a brief detour into an alley off West Brunswick, so I could get out and do a quick survey. The wind blew ferociously, lightning splitting open the sky, thunder rumbling and crashing. The sky was dark, the air heavy. By the time I walked to the end of the alley, the rain was coming down in sheets. I looked out over the large marina. The rain made it difficult to see clearly.

The one thing that heartened me was the fact that if I was right about the identity of the "boss," he had a supersized ego. What kind of sailing vessel would someone like that have? The largest in the marina, of course. That narrowed the options nicely. Only three yachts loomed among the many other boats, and of the three, one was significantly larger than the others. I was willing to bet that was the one, but I couldn't be sure.

I found the last call on my phone and pressed "call back." He picked up immediately.

"I'm lost," I said, doing my best to sound both frightened and annoyed.

"Where are you?" he asked, impatiently. "Can you see a cross street?"

"The last I knew I was on Moore, but I don't see a street sign now. It's raining so hard it's difficult to make out the street names."

He let out a string of swear words, and I held the phone away from my ear. "Okay," he said. "Get out of the truck and walk to the nearest sign."

"All right," I said, staying where I'd planted myself earlier. "Oh, here it is," I said. "It's Herring and Longleaf. Yes, I believe that's it."

"How'd you get up there?" He swore again, and again, I held the phone away from my ear.

"Maybe it would be better if you sent someone to get me, and I'll follow them to the gate."

"This better not be a trick," he said.

"You've made it very clear to me what would happen if I attempted anything like that."

"I'll send someone."

I hung up and put the phone in my pocket, pulled out my binoculars, and focused in on the three yachts from where I'd stationed myself. Just as I'd hoped, someone came out of the largest boat, put up an umbrella, and ran down the dock toward the gate. The sheets of rain made it difficult to tell, but even covered in rain gear, the figure was obviously female.

Female? I wasn't expecting that. I frowned, keeping my binoculars trained on her as she ran and her face came into better focus. Pretty features, beautiful even. Dark reddish hair swept back into a loose braid of some sort. I'd seen her before and tried to remember where.

Just before she headed toward the parking lot across from the marina, it came to me. Max's dinner. After the poisoning. She'd sat next to him, was one of the first to reach him, and then came for me to tell me he needed me.

I gaped as she lowered her umbrella and threw back her hood just before entering her car. Even in the rain, her dark red hair gleamed. Jane Fletcher.

I swept the binoculars to the yacht then hurried down the wharf to the gate. In her hurry, she had left the gate open.

I watched Jane back out of her parking place in the dark SUV and head off in the direction I'd sent her. Of course. She was the insider.

Another puzzle piece flew into place. I remembered that she had been among the first to be admitted to the hospital after the poisoning, but she must have faked her illness. She probably left just long enough to go after Enrique and my van with a crowbar then returned to the hospital as if she'd been there all along.

Did she cause the poisoning as well? She had access.

She knew about the figurehead and its value as an antique, but how did she know about the map it contained?

I was willing to bet she was the one in charge. I tried to put the other pieces together. I thought of Sandy and his new position in Wilmington at the pharmaceutical company. Was he involved? Was he trying to become a drug lord?

There was no doubt that they had been together at the farmhouse. One of them shot the third thief.

Sandy had tricked Katie into thinking he had changed, that he wanted to be a real father to Chloe Grace, all to get close to the banquet plans. And now he held them captive.

A jagged bolt of lightning flashed over the ocean, followed by a rolling, banging clap of thunder so loud it shook the ground. The blue-black clouds moved closer, sheets of rain falling over the water.

Shivering, I turned my attention again to the marina. It was time to make my move.

Chapter Thirty-nine
The Professor

• • • • • • • • • • • • • • • •

In his time Max had traveled by camel, by donkey, and by horseback but never in a crate in the back of a rental truck with a woman behind the wheel whose average speed rivaled that of a NASCAR driver. He slid one direction, then the next, wondering why no one had thought to brace the crate with the concrete blocks he'd earlier asked one of the deputies to place in the cargo area. Probably because the men couldn't have imagined that the crate carried human cargo. He was glad they hadn't blocked the air holes he'd made for himself.

He felt queasy for most of the trip, but he had plenty of time to plan what he would do once they arrived. Even so, he was afraid for El. She was smart, no doubt about that, but she was also impulsive. And when it came to protecting those she loved, she was fierce and unrelenting.

He attempted to push away his fear and think clearly. If she needed him, he wanted to be there for her.

After the vehicle stopped, he heard the muffled sounds of the cab door open and close. He waited a minute or two longer, then pried open the container, crawled out, and stretched his creaky limbs.

Grabbing his binocular case and hanging the strap around his neck, he stepped to the window between the cab and the cargo area. El had made her way through the rain toward the wharf. He took his binoculars out and watched as she let herself through a gate. She seemed to know exactly what she was doing as she headed toward a large yacht berthed at the end of the dock.

Chapter Forty
Mrs. Littlefield

. . . .

The rain fell in buckets, the lightning and thunder violent and terrifying—or they would have been under different circumstances. Right now, my fears were focused on my family.

I tightened the sash around my trench coat, drew in a deep breath, and hurried across the street to the marina gate. Unlocked, thanks to Dr. Fletcher—or, if I'd figured correctly, Mrs. Ainsley. I sauntered down the dock as if I belonged there.

I headed directly for the large yacht. I noticed that many of the larger vessels had small dinghies tethered to their sides.

The phone with the mechanical voice buzzed. I pulled it out of my pocket and tossed it into the water. Then I ducked out of sight between two of the larger boats, keeping an eye out for anyone else who might be nearby, especially someone from Sandy's yacht.

The squall passed, and the rain turned to sprinkles. The marina gate slammed in the distance, and soon the sound of hurried footsteps carried toward me. I caught a glimpse of Jane before dropping to my knees behind a large pile of ropes. Jane didn't even glance in my direction but tromped angrily to the yacht and up the gangway.

Even from my hiding place two yachts down, I could hear her voice. Just a few words here and there, but from her tone, I got a sense of her foul mood. She was suspicious of a "double-cross" and wanted them to "set sail immediately."

Staying close to the ships, I slipped down the dock toward the largest yacht. Another voice pierced the air—the distinct wail of a child: Chloe Grace.

"I want my mommy," she cried. "And I want to go home."

My heart threatened to stop beating.

Just then, Jane spotted me. I heard voices and shrank back to hide. I scanned the dock and then ran toward a small yacht. It looked unoccupied, but as I got closer, I could see no way to get in and hide.

"Where is the figurehead?" demanded a male voice that sounded like Sandy's. Anger compounded my fear, and I turned to give him a piece of my mind.

"You can't hide from us." Jane yelled. She lifted a gun over the rail and aimed it in my direction. "If you do, you'll never see your loved ones again. That's the deal. Tell us where the figurehead is, and we'll make the exchange, just as promised."

"I want to see my family first," I yelled back. "And right now—or you'll never see your precious figurehead again. That's my deal." My heart beating so hard my ribs hurt, I looked around. There was no place to hide except the deep murky water.

Chloe Grace cried out again. I took in Jane's grim expression and the gun aimed at me. They weren't about to let any of us live. We knew too much.

I couldn't wait. I held my nose and jumped into the water.

The weight of my raincoat pulled me under. I fought against it as I tried to get my arms out of the too-tight sleeves. And my tennies, now waterlogged, made my feet nearly immoveable. I kicked them off and, letting myself float downward, finally managed to free myself from the coat.

My plan had been to create a diversion and then carry out the rescue. I kicked hard to reach the surface, spotted a dinghy nearby, and swam to it. I struggled but was able to climb aboard, then untied the knot that attached it to the dock. Breathing hard, I tried to get my bearings. Sandy's yacht was to my right. I prayed I hadn't been seen, and with the oar I'd found attached to the side, I paddled toward it under the cover of the dock.

I heard voices on the dock overhead, Sandy's and one or two others. I held my breath, willing them not to look down. They were arguing. I could hear Sandy's voice above the others, but I couldn't make out the words.

"We'll have to smoke her out," one of them said. "Get her to come to us."

Smoke me out? Did they mean fire? Of course they did. Sandy knew my secret phobia. He was putting me to the test, hoping I would fail in the process. He would get the figurehead, at least he thought he would, then do away with me. My eyes filled. What was his plan for Katie and Chloe Grace? None of it made sense.

I'd paddled close to Sandy's yacht, almost even with the bow. Chloe Grace was sobbing now, crying for her mother. I had to get to her. I couldn't wait any longer.

The sound of the anchor chain rattling against the yacht

carried toward me. Were they raising the anchor? The engines came to life. They were preparing to leave—with Katie and Chloe Grace.

Frantically, I looked around for a way to climb up the side of the boat but saw nothing. Then the acrid smell of gasoline stung my nose. I looked up. Some sort of fuel was being poured onto the dock above me. It dripped through the rail and splashed onto the dinghy. I grabbed the oar and paddled hard. I was heading opposite of where I needed to go, just to keep ahead of the flames.

I turned to look back. An orange glow covered the dock, blocking my way to the yacht. Flames were rising fast with heat so intense I thought my skin would blister, my lungs burn to a crisp. It seemed the entire dock was on fire. The substance they'd poured out created a ring of fire between the yacht and me.

I stared at the leaping flames. My mouth went dry. My nightmares … I closed my eyes and breathed a prayer for strength … The only way to reach Chloe Grace was to paddle around the yacht and hope that somewhere I would find a ladder that reached to the water. It didn't matter if I had to run through the fire. I would do it.

I heard shouting from the yacht, and from my hiding place I saw Sandy come out on deck. He looked directly at me and shouted something I couldn't understand. Then he frantically motioned with his hands. It was as if he was showing me a way through the fire. Behind him, the flames now licked higher, the fire spreading both directions. Fast. The air was heavy with moisture. How could this happen? What had they used?

It didn't matter. I had to go through it to get to Katie and Chloe Grace.

Sandy ran inside and then came back with his phone to his ear, probably calling the fire department. Jane was right behind him. "Hurry, hurry, hurry!" she shouted. "You got to move the yacht!" Neither one seemed concerned about their captives.

The fire that was supposed to smoke me out had gotten away from them. By now the flames licked skyward, and I could feel the heat from several feet away. I paddled the dinghy around the yacht. The fire had spread to this side as well. The paint on the gleaming yacht had begun to bubble and blister from the heat.

But I had no time to gloat. My worst nightmare was before me. The only way to my family was through the fire. A wise person once told me that there are some things in life you can't go around, you can't go over, you can't go under. You have to go through.

I reached for the ladder that led to the deck.

The flames were growing higher by the second. If I waited any longer, I might not make it through. I clambered up, Katie and Chloe Grace occupying my every thought. I dashed around the deck and saw no one. I went below, down the steps, through the galley, and then into a hallway. I opened each door I passed.

"Katie," I shouted. "Are you here?"

"Gramsy, is that you?" a little voice called, sounding distant.

"Yes, Pumpkin, it is. Where are you?"

"We're down here," she called. "Hurry." The sound seemed to float through a vent at the end of the hall.

I moved closer to the vent. "Tell me again, sweetie."

"Down here," she said. "Where there's big machines and things."

Behind me a man's voice jarred my senses. Before I turned I knew it was Sandy. "Follow me," he said. "Quickly."

I didn't have time to question or ponder. I just followed as he ran down the corridor. "In here," he said in front of a closed door. He touched my shoulder. "I don't have time to explain. They haven't been hurt. I've done everything I could to protect them. Please believe me."

He unlocked the door. "I love them, you know. Make sure they know that."

I nodded and opened the door. "Chloe Grace, are you in there?"

"I'm here, Gramsy."

"Is your mommy with you?" I rummaged in my bag for my B & E tools, then found what I needed and quickly unlocked the door.

"She's sleeping," Chloe Grace said as I stepped inside. "She's been sleeping for a long time." As the child raced into my arms, I caught a glimpse of my daughter's body, crumpled against a generator.

Panic like I'd never known before welled inside. *Katie*!

I held Chloe Grace tight. "Everything is going to be all right," I crooned and then put her down gently. I went over to where Katie lay, knelt beside her, and lifted her wrist to be sure Sandy had spoken the truth. Her pulse was strong. She was alive. Waves of relief flooded through me. Outside, sirens wailed as fire trucks and EMTs arrived. I knew other law enforcement personnel would arrive soon, just as Max and I had planned.

Shouts carried through the open door. Sandy's voice rose above the cacophony, but there wasn't a hint of triumph in the sound.

"Katie," I said softly. "Katie, can you hear me?" She moved almost imperceptibly. "Katie, it's Mom. I'm here. Everything is going to be all right. You're safe."

Chloe Grace stood beside me. I looked at her worried little face. "Is there water anywhere in here?"

She nodded and brought me a plastic bottle with water in it. I poured a little on my hand, and gently patted Katie's face with it. She opened her eyes, tried to focus, and closed them again. "Katie, listen to me. We need to get you out of here. I need to see if you're strong enough to stand."

Katie shook her head.

"Let's try some water." I held the bottle to her lips and lifted her head at the same time. She took a few sips. Her eyes fluttered open again. This time she focused on me and then moved her head to search for Chloe Grace.

"C.G.," she whispered. "Are you okay, sweetheart?"

"Yes, Mommy."

I helped Katie sit up. She groaned and put her hand to her head. "I must have fallen."

"You don't remember?"

"Where's Sandy?" She looked around, realizing she was in the engine room. "Where are we?"

I didn't want to answer her first question. "We're on a yacht."

"We were coming with Sandy. Is he here?"

"No," I said. "But we need to hurry. There's been a fire, and we must get off this ship."

More vehicles had arrived outside. Sirens continued to wail. Bullhorns called for everyone on the ship to disembark.

Katie looked confused but let me help her to standing. "How long have I been out?" She looked to Chloe Grace for an answer.

"A long time, Mommy. You fell down and bumped your head when we were playing pirates. I couldn't wake you up. Not even when they brought us food."

Katie wrapped her arm around my neck, and I wrapped mine around her waist. I took Chloe Grace's hand. We inched our way out into the hallway and up the stairs. I saw the rescue personnel had connected a gangway, so I directed us toward that and slowly down toward the marina. The firemen were still aiming their hoses at hot spots on the ship. We stepped around some wet, charred wood, and continued walking toward shore.

Chloe Grace wrinkled her nose. "Yuck, that smells bad," she said.

I squeezed her hand. "It sure does."

I looked up to see Max running toward us. Sheriff Doyle was right behind him. Then I blinked in surprise to see Bubba and Junior, grinning to beat the band, come running from behind. And EMTs rolling a stretcher, looking as though they were in a race with the others to reach us first. And they did.

The paramedics lifted Katie onto the stretcher, then glanced at Chloe Grace. "I'm fine," she pronounced, grasping my hand even tighter. I nodded indicating that she was.

Sheriff Doyle had joined us, and stepped forward to greet me. "Job well done," he said.

I narrowed my eyes at him. "First you tell me you're going to arrest me for everything from manslaughter to drug possession, and now you're praising my work?"

"Point taken," he said, backing off. "I admit I get on my high horse sometimes. I'm sorry." He held up both hands as if in surrender. "It won't happen again. I promise."

"I've heard that before," I said, then smiled. "Something tells me I'll hear it again."

I turned to Max, but Bubba and Junior got in the way. They were still grinning when the sheriff came up again and gestured toward them. "Meet my newest recruits."

"Recruits?" These two hellions? I exchanged a glance with Max. He stood open-mouthed too.

"We just graduated from the academy," Bubba said, looking a lot more professional than the last time I laid eyes on him.

The sheriff stepped up, his grin widening. "I recruited them to go undercover to help us solve the puzzle of the ipecac epidemic."

Not to be outdone, Junior elbowed his way into the group. "We've been working behind the scenes."

The sheriff gave Junior a good-natured slap on the back. "We'd suspected Dr. Fletcher for some time but had no proof. Sorry I kept you out of the loop, but I had to be sure."

I was dumbfounded.

"We're sorry for the things we said to you, Mrs. Littlefield," Bubba said, looking appropriately contrite.

"You should be." I looked at his brother. "And you too."

"We got into our roles a little too eagerly," Bubba said. "Even Mama said she was ashamed."

"My turn," Max said stepping up and nudging the Sutherlands out of the way. He drew me into his arms and held me as if he never wanted to let me go. Then he stooped down and hugged Chloe Grace.

"Did you know it was Jane and Sandy?" I asked Max.

"Jane was on board the *Black Watch* with me when the figurehead was found."

"She had access to your gear?"

He nodded. "I think she also guessed that because of what the figurehead meant to me, I'd be in the water a second time. But Sandy …" He frowned. "But as for Sandy … I'm haven't yet figured out his role."

By the time we reached the marina office, the EMTs had loaded Katie into the ambulance.

"She's suffered a possible concussion," one of them said to me. "It appears that she fell. The patterns of bruising aren't consistent with blunt force and she doesn't seem to have any broken bones."

"Which hospital?" I didn't want my daughter out my sight for longer than a few seconds.

"Mercy General," the same EMT said.

"I'll follow you."

"They'll be running tests on her, probably a CT scan and an MRI," the EMT said. "Give us half an hour or so, then they'll let you see her."

I turned to Max. "Can we ride with you?"

"Oh dear," he said. "I'm afraid I have a confession to make."

"You? A confession?"

"I rode with you."

"What?" Then it dawned on me. "You were in the back of the truck?"

"Actually, in the carton. In place of the angel."

I felt my jaw drop. All along, I'd held close that image of an angel riding with me. And it had been Max.

He laughed. "I'll drive this time. We have a lot to talk about," he said. "I discovered the connection between Sandford Ainsley and William MacDonald. Sandford, aka Sandy, is William's grandson. He grew up hearing stories about the *Lady*, much as I did."

"How did you find that out?"

"Online research last night after we talked. I found a neighbor whose children played with Sandy when he was young. He's always been obsessed with the idea of finding the figurehead, and the romance of finding the buried treasure."

I frowned. "How did Sandy and Jane get together?"

"That I don't know, but with a little digging we could probably find—"

I touched his lips with my fingers to shush him. "I'm ready to let the law enforcement officers do their job."

"Ladies," Max said, giving us a little bow, "Our chariot awaits your charming presence."

Chloe Grace giggled.

"I say we go by the hospital and see how your mama is doing, then we'll find a Cracker Barrel for some fried chicken." He winked at Chloe Grace.

"Yay!" she yelled, "I like that plan!"

"But first, Mercy General," I said, holding his gaze with mine, "I won't be able to rest until I see that Katie is all right."

Chloe Grace's eyes grew big when she saw the truck. "It's so big," she said. "I bet a horse could fit inside it."

Max grinned. "I bet it could."

"Wow!" she said.

Max buckled Chloe Grace into her seat belt and then took my hand to help me in. His touch made my heart do a little dance. Imagine such a thing at my age. Before he closed the door, he took both my hands in his. "You're a wonder, Mrs. Littlefield. I can say unequivocally, this has been the best week of my life."

"Well, thank you, Professor," I said. "You're a bit of a wonder yourself. And I agree."

He rounded the truck and got in on the driver's side. "Are all your cases this exciting?" He started the engine and backed out of the parking space. The sound of the engine's rumble—with Max driving —calmed me. He turned to smile at me, and I got lost in those blue eyes of his.

"No." I reached over and touched his cheek. "Not even close."

Chapter Forty-one
Mrs. Littlefield

. . . .

The following afternoon, I had just grabbed a chocolate-chip cookie out of the freezer and dunked it into my coffee when my home phone rang. The caller ID read: New Hanover County Jail, Wilmington, North Carolina.

Sandy.

My feelings were mixed. I'd mulled over his words to me the day before, about his love for my daughter and Chloe Grace, wondering, no, believing, that he was sincere. I'd been talking to God a lot about forgiveness and grace. Do we ever have reason not to forgive? What if he lied to me yesterday? Did that excuse me from having a forgiving heart?

I picked up the phone. "Hello, Sandy."

"I can't talk long," he said. "I just want you to know that everything I said to you about loving Katie is true. I want a second chance. I also realize that everything you said to me is true as well. I didn't deserve a second chance. I will be out of her life now, until I pay for my actions since I plan to plead guilty."

He let out a long ragged breath. "I'd so hoped to get to know my daughter. Maybe someday she'll know how sorry I am for what I've done—both for my abandonment of her and her mother and now, after deceiving them both."

"Sandy—"

"No, please, let me finish," he said. "Little by little, I let greed and self-centeredness control my actions. I didn't know about the kidnapping plan. By the time it happened, it was too late to get out."

"Who's idea was it?"

"Some people Jane's father is in cahoots with. They wanted to get their hands on the figurehead for the 'loot,' as they called it. Jane willingly went along with it, even talked me into taking a position with the pharmaceutical company they run." He dropped his voice to a whisper as if to not be overheard. "The company is a front for drug running. The relatively 'harmless' ipecac was a foil."

He paused. "But to back up, I told Jane about the treasure off the coast of NC, and she became obsessed with finding it. She found the connection with Dr. Haverhill and his search. She already had her doctorate in social science so she applied for a teaching position at his school, and landed a spot on the *Black Watch*—just as she had planned.

"It wasn't until she, her father, and his thug friends found out that you were connected to Dr. Haverhill and actually catering his retirement dinner that she pushed me to make a move on Katie." He paused, and I thought I heard him crying softly. "But the minute I set eyes on Katie and … Chloe Grace … the past seven years flashed in front of me, and I realized what I'd lost and how much I wanted them back. I foolishly thought I could turn back the clock and start all over again. Again, my self-interests overruled what in my heart I knew would be best for them both. I was too far gone to be in their lives."

"Sandy, you don't need to tell me this."

"Jane quickly figured out that Katie and C.G. were my Achilles' heel, and used them to get me to cooperate. Her threats ensured my cooperation. I played along, too greedy and weak to say no."

"I will tell Katie."

"I know it's too late to ask forgiveness …"

"It's never too late," I said softly. "It doesn't mean that things can return to the way they were. But I think you underestimate my daughter's heart."

Again, I heard the barely audible sobs of a broken man.

"There's One who tells us we are to forgive seventy times seven … just as we are forgiven. He's the One you need to turn to first," I said softly. "I will pray for you, and visit if you need a friend."

"I … do," Sandy said. "Thank you." A moment of silence followed, then he cleared his throat. "Tell Katie I am so sorry …" He ended the call.

Chapter Forty-two
Mrs. Littlefield

• • • • • • • • • • • • • • • • •

I'd gone to bed early to read and had just turned the last page of *Thoughts in Solitude* by Thomas Merton when my cell phone rang. I placed the book on the bedside table and picked up the phone. I smiled. It was Max. He'd been shuttling between Eden's Bridge and Washington for the last few weeks. Each time he left, I missed him more.

"I finished the Merton book," I said without preamble. His low chuckle made my toes curl.

"Do you still think he's too Catholic for your tastes?"

I laughed with him. "Well, he was a monk."

There was a beat of silence, and then he said, "So am I."

"Wait, what did you say? You're a monk?" My voice came out in a squeak. "A monk like Thomas Merton?" Images of sackclothes and ashes, honey and locusts whirled through my head.

He laughed. "Actually, I should say I was a monk. But not like Merton. He was Roman Catholic. I'm Episcopalian. There is a difference. I lived in a monastery for a few years after my profession, then I felt called to teach and to live in the world. To do what I could to make a difference in the lives of others, to love others as Jesus did, as Saint Francis did, with simplicity and joy. The only habit I wear is my cross."

"Why didn't you tell me sooner?"

He sighed. "I was afraid you'd run the other way if I told you."

"Why would I do that?"

"You might think me odd to have chosen to live my life this way."

A question that I didn't know quite how to ask popped into my head. "Um, what about … well, are you … I know that Catholic priests and, well, monks too I suppose, take a vow of cel—" I couldn't get the word out.

"Celibacy?"

"Yes."

"I did when I first took my vows and lived at the monastery. But when I left I was no longer bound by the same commitment. Though there are other vows I keep in my rule of life."

I fell quiet, taking it all in. Other commitments? Rule of life?

"Earth to El," he said quietly. "Are you okay?"

"What is a rule of life?"

He laughed lightly. "It's a sort of plumbline I follow that keeps me available for whatever or whomever God brings into my life. I have a set hour of prayer daily, I say the Daily Office …" He went on to explain the twelve rules that included a vow of poverty—living simply and giving to the poor, loving God and his neighbor with all his heart, examining his heart at the end of each day.

When he finished, I said, "I don't think I could live like that. It's too … too confining." And honestly, though I didn't say so, it sounded boring.

Give me a fiery sermon from Pastor Billy Joe Newborn any day. Let me lift my voice with the worship team and their guitars, bass, and drums. My Bible was worn from reading, its pages crinkled from being underlined and highlighted and filled with margin notes. Yet somehow, I didn't feel holy enough for Max.

The other truth was that Max's commitment to his order made it clear that there was no room in his life for me. And what about the church and spiritual practices that were part of my life? Did he look down on those?

Maybe he didn't understand it yet, but I did. When it came right down to it, we were incompatible.

"I should have waited to tell you in person."

Tears filled my eyes. "Yes," I said. "That might have been easier." I took a deep breath and changed the subject. "Tell me the latest about the *Lady*. Is there any news about the code or map?"

"Nothing, not even a hint," Max said. "We've examined the *Lady* with every instrument the Smithsonian has at its disposal. We've brought in experts from around the world. We're all disappointed, but it's time to release her to the museum in Boston where she belongs. I should be home by the end of the week."

Our good-byes were rather awkward. I put down the phone and buried my head in my pillow, my tears flowing.

Max didn't call for the rest of the week. I wondered if maybe his thoughts had been similar to mine during our last conversation. Maybe we were incompatible after all.

Friday morning I rose at dawn, showered and dressed, and then headed to the kitchen. I wondered if Max might stop by when he arrived back in Eden's Bridge. After my first cup of coffee, I called Pastor Billy.

I told him the sad tale of Max's devotion to the Franciscan order, that he was practically a monk, and I didn't know what to do.

"You've got to hit this hard and fast," he said. "You come right over here and I'll give you the weapons you need to fight this."

"It's not a war," I said when he stopped to take a breath.

"It is in my book, Elaine, and you've got to nip this thing in the bud. I'm in my office at the church and I'll wait for you. You hurry on over. No telling when that professor will be dropping by. You need to be ready for him."

A wave of sadness washed over me as I slid behind the wheel of the catering van. I missed the Ghia. When I arrived at the church, the pastor was waiting for me in the parking lot. He handed a tote bag to me and then patted me on the hand.

"Now, you skedaddle," he said, mopping his face with his hand-kerchief. "Get on home and get prepared for the homecoming."

I grinned and did as he said.

Just before sunset, the doorbell rang. I swallowed hard and went to the dining room window and looked out at the driveway. It was empty. Puzzled, I started back toward the kitchen. The doorbell rang again. This time I went to the entry hall and looked through the peephole.

It was Max, grinning to beat the band. I opened the door and hesitated even after he opened his arms for me to step in.

In a heartbeat he'd closed the distance between us and wrapped his arms around me, holding me close. I pulled back and searched his eyes. All I saw was warmth and joy and love. Had I imagined the distance between us?

He gently reached for me again, gazed into my eyes, and then, glory of all glories, he bent to kiss me. I didn't want to kiss him back and tried not to. We had too many things to talk about, to figure out ... but I lost myself in his kiss.

He pulled back slightly and grinned at me as if expecting some reaction. But all I could do was stare into his eyes, memorizing everything I loved about them, their color, their depth, their emotion. Oh, how I'd missed him.

"I have a gift for you." He turned and looked away from me. I followed his gaze and gasped.

It had been there the entire time, but I was so caught up in Max's presence—and the familiarity of it—that I hadn't noticed.

My smile spread as I walked toward the car.

A Karmann Ghia.

"How ...?" I looked up at him. His smile was as wide as mine.

"It took some doing," he said.

I walked closer to examine it. I touched the smooth Naugahyde, which was not as worn as my Ghia's had been. "Someone has lovingly restored this one," I said.

"Yes," he said. "They did. You can see the love that went into it." He ducked inside, reached under the dashboard, unlatched the convertible top, and with a gentle push let it settle into folds behind the backseat.

"It's just like mine," I said putting my hands together. I circled the car, admiring its shiny chrome bumpers and hubcaps. "It's even the same color. It even looks like it could be the same year."

Then I saw the license plate. "The same ..." I read off the numbers and letters, tilted my head, and looked up at him, remembering
that terrible sound of my Ghia tumbling into the quarry. "How
did you do this? How did you find one just like it? How in the
world ...?" I was so flabbergasted—a word I don't use often, by the
way—I could only sputter.

"I enlisted the help of one of the coaches who gave me the name
of some super athletes," he said, laughing. "Turns out a couple are
into rock climbing and are experts at repelling. They enjoyed the
challenge of retrieving plates from the quarry." He opened the door
on the driver's side and gestured to me to get in.

"Wait, I'll need my handbag." I raced back to the house and
grabbed one of Pastor Billy's "weapons" off my kitchen table. I stuffed
it into my purse and headed back outside.

Max was leaning against the car, a satisfied smile on his face. I
tossed my purse into the back and slid under the steering wheel. He
got in on the passenger side and we both buckled up.

The key was in the ignition. "The dash looks different," I said as
I started the engine.

"I had them add a CD player." He reached into an inside pocket
of his jacket and pulled out three CDs. "I thought you might like
these." He opened a jewel case and pushed a disc into the slot. A song
by one of my favorite groups filled the air.

I turned to him and grinned. "Contemporary. Drums, bass,
guitar."

"I thought maybe it was more your style than stodgy old hymns
from the last century."

"How did you know?"

"I called Pastor Billy Joe Newborn."

Pastor Billy had known before I talked with him this morning. I shook my head in wonder and turned up the speakers, noting the lack of a rattle. "Beautiful."

When I looked up, Max was gazing at me with so much love in his eyes. "You understood," I said.

He reached for my hand and nodded, his gaze still on mine. He didn't have to say a word. The soft music continued, "There's a sweet, sweet Presence in this place …"

"I have something to show you." I reached for my handbag and pulled out a small copy of the Book of Common Prayer. I held it close to my heart. "I began reading this morning. The prayers are beautiful." I felt the sting of tears and blinked to keep them from spilling. Maybe there wasn't such a chasm between us after all. "Pastor Billy told me I needed weapons to fight with. After I saw what he'd given me, I realized he meant weapons to fight my prejudices."

She patted the dash affectionately. "And this … this wonderful car." I knew I would cry for sure if I didn't start driving.

He chuckled. "I couldn't go a lifetime without another drive with you in your Ghia," he said. He winked at me and clutched the edge of his seat, his knuckles turning white as I put the car in reverse and turned it around.

The tires screeched as I headed out of the driveway. Oh, how I'd missed that sound. The traffic was light, the sun was just dipping below the horizon, turning the sky golden with hints of pink and orange. I drove onto the interstate and into the sunset. The feel of the wind in my hair, the wonder of Max at my side, the beauty of that moment made me catch my breath. It was a gift from the Giver of all good things. I glanced at Max and could see by his expression that he felt it too.

That evening, after another candlelight picnic by the fireplace, we moved to the sofa to avoid getting up and down from the floor. Max told mè how he'd found my new Karmann Ghia online. It turned out there had been one east of the Rockies in the right color, owned by a doctor in Old Beau who'd put it up for auction on eBay. Max put in a bid—he wouldn't say how much—won, and then enlisted Enrique's help to pick it up and deliver it to Max's house.

We talked about the mystery that brought us together, even the strange little puzzle pieces we hadn't put together until later.

Juan had explained that he'd taken my street to the university the day of the explosion. He'd been so astounded to see Dr. Jane Fletcher, his History 101 professor, placing a package in my mailbox that he'd run into her car. Each had their own reasons for fleeing the scene. She, of course, didn't want to be caught. He got an A that quarter, but he wasn't too proud of it.

Katie had recovered from her concussion. She remembered that Sandy had tried to get them off the ship, and Chloe Grace had thought it all a wonderful game of pirates, thanks to Sandy's quick thinking. Chloe Grace's greatest worry was over the ballerina sock monkey that she'd left aboard the yacht. You can imagine her surprise when another just like it arrived in the mail from Washington, DC.

"What happened to Marcel Devereaux?" I hadn't seen him around town since the night of the fateful banquet.

Max sat back and put his arm around me, and I snuggled up against him. "He called me a couple of times while I was in DC with some pointed questions about the figurehead. Strangely, though, he was calling from Paris. During our last conversation he asked if the museum in Boston would have the *Lady* on exhibit. The question made me nervous after all we'd been through with him, but I gave him the information." He shrugged. "I figured he would find out anyway. Another strange thing: he asked if I was going to be at the exhibit."

I looked up at him, suddenly not wanting him to leave my side. Ever. "And will you?"

"Only if the beautiful Elaine Littlefield will accompany me."

I sighed and leaned against his side again. "I believe I can arrange that."

"I don't ever want to be away from you again," he said, his voice husky.

Startled, I leaned forward so I could better see his face. "I was just thinking the same thing."

"I've never done this before," he said. "Shall I get down on one knee?"

"Oh, please, no," I said with a soft laugh. "Creaky knees, you know."

He took my hand, turning to me as he spoke. "I've fallen in love with you, El. I want to spend every day of the rest of my life with you, laughing with you, taking joy in life with you, watching sunsets, holding hands ..." His eyes welled. "I can't imagine my life without you."

"But our differences ... your vocation ... your vows ... your rule of life ... your ..."

His lips covered mine and I couldn't finish speaking. I couldn't even remember what I was going to say.

I pulled back slightly and looked into his eyes, losing myself in their depths.

He pulled me into his arms again. I rested my cheek against his chest. "I've loved you forever, I think, but I didn't know it until I saw you the first time."

I felt a soft laugh rumble from his chest. "And when was that?"

"When I saw you baking cookies in your sock monkey pajamas and line dancing to Mozart. Though you were wearing your earbuds, so I didn't know it was Mozart until later."

"If nothing else, I'm eclectic," I said.

"That's just one of the things I love about you." His whisper tickled my ear, and I felt my toes curl. "I love you, El. Please say you'll marry me."

I leaned back, taking in every detail of his face, his jaw, his eyes, so filled with compassion and expectancy. I touched his cheek. How could I begin to express all that was in my heart? The joy of unexpected love at this time of my life ... the amazing depths of this man's heart and soul ... and to think that he loved me? I didn't think I could breathe for the amazement of such a thing.

I placed my hands on either side of his face, and then I kissed him. "I would love to," I said. And when I could breathe again, I whispered, "I love you, Professor Haverhill."

Epilogue
Mrs. Littlefield

• • • • • • • • • • • • • • • •

Never be afraid to trust an unknown future to a known God.

Corrie ten Boom

Max's speech at the exhibit opening at Boston's Maritime Museum stirred my heart. The well-heeled patrons and guests around me seemed equally spellbound by his description of the hunt for the figurehead. We were right there in the water with him, through the storm, the rescue, and his first look at the *Lady*.

He showed a number of slides on a screen behind the dais, while he stood to one side where he could see the screen and the audience.

He caught my eye and gave me a wink and a half smile. I loved that, but then I loved everything about this man. I twirled the engagement ring on my left hand.

"The tension was immense," Max said as he showed a photo of the approaching storm. "After all these years you can imagine my father's devotion to the search as well as my own, and what it felt like to surface with the pod ... and finally have discovered the prize."

He shook his head slowly. "We used a smaller backup crane to get the thing out of the water and on board the ship. The container was taken immediately to the hold, where I, of course, followed.

"The figurehead pod was covered with barnacles. They looked like clusters of rock, but they were colonies of live barnacles. The best way to get rid of them is to let them die and then power wash the surface. I also knew it takes ten days for a barnacle to die. But I was in a hurry, as you can imagine." He laughed lightly, and the audience laughed with him. He clicked and another slide came up. It was a photo of the barnacle-covered pod, Max standing beside it, hair rumpled, goggles and gloves on, but looking deliriously happy.

"I inspected the container, looking for the metal shipping label I'd seen on an earlier dive. It took more barnacle scraping, followed by several inspections with a high-powered magnifying glass, but I finally found it."

He clicked the remote and a new slide appeared, a close-up of a shipping label.

He paused to take a sip of water. "I don't know if you can make out the address. The years housing colonies of barnacles took its toll on the pod. But if you can't see it, I'll read it to you: Centr Bost Muse 1425 Beac St Boston Mass USA and freight no 3725818122.

"Central Boston Museum, Beacon Street," he translated. "This was the proof I needed, even before we opened the container. This was our *Lady*. At this point, we knew we had found her, but we didn't know if she'd been damaged."

Max showed a few more slides of the container being opened, but one stood out: The photographer, who Max had said was one of the ship's crew, caught the expression on Max's face the moment he saw the figurehead. He fell to his knees almost reverently, with a look of pure joy on his face.

As the last slide faded—that of the figurehead herself—and the curtain lifted to reveal the real *Lady*, the crowd stood and applauded.

"Please, please, sit down, if you would. I have something important to add to the story. It was the bravery of a few good people in Paris—young men and women, older folks, fathers and mothers— who, in the midst of the horror and thievery of the massive Nazi machine, saved the treasure of the *Lady*. Though I'm proud of the honor you've given me tonight, the courageous people of the French Resistance are the true testament to heroism.

"These heroes and heroines kept track of millions of dollars worth of art and antiquities. No matter the cost, even if it meant capture or death, they were ready to act. When orders came from the highest levels of the Nazi government to transport the treasures of France and the French people by train and by trucks across the border into the Reich, these few tracked every stolen item they could get hold of, kept what records they could, and secreted untold items away.

"The treasures may never be found, but the story of these brave individuals will never fade." He moved his gaze to the pedestal where the *Lady* now stood. "And this figurehead, ladies and gentlemen, is not just a reminder of the hidden treasure that might someday be found. She is a reminder of those who worked tirelessly in the face of almost impossible odds."

I jumped from my seat, applauding, as the crowd at Boston's Maritime Museum gave Max another standing ovation.

Max flashed me a wide smile as the curator of the museum spoke a few words in closing, then trotted down the stairs to where I waited.

"That was wonderful." I squeezed his hand when he took mine. "Inspiring. Exciting. Dangerous. Now I want to go on your next grand expedition."

He laughed. "I wouldn't have it any other way."

Friends gathered around us. Max introduced me to Captain Donnegan of the *Black Watch*, two former students, MacFie and Dirk, and several other seamen who'd been on the salvage ship.

"These are the divers who brought the *Lady* to the surface," Max said, nodding toward the two young men.

"So nice to meet you." I stepped forward and shook their hands.

"She doesn't know, does she?" The young man named MacFie searched my face.

"Know what?" I glanced from one to the other of the young men.

"If she knew," Dirk said to Max, "she'd be hugging our necks right now, congratulating us for being alive."

The captain came up and slung his arm around Max's shoulders. "This one never toots his own horn." He looked at the young men. "You two ought to know that by now."

MacFie grinned at Dirk and looked back to Max. "If you aren't going to tell your bride-to-be, then I—"

Dirk stepped up and interrupted. "No, I will. I got a better look at what this Houdini did."

"For the sake of time," the captain said, "I'll be the one to tell Mrs. Littlefield." He smiled at me as he continued. "Max saved their lives. We were caught in a storm and lost the crane that was bringing up the divers. It was headed to the ocean's floor, taking the cage with it. Your man's fast thinking saved them. The crane landed on a cliff not too far under the surface, but it wouldn't have stayed put long. Not in that chop."

"Anybody would have done the same thing," Max said, looking uncomfortable.

"You were already in the water. It was as if you knew …" The captain glanced at me. "He got to them in the nick of time, broke them out of the cage, and somehow, the three of them were able to get the pod carrying the figurehead to the surface." He shook his head slowly. "If I hadn't been there to see it, I never would have believed it."

Max took a sudden interest in his shoes, absently resting his hand on his chest where I knew he wore his cross.

"Hey, man," MacFie said, "we owe you big time, th—"

"Excuse me," a man's voice interrupted. I recognized the French accent and turned to see Marcel Devereaux pushing a woman in a wheelchair toward us.

"I have someone who wants to meet you," Marcel said, his eyes on Max. The captain and the two young men moved to the side of the room, where dessert and coffee were being served.

"Yes, of course." Max took my elbow and drew me to his side.

Marcel laid his hand on the elderly woman's thin shoulder. "This is my mother, Madeleine Devereaux," he said. "Come with us, please."

Marcel pushed the wheelchair across the room. Max and I exchanged puzzled looks and then followed them to the figurehead display. I was a bit put off by their lack of manners, and if it hadn't been such a grand and wonderful night, I would have said so. I mean, really, we should have been properly introduced.

For a long time, Mrs. Devereaux stared up at the figurehead. "She's as beautiful as I thought she would be," she said. "All those decades ago, and now at last, I see her in person." She smiled, and I could almost see the lines disappear from her face.

She gestured toward a bench on one side of the display. "Please sit, and I shall tell you how to find the *Lady's* treasure." Her smile reached her eyes, lighting her entire face. From her expression it was obvious she'd been waiting years for this moment.

"It was right in front of you all along," she said. "The freight number isn't about freight at all. Break it up and see where you land if you follow the coordinates." She waved her hand. "You may have to play with the numbers, but you'll eventually get there. You know, latitude, longitude, that sort of thing. Not all of the numbers are on the photograph you took. I could see some were missing, but I'm sure you'll soon figure out the rest."

Max had turned pale. For a moment he didn't speak. Finally, he stood and started pacing. He put a hand to his forehead and rubbed his temples. Finally, he turned to Mrs. Devereaux. "If you knew this, why didn't you come forward sooner?"

She straightened, pulled her shawl around her thin shoulders, and lifted her chin. "I was never told the numbers; I was only told where they would be found. I had to wait to see for myself, if you had indeed uncovered them." She laughed lightly. "Is it not clever that those who hid the so-called code did not put it on the *Lady* at all?"

She laughed, looking up at her son. "I'm ready to go now, Marcel. It's been a long journey."

He had wheeled her a short distance when she stopped him and looked back at Max. "Did you wonder why my son was following you earlier this year?"

"Yes, I did," Max said.

She laughed. "I sent him to America to find out if you were worthy of receiving the *Lady*'s final burden. And believe me, the knowledge you now hold may be the greatest burden you will ever bear. He said you were worthy. And another thing, my granddaughter Natasha will be enrolling at your college next fall. I sent my daughter with Marcel to find out if your campus was suitable for young girls."

Lifting her chin high, she motioned her son to move on.

"Godspeed, Dr. Haverhill. Godspeed," she called over her shoulder.

I stood in an almost reverent silence next to Max as Marcel and his mother disappeared into the lobby. Judging from Max's trembling hand as he took mine, he felt the same way. I tried to take it all in, the millions of dollars in antiquities, irreplaceable art, personal treasures … all stolen in such a vicious and horrible manner. Now it all had to be sorted and returned to the families of the victims. It was too much to get my mind around.

Max looked shaken. The same thoughts … and more … were surely whirling through his mind. He slid one arm around me, and with his opposite hand he reached for his cross, pulling it right out from underneath his shirt. He held it like a rosary.

"This has been quite a ride," I said.

"And it's only begun."

"I suppose this means we need to watch out for bad guys."

"I hope no one else knows we're the only ones who have the code."

We turned back toward the room featuring Max's exhibit. It was mostly empty now, and some of the lights had been dimmed as a signal that the event was over.

We stood facing the spotlighted *Lady*. The play of light and shadow made her more stunning than before.

"She brought us together," Max said softly.

"Indeed she did."

"The greatest treasure of all …"

"Love," I said simply. "And we didn't need a code for that."

"We certainly didn't." He laughed lightly, pulled me into his arms, and kissed me.

"Holy cannoli," I whispered, feeling my knees turn to jelly.

... a little more ...

When a delightful concert comes to an end,

the orchestra might offer an encore.

When a fine meal comes to an end,

it's always nice to savor a bit of dessert.

When a great story comes to an end,

we think you may want to linger.

And so, we offer ...

AfterWords—just a little something more after you

have finished a David C Cook novel.

We invite you to stay awhile in the story.

Thanks for reading!

Turn the page for ...

- **Note from the Author**
- **Discussion Questions**
- **Author Contact**

From the Author

For the LORD your God is living among you.
He is a mighty savior.
He will take delight in you with gladness.
With his love, he will calm all your fears.
He will rejoice over you with joyful songs.

Zephaniah 3:17 NLT

Creating and populating a new fictional world is a process I love. This book, more than any of my others, gave me three characters I couldn't wait to get back to at the end of each writing stint: El with her undaunted spirit; Max, and his growing fascination with El; and Hyacinth with her irrepressible antics (who would have thought she would get herself kidnapped on purpose?).

Discussion Questions

1. There are four spiritual threads woven through the storyline: friendship, love, sacrifice, and forgiveness. Discuss instances in the book when El, Max, and Hyacinth handled any of the challenges or tests, and displayed one or more of these threads.

2. John 15:13 says, "Greater love has no one than this: to lay down one's life for one's friends." Who do you think was the most willing to sacrifice and risk his or her life to save a colleague or loved one? Examples?

3. El is exuberant in everything she does and she loves God with all her heart. Her idea of the perfect worship service is one with upbeat music and loud instruments. She talks to God as she would a friend, and is not afraid to let her emotions show. At one point, she tells Max that she likes to try to make God laugh. Reread Zephaniah 3:17 (above), and discuss how you feel about this. What do you think about the Almighty God of the universe taking joy in you and rejoicing over you with singing?

4. Close your eyes and picture a toddler, perhaps your own little one, or a grandchild, niece, or nephew. Remember how you've laughed at their antics. Remember the joy you've taken in them just because of who they are. They didn't have to earn your delight—it just bubbled up inside you. Pure joy. Pure laughter. Can it possibly be that God experiences us in the same way?

5. Early on we find that Max follows Jesus by walking with humility, love, and joy in the manner of Francis of Assisi, a thirteenth-century monk. Max is a contemplative who loves the older traditions and liturgies of the church, and his conversation with God is most often silent. How did you feel when El found out the details of his Franciscan side? How do you think it might affect their relationship? How do you handle theological differences of opinion with friends? Doctrinal differences? (Dare I say ... political differences?) How does the following verse from Isaiah 54:2 relate to these differences: "Enlarge the place of your tent, stretch your tent curtains wide, do not hold back; lengthen your cords, strengthen your stakes"?

6. In today's world we have some huge spiritual and political divides. How do you think we can bring

about a spirit of reconciliation among those in our circles of influence?

7. Prayerfully read and discuss the following prayer attributed to Saint Francis of Assisi. How can you be an instrument of God's peace?

> Lord, make me an instrument of Your
> peace;
> Where there is hatred, let me sow love;
> Where there is injury, pardon;
> Where there is discord, harmony;
> Where there is error, truth;
> Where there is doubt, faith;
> Where there is despair, hope;
> Where there is darkness, light;
> And where there is sadness, joy.
> O Divine Master, Grant that I may not so
> much seek
> To be consoled as to console;
> To be understood as to understand;
> To be loved as to love.
> For it is in giving that we receive;
> It is in pardoning that we are pardoned;
> And it is in dying that we are born to
> eternal life.

I love hearing from my readers. If you would like to contact me, please visit my website, or follow me on Facebook or Twitter. If you prefer, you can also send a letter to me at PO Box 141, Indian Wells, CA 92260.

Grace to you, and abundant joy,

Diane Noble
dianenoble.com
facebook.com/BooksbyDianeNoble
twitter.com/dianenoble